SPELLSLINGER

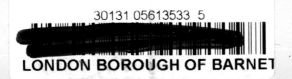

THE SPELLSLINGER SERIES

SPELLSLINGER
SHADOWBLACK

Look out for
CHARMCASTER

Coming in May 2018

SPELLSLINGER

SEBASTIEN DE CASTELL

HOT
KEY
BOOKS

First published in Great Britain in 2017 by
HOT KEY BOOKS
80–81 Wimpole St, London W1G 9RE
www.hotkeybooks.com

This paperback edition published 2017

A CIP catalogue record for this book is available from the British Library.

ISBN: 978-1-78576-132-4
also available as an ebook

1

Typeset by Palimpsest Book Production Ltd, Falkirk, Stirlingshire

Printed and bound by Clays Ltd, St Ives Plc

Hot Key Books is an imprint of Bonnier Zaffre Ltd,
a Bonnier Publishing company
www.bonnierpublishing.com

*For my brother Peter, who always had a
soft spot for obnoxious animals.*

TWO of SPELLS

THE FIRST TRIAL

There are three requirements to earning a mage's name among the Jan'Tep. The first is the strength to defend your family. The second is the ability to wield the high magics that protect our people. The third is simply to reach the age of sixteen. I was a few weeks shy of my birthday when I learned that I wouldn't be doing any of those things.

1

The Duel

The old spellmasters like to say that magic has a taste. Ember spells are like a spice burning the tip of your tongue. Breath magic is subtle, almost cool, the sensation of holding a mint leaf between your lips. Sand, silk, blood, iron . . . they each have their flavour. A true adept – the kind of mage who can cast spells even outside an oasis – knows them all.

Me? I had no idea what the high magics tasted like, which was why I was in so much trouble.

Tennat waited for me in the distance, standing inside the seven marble columns that ringed the town oasis. The sun at his back sent his shadow stretching all the way down the road towards me. He'd probably picked his spot precisely for that effect. It worked too, because my mouth was now as dry as the sand beneath my feet, and the only thing I could taste was panic.

'Don't do this, Kellen,' Nephenia pleaded, quickening her step to catch up with me. 'It's not too late to forfeit.'

I stopped. A warm southern breeze shook the flowers from pink tamarisk trees lining the street. Tiny petals floated up into the air, glittering in the afternoon sun like particles of fire magic. I could have used some fire magic just then.

Actually, I would have settled for just about any kind of magic.

Nephenia noticed my hesitation and unhelpfully added, 'Tennat's been bragging all over town that he'll cripple you if you show up.'

I smiled, mostly because it was the only way I could keep the feeling of dread crawling up my stomach from reaching my face. I'd never fought a mage's duel before, but I was fairly sure that looking petrified in front of your opponent wasn't an especially effective tactic. 'I'll be fine,' I said, and resumed my steady march towards the oasis.

'Nephenia's right, Kel,' Panahsi said, huffing and puffing as he struggled to catch up. His right arm was wrapped around the thick covering of bandages holding his ribs together. 'Don't fight Tennat on my account.'

I slowed my pace a little, resisting the urge to roll my eyes. Panahsi had all the makings of one of the finest mages of our generation. He might even become the face of our clan at court one day, which would be unfortunate, since his naturally muscular frame was offset by a deep love of yellow-berry sweetcakes, and his otherwise handsome features were marred by the skin condition that was the inevitable result of the aforementioned cakes. My people have a lot of spells, but none that cure being fat and pockmarked.

'Don't listen to them, Kellen,' Tennat called out as we approached the ring of white marble columns. He stood inside a three-foot circle in the sand, arms crossed over his black linen shirt. He'd cut the sleeves off to make sure everyone could see he'd sparked not just one, but two of his bands. The tattooed metallic inks shimmered and swirled under the skin of his forearms as he summoned the magics for breath and iron. 'I think it's sweet the way you're throwing your life away just to defend your fat friend's honour.'

A chorus of giggles rose up from our fellow initiates, most of whom were standing behind Tennat, shuffling about in anticipation. Everyone enjoys a good beating. Well, except the victim.

Panahsi might not have looked like the gleaming figures of ancient war mages carved into the columns in front of us, but he was twice the mage Tennat was. There was no way in all the hells that he should have lost his own duel so badly. Even now, after more than two weeks in bed and who knew how many healing spells, Panahsi could barely make it to lessons.

I gave my opponent my best smile. Like everyone else, Tennat was convinced I'd challenged him for my first trial out of recklessness. Some of our fellow initiates assumed it was to avenge Panahsi, who was, after all, pretty much my only friend. Others thought I was on some noble quest to stop Tennat from bullying the other students, or terrorising the Sha'Tep servants, who had no spells of their own with which to defend themselves.

'Don't let him goad you, Kellen,' Nephenia said, her hand on my arm.

A few people no doubt suspected I was doing all this to impress Nephenia, the girl with the beautiful brown hair and the face that, while not perfect, was perfect to me. The way she was staring at me now, with such breathless concern for my well-being, you'd never have guessed that she'd hardly noticed me in all the years we'd been initiates together. To be fair, most days no one else had either. Today was different though. Today everyone was paying attention to me, even Nephenia. Especially Nephenia.

Was it only pity? Maybe, but the worried expression she wore on those lips that I'd longed to kiss ever since I'd first figured out that kissing wasn't just two people biting each other made my head spin. The feel of her fingers on my skin . . . was this the first time she'd ever touched me?

Since I really hadn't picked this fight just to impress her, I gently removed Nephenia's hand and entered the oasis.

I once read that other cultures use the word 'oasis' to describe a patch of fertile terrain in a desert, but a Jan'Tep oasis is something completely different. Seven marble columns towered above us, one for each of the seven forms of true magic. Inside the enclosed thirty-foot circle there were no trees or greenery, but instead a glimmering carpet of silver sand that, even when stirred by the wind, never left the boundary set by the columns. At the centre was a low stone pool filled with something that was neither liquid nor air, but which shimmered as it rose and fell in waves. This was the true magic. The Jan.

The word 'tep' means 'people', so it should tell you how important magic is to us that when my ancestors came here, like other peoples before them, they left their old names behind and became known as the Jan'Tep, the 'People of True Magic'.

Well, in theory, anyway.

I knelt down and drew a protective circle around myself in the sand. Actually, 'circle' might have been a bit generous.

Tennat chuckled. 'Well, now I'm really scared.'

For all his bluster, Tennat wasn't nearly as imposing a figure as he imagined. True, he was all wiry muscle and meanness, but he wasn't very big. In fact, he was as thin as I was and half a head shorter. Somehow that just made him meaner.

'Are you both still determined to go through with this duel?' Master Osia'phest asked, rising from a stone bench at the edge of the oasis. The old spellmaster was looking at me, not at Tennat, so it was pretty clear who was supposed to back out.

'Kellen won't withdraw,' my sister declared, stepping out from behind our teacher. Shalla was only thirteen, younger than the rest of us, but already taking her trials. She was a better mage than anyone present except for Panahsi, as evidenced by the fact that she'd already sparked the bands for breath, iron, blood and ember magic. There were mages who went their whole lives without ever being able to wield four disciplines, but my little sister fully planned on mastering all of them.

So how many bands had I sparked? How many of the tattooed symbols under my shirtsleeves would glow and swirl when I called on the high magics that defined my people?

Zero.

Oh, inside the oasis I could perform the practice spells that all initiates learn. My fingers knew the somatic shapes as well or better than any of my fellow initiates. I could intone every syllable perfectly, envision the most esoteric geometry with perfect clarity. I was skilled at every aspect of spellcasting – except for the actual magic part.

'Forfeit the duel, Kellen,' Nephenia said. 'You'll find some other way to pass your tests.'

That, of course, was the real problem. I was about to turn sixteen and this was my last chance to prove that I had the calibre of magic worthy of earning my mage name. That meant I had to pass all four of the mage's trials, starting with the duel. If I failed, I'd be forced to join the Sha'Tep and spend the rest of my life cooking, cleaning or clerking for the household of one of my former classmates. It would be a humiliating fate for any initiate, but for a member of my family, for the son of Ke'heops himself? Failure was inconceivable.

Of course, none of that was the reason why I'd chosen to challenge Tennat in particular.

'Be warned, the protection of the law is suspended for those who undertake the trials,' Osia'phest reminded us, his tone both weary and resigned. 'Only those whose calibre gives them the strength to face our enemies in combat can lay claim to a mage's name.'

Silence gripped the oasis. We'd all seen the list of past initiates who'd attempted the trials before they were ready. We all knew the stories of how they'd died. Osia'phest looked to me again. 'Are you truly prepared?'

'Sure,' I said. It wasn't an appropriate way to speak to our teacher, but my strategy required that I project a certain confidence.

'"Sure",' Tennat repeated in a mocking whine. He took up a basic guard position, legs shoulder width apart and hands loose at his sides, ready to cast the spells he'd use for our duel. 'Last chance to walk away, Kellen. Once this starts, I don't stop until you fall.' He chuckled, his eyes on Shalla. 'I wouldn't want the tremendous pain I'm about to inflict on you to bring any needless suffering to your sister.'

If Shalla had noticed Tennat's childish imitation of gallantry she gave no sign of it. Instead she stood there, hands on her hips, bright yellow hair billowing gracefully in the wind. Hers was straighter and smoother than the dirt-coloured mop I struggled to keep out of my eyes. We shared our mother's pale complexion, but mine was exacerbated by a lifetime of

10

intermittent illnesses. Shalla's accentuated the fine-boned features that drew the attention of just about every initiate in our clan. None of them interested her, of course. She knew she had more potential than the rest of us and fully intended doing whatever it took to become a lord magus like our father. Boys simply weren't part of that equation.

'I'm sure she'll weather my screams of agony just fine,' I said.

Shalla caught my glance and returned a look that was equal parts bemusement and suspicion. She knew I'd do anything to pass my trials. That was why she was keeping such close watch on me.

Whatever you think you know, Shalla, keep your mouth shut. I'm begging you.

'As the student who has sparked the fewest bands,' Osia'phest said, 'you may select the discipline of magic for the duel, Kellen. What is your weapon?'

Everyone stared at me, trying to guess what I'd choose. Here in the oasis, any of us could summon some tiny portion of the different forms of magic – just enough to train in spellwork. But that was nothing compared with what you could do once you'd sparked your bands. Since Tennat had iron and breath at his disposal, I'd be crazy to choose either of those two.

'Iron,' I said, loud enough to ensure that everyone heard.

My classmates looked at me as if I'd lost my mind. Nephenia went pale. Shalla's eyes narrowed. Panahsi started to object, but a glance from Osia'phest shut him up. 'I did not hear you correctly,' our teacher said slowly.

'Iron,' I repeated.

Tennat grinned, a greyish glow already winding itself from the iron band on his forearm, slithering around his hands

11

as he began summoning the power. Everyone there knew how much Tennat loved iron magic, the way it let you tear and bludgeon at your enemies. You could see the excitement building up inside him, the thrill that came from wielding high-calibre magic. I wished I knew what it felt like.

Tennat was so eager that his fingers had already begun running through the somatic shapes for the spells he'd be using against me. One of the first things you learn in duelling is that only an idiot shows his hand before the fight starts, but since there was no possible way I could beat Tennat in iron magic, he probably figured there was nothing to lose.

That was the real reason why I was smiling.

See, for the past several weeks I'd watched every single duel Tennat had fought against the other initiates; I'd noticed how even those students with more power – those who should have been able to beat him with ease – always ended up forced to yield.

That was when I'd finally figured it out.

Magic is a con game.

The oasis was quiet, almost peaceful. I think everyone was waiting for me to giggle nervously and announce before it was too late that it had all been a joke. Instead, I rolled my shoulders back and tilted my neck left then right to make it crack. It didn't help my magic any, but I thought maybe it would make me look tougher.

Tennat gave a confident snort. It sounded like his regular snort only louder. 'You'd think someone who can barely light a glow-glass lantern without giving himself a heart attack would be a little more cautious in his choice of opponent.'

'You're right,' I said, rolling up my sleeves to let him see the flat, lifeless inks of my own six tattooed bands. 'So you've got to ask yourself, why would I challenge you now?'

Tennat hesitated for a second before he said, 'Maybe you've been having death-dreams and you know I'm the best person to help usher you into the grey passage and end your suffering.'

'Could be,' I conceded. 'But let's say for the sake of argument that it's something else.'

'Like what?'

I had a whole speech planned about how I'd banded myself with shadow – the seventh and deadliest of magics, the one forbidden to us all. If that didn't scare him I had a different bit about how the truly great mages among our ancestors could wield the high magics without sparking their bands at all. Just as I was about to speak though, I saw a falcon flying overhead and decided to switch tactics.

'You don't need to spark your bands if you've found your power animal.'

Everyone looked up to see. Tennat's smirk was just angry enough to tell me he was getting nervous. 'Nobody bonds with familiars any more. Besides, how would someone with as little magic as you ever attract a power animal? And a falcon? No way, Kellen. Not in a thousand years.'

I noticed the falcon was about to swoop down on a smaller bird. 'Dive, my darling,' I whispered, just loud enough for everyone to hear. There was a sudden nervous intake of breath all around me as the falcon's claws took merciless hold of its prey. It occurred to me then that I might have made a decent actor if it hadn't been a forbidden profession among the Jan'Tep.

'All right, all right,' Osia'phest said, waiving his hands in the air as if trying to cast a banishing spell on all our nonsense.

13

I was fairly sure the old man knew I hadn't acquired a familiar, but I guess it's bad form to reveal another mage's secrets, even when they happen to be lies. Or maybe he just didn't care. 'I recognise that it's traditional for there to be a certain amount of . . . posturing prior to a duel, but I think we've all had just about enough. Are you ready to begin?'

I nodded. Tennat didn't bother, as if the implication that he might not be ready were an insult.

'Very well,' Osia'phest said. 'I shall commence the counting.' The old man took in a deep breath that was probably excessive given that all he said next was, 'Seven!'

The breeze picked up and my loose linen shirt flapped noisily against my skin. I dried my hands on it for the tenth time and cleared my throat to get rid of the tickle. *Don't start coughing. Don't look weak. Whatever you do, don't look weak.*

'Six.'

Tennat gave me a wide grin as if he had some big surprise waiting for me. I would have been more scared if I hadn't seen him give every opponent that same look prior to each duel. Also, I was already as terrified as I could possibly be without collapsing to the ground.

'Five.'

The bird swooped overhead again so I looked up and winked at it. Tennat's smile wavered. Evidently he was capable of simultaneously believing I was a weakling and yet had also acquired a power animal. *Moron.*

'Four.'

His left hand formed the somatic shape necessary for his shield spell. I'd never seen him prepare the shield before the sword. He looked down at his hand to check the form. Tennat was just a little worried now.

14

'Two.'

Two? What happened to three? *Pay attention, damn it.* Tennat's right hand made the somatic shape for the iron attack spell we informally call the *gut sword*. His fingers were perfectly aligned to cause the maximum pain in his opponent. His head was still down, but it was starting to look as though he might be smiling again.

'One.'

Okay, Tennat was definitely smiling. Maybe this hadn't been such a good idea.

'Begin!' Osia'phest said.

The next thing I felt was my insides screaming in pain.

Like I said, magic is a con game.

Mostly.

To an observer, it wouldn't have looked as if anything was happening. There was no flash of light or roar of thunder, just the early evening light and the soft sounds of the breeze coming from the south. Iron magic doesn't create any visual or auditory effects – that was why I'd picked it in the first place. The real fight was taking place inside our bodies.

Tennat was reaching out with his right hand, carefully holding the somatic form: middle fingers together making the sign of the knife, index and little fingers curled up – the shape of pulling, of tearing. The horrifying touch of his will slipped inside my chest, winding itself along my internal organs. The pain it created – more slithering horror than anything blunt or sharp – made me want to fall to the ground and beg for mercy. *Damn, he's fast, and strong too. Why can't I be strong like that?*

I responded by letting out the barest hint of a laugh and

smiling effortlessly. The look on Tennat's face told me I was creeping him out. I was probably creeping everyone out, since confident smiles weren't exactly my customary expression.

I let the corners of my mouth ease down a bit as my gaze narrowed and I stared straight into Tennat's eyes. I thrust out my hand as if I were stabbing the air – a much more pronounced gesture and by all rights much too fast for an initiate like me to do while holding on to the shielding spell. Where Tennat's hand formed the somatic shape with care and precision, mine was looser, almost casual, something few would dare because of the risk of breaking the shape.

At first nothing happened. I could still feel Tennat's will inside my guts, so I let my smile grow by a hair – just enough to let him see how sure I was that he was completely screwed. The painful pulling at my insides began to subside just a little as Tennat's gaze lingered on me for several agonising seconds. Suddenly his eyes went very, very wide.

That's when I knew I was going to win.

The other reason I'd chosen iron magic even though I couldn't wield it myself was because when a mage uses the gut sword to attack, he has to use a second spell – the heart shield – to protect himself. But it's not a shield the way you might think of a big round thing that acts as a wall. Instead, you use magical force to maintain the shape and integrity of your own insides. You have to picture your heart, your liver, your ... well, everything, and try to keep them together. But if you start to panic – say, if you think the other mage is beating you and nothing you're doing is working – you can inadvertently compress your own organs.

That was how Tennat had beat Panahsi. That was how he'd hurt him so badly, even though nobody but me – not even

16

Tennat himself – had realised it. Pan had been trying so hard to protect himself that he'd actually ended up crushing his own internal organs. Now it was Tennat who was so convinced that his spells were failing that he was pushing them too hard. I was still in blinding pain, but I'd expected it. I was ready for it. Tennat wasn't.

He struggled for a while, increasing his attack on me even as he unconsciously tore at himself with his own shield spell. I felt my legs shake and my vision start to blur as the pain became too much for me. It had seemed like such a good plan at the time, I thought.

Suddenly Tennat stumbled out of his circle. 'Enough!' he shouted. 'I yield . . . I yield!'

The fingers of his own power disappeared into nothingness. I could breathe again. I tried my very best to keep my tremendous sense of relief from showing on my face.

Osia'phest walked slowly over to Tennat, who was on his knees gasping. 'Describe the sensation,' our teacher demanded.

Tennat looked up at the old man as if he were an idiot, which was a fairly common impression of our teacher. 'It felt like I was about to die. That's what it felt like!'

Osia'phest ignored the belligerent tone. 'And did it feel the same as with the other students?'

A jolt of fear ran through me as I realised Osia'phest was testing his suspicions. Tennat looked over at me, then at the old man. 'It . . . I suppose not at first. Usually it feels hard, like a strong hand grabbing at you, but with Kellen it's different . . . worse, like tendrils insinuating themselves all around my insides. By the end I could feel him crushing my organs.'

Osia'phest stood in silence for a long time as the breeze picked up and drifted off again around us. The other initiates were still staring at me, wondering how someone who hadn't broken any of his bands had beaten the best duellist in our class. But they'd all seen Tennat falter and heard him describe what sounded like someone being overwhelmed by superior magic. Finally Osia'phest said, 'Well done, Kellen of the House of Ke. It would appear that you've passed the first test.'

'I'll pass the other three too,' I declared.

I did it, I thought, as a surge of joy erupted inside me. *I beat him. I won.* No more spending hours and hours staring at the bands on my forearms, praying without success to break the bindings between the sigils to spark them. No more sitting awake at night wondering when I would be sent away from my family home, doomed to become Sha'Tep and take a position as a tradesman, clerk or, ancestors help me, Tennat's personal servant.

A few of the other initiates applauded. I doubted any of them other than Panahsi and maybe Nephenia had wanted me to best Tennat, but among my people? Let's just say everyone loves a winner. Even Tennat bowed to me, with about as much grace as you'd expect given the circumstances. I hadn't hurt his standing in the trials. Every initiate was allowed three attempts at the duel and he'd already won several.

'All right,' Osia'phest said. 'Let's have the next pair and—'

'Stop!' a voice called out, cutting off our teacher and, with more force than any spell I could imagine, shattering everything I had done and everything I would ever do. I watched with a sinking heart as my sister pushed past Osia'phest and strode forth to stand in front of me, hands on her hips. 'Kellen cheated,' she said simply.

And, just like that, all my hopes and dreams came crashing down around me.

2

The Betrayal

Everyone was staring at me, waiting for an answer to the charge that my own sister had just levelled at me. My mind, not good for most things but usually quick to come up with a wide range of excuses, bluffs, and out-and-out lies, failed me. It wasn't as if I couldn't have made something up (*Shalla's possessed by a demon! Mine is the secret eighth form of magic! The council of mages sent me to test all of you! It's a dream! You're all dreaming!*) but what possible explanation could I give that wouldn't be tested by simply having me retake the trial, this time with someone who wasn't going to be fooled by my trick?

I did the thing that you should never do in these situations. I looked at the faces of the people around me, hoping someone would intervene. If there's a surer way of demonstrating one's own guilt, I haven't encountered it. Oddly it was my teacher, Osia'phest, who tried to come to my rescue. The old man put on an annoyed expression and waved a dismissive hand in the air. 'Girl, I may be forced to allow you to be part of these trials, but I am *not* required to let you interrupt them. Go bother Master He'met.'

'But he's cheating!' she said, pointing at me. 'Kellen's not even doing the—'

19

'Shalla, get out of here,' I said between gritted teeth. I tried to signal her with my eyes. *Please. If you love me at all, let it go.*

If she caught my meaning, she gave no sign of it. Shalla crossed her arms and stood there as if she were about to hold her breath until she got her way. 'He's cheating, Master Osia'phest. He didn't cast any spells.'

Tennat, who was not yet aware that Shalla had long ago decided he wasn't quite impressive enough a mage to become her lover when the time came, took the opportunity to put a hand on her arm and give her a patronising smile. 'Trust me, Shalla, I was there. Your brother—'

'Oh, shut up,' she said, shaking him off. She pointed at me again. 'Kellen's not doing the spell. He just made you think he was, and you fell for it because you're an idiot. He convinced you that he was winning and tricked you into turning your own power against yourself. It's almost clever, but it's not magic.'

They turned to look at me. Panahsi. Nephenia. All of them. Tennat's expression was uncertain and I could tell he was trying to relive the experience and decide whether or not his feelings had been real. Some of the other students started to snigger a bit, not sure quite whom they were laughing at.

The ruse had been so simple that no one could have expected it. But now they all knew. *Why couldn't you have let me have just this one thing, Shalla?*

Osia'phest frowned, his eyes strangely soft as they caught mine. *He already knew*, I realised. *He's known all along. But why didn't he say anything?* 'Very well,' he mumbled. 'I will have to take the matter up with –'

'He can do the spell if he just tries harder,' Shalla interrupted,

20

stepping into the circle Tennat had occupied moments before. 'You don't need tricks, Kellen. You think you do, but that's only because you don't believe in yourself.'

Despite how betrayed I felt, I almost laughed. *She thinks she's helping me!* I realised. *This is Shalla, trying to make me into the man she believes I ought to be.*

'You can do it,' she insisted. 'I know you can. You're the son of Ke'heops! You're my brother, not some Sha'Tep weakling. Prove it to them. Show them. Now!'

She reached out and suddenly I felt her fingers around my heart. *Stop,* I tried to say, but nothing came out. She was attacking me, just as fast and hard as Tennat had done. But this time I wouldn't be able to trick her into defeating herself. I had to try to fight back with whatever real magic I had inside me. My left hand formed the somatic shape of the shield, four fingers curled closed in front of my chest and the thumb extended, as I tried in vain to draw on the power of the oasis. With the inks of the iron band flat and dead around my right forearm, I couldn't summon enough. *Spark,* I commanded the tattooed bands. The coloured metallic inks briefly glinted in the sunlight, mocking me. *Spark. You will light! I'm the son of the most powerful mage in the clan. I can do this. Spark, damn you. Spark!*

The pain of Shalla's attack continued unabated and I cried out. Even seeing me in agony didn't lessen her will in the slightest. She was so sure that I was as powerful as any of them, that big enough stakes were all I needed to shake me from my weakness. 'Find the stillness, Kellen,' she murmured. 'Let it flow.'

Despite how angry I was with her, I did try. I tried to be still the way the masters taught us, but all I could feel was the force of Shalla's will crushing my heart. *Oh ancestors, this is really starting to hurt now.*

'Come on, Kellen,' Panahsi urged.

I poured everything I had into my shield – every shred of will I could muster and more. I pushed at my limits. I pushed beyond them, tearing through the barriers like parchment. The bands were still there, but I didn't care any more. *You want to see my will, sister? Well, here it is, you stupid, arrogant, mean-spirited wretch. Here's all of me.*

All at once, I felt the stillness, the emptiness. *Is this what the masters go on about? The 'deep silence of the mind'?*

But the silence wasn't in my mind – it was in my body. I had stopped breathing some time ago . . . why had I stopped breathing? The answer came to me as my knees buckled and I felt myself falling to the ground.

My little sister had just stopped my heart.

3

The Grey Passage

Among my people the space between life and death is called the *grey passage*. It is a shadowy place where every mage must one day await the three thunders that will summon him to the judgment of our ancestors.

This isn't fair, I thought, watching the world tilt before me as I fell backwards like a blade of grass freshly cut by a gardener's scythe. Bad enough that I was dying, but did it have to be in such a completely humiliating way, killed by my own sister? I hadn't even turned sixteen years old. I'd never kissed a girl. In fact, I hadn't done much of anything with my life yet. There would be no tales of grand accomplishments with which I could purchase my place in the afterworlds from our ancestors, the first mages.

I heard a loud thud, which I assumed was my back hitting the sandy ground of the oasis. I tried (somewhat heroically, from my perspective) to draw in breath. Nothing came.

I thought about lying to the ancestors – making up stories in which I'd fought fiery mages to the death or saved small animals from harm, but I suspected that deities were actually quite difficult to trick, and besides, lying hadn't been working out that well for me lately.

The revered elders of my clan tell us that reincarnation is the penalty the gods levy for the sins of a life poorly lived, and the punishment is to come back somewhere lower on the ladder of life, as, say, a rat or maybe a small fern. But just as I hadn't achieved anything yet, neither had I committed any great sins. So, as my body settled into the sand beneath me, I came to the inevitable conclusion that I was about to traverse the grey passage only to be sent back to start all over again as a somewhat sickly Jan'Tep initiate possessed of almost no magic. *Please, please don't let me die like this.*

The elders would have chided me for such insolent thoughts and reminded me that the grey passage is a time of peace and warmth, when the dying mage hears the soothing sounds of music and the voices of those he admires most praising his name.

Me? I heard screaming.

It came from every different direction. Osia'phest was loudest. He bellowed for the other initiates to get out of the way and then launched into a spell which, if I heard it properly, had many of the same syllables as the one cooks use to keep food from spoiling. Osia'phest is a kind old man, but he isn't exactly the most powerful mage you'll ever meet. His voice was shrill and desperate, which is a bad way to start out since the high magic requires complete calm and perfect focus.

Get up, I told myself. *Breathe. Osia'phest is going to end up preserving you like a dried apricot. Get up!*

Panahsi was shouting too, calling out for someone to find one of the healers. I think he had even less faith in Osia'phest's abilities than I did.

One voice was quiet and almost soothing. Nephenia was

24

calling out to me. 'Try to breathe, Kellen, just try to breathe.' She repeated the phrase over and over as if she might persuade me through repetition.

Dearest Nephenia, you're not doing me any good at all, I thought. *Try a kiss, maybe that will get my heart started. At least it'll give me something to tell the ancestors.* I would've laughed at myself if I'd had the requisite bodily function to do so. Who knew that even dying couldn't put a stop to teenage lust?

'His skin's going grey,' someone said. That set off even more shouting.

In among all the noise, the one voice I didn't hear was that of my sister Shalla, though I swear I could hear her breathing.

When we were children and shared a bedroom, I could always tell when Shalla was having nightmares. Her breath would go in and out in this peculiar pattern ... fast and shallow, as if she were racing up a hill. Listening to it now gave me an absurd impulse to hold her hand and comfort her the way I did when we were kids – when neither of us had any magic and we would stay up late at night talking about how powerful we'd both be when we grew up. I liked her better in those days. She probably felt the same way about me.

How long has it been since my heart last beat? I wondered. A minute? Two minutes? How long can you survive without something pumping the blood through your veins? And if this is the grey passage, why does it seem to involve so much standing around, figuratively speaking?

The elders promise that visions will appear to the dying mage of those he loves best, and who love him in return. That too turned out to be something of an exaggeration. All

I could see now was a burning ember that remained perfectly still. *It's the sun*, I realised. When I'd hit the ground, my head had landed facing west, and now I was staring straight into the last light of the sun with unblinking eyes. *That explains the burning sensation anyway.*

On the positive side, the fact that I was aware of anything despite my heart's not beating suggested that Osia'phest's desperate spell might be doing something useful.

The amber light became a blur that slowly resolved into the sight of Shalla kneeling in front of me. Some of the pain in my eyes subsided. She'd had the presence of mind to realise I was going blind from staring into the light. As her face became clearer her expression settled into one of fear and sorrow and . . . something else. Disappointment. *She killed me and she's actually disappointed in me for dying.*

I felt strangely calm. I suppose that made sense, since the symptoms of panic – pulse racing, rapid breathing, or profuse sweating – all required a beating heart.

The weary repetitions of Osia'phest's exhausted voice shook me from my thoughts. The harder I tried to focus on his face, the less I could make anything out. *Is it getting darker?*

'The preservation spell is fading,' Panahsi said anxiously.

'I cannot continue. We need the healers. Now.' Osia'phest's voice was hoarse and almost pitiful.

'Use a blood sympathy spell!' Panahsi demanded. 'Make his heart beat again!'

'I can't,' Osia'phest replied. 'I'd have to link his heart to mine and I'm too old.'

'You're afraid!'

'Of course I'm afraid, you fool. If I die now, the spell preserving him will disappear completely.'

Shalla finally spoke. 'Then I'll do it. Show me how!'

'You cannot,' he replied, his voice strained. 'You . . . lack the training. I'll not be . . . the one to tell your father that . . . that I . . .'

I heard a thump next to me.

'Master Osia'phest?' Shalla called out, her voice shrill.

'The old fool has passed out,' Panahsi said. 'He couldn't keep up the spell.'

Perfect, I thought. *I'm surrounded by mages and no one's going to save me.*

Someone was crying now, their sobs sounding like raindrops falling down a deep well. *Where's that soothing music the elders promised? Where are all those voices praising my name?*

I heard the thump-thump of boots coming towards me across the sand. 'Out of the way, idiots,' a woman's voice growled. She made the last word sound like *idgits*. Her accent wasn't Jan'Tep at all, but a thick drawl that made me want to giggle. 'Y'all stay far back unless you want to spend the next week tryin' to scratch your own damned skin off right through those fancy skirts of yours.'

Something light and powdery fell on my skin. I wondered if this was what snow felt like. At first it tingled, then it burned, and finally it itched so badly I began to fear that I would go mad.

'Sorry, kid,' the woman whispered close to my ear. 'This ain't gonna be much fun for you.'

The itching spread to my eyes and for a moment my vision cleared. I could see her now, kneeling over me. Her face was pretty but sharply angular, framed by long red hair with a single lock of white sticking out from under a frontiersman hat – the sort of thing I'd seen Daroman riders wear as they

27

travelled their lands, following herds of cattle. We didn't see many Daroman in the Jan'Tep territories these days. This particular one wore a soiled white shirt under a black leather waistcoat. She had something in her mouth – a stick with a flicker of red light that generated little billowing clouds of grey fog. *A smoking reed? Who smokes in front of a sick person? And gods, why won't this itching stop?*

There was some kind of scuffle as Shalla tried to take control. 'Who are you? Get that stuff off of him. He's—'

'Shove off, girly,' the woman replied, easily pushing my sister away. She turned her attention back to me. 'That itch you're feeling is the powder making your nerves go wild. That idiot spell the old man was mumbling would have left you paralysed and brain damaged.' Then, almost as an afterthought, she said, 'Not that all Jan'Tep aren't at least a little brain damaged.'

'He needs *real* magic, not some stupid frontier hedge medicine,' Shalla insisted.

'"Real magic",' the woman snorted. She turned her attention back to me. 'I know it's uncomfortable, kid, but if it makes you feel any better, this next part is *really* going to hurt.'

I felt something slam down onto my chest, as if I were being hammered into the ground. The woman's hands were bunched into fists. She lifted them up, only to bring them crashing down on me again.

'Stop that!' Shalla screamed. 'You're killing him!'

I'm pretty sure you already took care of that, Shalla. On the other hand, I was going to end up a remarkably battered and bruised corpse if this kept up. Maybe I could turn this into a story the ancestors might like enough to let me through the gates. *There I was, Your Godlinesses, lying on the ground, when a crazy woman started beating the hells out of me with her fists.*

'I'll cast a binding spell on you if you don't stop,' Shalla threatened.

'Little girl, you're starting to bug me.' The woman struck my chest a third time, then a fourth. Then she leaned forward and I felt something soft and wet on my lips. The sensation was strange and gentle. Was she kissing me? *The gods have a strange sense of humour.*

Apparently they don't like being mocked, because a moment later the kissing stopped and the pounding resumed. It didn't hurt as much as before though, and the itching had gone too. In fact, I really didn't feel anything. *This is it . . . I'm about to die.*

The elders say that when you reach the end of the grey passage the thunder will strike three times to summon you for judgment. I heard that thunder.

The first time it sounded like a loud crack, followed by a sudden sharp pain in my left side. One of my ribs had broken.

The thunder struck again, this time as a loud boom coming from somewhere deep inside me. My heart had just given its first belligerent beat.

I'm alive, I realised, as my chest expanded in a sudden, agonising rush. *I'm breathing!* Absurdly, my next thought was to try to think of what I could say when I got up that would make me sound clever and brave. Then I heard the thunder strike its third and final blow – a roar so loud it threatened to shake the whole world apart and send us all tumbling away.

It wasn't really thunder, of course, just as it hadn't been the other times. What I'd heard just then was the voice of my father.

He sounded very, very angry.

The gods, it seemed, were ready to pass judgment.

4

The Thunder

What happened next came mostly in flashes – little sparks between the shadows that would envelop me on the journey from the city's oasis back to my family home. It began with my father lifting me up from the ground and whispering in my ear.

'Do not cry in front of them. If you must cry, hold it in a little while longer.'

A Jan'Tep must be strong, I told myself. I'm usually not much of a cryer anyway, never having seen any evidence that it does any good. But I was exhausted and frustrated and more than a little scared, so it took a surprising amount of self-control for me to say, 'I'm not going to cry.'

My father gave me a small nod followed by the barest hint of a smile. I felt a warmth inside me that made me wonder if he'd just cast a fire spell, though of course there was no way he could have made the somatic forms while holding me in his arms.

Everyone in the oasis stood stiff and silent, except for Osia'phest, who still lay on the ground, though from the mumbling noises he made I presumed he was gradually regaining consciousness. Panahsi, Nephenia, Tennat and the rest of my fellow initiates just stared at us.

My father was a big man, over six feet tall with deep black hair – a sharp contrast to the blond colouring that both Shalla and I had inherited from our mother. He kept his moustache and short beard meticulously trimmed and exuded an air of imposing dignity wherever he went. He was strong in all the ways a Jan'Tep was supposed to be: physically, mentally and, above all, magically. Even Panahsi's eyes reflected a kind of disbelief that I was really the son of someone as powerful as Ke'heops.

'I can stand,' I said to my father, embarrassed to appear so weak in front of the other initiates. He didn't let go of me.

Shalla walked gingerly towards us. 'Father, don't be cross with—'

'Be silent,' he said, and my sister closed her mouth. I watched as my father scrutinised the scene in front of us, his eyes moving to each of the participants in turn. I knew he was reading them as easily as if he could unlock their minds, watching their reactions to his presence, sifting through furtive glances and shifting eyes. I could see him work through recent events by considering and cataloguing each person's fear or guilt under his gaze. Then his face took on a slightly puzzled expression. I turned my head and saw him looking at the woman who'd saved my life.

'You. What is your name?' he asked.

She took a step closer as if to prove she wasn't afraid of him. 'Ferius Parfax,' she said, and reached out a gloved hand to wipe something from my face. I saw grains of green and grey dust against the brown leather of her glove. 'You'll want to bathe him. That powder can start acting up again something fierce when it settles into the skin.'

My father barely let her finish the sentence before he said, 'You will come with us now.'

Ferius Parfax, who, despite the single lock of white sticking out from the red tangle kept in check by her frontiersman hat, looked to be several years younger than my father, nonetheless put her hands on her hips and laughed out loud. 'Now, see, I thought you Jan'Tep were supposed to know *all* the magic words.'

There was grumbling and sharp intakes of breath from my fellow initiates, the loudest coming from Shalla. No one spoke to Ke'heops that way, especially not some magic-less Daroman wanderer. I looked up at my father and saw his jaw tighten just a little, but then he said, 'Forgive me. Would you please accompany us to my home? I have questions that may be important to my son's recovery.'

Ferius looked at me and winked as if she'd just conjured a thunderstorm on a dry day. 'Surely I will.'

I felt oddly compelled to contribute to the conversation, so I said, 'My name is Kellen.'

'Nice to meet you, Kellen,' she said, taking off her hat only to put it right back on her head a second later. The Daromans have weird little rituals like that.

A commotion nearby drew our attention. Osia'phest, with precious little help from the students standing next to him, was struggling to rise. 'My Lord Ke'heops –'

'Someone assist him,' my father said.

Immediately two of the nearest initiates took Osia'phest by the arms and lifted him to his feet. The old spellmaster took a few awkward steps towards us. 'If I could perhaps explain more fully the circumstances . . .'

32

'Rest,' my father said. 'Some of these others will help you home. We will speak tomorrow.'

Osia'phest looked as though someone had just read out his prison sentence. Ferius gave a snort of disgust. 'Mages,' she said, as if the word meant something different in her language than it did in ours.

Watching the old man having to be practically carried by his students, seeing the way they rolled their eyes at him and the way they glanced back at me, filled me with shame. 'I can stand by myself,' I said to my father.

His eyes narrowed for an instant but he set me on my feet. The sudden weakness in my legs and blurring of my vision were the first clues that I'd made a terrible mistake.

'Never seen a man recover so fast from a stopped heart,' Ferius said, patting me on the back. Only she wasn't patting me on the back, not really. Her hand was gripping the back of my shirt as she kept me from falling forwards onto my face.

My father did an admirable job of pretending not to notice. He took a step forward, blocking the view of the others as Ferius now used both hands to keep me up. 'The rest of you have homes and families to return to,' he said. 'Do so now.'

It took only seconds for the oasis to clear out. No one stopped to say anything to me. Not Panahsi or Nephenia. Tennat didn't even bother to insult me.

When everyone but Shalla and Ferius had gone, my father turned to the Daroman woman and nodded. She removed her hands and I immediately felt myself falling backwards. My father caught me effortlessly in his arms. 'You should sleep now,' he said.

It wasn't a command or a spell. I could have stayed awake if I'd tried hard enough. But, see, there was this tiny, almost infinitesimally small possibility that if I fell asleep I would wake up later to find that this had all been a terrible, humiliating dream. So I closed my eyes and hoped.

5

The Stand-Off

I woke several times on the journey back home. My father kept a steady pace despite the weight of carrying me. Whenever I opened my eyes I'd see the sky had got darker, only to suddenly blaze with light whenever we passed under one of the city's glow-glass street lanterns.

'You're going to blow one of those things up if you don't keep that will of yours under wraps,' Ferius Parfax said, leading her mottled black-and-grey horse beside us.

'You question my father's control?' Shalla demanded, her voice full of righteous fury.

My father spoke a single word – *'Daughter'* – and Shalla's eyes darted back to the sandstone sidewalk beneath us.

Ferius gave a little laugh and shook her head.

'What's so funny?' I asked.

'So many magic words in your language. Who knew the word for "daughter" was the same as the word for "silence"?'

I felt my father's arms tense beneath my back and legs. 'How clever. I take it you must be some sort of travelling entertainer? Should I offer you a few coins for your performance?'

My father considers actors and troubadours to be slightly less useful than sand lice.

'Why, thank you, Great Ke'heops,' Ferius replied, either not picking up on his sarcasm or not caring to. 'But no, I'm more of what you'd call a cartographer.'

'You make maps?' I glanced back at her horse's saddlebags, expecting to find the kinds of long wooden tubes my mother uses to protect her fragile charts. 'Where do you keep them?'

Ferius patted one of the front pockets of her black leather waistcoat. 'Right here.'

There was no way you could keep proper maps inside a pocket. I was about to point this out to her when I noticed that the buildings along the street on either side of us were getting shabbier and shabbier. No longer the three- and four-storey trimmed limestone houses and marble sanctums we'd passed on the Way of Ancestors, these were squat little buildings made from rough timber or unpolished slabs of sandstone. The exteriors had none of the brass or silver finishings typical of Jan'Tep homes, nor statues or any decoration other than the occasional worn shop sign hanging out front. What little illumination leaked out onto the street came from the flicker of mundane oil lanterns through the wooden slats of unevenly cut windows.

'Why are we going through the Sha'Tep slums?' I asked my father. 'The Way of Ancestors is faster.'

'This path is . . . quieter.'

Quieter. You know you've sunk pretty low when your own father is embarrassed to be seen with you in public. My chest felt tight. It made no difference that I'd managed to beat Tennat even without spells of my own. No one thought that I'd been clever or brave, not even my own father. All that mattered was that my magic was weak.

'Guess it makes sense to take the quiet route if you're

looking to avoid trouble,' Ferius said, reaching into her waist-coat and pulling out a thin smoking reed.

The comment struck me as innocuous, but Shalla was always sensitive to any implied insult to our father. 'How dare you suggest that Ke'heops would ever—'

'*Daughter!*'

The word had come so fast and forceful that it took me a second to realise it was Ferius who'd said it. Shalla looked stunned and stood there for a moment as if someone had cast a chain binding on her.

'Will you look at that?' Ferius chuckled. 'It really works. My very first magic spell.' She stuck the smoking reed between her teeth and leaned towards Shalla. 'Give me a light, will you, kid?'

Shalla gave her a look that made it clear she had no inten-tion of obliging her with even that simple spell. Despite knowing better, I lifted up my right hand and called on the magic of ember to flow through me. I turned the full force of my mind and will to envisioning the gap between my thumb and forefinger igniting in flame. When I was sure I had it ready I whispered the single-word incantation, '*Sepul'tanet.*'

Nothing.

This far from the oasis, I couldn't even make a candle spell work. All I got for my troubles was a sudden wave of exhaus-tion and the sensation that the tattooed ember band on my arm was cutting into my skin.

'No need to trouble yourself,' Ferius said. 'Got my own magic for this.' She snapped her fingers and a match appeared between them. She flicked her thumb against the head of the match and it ignited. A few seconds later she was blowing thick rings of hazy red smoke into the air behind us. 'Someone's following.'

'No one of consequence,' my father said, resuming his progress down the street. 'Probably just some curious Sha'Tep.'

'My father cast a warding spell when we left the oasis,' Shalla explained. 'He'll know if any mage comes within a hundred yards of us.'

'Really?' Ferius asked. 'You can do that?'

Shalla smirked at her. 'We have spells for everything, Daroman.'

Ferius took a drag from her smoking reed. 'I wonder then, oh great and powerful mages, if there might also be a spell that counters those sorts of wards.' Before either Shalla or my father could answer, she added, 'Because those people I mentioned are here, and they ain't Sha'Tep.'

Voices came shouting from the darkness behind us, followed swiftly by several sets of sandalled feet slapping along the street. 'Ke'heops! Stand and answer for the crimes of your house!'

My father set me down on my feet. My legs were still wobbly so I leaned against the rickety door frame of a cloth merchant's shop. When I looked back down the street, I saw the red flapping robes of Ra'meth coming towards us.

Like my father, Ra'meth was one of the lords magi of our clan. He was, quite possibly, the only person who disliked me even more than his son, Tennat, who came alongside with his two older brothers.

'Good evening, Lord Magus,' my father greeted Ra'meth. He nodded to the others and added, 'Adepts. Initiate.'

Both the older boys had passed their mage's trials a couple of years ago. Ra'fan was a chaincaster now, and Ra'dir a war mage. They both appeared calm, almost cordial, which is how you look when you've been preparing yourself for spellcasting. This wasn't going to be good.

My father showed no sign of concern. 'I doubt you've forgotten the clan prince's edict, Ra'meth. Our two houses are forbidden from feuding.'

Tennat sniggered, which is the kind of thing you do when you're too stupid to understand quite how dangerous it is to break an edict. There are all sorts of concealment spells in Jan'Tep magic, but none that will hide you from the clan prince's wrath if you cross him.

'We come on a matter of law,' Ra'meth declared. 'That foul creature of yours comes with us!'

My father made a show of looking around at Shalla, Ferius and myself. 'Of which foul creature do you speak? I seem to be plagued with them tonight.'

Ra'meth pointed an elaborately carved oak-and-silver rod about two feet long at me. It was the symbol of his office and a potential conduit for his magic. 'That filthy wretch cheated in a sanctioned initiates' duel,' he said. Ra'meth's voice had a clear, almost musical quality to it so that, even angry as he was, there was a certain beauty to the way he added, 'I will see Kellen, son of Ke'heops, bound in copper and buried in a cell this very night.'

My father hesitated. Lying to a fellow member of the mage's council was grounds for sanction, but if he admitted that Ra'meth's accusation was true, I'd be dismissed from the mage's trials. I had put my father in an untenable position.

Damn all you ancestors a thousand times for making me so weak. 'My spell failed,' I said. That part was technically true, and not all that uncommon during the trials. 'I just need another chance to—'

'So you beat my son with lies and trickery!' Ra'meth's glare slid from me to my father. 'You see? The boy admits his magic is weak. He should never have been allowed among the initiates. How many times have we told you that he should have been declared Sha'Tep years ago?'

'I . . . I didn't beat Tennat,' I muttered, reeling from the idea that my fate might have been sealed so long ago. 'My spell failed, that's all. I just need a little more practice. Just until—'

The end of Ra'meth's oak-and-silver rod twitched and for a second I couldn't tell if he was going to hit me with it or cast a spell. A fleeting motion to my left caused me to turn. Ferius had slipped a hand into her waistcoat. 'Maybe you should stop shaking your little stick there, fella. It's starting to annoy me.'

Tennat, having been quiet up until now, finally found an opponent he was comfortable threatening. The tattooed iron band on his forearm began to glow, the eerie grey light cutting through the darkness around us. 'Speak again, Daroman, and I will make the next words out of your mouth a scream for mercy.'

Ferius took a drag from her smoking reed and nodded as if giving his words deep consideration. 'Sounds serious,' she said, and let out a puff of smoke that sent Tennat and both his brothers into a coughing fit. 'Sorry about that. Guess you got me all flustered.'

Tennat did his best to utter a few curses in between coughs.

'Shut up, Tennat,' Shalla said. 'You're just upset because you lost the duel.' She turned to his father, favouring him with a little more respect. 'Lord Magus Ra'meth, Kellen didn't violate the terms of the duel. He didn't set any traps or use weapons. The fact that Tennat thought he was losing and gave in wasn't Kellen's fault and it wasn't against the rules.'

40

Ra'meth was about to say something when my father cut him off and spoke directly to Tennat. 'Were you injured, boy? Did my son hurt you with . . . whatever it was he did?'

Tennat's chin came up. He looked a little green. 'I'm fine. Kellen could never hurt me. He's too weak.'

My father nodded, though I could see the skin around his eyes tightening. 'Then the question is settled.' He turned to Ra'meth. 'Your boy wasn't harmed. This was a simple misunderstanding and is now an issue to be resolved by the respective families, not by the court.'

For a moment it appeared as if the matter was done with and we could all return home, but Ra'meth suddenly pointed his rod at Shalla. 'You. You duelled your brother without sanction or agreement.' With increasing confidence he turned his fury back on my father. 'This precocious little wretch of yours attacked an initiate who had only just completed a duel. This crime cannot be ignored. The girl must be counterbanded. Permanently.'

Shalla's eyes went wide with terror. The very thought of what Ra'meth proposed – of my father being forced to burn counter sigils into her bands, forever denying her the ability to perform any magic whatsoever . . . For a moment I thought she might actually make a run for it.

My father looked pained. Ferius just laughed.

'You find our laws funny, Daroman?' Ra'fan asked, stepping forward to stand by his father's side.

'Nah, I just think it's sweet how you're all so worked up over Kellen's well-being when a minute ago you wanted to arrest him. You're quite the little troop of concerned citizens.

Ra'meth's rod began to smoulder with shifting blue and red light so thick it was like watching twin snakes slithering

41

around the shaft. 'Watch your tongue, woman. You know nothing of Jan'Tep power.'

Ferius kept a hand on whatever it was she was holding inside her waistcoat pocket. She let out a smoky breath that filled the air between her and Ra'meth and set him to coughing. 'I know that if you keep pointing that little stick of yours in my face you're going to find it lodged somewhere mighty uncomfortable.' Her lips kept their casual smile but her eyes looked deadly serious.

Ra'meth caught his breath and laughed. 'Would you draw a weapon on me, Daroman? Would you do battle with a Jan'Tep lord magus? Say yes, I beg you, or simply nod and the duel is sanctioned.'

As if on cue, all three of Ra'meth's sons lined up in front of us, raw magical force twisting and turning around their arms while their hands prepared the somatic forms for a range of assault spells.

I saw Shalla tense up next to me, then try to calm herself, hands at her sides, fingers twitching with her own spells. Ferius still had her hand inside her waistcoat, no doubt holding some kind of weapon. And me? *I guess I can throw myself at them and hope it breaks someone's concentration.*

'Have you lost your minds?' my father demanded. 'By the clan prince's decree we are forbidden from feuding. He will see your entire house exiled for this!'

The threat of exile should have brought them to their senses, but it didn't. Ra'fan and Ra'dir smirked. Tennat openly giggled. They looked like jackals grinning over wounded prey. *They know something we don't.*

'I suppose you've been distracted this night by the plight of your failed children,' Ra'meth said. He nodded back towards the centre of the city. 'How else could you have missed the lights above the palace?'

I looked back, past the homes and shops, all the way to the palace itself. Seven beams of coloured light, so pale they almost disappeared against the backdrop of stars, rose from the roof of the palace to meet the sky. I was too young by far to have ever seen the seven sacred lanterns lit, but even I knew what they meant: the clan prince was dead.

'A tragedy,' Ra'meth said, his tone making a lie of his words. 'By tomorrow the council will open the election for the next clan prince. Naturally they'll forbid any acts of vendetta between the great houses, but that is tomorrow. Tonight is for the kind of justice that is quickly forgotten once an election is called.

My father's next words echoed through the street. 'Enough!' He stepped in front of Ra'meth. 'You come at me like a shadow thief in the night with your accusations and your arrogance? Go home, Ra'meth. Make whatever complaints you wish to the council in the morning, or, if you are so determined to settle this matter here in the street like dogs fighting over a bone, then we have the means to do so. But it is me you will duel, Lord Magus, not my children and not this woman.'

For a moment Ra'meth looked genuinely worried by the cold, hard stare my father gave him. I thought he was about to walk away, but then he said, 'My whole life I have watched you strut and stride among our people, Ke'heops. You act as if you are so much better than the rest of us, but for all your strength, you are only one man.' Ra'meth nodded to his sons. 'My blood is strong. Every one of my children carries the magic of our people in their veins. You have forgotten the wise words of our ancestors, Ke'heops: it is the house that matters, not the man.'

This is it, I realised. *They're going to attack.* My father, powerful as he was, couldn't hope to overcome Ra'meth and his sons by himself. Shalla had potential, but that wasn't going to be enough against a lord magus, a chaincaster and a war mage. *Do something,* I told myself. *Anything.*

A light chuckle broke the silence. It came from Ferius. 'A little free advice? Next time you're planning an ambush, don't give the other guy so much time to prepare.' She took one last drag from her smoking reed before letting it fall to the ground and crushing it under the heel of her boot. She still had a hand inside her waistcoat.

'Show us your little weapon then, woman,' Ra'meth said. 'You think a knife will save you?'

Ferius withdrew the hand and held it up for all to see.

It was empty.

'Look, see?' Tennat laughed. 'She's a fake, like Kellen. She doesn't even have a weapon.'

She smiled, then blew the last of her smoke into the faces of Ra'meth and his sons. 'Who needs a weapon?' she asked, as the three of them began coughing even worse than before. It was only then that I realised how careful she'd been to always blow the smoke out towards them and not us. 'Yeah, that stuff's awful rough on the lungs the first few times. Gives you a terrible headache too.' She turned to me. 'Say, I don't suppose you need to be able to speak and think clearly to cast spells, do you?'

Ra'fan, the skin on his face looking remarkably green, extended his right hand, middle two fingers bent in towards the heel of his palm and the outer two extended towards

Ferius. '*Medran'e'fe*...' The intonation of the spell was broken as he launched into a coughing fit. Ra'dir tried next, but barely got the first syllable out before he turned and vomited into the street.

Ferius looked down at the remains of her smoking reed on the ground. 'I should give those up. Filthy habit really.'

Ra'meth drew in a deep breath, his eyes focused, expression calm. Like his sons, he looked ill from the smoke, but unlike them he had the strength and experience to resist its effects. Before he could open his mouth however, my father spoke, hands held out in front of him. His fingers didn't twitch nor did his hands glow. My father never showed off. 'Think before you speak, Ra'meth of the House of Ra, because in the next ten seconds I will use these hands either to carry my son home so that his mother can see to his injuries or to settle our dispute once and for all. The choice is yours.'

Ra'meth stiffened. He gave no more threats, no more demonstrations of power. My father had made it clear that there were only two choices. Without Ra'fan and Ra'dir to back him up, Ra'meth knew he couldn't take my father. He signalled for them to leave, then turned to me. 'You will receive no gold disc for your duel, boy. You will fail the other three trials as you failed the first. Then you will find yourself here among the Sha'Tep where you belong.' He grabbed Tennat, who was still choking and gagging from the smoke, and turned to leave. 'Where even your parents have always known you belong.'

The words were callous and cruel and I knew they were calculated to wound my father as much as me. Still, my heart would have sunk then had it not been for Ferius, who gave a little snort and punched my father in the arm. 'All that

45

magical posturing with glowing rods and mystical fireworks, and in the end you sent him packing with nothing more than a stern look. I see where the kid gets his nerve.'

I felt strangely proud of that.

6

The Household

I convinced my father to let me walk the rest of the way home but I suspect I didn't make it very far because I woke up sometime later in my mother's private room. She and my father shared a bedroom, but each also kept a separate chamber for their personal use. In my mother's case, it was for her two passions: medicine and astronomy.

A wall of beautifully framed star charts greeted me when I opened my eyes. I was lying on my side on her silk-covered settee.

From the age of six I'd spent countless hours in this room, sitting anxiously as my parents cast evocations in the hope of strengthening my pathetically weak connection to the six foundations of magic. The process exhausted them and left me so weak I was unable to do more than lie on the settee for hours. By now I knew every inch of every wall and every scratch on every piece of furniture in the room, so I was unsettled to see one of my mother's silver telescopes lying haphazardly on the floor in the corner. Her writing desk held a large piece of parchment and small bottle of black ink left open, which meant she'd been in the middle of working on a new chart when my father had brought me to her. On the opposite side of the room, cabinets of healing draughts and medical supplies sat wide open, pieces of linen bandaging strewn on the floor. *Guess I was in even worse shape than I thought.*

Voices carried from outside the door but I couldn't make them out. My first attempt to get to my feet failed as nausea and the sensation of dozens of rusty iron spikes piercing the inside of my skull forced me back down. One of my ribs screamed in protest. It didn't feel broken any more, but it still hurt. *A Jan'Tep must be strong,* I imagined my father saying. *An eavesdropper must be stronger,* I added.

I clambered down to the floor and crawled on hands and knees until I reached the door and put my ear against it. Normally I wouldn't have been able to hear through the thick wood, but normally people weren't yelling quite this much.

'It wasn't my fault!' Shalla shouted, her voice a half-octave higher than usual. 'Kellen's the one who cheated! He *cheated!*'

My father's reply wasn't shouted at all and yet the deep tones of his voice practically made the walls shake. 'And in your pride, you betrayed your brother. Your family. Your blood.'

'But—'

Whatever she was about to say next ended in a strangled cry.

'Ke'heops!' my mother said, her voice pleading rather than commanding.

'The one is a liar and the other a traitor to her family,' my father said. 'Is our blood so weak? So flawed? The House of Ra seeks our downfall, and how can I present myself as candidate for prince of our clan when my own progeny shows the seed of our line to be so foul?'

'She is a child! She doesn't know what she—'

48

'A child? She sparks one of her bands every other week. Her power grows daily. What manner of mage will she become, when her spells are tempered not with humility and conscience but instead amplified by arrogance and pride?'

There was a long pause in the argument while the sound of my father's pacing rumbled along the floorboards of the house. 'I could counter-band her,' he said. 'Permanently. I have the metals waiting in my study. I know the sigils. I needn't even ask the council.'

'Husband! You cannot!'

'Father, no! Please!'

His footsteps stopped. 'I am the head of this house. It is my right and my responsibility both to protect this family and to protect the clan from the threat of another rogue mage. I will bind her forever if I must. Do not doubt it.'

My mind suddenly filled with visions of Shalla being held down by the force of my father's will as he pushed banding needles into her forearms, coloured inks of copper and silver insinuating themselves under the skin, the counter-sigils binding the magic inside her forever. I rose to my feet and reached for the doorknob.

'You say things you do not mean to,' my mother said. Her voice held a stiff tone she used only rarely, like a steel bar fresh from the forge. Even my father knew not to test that strength.

'I'm sorry, Father,' Shalla whimpered. I let out a breath I hadn't realised I was holding in and stepped back from the door. I knew my father loved Shalla fiercely, and yet now he seemed to be contemplating the unthinkable.

'Go to your room,' he said. His voice had lost its imperious edge, replaced by a weary resignation. 'I will take time to consider the appropriate course of action.'

Several minutes passed before I heard my mother speak again, this time her tone softer, gentler. 'Shalla is not like your mother, Ke'heops, nor was she to blame for what she did. Seren'tia was sick, she was –'

'She was shadowblack,' he said.

The world became silent and still, shut down by the word my father had just uttered. *Shadowblack?*

There are seven fundamental sources of magical force, but Jan'Tep mages are banded with only six: iron, ember, silk, sand, blood and breath. No mage is ever banded with the seventh, because shadow is the magic of emptiness, of the void, of the demonic. Our ancient enemies, the Mahdek, drew upon shadow for their spells. That's why the Mahdek are long dead.

My grandmother had died when Shalla and I were still small children. I knew she'd lost her mind – something that can't be allowed for a mage with her power – but could she really have been shadowblack?

No wonder our father was concerned about Shalla's behaviour.

'Nice family you got there.'

I spun around and lost my balance, tripping over my own feet and stumbling forward. If Ferius hadn't caught me I probably would've tumbled out the open window beside her.

'Reckon you can fly now, kid?'

Looking up at her I was again struck by the unruly curls of copper-coloured hair that tumbled across her features. They might have suited a lady of the high court had they not seen more sun than a broad-brimmed frontier hat could hold at bay. Her black leather waistcoat was scuffed, and her linen shirt had long ago traded its original colour for a thousand miles worth of dust. But it was the smile – curled up on one side as if she was holding back the best joke in the world

– that really set Ferius Parfax at odds with the refined elegance of my mother's study.

'How did you get in here without me hearing you?' I asked.

She steadied me and gave me a little wink. 'Who can say? Maybe it was magic.'

'I didn't know Daroman could—'

Ferius sniggered. 'You Jan'Tep. So reliant on your little spells that you can't imagine getting through the day without them. You were distracted, kid, that's all. I've been tapping on that window for the past five minutes, but you were so focused on listening to your parents through that big old door that you were oblivious to what was happening right behind you. A roof snake looking for a midnight snack would've made a meal of you by now.'

'I nearly died from having my own sister hit me with a sword spell,' I said, irritated. 'I'm not exactly at my best. What time is it anyway?'

She shrugged. 'I don't pay much attention to clocks, but I'd guess I left you here around four hours ago.'

'I've been unconscious for four hours?'

'Probably longer than that, seeing as how I had to spend forever explaining to your mom how I revived you.' Ferius shook her head. 'And the woman calls herself a healer? Anyway, your dad had a bunch of questions, your sister had a bunch of excuses – but no one offered me anything to drink. So I left and spent the next couple of hours discovering that nothing remotely resembling a saloon stays open after midnight in this hick little town of yours. Thought I may as well come back and check on you.'

It struck me as a little odd that a Daroman cartographer – not that I believed that's what she really was – would go to

51

the trouble. Maybe she was hoping to get paid for saving my life.

I walked carefully back to the door to see if I could hear any more of what was happening on the other side. My parents were still arguing, though not loud enough for me to make out anything but the occasional word like 'weakness' and 'flaw' and, of course, my name.

Shame and exhaustion drove me back to sit down on the settee. Ferius took a seat next to me and reached into the pocket of her waistcoat to pull out a short, stubby smoking reed. 'I don't think I like your family, kid.'

Despite the fact that I'd be a corpse right now if it weren't for her, it irked me that this woman thought she could come into my family's house and pass judgment on us. 'I suppose your family is so much better?'

'Well, my family's all dead,' she said, lighting the reed with a match and taking a puff from it. 'So they're not nearly as noisy.'

A quiet knock at the door startled me. Abydos, our steward, entered the room with a tray. The aroma of freshly baked bread and poppy-seed cheese filled the room and tugged at me, helped along by the sharply sweet scent of mulled pomegranate juice. When Abydos caught sight of Ferius he stiffened. 'I see you've returned, Lady Ferius.'

'I'm no lady, but yeah, I'm back.'

Abydos set the tray down on the table in front of me. 'I wasn't sure when you last ate, Master Kellen.' His eyes flicked from me to Ferius and back again.

'Oh, relax, Aby,' she said, laughing. 'You look as if you're trying to decide whether I'm here to kill the kid or seduce him.'

'And which is it?' he asked.

'Abydos!' I said, my voice rising. 'This woman is a guest in our house. You will—'

'Don't worry about it, Aby,' Ferius interrupted, casting me an angry sideways glance. 'Neither murder nor seduction's in the cards today.'

'Well then, that's all to the good. I'll leave you to . . .' The steward gave a quick nod to me, then left.

I was voraciously hungry and halfway through the bread and cheese when I saw the curious expression on Ferius's face as she looked towards the door. 'What is it?' I asked. 'Abydos didn't mean to be rude. He's just protective of me.'

'He looks a lot like your father,' she commented.

'Oh, that. He's my father's brother,' I explained, taking another bite of bread before washing it down with some pomegranate juice.

'You mean he's your uncle.'

'I . . . technically, yes.'

'And you talk to your uncle like a servant?'

'He's Sha'Tep,' I said, though I was fairly sure she knew that already. The look in her eyes made me feel small. 'He's well treated, you know. Some Sha'Tep work in the mines or are sent to serve other households. Most of them live in the slums at the edge of town. Abydos lives here, with us. My father treats him like family.'

Ferius took a puff from her smoking reed. 'That's decent of you.'

She'd said it as if it was a joke but I felt guilty anyway, so I changed the subject. 'Were you really just pretending to have a weapon before?'

'Weapon?'

53

I pointed to her waistcoat. 'When Ra'meth was—'

'Oh, that.' Ferius reached a hand into her waistcoat and pulled out a small stack of rectangular paper-thin boards, each one about the size of one of her hands. Gambling is forbidden among the Jan'Tep so it took me a moment to realise what she was holding.

'Playing cards?' I asked, dumbfounded. 'You threatened the leader of my clan's council of mages with nothing but a deck of cards?'

Her face took on a theatrically offended expression. '"Nothing but a deck of cards"? I'll have you know that I'm deadly with these things.'

I watched as she laid them out on the table in front of us. Now that I had a better chance to see them I found myself entranced by the cards' bright colours and beautiful, elaborate paintings. Even the ones bearing nothing but numbers and symbols were elegantly composed and stirred up stories of deadly battles and courtly intrigue in my mind.

Ferius split the cards into four stacks, each decorated with a different symbol. She picked up the first stack and fanned it out in front of me, pointing first to a card with an elaborately drawn number nine surrounded by shields. 'This is a numbered card.' Then she pointed to one showing an illustration of an oddly dressed man bearing a crown seated on a golden throne decorated with chalices. 'This is a face card.' She closed the fan and put the four stacks back together. 'There are four suits, each with ten numbered cards and three face cards.'

'What's that one?' I asked, pointing to a card that didn't seem to be part of any of the suits. Instead it showed a woman carrying fire in one hand and ice in the other.

'We call those discordances,' Ferius replied, quickly removing it from the deck and stuffing it back into her waistcoat. 'Those cards are a little too dangerous to mess with for now.'

Before I could ask how a card could be dangerous, Ferius launched into an explanation of the basic mechanics of the deck and described some of the games that could be played with them. She rattled off names: Country Twist, Royal Courts, Desert Solitaire, Six-Card Standoff . . . they went on and on. Each game had its own rules and strategies. I was utterly confounded by the complexity of it all. It had never occurred to me that there was more than one game that people played with cards.

I stared in awe as Ferius shuffled the deck, her hands moving smoothly and confidently as the cards flipped around her fingers. It was like watching a master mage performing a dazzling series of somatic shapes one after the other.

It was like magic.

'So,' Ferius said, grinning at my expression, 'want me to show you a few spells?'

7

The Cards

I don't know how long we sat up playing cards, but by the time we stopped the first rays of sun had made their way through the open window of my mother's study. *Playing* cards. The term didn't even begin to describe what it felt like to me.

I had no difficulty memorising the rules of each game or learning the different ways of handling the cards. I'd always been quick with both my head and my hands. It was too bad that magic wasn't just twirling your fingers and saying the right words.

'You got me, kid,' Ferius said, miming an arrow to the chest as she pretended to fall backwards.

I looked down at the cards on the table. I had beaten her at a game of Speared Jacks. My first game of it in fact.

'All right,' she said. 'Don't go getting a swelled head.' She picked up the cards and shuffled them back into a tidy stack.

'Are we stopping?' I asked, disappointed.

She shook her head. 'Just want to see you try something else.' Ferius took one card off the top of the deck and held it between her thumb and forefinger. 'See that knot of wood in the centre of the door there?' Before I could answer she snapped her wrist and the card flew through the air, striking dead centre in the little imperfection of the door's wood before bouncing off onto the floor.

'How did you do that?' I asked, utterly amazed.

She handed me a card and showed me how to place it between my own thumb and forefinger. 'It's all in the wrist.'

I gave a toss of the card. It landed a few inches in front of my foot.

'Again,' she said, handing me another card.

'What's the point? It's not like—'

'Just throw the card.' I did, and this one flew a little further, maybe two whole feet before flopping to the floor. The third did better than that. On the fourth try, I hit the door. By the time I'd worked my way through the deck and we'd picked up all the cards again, I could hit the target easily, and all I could think was, *I'm good at something*.

It's hard to describe the sense of elation I felt. Maybe it was because I'd spent the last several weeks failing at everything I tried, or perhaps just because I'd almost died and my head still wasn't right, but for whatever reason, I was smiling a big, stupid grin.

'Feels good, don't it?' Ferius asked.

I flicked a card towards the edge of the door. I could almost line it up so that it would stick in the gap between the door and the frame. 'It's all right,' I said, not wanting to sound too eager. 'It's not like it's real magic or anything.'

Ferius raised an eyebrow. 'Not real magic? Of course cards are magic, kid. I've got all kinds of spells I can do with them.'

'Like what?'

She flipped a card into the air – a three of shields. When it landed back in her palm it was the ace of spells. 'Like using them to make someone else's money magically move from their pocket to mine, for example.'

'How?' Then I realised she was just talking about gambling, not actual magic. 'Oh, right.' I turned away and pulled back my wrist to fling another card at the door.

'"Oh . . . right",' Ferius repeated, mimicking me in a way that made me feel stupid. 'You Jan'Tep. You wouldn't know real magic if it hit you in the face.'

Just then the door opened. I hadn't been paying attention to the sounds of approaching footsteps. The card I'd been hurling at the door left my hand before I could stop it and an instant later hit my father right between the eyes.

I watched my father's hands go up reflexively into the somatic form for a fire spell. I flinched, immediately bringing my arms up to cover my face and dropping the cards all over the floor in the process. When I noticed that I wasn't engulfed in a ball of flame, I opened my eyes again and saw my parents standing by the door. My father looked more disappointed than angry.

My mother took immediate notice of Ferius sitting next to me. 'Lady Ferius, I wasn't aware that you'd returned. Can I—'

'No "Lady",' Ferius interrupted.

'Excuse me?'

'I'm not a . . .' and here Ferius waved her hand deferentially towards my mother before finishing with, 'whatever.'

While I wasn't sure what would qualify a Daroman woman as a 'lady', it was certainly true that Ferius had nothing in common with my mother. Ferius's features might have been attractive on a woman who, well, dressed like a woman, but everything about her was sharp edges and hard angles. It was as if some mischievous god had designed her entirely for the purpose of smirking, making lewd remarks or sauntering into other people's homes uninvited.

My mother, on the other hand, could have walked right out of a painting of the three goddesses of love and would have put the other two to shame. Her straight blonde hair was like Shalla's, but with a deeper colour, as though lit from underneath by warm fires. She rarely wore excessive finery, yet her simple kasiris dress – a sheath of white muslin that went down to her ankles – drew no end of attention from the men in our city, sometimes annoyingly from my fellow initiates.

My father glanced at the open window and then at Ferius. He reached into a pocket of his coat and pulled out a small bag of blue silk. 'I was going to seek you out later in the day, but since you're already here, I wish to repay you for your service to my family.'

'What, you mean chasing off old Ram . . . Ramey . . .' She raised an eyebrow. 'Heck, I can't keep track of all the weird names your people have. Anyway, don't think nothing of it.'

A flicker of irritation passed over my father's features. 'I would have dealt with Ra'meth and his sons myself. I was referring to Kellen's weakness nearly costing him his life earlier.'

'Well, in that case it's the kid who owes me a debt, not you, Mister Ke'heops.'

My father's jaw clenched. The implication that anything involving a member of his family might not be his concern was not something my father tolerated. This was getting ugly, fast.

'Master,' my father said.

'Pardon me?'

'A Jan'Tep mage of my rank is referred to as "master".'

Ferius shrugged. 'I've made it a policy never to call any man "master", so I suppose we'll just have to pretend we're friends and I'll call you Ke'heops.'

'And you? Shall I call you Ferius Parfax?' He jiggled the silk bag. Coins tinkled against each other. 'Or do you go by Ferius *Argos*? That is how your kind are named, is it not?'

I glanced between my father and Ferius. 'What's going on?' I asked.

'The woman is an Argosi,' he replied.

'What's an Argosi?'

Ferius reached out and plucked the small bag from my father's hand. 'Someone your people don't understand very well, I'd say.'

My father nodded towards the coins that Ferius was now stuffing inside a pocket of her waistcoat. 'It seems we understand you well enough.'

'Were you not able to find a place to stay in the city?' my mother asked. 'You could stay here with us...' Her words drifted off just enough at the end that even I caught her meaning.

'That's all right, ma'am,' Ferius said. 'Not enough booze in this house.' She rose and walked past my mother and father to the door. 'Besides, you've got too many spies.' She abruptly banged the door right in its centre. From the other side I heard Shalla squeal a loud 'Ouch!' Ferius gave a little laugh and shook her head, the red curls shivering as if they too thought it was funny. 'You Jan'Tep. You knock me out, you know that?' She turned back to look at me briefly. There was a strange softness in her eyes. 'Keep the cards, kid. You'll need 'em.' Then she opened the door and walked out, leaving me alone with my parents.

My mother came to me immediately and brought a hand to my forehead.

'I'm fine, Mother,' I said.

'Unless you've become a healer without my knowing, that is for me to judge,' she said, lightly tracing a finger around my left eye. It was something she did when I was sick – her way of reassuring me.

My father walked back to the door, picked up the card I'd hit him with and then slowly collected the others and placed the deck on the table. 'Later today you will send one of the servants to return these to the Daroman woman.'

'She said I could keep them.'

My father sat down on the table next to the settee, which was unusual for him. 'Kellen, a son of the House of Ke doesn't play with cards. He doesn't gamble. He doesn't cheat at his trials.'

'I beat Tennat,' I said, the combination of exhaustion and my earlier elation at learning to throw cards making me foolish. 'Does it really make a difference how I did it?'

'Cheats. Deceptions. Tricks. It is always tricks with you, Kellen. Tricks will not keep our family safe.'

I found myself tensing up. I resented my father in that moment, resented his lofty words and his honour and, above all else, his magic. Was it my fault the damned bands around my forearms wouldn't spark? Was it my fault I had so little power inside me I could barely light a glow-glass lantern? Ever since I'd been a child I'd had to find ways around my problems, never able to force my way through them the way Shalla or my parents could do. 'Tricks are all I have,' I said.

He turned to my mother. 'Clever. The boy seeks always to be clever.' My father uses the word 'clever' the way other people use terms like 'unsavoury disposition' or 'unsightly skin condition'. He walked over to her writing desk and returned with a small glow-glass ball, the kind children use to learn to focus their will. He handed it to me. 'A Jan'Tep must be strong.'

I held the ball in the palm of my hand. It was burning brightly, but when my father and mother walked to the door, the light disappeared. Not dimmed. Disappeared. I focused my will on it, urging it to light, but nothing happened. *Come on*, I told myself. *You've done this a thousand times before.* Nothing. The light was dead. Ra'meth's cold voice came back to me. *You will soon find yourself among the Sha'Tep, where even your family knows you have always belonged.*

'A Jan'Tep must be strong,' my father repeated from the doorway. I looked up and saw that he wasn't talking to me – he was talking to himself, the way people did when they were preparing themselves for something that was going to be very hard, or very sad. The last days before my sixteenth birthday were upon me and, for the first time in my life, I was truly afraid of my father.

8

Abydos

I spent most of that day in my own room, sleeping, waking and, in between those two states, staring at the little glow-glass ball I still clutched in my hand. I could get the barest glimmer out of it now, just enough that if I pushed myself to the point of collapse I might make it compete with a small candle. Eventually I threw the ball against the wall of my room. It didn't even have the courtesy to break. One more test failed. No messenger was going to be coming to bring me the gold disc that would symbolise passing the first trial.

I lay in my bed for hours at a time, holding my arms out in front of me, willing the tattooed metallic inks of the six bands to break apart, for the sigils to spark, igniting the symbols of the spells that I should be able to cast by now. It wasn't fair. My whole life I'd done everything a Jan'Tep initiate was supposed to do. I'd memorised the perfect pronunciation of every spell, mastered every somatic form. I could hold the image of a spell in my mind with perfect clarity even in the middle of a raging thunderstorm. None of it mattered. The bands wouldn't spark.

At one point I became so consumed with frustration and resentment that, even though I knew it wouldn't work, I scratched at the bands with my fingernails, breaking the skin until I bled. But no amount of scraping or cutting would bring them to life. Only magic. Only strength. Only the things I didn't have.

I bit into my blanket, fearing my mother or father – or, worse, Shalla – might hear me crying. I raged silently against the whole world, only to later try to force myself into accepting the fate laid out before me, imagining my life as a Sha'Tep clerk or servant. By evening I came to the conclusion that neither petulance nor subservience suited my temperament.

I needed to do something about my situation. *A liar*, my father had called me. *A cheat. A trickster.* Well, if that's what I was, then I was going to lie, cheat and trick my way to a mage's power, because there was no way in any hell I was going to stay like this. We had plenty of stories among my people of the Mahdek tribes who stole magic from the gods or spirits, who drank deadly concoctions and performed secret rituals that led them to discover powerful spells. Of course, being thieves, the Mahdek weren't exactly considered the heroes of those stories. *Fine then*, I thought, *I'll be the first.*

A knock at the door brought me back down to earth.

'Come in,' I said, not wanting to see other people but determined not to let it show.

There were no lights in my room so it took a moment for the shadows coming through the door to resolve themselves first into hands, then a tray, and finally Abydos. *Uncle Abydos*, I reminded myself.

'You haven't eaten all day,' he said quietly.

I was a little surprised at his coming to me with food. My father had a strict policy that meals were to be eaten as a family, and if either Shalla or I ever chose to sulk in our rooms then we could go without. Last night I'd been ill, so it was an excusable lapse. But tonight? 'Does my father know that you're bringing me supper?'

Abydos came and set the tray down on the small desk in the corner of my room and sat at the chair that was already too small for me and made him look like a giant. He lifted the red-clay cover from the tray, revealing a plate laden with some kind of roasted lamb dish that smelled wonderful. 'The family has already been served, Master Kellen. This is my supper and I'm entitled to eat it where I please.'

'You want to eat in my room?'

'Do you mind?'

I got up from the bed, my clothes from the day before feeling rough and stiff against my skin, and joined him at the desk. When I looked at the tray I noticed he'd put together a rather large portion for one man. I noticed something else as well. 'You seem to have two sets of cutlery on your tray.'

'Hmm?' He looked down at the extra pair of utensils in mock surprise. 'Why, I do indeed. How odd.' Then he looked at the plate of lamb. 'I also seem to have taken more food than I can eat. I don't suppose you might . . . ?'

I picked up a knife and fork and grinned, more for Abydos than out of any real sense of pleasure I felt, but even fake happiness was better than sitting alone in my room staring at a blackened glow-glass ball.

At first we ate in silence. I'd never spent much time with Abydos. He'd always struck me as a rather simple person – utterly unlike my father. But now, as I watched him eat with a kind of methodical patience, I could see similarities emerge. They were close in age, Abydos being a year or so younger, and shared the same colouring and powerful build. But my uncle didn't exude that sense of power, of command, that my father did. He was, I suppose, what a Daroman farmer or a Berabesq soldier might seem like. Unimposing. Unremarkable. Ordinary. And yet, did I see him that way simply because he had no magic?

'Did you always know you were Sha'Tep?' I asked, dimly aware of how rude the question was but suddenly desperate to know the answer.

My uncle took it with remarkable grace. 'I suppose I did,' he said, his eyes gazing somewhere far away. 'I could do a little magic, as a child. Most of us can, close to the oasis, but my ability faded as I approached my naming year.'

Which was exactly what was happening to me! A sudden panic began to rise up from somewhere deep inside me, as though my very soul were screaming for help. *This isn't right! I was born to be a mage like Mother and Father and Shalla, not some useless Sha'Tep like* . . . Abydos was looking down at me. His eyes were gentle . . . patient. Shame drowned out my terror and rage, and my breathing slowed, but the underlying desperation remained. 'When your magic began to fail . . . did you . . . did you ever try to fight it?'

Abydos held out his forearms, the coloured bands long faded but still visible. 'I used to sit and stare at these things for hours, trying to will them away, praying for the spirits of our ancestors to ignite them for me.' He ran a fingernail down the length of one forearm. 'I even tried . . .' Abydos shook his head. 'I sometimes had foolish thoughts as a boy.' He went back to eating his food.

'Tell me,' I said. A subtle change in my uncle's expression made me realise I'd sounded as if I were giving him an order.

'I mean, I've read . . . I've heard other initiates talk about ways of breaking the bands with copper sulphides and . . .'

Abydos smiled, swallowing a mouthful of lamb and then setting his knife and fork down on the tray. 'Ah, yes, the tales of potions concocted from the banding metals we mine deep beneath the oasis. Do you envision formulating exotic potions fuelled by the spells of three young mages working in concert, nobly sacrificing a portion of their own magics . . . Kellen, can you imagine in your wildest dreams that your fellow initiates would ever do such a thing?'

'Why wouldn't . . . ?' The question died on my lips. I already knew the answer. Magic was the most prized possession of my people. Who would ever want to give up a piece of that power? And yet, that was precisely the strategy I'd been contemplating. Panahsi had so much potential that I hoped he might be willing to give up a little for me. My sister – if she felt guilty enough and if I stoked her ego sufficiently. *But, Shalla, you're so powerful . . . you've got more magic than our whole clan combined, don't you?* It was a far-fetched plan, but, as I'd learned from Ferius last night when she'd taught me an odd game called Poker, sometimes you have to play the cards you're dealt.

'Don't,' Abydos said, shaking me from my thoughts. 'I've seen that look on the face of many a young initiate, but for every legend of a mage finding their power through dark magics, there are a hundred very real stories of those whose lives were shattered in the attempt. There is a cost to pay for seeking greater power than the spirits of our ancestors would willingly grant.'

Unbidden, something my father said the night before came back to me.

'Is that what happened to my grandmother?' I asked. 'Did she really have the shadowblack?'

The question would have shocked anyone, and I think it did give Abydos a jolt, but he hesitated only for a second before answering. 'She had an illness,' he said, almost absently. He brought the index finger of his right hand up to his face and traced a pattern on his cheek. 'Black, swirling markings that grew over time and, as they grew, so too did the darkness inside her.'

'I don't understand. What darkness? What do you mean?'

Abydos leaned back against his chair and I saw deepening lines on his forehead, his eyebrows rising at the centre. 'It just seemed to take her over. An . . . ugliness inside her, changing her. She became someone utterly different from the woman I'd known as a child. In the end, it fell to your father to stop her.'

My father's words rang out in my head. *It is my right and my responsibility both to protect this family and to protect the clan from another rogue mage.* But he'd said something else too – about Shalla. *I will bind her forever if I must.*

'I don't understand,' I said, my voice rising. 'Mother is a healer! Why didn't she—'

'There is no cure. If it's true, what the masters say, that the shadowblack is a curse cast upon us by the Mahdek in the final days before they fell to our spells, then I doubt any magic of ours can remove the disease. We can only cut out the infection before it spreads.' He placed a hand on my shoulder – an unusual gesture for him. 'Do not dwell on the past; the present has more than enough perils of its own.'

I thought about last night and Ra'meth with his sons.

Could they have killed Father if Ferius hadn't interfered? I looked up at Abydos. 'Is our family in danger from Ra'meth?'

He turned back to the food. 'Not if your father becomes clan prince.'

'But will he? The House of Ra has a lot of supporters. What if . . . ?'

Abydos had been in the process of raising a forkful of lamb to his mouth. He stopped and gave me a raised eyebrow. 'Have you ever known your father to fail at anything?'

He had a point. On the other hand, I doubted Abydos knew anything about Jan'Tep politics. Before I could think of a polite way to make that point, the door to the room opened again. It was Shalla.

I should have known she would come. Almost a whole day had passed, and no doubt she expected me to be over any misguided anger I might feel towards her. 'Look, Kellen, I know you're cross with me, but I . . .' It was only then that she seemed to take any notice of our uncle sitting at my desk. 'What are you doing here, Abydos?'

'Get out, Shalla,' I said.

Abydos gave me a stern look. Normally I would have found the idea of being reprimanded by a Sha'Tep preposterous, but in a few weeks' time chances were very good that I'd be reporting to him every morning to receive my duties for the day. He squeezed my shoulder and gave me a sympathetic smile. There was real warmth there, maybe more than I was used to seeing from my parents.

'I was just leaving, Mistress Shalla,' Abydos said. He rose and was about to reach for the tray still half full of food when he turned to me. 'Forgive me, Master Kellen, but I have some pressing duties. Would you mind terribly if I left my supper tray here for a little while longer?' He didn't wait for an answer, but simply stood and walked to the door.

'Thank you, Ab . . . Thank you, Uncle,' I said.

He turned back and gave me a smile underneath sad eyes.

'"Uncle"?' Shalla asked dubiously, depositing herself on the chair Abydos had just vacated.

'What do you want?'

'I . . .' She hesitated for a good long while. 'I just wanted to see if you were all right.'

Why do people ask questions like that? *I see your arm has fallen off, are you all right? Oh, hello there. I understand your entire family burned in a fire. Are you all right?* My magic was fading and in a matter of weeks I would find myself consigned to the Sha'Tep. From that moment forward Shalla would view me with no more respect than she did our uncle. So the correct answer was, *No, I'm not all right. I'll never be all right, and it's your fault, Shalla.*

Had it been five years ago, when we were little children, I would have picked up the tray and dumped its contents on my sister's head. Had it been yesterday, I would have yelled at her, shouting until the roof came off for the way she'd helped to destroy my life. But it was today, and I could no longer afford to be that person. I needed to be someone who thought about the future.

'Shouldn't you be preparing for your own tests?' I asked, hoping to change the subject.

She opened up the palm of her hand and revealed a gold disc. 'My duel was this morning. I almost refused when that old fool Osia'phest told me I had to fight Enyeris. She's the weakest student among all those taking the trials.'

70

Not the weakest any more, I thought bitterly. When I caught Shalla looking at me as if I was some kind of invalid I said, 'I'm fine. Thanks for asking.'

Her mouth opened but no words came out. I let her hang that way for a few seconds, hoping a bug might fly in through the window and land in her mouth. At last she said, 'You're *fine*?'

I nodded and patted the left side of my chest. 'Heart's beating just how it should.' I had no idea if that was true of course. It might have been ticking backwards for all I knew. I stood up and opened my wardrobe and began searching for a clean shirt. 'Really, Shalla, I'm doing great, but I've got some important errands, so if you don't mind . . . ?'

'Your magic is fading, Kellen. Soon it'll be completely gone. And you're saying you're *fine*?'

I didn't respond. She was trying to pick a fight with me. In Shalla's world, a fight was a chance to prove how smart she was; a test of wills to be quickly won – after which she would magnanimously declare that the conflict and anger could now be forgotten. Shalla was my sister and one of the three people I loved best in the world, but I didn't want to 'fight and forget'. Despite how much I was soon going to need my sister's help, at that moment I couldn't stand even to look at her.

I exchanged my dust-covered shirt from the day before for a dark grey linen one from the wardrobe that suited both the evening sky and my mood.

'And what "errands" do you have tonight?' she asked, idly picking at my food. 'Is this because Mouse Girl came around asking about you?'

'"Mouse Girl"?'

71

'The dull one from your class. The one with the pointy face. Nephi . . . Neph . . .'

'Nephenia?' I asked. 'She doesn't have a pointy face. She's the most –' The smug look on Shalla's face stopped me from saying any more. The last thing I wanted was to give her one more thing to hold over me. I looked away and my eyes settled on the deck of cards sitting on the edge of the little table next to my bed. I walked over and retrieved the deck, feeling the cards slide smoothly into my palm. I resisted the urge to fan the cards out and start flipping them in the air. 'I have to go. Father said I was to return these to Ferius Parfax right away.'

Shalla stopped playing with my food and turned to me, her expression suddenly very serious. 'No, he said to send a servant. You should stay away from that woman, Kellen. People are saying she's a spy for the Daroman king, come to interfere in the election of the next clan prince.'

'It's going to be Father,' I said reflexively.

'Of course it's going to be Father. So why is this Ferius woman here? What does she want?'

'I don't know,' I replied, tucking the deck into the pocket of my shirt. 'I'll be sure to ask her when I see her.'

I turned to open the door, only to have it open in front of me. Our father stood in the doorway, his tall frame lit by the lanterns in the hallway behind him, casting a shadow over me. He held out his right hand and there, across his palm, was a rolled piece of parchment sealed with black wax. *An edict*, I realised, suddenly terrified. *Ra'meth has got the council to issue an edict against me.* 'You've been summoned,' he said.

I couldn't tell from his voice how much of what he felt was concern for me and how much was anger over whatever infamy I'd brought down on our house. 'You have to open

72

it, Kellen,' he said. 'There is a guard from the palace waiting outside.'

I reached out and took the scroll, hands shaking. It felt heavier than it should, and when I opened it something fell out onto the floor. I looked down and saw the light reflecting off a small gold disc, just like the one Shalla had received for winning her duel. 'I don't understand,' I said, reaching down to pick it up.

Shalla took the disc from me and held it up to examine it next to her own. They were identical. 'What does the summons say?' she asked.

I began to unroll the scroll and only then noticed the symbol pressed into the black wax: a star rising above waves in the water. 'That's the sign of the clan prince,' I said, turning to my father. 'But . . . he's dead. How could . . . ?'

My father's eyes narrowed, examining the seal as if he might find some flaw in its design. 'The prince is dead, but there is one other who may still use his symbol.'

'The dowager magus,' Shalla breathed. 'But she hasn't held court in . . .'

Neither of us knew the answer. The dead clan prince's wife hadn't left the palace since long before either of us was born. To us, she was little more than the stern, cold features carved onto the face of the statue outside the palace gates bearing her name. I opened up the scroll and found written on its surface a single sentence. *I have questions for you.*

I glanced up at my father, the scroll in my right hand and the gold disc in my left. 'What do I do?'

The uncertainty in his eyes settled on a look of concern for me. 'You have no choice. She is the dowager. There will be a price for refusing her.'

9

The Dowager

I had never been through the palace gates before. Inside was a huge expanse, lit by nothing but the stars overhead, walled in by stone colonnades that rose twenty feet from the swept sandy ground. In the centre stood the palace itself, a large single-storey building with seven walls that sloped inwards, making the heptagonal roof smaller than the foundations. I could still see the seven pale lights rising up from the roof and shining towards the stars, a reminder that the clan prince was dead, and that these were dangerous times.

The lone guard who'd delivered the edict walked me right past the palace, leading me instead to the seemingly endless gardens behind. The darkness, the emptiness, made me feel very alone. Was this why my parents had been forbidden to accompany me? With the shadows all around, this would be an excellent place to murder someone.

By now the council would certainly have banned any feuding while the election of the next clan prince was under way, but would Ra'meth *really* fear their judgment? How much would it cost to bribe one guard into eliminating the son of a rival?

I glanced at the guard, who kept his arms at his sides,

index and little fingers of each hand touching lightly. A *trib-*
ulator, I thought – a mage who specialises in iron and blood
magic. If I tried to run or make a move against him he'd
have me paralysed in agony in an instant. He raised one arm
and I flinched. 'She awaits you inside,' he said.

I looked out past the rows of brightly blooming trees and
dark rectangular ponds. There was a copse of tall wooden
structures that looked like skinny dancing figures, each with
many arms. At the end of each arm was a pot with lush
flowers of pink and gold. 'Inside what?' I asked. 'All I see
are—'

The guard's eyes flickered annoyance. 'There,' he said,
pointing more clearly.

Deeper inside the gardens I finally saw the small, darkened
cottage hidden among the flora. It couldn't have been more
than ten by ten feet and the walls barely rose to the height
of a man.

'The dowager is in there?' I asked incredulously.

The guard gave no reply. He just kept standing there, arm
pointed towards the cottage, waiting for me to proceed. My
father's words came back to me: *There will be a price for*
refusing her.

Having never been inside the palace grounds, I hadn't known
what to expect – but it certainly wasn't a ramshackle cottage
that looked as if it belonged in the Sha'Tep slums. Unfinished
logs supported the roof in each corner, while rough wooden
slats made up most of the walls and the ceiling that sloped
down on one side, presumably to keep rain from collecting.
The inside was clean and reasonably well kept. I saw no signs
of mould or filth. Had the cottage been a human being you

75

might have said it carried itself with a quiet dignity, but to me it just looked old and tired. Its lone occupant gave much the same first impression.

'Is this the obeisance one may expect from the House of Ke?' she asked.

The dowager magus sat in the cottage's lone chair, a book in her hand. She wore black from head to toe, the garments appearing to have been made from a single long bolt of silk that she'd wrapped around her arms and body and tied here and there with blue cords to keep it from billowing out. It looked rather a lot like the kind of thing the undertaker dresses a body in for burial. Only her face and hands were visible, and what I saw of them confused me.

'Forgive me . . .' I mumbled, stumbling through a series of bows, realising I had no idea how to do so properly nor how to address her. 'My . . . Lady?'

'You may call me Dowager Magus.' Then she added, 'But only if you close the door before I catch cold.'

I quickly closed the door behind me, careful not to turn my back on her. That, at least, I knew would be impolite.

The dowager appeared at first to be my mother's age, but as the single glow-glass lantern hanging overhead swung back and forth, I would have sworn she aged deep into her seventies and then back again. 'Distressing, isn't it?' she asked.

I cursed myself for staring. 'What is, My Lady . . . I mean, Dowager Magus?'

She rose to her feet and folded her hands in front of her. 'The sight of someone so long past the appointed time of her death.'

She took in a deep breath and her features seemed to shift again, to those of a much younger woman.

I really had no idea what I was supposed to say. 'You look . . .'

She smiled. 'Beautiful?'

Not exactly the word I would have used, but I was a little too nervous to judge. 'Yes, Dowager Magus.'

She gave a tired laugh that, even though her appearance stayed the same, made her seem much older. 'I will save you a great deal of awkwardness, Kellen, son of Ke'heops.' She spread her hands wide and with that gesture I saw lines of energy sliding all around her, glowing beneath the folds of her black silk garment, lighting up her skin from the inside. 'I am some three hundred years old, held together by nothing more than spells and will. I stopped caring about what a callous boy might think of me roughly two hundred and eighty-three years ago.'

I suppose on some level I'd known this would have to be the case. The recently deceased clan prince had been the same man who'd fought and defeated the Mahdek nearly three centuries ago. He and his wife had never sired an heir, which was why we were about to have our first ever election for a new prince. I found I was holding my breath just watching her. It's one thing to hear such stories and quite another to come face to face with them. 'How do you . . . ?'

'Stay rooted to this place, foregoing the dubious honour of the grey passage?' She set aside her book and raised a hand. As I watched, tendrils of force slid along the lines of her fingers. 'Spells to hold my bones together, spells to make the blood course through my veins, spells to keep my mind sharp, spells to . . . well, I imagine you get the idea.'

The amount of magic for such effects – not to mention the skill and precision required to work them – was staggering.

A thought occurred to me then. 'With such power, why do you not—'

'Heal myself permanently? Simply make myself younger?' She sat back down in the chair. 'Some costs cannot be avoided, even with magic.'

I shook my head. 'Forgive me, but I was going to ask why *you* are not the clan prince now.'

She looked up at me from her chair, one eyebrow arched, and then she reached out a hand. 'Come here.' I did, and she took my hand and kissed it. 'Thank you, Kellen. I find I'm so rarely surprised these days. The heaviest price of a long life is that people become so predictable. One needn't even ask most of them questions, for their responses are so dependably calculated by the simple equations of self-interest. From now on, you will call me Mer'esan.'

I took my hand back, feeling distinctly uncomfortable at the odd intimacy. 'Is that why you summoned me, Mer'esan? To ask me questions?'

'Why? Have you any answers?'

'To some things,' I replied, then thought about it for a moment. 'But probably not to anything that would interest you.'

She smiled again. 'Good – clever. I like clever.' She rose to stand in front of me, looking much younger now, perhaps in her late twenties, and beautiful indeed. I wondered if she were truly as unconcerned with appearances as she pretended. 'I have many questions, Kellen. None of which you can answer, of course, but my hope is that together we might work them out.' She tilted her head for a moment. 'Ah, but you are in the midst of your mage's trials, aren't you? So it is incumbent upon us to *test* this mind of yours. Ask me the question.'

A hundred questions bubbled through my mind. Why had she summoned me? Why did she live in this shack in the gardens instead of the palace itself? Why had she given me the gold disc that allowed me to continue in the mage trials? All questions to which I very much wanted an answer; none of which, I suspected, she cared about at all. She had no intention of answering my questions. She wanted to know if I could discern hers.

I worked through the permutations of what I had seen of her so far: she chose not to live in the palace, made no attempt at taking power for herself, and thus had little interest in the machinations of clan politics. After staying out of our people's daily affairs for decades, she'd chosen to involve herself in something as small as the mage's trials. Further, she'd taken an interest in me. Why? Because my father was the most likely person to become clan prince? There were others in contention, including Ra'meth. Had she spoken to him, or to Tennat? Looking around the cottage, I doubted she'd had any other visitors here for a long time.

'Take your time,' she said, betraying impatience in her voice.

She's nervous. Concerned. It had to be something else . . . something that would trouble someone who'd long ago lost interest in either dying or living. Something new. Something her own magic couldn't answer. I let the possibilities and permutations roll through my mind a while longer until I decided to trust the answer – or rather the question – to my intuition. 'There is only one question that interests you, Mer'esan. It is the one you cannot answer yourself.'

'Really? I am a learned woman, Kellen. What is this riddle you believe befuddles me so?'

'Who is Ferius Parfax?'

79

There was silence between us for a long time before Mer'esan gave a slight bow of her head in recognition. 'Well done, Kellen, son of Ke'heops. You have earned that little disc in your pocket.'

Mer'esan walked over to a kettle sitting on a small shelf. 'I would offer you something to eat or drink, but I'm afraid the things I consume at my age would likely make you quite ill.' She poured something thick and viscous into a blue glass and took a sip. Finally she looked at me over its rim. 'Did the Argosi show you her cards?'

Instinctively my hand went up to the pocket that held the deck. Mer'esan caught the motion and held out a hand to me. 'Give them to me,' she said. I complied and watched as she spread them face up on a wooden countertop. After a moment her eyes narrowed. 'This isn't her true deck.'

'It is,' I said. 'She gave it to me yesterday.'

Mer'esan slid the cards back together and handed them to me. 'This is, indeed, a deck of cards and I've no doubt it belongs to this Ferius woman. It does not, however, contain her *Argosi* cards.'

'But what is an "Argosi"? Are they related to the Daroman or the Berabesq?'

'The Argosi aren't a people,' Mer'esan replied, taking another sip from her glass. 'They're more like. . . a collection of outcasts. They wander the world, making their way by doing whatever little services will get them money.'

I looked down at the deck of cards and remembered Ferius's joke about using them to cast spells that moved other people's money into her pockets. 'They're gamblers.'

'Yes – but that is, I believe, something of a ruse. In truth, one might think of them as . . .' She looked up as if reaching for a word.

'Cartographers?' I suggested.

The dowager seemed surprised, but then gave a light laugh. 'Is that what she called herself?' She didn't wait for a reply. 'I suppose "cartographer" is as good a description as any, but the Argosi do not draw maps of places, but rather of people . . . cultures.' She tapped the deck in my hand. 'You understand the meaning of the suits?'

I nodded. 'Shields for Darome, spells for the Jan'Tep, chalices for—'

'Chalices for the Berabesq, yes. But look more closely at the individual cards and you'll see that the particular design on each card reflects part of the fundamental power structure of that society. They call these the "concordances".'

I rifled through them, picking up one of the face cards in the suit of spells, and noticed then that it showed a picture of a lord magus on it. Another card, this one in the suit of shields, showed a man in armour, a long red cape flowing from his shoulders. The card was titled 'General of the Armies'. The ace of spells showed an oasis, while that of shields depicted some sort of siege engine about to strike a great stone wall. *So each suit shows the foundation and hierarchy of its culture.* 'Ferius had other cards,' I said then, remembering the ones she'd stuffed back into her waistcoat. 'She called them "discordances".'

Mer'esan nodded. 'They are trumps, of a sort. The Argosi travel to witness the great events that have the power to reshape the world around us; they watch the people and forces that can build and destroy civilisations. They paint these new cards – the discordances – believing that by

81

creating the truest deck they can interpret the course of history.'

There was a strange, twisted logic to it all. If you had a deck that perfectly mirrored the people and events that shaped a culture, it might help you see where that society was headed. 'Is that why she's here? Because the clan prince . . .'

'You needn't protect my feelings,' Mer'esan said drily. 'It's not as if I was unaware that my husband is dead.'

The casual way she spoke caught me off guard. I found myself staring at her, searching for some sign of grief, or anger, or even relief. I guess I stared too long, because when she looked back at me I suddenly felt very cold. 'Watch where you swim, son of Ke. Men are apt to drown when they dive too deep into unknown waters.'

'Forgive me, Dowager . . . I meant no—'

'I told you to call me Mer'esan.'

'Forgive me, Mer'esan.' I decided to keep my mouth shut for a while and see if that worked out better.

The dowager stared at me for what felt like a very long time. I grew increasingly uncomfortable, which I suspected was the point. I think she wanted me to speak again, to say some other foolish thing so she could mock me once more. But I have a stubborn streak sometimes, especially when someone is goading me.

'Good,' she said, after what felt like eternity. 'Now perhaps we can return to matters of consequence.' She took the cards from me and fanned them out, picking one at random. When she flipped it over it showed the highest face card of the suit of spells: the clan prince.

'Ancestors . . .' I swore. Could Ferius have been responsible for his death? *No, Mer'esan would have already cast a scrying*

82

spell, sand and ember magic most likely. She'd know if her husband had been murdered. It's just another test.

'Better,' she said, as if she could read my thoughts, which was entirely possible. I doubted even silk magic was beyond the dowager magus. She handed me back the cards. 'My husband had been declining for decades, and half the world knew he was in his final months. The Argosi's timing was simply coincidence. She's here for another reason.'

I flipped through the cards. If the Argosi always made sure their decks represented the true state of the world, then wouldn't a new clan prince be important to them? I sorted through until I found the card titled 'The Clan Prince'. It showed a man in a crown with a septagram behind him, the sigils of all seven forms of magic glowing. 'Whether we have an old clan prince or a new one, it's still the same card, still the same deck.'

I hadn't intended to speak aloud, but Mer'esan smiled and reached out to put a hand on my cheek. The gesture was far more affectionate than I would have expected. 'Better, son of Ke. Much better.'

It seemed the degree to which the dowager liked me was entirely dependent on whether the last thing I said was clever or not. 'You said the Argosi only painted their other cards . . . the discordances . . . to represent people or events that could change the world. You believe that Ferius Parfax is here because something dangerous is coming. Something that could . . .' *How had she put it?* 'Something that could build or destroy a civilisation.'

Mer'esan nodded. 'Try and sleep with that thought burrowing around your head.' Her shoulders slumped and her eyes looked sunken in their sockets. 'Finish now, Kellen

83

of the House of Ke. This conversation is the longest I have suffered for more than twenty years. I grow tired.'

I was about to suggest that it could have gone a lot faster if she hadn't kept testing me. *Unless that was the point. She wanted to know if I was clever enough, but clever enough for what?* I reached into my pocket and dug out the gold disc that the dowager magus had sent to me. 'You want me to spy on Ferius Parfax.'

Mer'esan turned away from me, suddenly busy with arranging her glass and her book and her kettle. *She's ashamed,* I thought. *Ashamed of what she's asking me to do.* 'The Argosi are full of secrets,' she said. 'This one seems to have taken an interest in you. You will do whatever is required to maintain that interest. You will do so without revealing my request to her or your father or to anyone else.'

So, spy on the woman who saved my life. 'And in return you'll ensure I stay in the mage's trials,' I said, the words already sounding like a betrayal. 'But won't the trials be suspended until the new clan prince is selected? Doesn't the council have better things to do than decide who gets a mage's name?' Mer'esan turned back to me and gave me a hard look, but I was getting tired of being made to perform for her amusement. 'No, just tell me this time.'

I think she might have blasted me with a spell then and there if she hadn't been so exhausted. 'The trials are more important now than ever. They are all that matters.'

'But why?'

'Because I never gave my husband an heir,' she said, her voice barely a whisper and yet so full of . . . what? Sadness. Regret. Guilt. *And something else. Determination.* 'What matters more than the strength of a mage, Kellen?'

I thought back to Ra'meth's words the night before. 'The strength of his family.'

Mer'esan nodded. 'There is no mage left powerful enough to hold our people together solely on his own strength. Others could try to kill him and thus take the crown for themselves. So the next clan prince must have a powerful bloodline. A family too strong to challenge. A dynasty.' She gave a wry shake of her head. 'Besides, by using the trials to determine the strongest bloodline, those cowards on the council needn't fear voting against the mage who might become their ruler. Their hands are kept clean.'

It wasn't hard to imagine Ra'meth using his new position to punish those who'd failed to support him. He'd been ready to try to murder my father just to improve his chances. *Hells, what if he keeps coming after us?*

'You needn't fear Ra'meth, if that's what's creasing your brow. The council has made its decree – no vendettas until the new clan prince has been given the crown.'

'What happens then?' I asked, my rising voice betraying my fear. 'What happens to my family if Shalla and I don't . . . if my father isn't selected?'

'Exile,' she replied. 'Not by the new prince of course – that would be a terrible way to start a reign. No, if Ra'meth becomes prince, the council will banish the House of Ke.'

Exile. A Jan'Tep family wandering the world with no allies, no clan and no access to the oasis. Over the years even my father's magic would weaken. It was nothing less than a death sentence for all of us.

Mer'esan looked at me for a moment, an expression of sympathy on her face that made me feel even worse. 'We are a people of magic,' she said quietly. 'We cannot afford a mages'

85

war between houses. Better one quick and brutal injustice than decades, perhaps even centuries, of blood feuds fought with spells and murder and mayhem.' She reached out and closed my hand over the tiny gold disc. 'I suggest you find your magic quickly, son of Ke.'

10

The Spy

It was late into the night by the time I left Mer'esan's little cottage. I still had Ferius's deck in my pocket, along with the gold disc. I felt weighed down by these tools that were being used to manipulate me. I thought back to all the jokes Ferius had made about Jan'Tep magic. She made my desire for it sound petty and childish. *Except that the dowager magus tells me it's the only thing that will keep my family safe.*

I didn't know who to believe. I knew exactly what my family would think. *A Jan'Tep must be strong,* my father would tell me. My mother would just look at me, and make that little gesture of hers, drawing a finger around my left eye, assuring me that life was unfolding as it must. Shalla would do what she always did: tell me it was all my fault and I just needed to try harder. For once I just wanted to talk to someone who wasn't going to judge me or make fun of me.

Nephenia.

Shalla had told me she'd come looking for me. I wondered what she'd looked like, knocking at our door, asking after me. Had her eyes been full of concern and maybe, just maybe, something more? Had she cried when my parents had refused to let her see me?

It was a childish fantasy of course, as was my sudden desire to try to find her. It was late, and for all I knew the dowager magus might have one of her guards following me to see where I went. Besides, I was fairly sure that in the morning Shalla would put on a big show in front of my father, asking whether I'd returned the deck of cards to the 'Daroman woman', which was the only justification for not returning the instant my meeting with the dowager had ended. So finding Ferius had to come before any hopes of romance with Nephenia.

Ours isn't a very big city – it's barely five miles in diameter with about three thousand inhabitants – but trying to find one person among all those souls would have been almost impossible had I not been fairly sure where to look.

My people drink wine and beer along with an older, more traditional spirit made from apricots and pomegranate called *djazil*; for the most part, these are imbibed in the home, with family, in a quiet, dignified manner. Since that in no way described Ferius, I headed towards the city's guest houses. There were only five specifically intended for foreigners, and of those I was fairly sure only three served strong drink.

'She's not here,' the thin-lipped Sha'Tep man behind the counter said, ignoring me while he shifted a pair of small oak barrels onto the deep shelf behind him.

'But you're sure you saw her?'

The little belly awkwardly attached to his otherwise bony frame shook as he laughed. 'A red-haired Daroman woman in a frontiersman hat? How many of those do you think we get around here?'

'So when did she leave?'

He looked annoyed, or thoughtful. I couldn't quite tell which. 'Must have been about two hours ago. She said my beer tasted like cow's piss and went off in search of something better.' He pointed towards the door. 'Try the Night's Calling. It's in Veda Square, about a quarter-mile down the street.'

'Why not the Falcon's Pride? It's closer.'

'She said she'd already been there. Said *their* beer tasted like cat's urine, which, evidently, Her Ladyship considers even worse than cow piss.'

I left the guest house and over the next half-hour made the trip through the slums down to Veda Square. I don't know whether Ferius had been inside the Night's Calling, nor what particular type of urine she would have compared their house beer to, because by the time I found her, she had more pressing concerns.

The entrance to the square was blocked by the white-shirted backs of a dozen initiates, a few from my own class, making it impossible for me to see inside. It wasn't hard to tell Ferius was there though.

'Back off, you sap-faced little rat, before I clip your whiskers and use them to pick my teeth!' Her shouts were slightly slurred. I don't think I'd ever heard someone that drunk.

I recognised Panahsi's tubby frame nearby and yanked him around. 'What's going on in there?'

When he recognised me he ushered me back further from the square. 'Kellen! What are you doing here?'

'Looking for Ferius Parfax,' I said, shaking off his arm. 'Now tell me what's going on.'

'Go home, Kellen. You shouldn't be here.'

I was about to press him further when a couple of older initiates, maybe seventeen or eighteen years old, looked back and took notice of us. 'Hey, fatty, you're supposed to keep lookout.'

'It's all right,' Panahsi called to them. He turned to me and spoke in hushed tones. 'Go home, Kellen. You don't want Tennat and his brothers seeing you right now.'

I grabbed him by the shirt, which would have been a mistake if Panahsi's inclination for violence was even remotely in proportion to his potential to deliver it. 'She saved my life, Panahsi.'

Panahsi's eyes went straight to the ground. 'It's . . . Don't worry. They're not going to hurt her. Not really.'

'You're lying, Panahsi. Or you're stupid.' I shoved him out of the way and ran towards the entrance. The other initiates had their backs to me, their attention focused on the action inside the square. I spotted a small gap between two of them and made for it, pushing through them before anyone noticed me.

'Hey!' one of them shouted, making a failed grab for my arm.

I glanced back, expecting to see the initiates coming for me, but none of them, not even Panahsi, crossed the line into the square. They must have been ordered to stay outside.

'Kellen, wait!' Panahsi shouted to me. 'You don't know what you're doing. She's a spy!'

I ignored him and ran the hundred yards to the other end of the square where three figures were standing in front of Ferius. She caught sight of me and called out. 'Hey, kid. You probably shouldn't be running around like that, what with nearly dying and all.'

The three in front of her turned. I recognised Tennat first. His face shone with excitement mixed with a kind of hunger that made my stomach turn. Next to him stood Ra'fan, his brother, wearing the grey-and-blue silk shirt and loose linen trousers that are the ceremonial garb of chaincasters.

Ra'dir was on the other side of him, bigger and taller than his brothers; he wore the blood-red shirt and black trousers of a war mage.

Why are they all wearing their ceremonial garb? That was when I noticed the four braziers set around the square, each one burning with a different-colour fire. 'You're holding a trial?'

'She's a spy,' Tennat replied, his smile as ugly as anything I'd ever seen. 'My father says so.'

'Your father's an idiot,' Ferius said. 'No offence.'

'Shut your mouth, Daroman!' Ra'fan shouted.

I'd expected him to be deep in concentration, holding Ferius in a binding spell, but there was no way he could maintain focus while shouting like that. *Why are you just standing there, Ferius? Why aren't you making a break for it?*

I looked down at the ground where she stood and found the answer. A rough circle had been scratched into the gravel and dirt, barely visible to the eye, but I was sure there was a thin line of copper wire buried just underneath. Ra'fan was the chaincaster of the group – he must have imbued the wire with a trapping spell while Ferius was inside the guest house and then triggered it the second she walked out the door and into the circle. From outside it would be a simple matter to break the wire, but anyone inside was bound until Ra'fan released the spell.

'You can't hold a trial,' I said, trying my best to channel my father's voice. 'None of you has rank to attend court, never mind run one. When the masters find out—'

'Who's going to tell them?' Ra'dir asked, taking a step

towards me. He pointed to the initiates guarding the square. 'Everyone here is a loyal Jan'Tep mage. Everyone here knows we have to protect our people from spies.' To me he said, 'Besides, Ra'fan's found a mind-chain spell that'll bind her from ever revealing what happened here. She'll remember all of it, but she'll never be able to say it or write about it or do anything that would let anyone know. Ra'meth will—'

'Shut up,' Ra'fan said. He came over and put a hand on my shoulder as if he'd suddenly decided to be my big brother. 'Just wait over there with the others, Kellen. Nobody wants to hurt you. You might be Sha'Tep, but you're still one of our people. It's our job as Jan'Tep to protect you, don't you understand?'

Merciful ancestors, he actually thinks I'm dumb enough to fall for that.

Ra'meth couldn't come after our family now that the election had begun, so instead he had sent his sons after Ferius. Not only could he get revenge for her interference last night, he could also show everyone that allies of the House of Ke weren't safe. Of course, pointing that out wasn't going to get me anywhere.

I gave a laugh which I hoped didn't sound as fake to everyone else's ears as it did to mine. 'You think Ferius Parfax is a spy? She's no spy. A card-playing swindler, maybe, but nothing as grand as a spy.'

'Oh really?' Ra'fan said, removing his hand from my shoulder so he could push me with it. 'A card player who just happens to show up at an initiates' duel? Who just happens to save your life and then spends the night at your father's house?' He pushed me a second time. 'Who attacked a lord magus under cover of darkness?'

My heart was starting to beat too fast for my chest.

Meanwhile, my mouth was as troublesome as ever. 'Really? *That's* what you're going with?'

Ra'fan pushed me again, sending me stumbling backwards. 'Wouldn't it just serve that fat Daroman king perfectly if he could keep our clan weak by preventing a true, strong prince from rising up?' He turned to the initiates standing guard at the entrance. 'They fear us, those Daroman cowards. Even with all their military might and all their war machines, they fear our magic! That's why their spy threatened Ra'meth's life yesterday.'

I turned to the initiates at the entrance, hoping that at least some of them had figured out how ridiculous this was. All I saw in their faces was a mixture of gullibility, foolish pride and perverse excitement. They'd all convinced themselves this was some kind of noble defence of the Jan'Tep people. Even Panahsi, when I caught his eye, said, 'Fair's fair, Kellen. The Daroman shouldn't be interfering in clan business.'

'It's time,' Ra'fan said.

I turned and saw them lining up in front of the circle holding Ferius.

'Wait, what are you doing? If this is a trial you have to—'

Tennat laughed. 'We already held the trial, Kellen, before you got here. We found her guilty of conspiring against the Jan'Tep people. Now it's time for her punishment.'

'It's okay, kid,' Ferius said. 'Go on home.'

At first I thought she wanted me to go for help. The problem was, that wouldn't do any good: I'd never find anyone in time, and even if I did, I doubted they'd care. Nobody was going to stick their neck out for some Daroman gambler or Argosi wanderer or whatever she was at the risk of angering the family of the man who might be the next clan prince. I looked back at Ferius, trying to signal that going for help wasn't going to work, but then saw the uncertainty in her eyes, which I hadn't noticed before were a deep green. When she said, 'Go on, I can take these three,' I knew she was lying.

'Go home, Kellen,' Ra'dir said. He held up his hands and they started smouldering with a red-and-black glow. Even without his casting a spell, his will was strong enough for me to feel the heat. 'I promise, if you keep your mouth shut about what you saw here, nothing bad will happen to you.'

Nothing bad will happen to you. Sure, except that just about every bad thing that could happen to me already had.

'It's time,' Ra'fan said.

Ra'dir smiled. 'Come on, Kellen. Let's be friends about this. Our houses don't have to quarrel. What do you say?'

There was something ironic about the fact that, if I was going to find some way to recover my magic, it was probably going to require the use of forbidden spells and rituals. I would need people to help me – people willing to do dark and terrible deeds for their friends. People like Ra'dir.

Which was a shame, because the one bad thing that hadn't happened to me so far was my own death, and that was thanks to Ferius.

'I say . . . you're just about the biggest, dumbest oaf I've ever met, Ra'dir, and if you want to get to Ferius Parfax, you're going to have to go through me first.'

His eyes went wide right before he made a grab for me. I ducked under his arms and raced forward, pushing past Ra'fan and diving towards the circle holding Ferius. If I could break the spell, she'd be free. I didn't have a knife or anything else with me so I just dug my hands as hard as I could into the dirt and gravel and felt for the copper wire. I felt someone kick me in the side just as my fingers found it. The wind got knocked out of me, but I managed to break the wire, and as it came apart, so did the spell it held.

I scrambled awkwardly back up to my feet to see Ra'dir and his brothers spread out a few feet away from me, looking unsure of what to do next, or, more likely, choosing which spells to use against us.

'Thanks, kid,' Ferius said. 'That whole binding thing was starting to bug me.'

'Nothing's changed,' Ra'fan called out. 'It's three mages against two magic-less fools. We're ready for your dirty smoke trick this time.'

Ferius ignored him. She turned to me and said, 'Don't suppose you brought a weapon?'

I pulled her deck of cards out of my pocket. 'Just these.'

'Keep 'em,' she said. 'I've got my own.' She slid a hand into her waistcoat and when it came back out she was holding another deck of cards. She fanned them out. 'Here, kid, pick a card, any card.'

Not knowing what else to do, I took one from the middle. That was when I felt the cool metal surface and discovered that these cards weren't anything like the pack I was holding.

'Four of clubs?' she said, looking down at the card in my hand. 'That's the best you can do?'

'You said any card,' I replied, my eyes glued to the strange weapon in my hand.

'Ah, I guess it's okay,' she said, and turned back to the others. 'Always wanted to try my hand at a Jan'Tep duel.' She fanned out the deck in front of her so everyone could see the razor-sharp edges of the thin metal cards gleaming under the soft light of the moon. 'So, who wants it first?'

11

The Deck

The red glow coming from Ra'dir's hands reflected menacingly off the surface of the fanned-out deck Ferius was holding. 'You think you can fight a war mage with a deck of cards?' he scoffed. His fingers were bunched together, pressing against each thumb, the somatic form that would unleash a ball of wildfire once he spread them apart and said the spell.

'For you I just need one,' Ferius replied, and a single card slid up from the fanned deck, which she took and held between the thumb and forefinger of her left hand. 'In case you're wondering, this isn't your lucky card.'

Ra'dir began the spell, but even as he spoke the first syllable, Ferius flung the card. It spun through the air like an arrow and lodged itself in his open mouth. He started choking and his spell came apart before he could even cast it.

'That was the dull end I gave you there, boy. Next time you get the sharp.'

I prayed to our ancestors to put a stop to this – for Panahsi or the other initiates to realise this had gone too far and step in, but none of them moved. This was a duel now, and duels are sacred to my people. Even so, if it had just been Tennat facing us, or maybe even Tennat and Ra'fan, fear of facing an armed opponent might have put an end to the insanity then and there. But Ra'dir was a war mage and they're trained for the chaos of battle. He spat out the card, a thin line of blood sliding from the edges of his mouth down his chin. 'She can't take us all. Attack together,' he said. 'Now!'

I heard both Tennat and Ra'fan uttering spells. I knew Tennat would go for the gut sword – the same spell he'd used on me the day before and one of the few forms of offensive magic an initiate learns. But it was Ra'fan I was worried about. A chain mage has all sorts of binding spells, and in seconds he could paralyse Ferius and that would be the end of the fight. As he spoke the first word, *Kaneth*, I threw the deck of regular cards into his face. The painted surfaces filled the air with colour for an instant, momentarily breaking his line of sight to Ferius. He swatted the cards out of the way and began forming the somatic shapes for the spell again.

I heard a grunt from Ferius. Tennat had chosen to attack her rather than me. *Of course he did. He's stupid but not that stupid.* 'It's the gut sword!' I shouted to Ferius. 'His will is inside you.'

'Just . . . a . . . little . . . sting . . .' she said, doubled over in pain.

Tennat was grinning wildly, so excited at being able to exert his will over Ferius that he forgot she had no shield spell of her own. 'She's mine,' he told the others. The idiot was going to rip out her intestines.

Instinctively I formed the somatic shapes for a spell to break Tennat's concentration. Silk spells are hard to envision – you have to slither into the mind of your enemy. But I've always been good at the basic elements of magic, so my fingers were tracing the somatic forms even as I spoke the first syllables of the incantation and tried to channel my will into the tattooed band for silk magic on my left arm. I thought that maybe here, in a moment of crisis, a moment where I was trying to do the right thing and protect someone else, the magic would come to me.

It didn't.

The only break in Tennat's concentration was the giggle from watching me try. It wasn't enough to weaken his gut sword.

'Keep . . . smiling . . . you little rat . . .' Ferius moaned. She flung another card from her deck and Tennat screamed as the sharp edge dug into the palm of his hand.

I knew Ra'dir was already preparing another fire conjuration, but I couldn't think about that now. Ra'fan had a clear line of sight at Ferius and was readying a different kind of binding spell. Again I raised my hands to try another spell, but Ferius shouted, 'Enough with the parlour tricks, kid.'

She's right, I realised. No spell I attempted was going to help. I tried throwing the metal card she'd given me, spinning it through the air the way I'd learned to do with the paper ones, but these had a different weight and the surface was slippery. The card bit into the ground at Ra'fan's feet. Having neither more cards nor spells and not knowing what else to do, I ran for him.

Something hot scorched the side of my shoulder and I realised distantly that I'd nearly run straight into a blast of flame from Ra'dir's outstretched hand. The air was hot all around me. I ignored it, leaping the last few feet between me and Ra'fan. My burnt shoulder collided with his outstretched arms, breaking the somatic form. I nearly screamed from the agony and stumbled when Ra'fan's elbow slammed into the side of my head, blurring my vision. At least it took my mind off the pain in my shoulder.

As I fell to the ground, I heard him uttering the spell a third time. I swung out my arm and hit his shin, but the blow lacked any force. Something shiny caught my eye and I saw my metal card, the four of clubs, sitting next to me. I grabbed it and slashed wildly at Ra'fan, catching his hands. A thin line of blood appeared in the air as the razor-sharp edge of the card sliced across both palms. He gave a terrified scream that was music to my ears. It's possible that I'm not a very nice person.

'Kid!' Ferius shouted. I turned my head to see Ra'dir standing a few feet away, three separate metal cards stuck in his big chest, still firing blasts of fire from his hands. Ferius was limping and the side of her left calf was smouldering. I rolled towards Ra'dir and kicked out hard, smashing my foot into the side of his leg. His blast went high as he fell to his knees next to me. The next thing I saw was the heel of Ferius's boot connecting with the underside of Ra'dir's chin. His head went back and the rest of him followed. Even then, even as he grimaced in pain on his back, he began uttering the syllables of another fire spell, only to have his words end in a gurgle. Ferius Parfax had her boot on his throat.

Looking up at her was like staring into the face of an angry goddess. Her hat had come off and her red hair floated in the breeze like flames rising from a wildfire. In each of her hands she held several cards, sharp edges shining in the light of the nearby braziers. She was smiling, but not with her eyes. 'You keep talking about magic, kid,' she said to me. 'You keep talking about power. You want to know what *real* power looks like?'

'If you kill us you'll start a war,' Ra'fan said defiantly, though with his injured hands buried in his armpits he didn't look very impressive. Tennat was on his knees, crawling towards his older brother.

With her boot still on Ra'dir's neck, Ferius snapped both her wrists out and I watched in horror as the cards flew from her hands towards Ra'fan and Tennat. *She's killed them*, I thought. *They misjudged her. I misjudged her. She's . . .* I hadn't realised that I'd closed my eyes until the sound of Tennat crying forced me to open them again. Five metal cards were stuck in the dirt just inches from each of the brothers.

'Now *that*,' Ferius said, removing her boot from Ra'dir's neck and setting off towards the entrance to the square where the initiates were already scattering, 'that's magic.'

FIVE of SHIELDS

THE SECOND TRIAL

A mage's power either grows or weakens. Power never remains still and neither does the strength of a nation. Only those who can find new sources of strength may earn a mage's name. Those who cannot have no value to our people.

12

Outcast

When Shalla and I used to get into one of our interminable fights as children, my father would wait patiently until one of us had won or we'd both simply run out of energy and then he'd look at each of us in turn and say, 'So, done then?'

One of us – usually the one my mother had commanded to sit down so that she could place a cold compress on a swollen eye or bruised cheek – would take note of my father's tone and mumble, 'I suppose.'

'Good,' my father would say, and clap his hands once as if he were banishing a spell. 'Then we're all friends again.'

Most times we were too exhausted to question his rather dubious logic, but on the one occasion when I challenged him on it he took me aside and said, 'You fought. Victor and vanquished were decided. Whatever began the dispute is now resolved.'

'I'm supposed to be friends with her? She—'

'She won this time. Next time perhaps she will lose. Either way, there is no virtue in continued hostility. The Jan'Tep do not hold grudges.'

At the time the idea was inconceivable to me. Every fight, whether with Shalla or someone else, felt like a life-or-death struggle waged over the greatest of causes, even if that cause was merely determining the rightful owner of a toy. But Shalla would do just as our father requested and act as if nothing had happened. 'Just a little game Kellen and I were playing,' she would say when Abydos asked why one of us had an arm in a sling. Not knowing what else to do, I would just nod and agree, convinced that Shalla was somehow mentally defective for being able to so convincingly pretend a fight had never happened.

It wasn't until the day after my fellow initiates had tried to cripple Ferius Parfax and myself that I realised Shalla was the normal one.

'Will you be joining us today, Kellen?' Master Osia'phest asked. I looked up to see him standing a few feet away from where I sat on a bench between two of the columns. The other initiates, waiting around the oasis, pretended I wasn't there.

Osia'phest's question was stupid of course. He'd seen my magic fail – everyone had. I wasn't going to be able to draw a soul symbol, or craft a spellstone, or summon a power animal, or perform any of the other tasks that could be used as proof of passing the second test. So the old man already knew I wouldn't be participating in the trials today. But – and here's the ridiculous thing – for him *not* to have asked the question might have implied that there was some *other* cause for my present weakness, such as having got involved in an unsanctioned duel on the side of a suspected Daroman spy. By now the whole town must have heard about it, but legally I hadn't done anything worse than anyone else who'd been there. So now, just as my father used to do after Shalla and I got into a spat, we were all going to pretend nothing had happened.

'No, master,' I replied. 'I'll just watch from here for today. I'll continue the trials when . . .' When what? When the insane dowager magus decides to give me an object of power so I can fake my way through the test? *No, don't think like that.* I was going to find a way to make my magic work again. If I could convince Panahsi and a couple of others to help me, there were still things I could try to get my bands to spark. In the meantime I'd be damned if I was going to let Tennat or anyone else think I'd given up. 'I'll be coming here every day to observe,' I said defiantly.

He nodded sagely, and then came closer and quietly asked, 'Have you tried casting one of the simpler forms, perhaps one of the evocations of breath? Perhaps here in the oasis you can—'

'You know I can't,' I said, practically growling under my breath. I felt immediately guilty for my outburst. Master Osia'phest had been the most understanding of my situation out of everyone. And yet I still couldn't keep the anger down. 'Even if I could, what good is casting a stupid breath spell? It's the weakest form of magic.'

He took a seat next to me on the bench. 'Do not underestimate breath, Kellen.' He slid the right sleeve of his robe up to reveal the silver tattooed sigils representing breath shimmering brilliantly under the withered canvas of his wrinkled forearm. 'Breath is the power of movement, Kellen, of channelling. It can give voice to other forms of magic. Perhaps on its own it's not quite so impressive as ember or iron, but combined with other magics, breath can be . . . remarkable.'

At this point I'd settle for mediocre.

'Go on,' Master Osia'phest said. 'Show me the first evocational form for breath. Unless of course you've forgotten the fundamentals?'

'I haven't forgotten anything,' I said. I could recite by heart the intonations and cantillations for all the breath spells. I'd mastered the somatic shapes, the envisionings, the anchorings. All of it. Just like I had for sand and ember and iron and all the others. There wasn't a single initiate in my clan who knew the forms as well as I did, not even Shalla. It just didn't make any difference.

'The first evocational form,' Osia'phest prodded me.

I forced myself into a moment of calm, softened my gaze and envisioned the movement of air. That's always the hard part with breath spells: holding something that can't be seen in your thoughts. I reached out with my hands, extending my index and middle fingers to form the somatic shape of direction, pressing the tips of my ring and little fingers into my palms, the sign of restraint and control. My thumbs pointed straight up, the sign of *Please, ancestors, let me cast this one stupid spell.*

I set my will upon the air and spoke the single-word incantation. '*Carath.*'

A tiny sliver of wind passed through the space between my hands, following the line of my index and middle fingers. It was barely enough to trace a thin line in the sand at my feet no more than six inches long.

'Well . . .' Osia'phest said. 'It's not . . . so bad. Your abilities are not as promising as they used to be, but they are not entirely gone either.'

To understand just how pathetic that statement was, you'd only have to remember that this close to a Jan'Tep oasis you could take a deaf, dumb and blind Daroman sheep herder, show him the spell and he'd probably summon up a more vigorous gust of wind than I just had.

Osia'phest patted me on the leg before rising from the bench. 'As it turns out, you aren't the only student feeling unwell today.'

It was only then that I noticed Tennat some forty yards away across the oasis, sitting on a bench just as I was, hunched over and looking, from this distance, utterly miserable. He had none of the cuts and bruises he deserved though, no doubt because his father had healed them. Ra'meth, in what can only be an injustice on a cosmic scale, was an even better healer than my mother.

'Initiate Tennat found himself unable to perform the preparation spells this morning,' Osia'phest went on. 'In fact, his situation appears to be worse than yours. I had him attempt the same spell I requested of you, and he couldn't summon any of the breath magic whatsoever.'

Well, maybe there's some justice in the world after all.

'Four other initiates are similarly afflicted. The sudden onset of this condition among so many is . . . improbable.'

A thought came to me, and a sudden hope came on its heels. 'What if we're all suffering some kind of temporary illness? Maybe I'm not—'

'Your magic has faded gradually, over weeks and months. This is a natural occurrence for those called to the life of the Sha'Tep. What is happening to the others is *not* natural.'

Considering how casually Osia'phest spoke of my becoming Sha'Tep, I couldn't imagine anything I cared about less than Tennat's suffering, but I still found myself asking, 'What do you think is weakening them?'

'There are poisons known to cause such symptoms . . . though the formulations are complex and known to only a few. However, it's not impossible that a particularly clever and

109

determined person might uncover them, given time and motivation.' There was something in the old spellmaster's eyes as he gazed at me . . . Was it concern? No. Suspicion. It was as if he was waiting for me to confess something. 'Your house has feuded with that of Tennat in the past, has it not? One cannot help but note that most of those afflicted come from families who support the House of Ra, or who might make their own claim the title of clan prince.'

'You can't possibly think that I—'

Osia'phest put up his hands. 'I make no such accusation. I know you to be a good lad, though reckless and, forgive me, somewhat callow at times. But what I have noted, so too will others. They may seek justice even in the absence of proof.' He took in a deep breath and seemed to hold it for a while. 'A people bound together by magic, and yet so often we seek to unleash the worst of that magic upon each other.'

I was trying to imagine any way in which this day could get any worse. Without success. I stood up and grabbed his arm. 'Master Osia'phest, I didn't do anything to anyone. I'm not responsible.'

He gently took my hand away. 'Kellen, I'm afraid there is a great deal of difference between not doing something and not being responsible for it.'

I spent the next few hours watching and listening as Master Osia'phest ran the other initiates through recitations of incantations, hierarchies of mystical strictures and endless meditations during which, I was quite confident, Osia'phest took a few naps.

After a while I found it impossible to keep my own eyes open during the endless droning and repetition. Each time

I opened them, I instinctively looked over at Tennat across the way, expecting to see him charging at me, his hands blazing with magic. But he never moved. Sometimes he would glance back at me, but he never said anything. That suited me just fine.

What had happened to dampen his magic? And what about the others? I knew I hadn't caused their sickness. There was one explanation that didn't require anything nefarious: fear. Magic requires perfect concentration and indomitable will. Emotional trauma made those almost impossible, and Tennat had done quite a bit of sobbing last night.

'You look pleased with yourself,' Panahsi said, rousing me from a brief doze.

'I didn't see you coming.' I shuffled over on the bench to make room for him but he didn't sit down. He had his arms crossed in front of him and I noticed right away that something had changed with him. 'You sparked your ember band . . . That's great,' I said, struggling to inject sincerity into my voice.

He nodded with grim satisfaction. 'Did it this morning.'

'How did you do it? Maybe you could help me later. I have some ideas about how I might be able to—'

Panahsi cut me off with a sneer, which was an unusual expression for him and looked just comical enough that for a second I thought he might be joking, until he said, 'You know what, Kellen? I've figured out why you don't have any magic.'

'Really? Why?'

'Because you don't deserve any.'

He took a step closer to me, his wide frame blocking out the sun. 'Magic is the gift of the Jan'Tep. Not the Daroman. Not the Berabesq. Not whatever you are.'

I stood up, rather too quickly, and all my various cuts and

bruises from the night before came screaming back at me, making me dizzy. 'I'm just as much a Jan'Tep as you are,' I said, and tried to push him away. It was stupid for a number of reasons, not the least of which was that Panahsi had been, up until that day, my best friend. He was also very heavy. My shove didn't move him an inch. His sent me reeling back over the bench.

'You sided with that Daroman woman over your own people, Kellen.'

I looked up from the ground, past Panahsi, to where the other initiates were doing a poor job of pretending to be oblivious to what was happening while sneaking quick glances towards us. Tennat, sitting on the bench on the other side of the oasis, wasn't pretending at all. It was the first time I'd seem him smile all day.

I got to my feet. With the bench between Panahsi and myself I decided to try a different tactic. 'They were going to hurt that woman, Panahsi. Is that what magic is for? To lord it over and torment people who don't have any?' *Oh gods, please let that not be the case or I'm completely screwed for life.*

'Ra'fan says she's a spy.'

'Ra'fan is an idiot. So's his father and so's Tennat, who nearly crippled you last week in case you've forgotten.'

'Tennat beat me because he's strong, just like the rest of his family. He's going to be a mage who fights for our people. Just like I need to be.'

That made me snort. 'Panahsi, you've got more potential than Tennat's whole family. You're going to be three times stronger than—'

'Not if I keep hanging around with you I won't,' he said, his palms open by his sides.

112

My people learn not to clench our fists when we get angry. It makes it harder to form the somatic shapes needed for attack spells.

'Are you going to beat me up, Panahsi?' I asked.

He hesitated. 'I could, you know. Even without magic. I'm stronger than you, Kellen.'

'I never said you weren't.'

For a moment he just stood there as if he was about to say something else, or was waiting for me to say something, but neither of us did and so he just turned and walked away from me, back to the other initiates. I couldn't hear what he said to them, but I doubted he was singing my praises, because a few of them laughed and clapped him on the shoulder.

It should have been obvious to me what was going on, but I'm a little thick sometimes. It was Tennat who illuminated things for me when he came over shortly after Panahsi left.

'I told them you'd come today,' Tennat said, coughing through the words.

'You don't look so good, Tennat. Maybe you ought to—'

He ignored me. 'So arrogant. So full of yourself. We've all known for years that you're going to end up with the Sha'Tep, cleaning the floors of proper mages or, better yet, working in the mines where you belong. Kellen the magic-less trickster thinks he can lie his way through life, and worse, you act as if you're better than everyone else.'

'Not *everyone* else.'

'So clever, aren't you, Kellen?' He gave a fake little laugh followed by a more genuine-sounding cough.

'You should probably get some rest, Tennat. Sounds like you've got a nasty cold.'

'I'll get better,' he said, mastering himself. 'I'll get well again because *my* blood is strong. Whatever sickness you're carrying inside you that's infecting our people, it won't get a hold on me.'

There was a thought I hadn't considered. What if I carried some kind of illness? I'd spent most of my life with one cold after another. But then, why would it affect the others faster than it had me?

Tennat was grinning down at me as if he'd won some grand debating point. *Such an idiot.*

'Guess you'd better run on home, Tennat. Wouldn't want you to catch a double dose of my deadly magical disease.'

He actually looked scared for a second, which told me that whatever this was, he wasn't faking. 'No,' he said, turning and starting back towards his bench across the way. 'I think I'll stay and watch.'

It took me a while to figure out what was happening and recognise that by coming to the oasis today I'd managed to toss myself headlong into a trap. See, my people have a ritual for exiling a criminal. It requires that the outcast's family and friends, colleagues and teachers, all tell him or her that they are no longer welcome among the clan. It can take hours or even days for the ritual to be completed. Only once every person that the outcast knows has rejected them will the council finally exile the criminal forever. Without family, without a clan, it's rare that anyone ever tries to appeal.

The scene with Panahsi repeated itself over and over again for the rest of the afternoon. Every hour, when Master Osia'phest gave the initiates a few minutes to rest, someone would come over to me and make some snide remark to make it clear to me, and to everyone else, that we weren't friends any more.

114

Every time they did, my father's words came back to me. *The Jan'Tep do not hold grudges.*

Sure.

I wanted more than anything to get up off the bench and run back home, lock myself in my room and do my best to forget the first fifteen years of my life. It wasn't that the things people said to me were cruel – I mean, they were cruel, obviously – but rather the things they didn't bother to say which stung. I was the outsider. I was the *other*. I wasn't Jan'Tep or Sha'Tep or anything else.

I kept glancing over at Panahsi, hoping that he would stop the next person from coming or even just look back at me. He didn't. I was like some kind of unwelcome insect that had burrowed its way into the garden. It wasn't that he or the rest of them wanted to see me dead. They just didn't want to see me at all.

I guess that was why I couldn't leave. As much as every part of me was screaming to get up and run, as small and alone as I felt, somewhere inside me was a tiny shard of anger that wouldn't let me go. I swore to myself I'd still show up every day at that oasis to sit through those lessons, to make everyone see me. Every day until my naming day, when I'd be forced to join the Sha'Tep forever.

I'd just about convinced myself I was doing something noble by staying when Nephenia walked over to me.

13

Rejection

I really could have used a shield spell just then.

Nephenia was armed only with her beauty and my feelings for her. That turned out to be plenty.

She looked pretty that day, as she did every day. A pale beige linen dress that ended just above her knees offset the soft brown curls hanging loose around her shoulders. I always liked her hair that way. There was a scent that came with it . . . tamarisk petals and warm sand and . . . *No*, I told myself. *She's here to break you. Those are her weapons. Stay strong.*

A good counter-attack was what I needed. Something that would cut her to the quick and shake her from her no doubt well-rehearsed script. I came up with a dozen mean, nasty things to say to her. Things that would make me sound clever and her seem small and petty. *Good. You're ready.*

But when she stopped, no more than two feet away from me, all my brilliant insults fled. I was suddenly transformed into a small, petulant boy. 'I suppose you came over here to—'

'They think I'm here to cast you out,' she said quickly, her voice so quiet I had to replay the words in my head to make sure I'd heard them right.

I started to rise but she gave a little shake of her head so I sat back down. 'But you're not?'

'I think . . . I think what you did was brave, standing up for that Daroman woman. I'm not sure if it was right. Jan'Tep are supposed to stick to their clan.' She stood there for a moment and then shook her head as if banishing the thought. 'This Ferius person saved your life and, when the time came, you saved hers. That can't be wrong.' She turned away, looking to the south, away from town. 'Three of them, Kellen, and you with no magic. Yet you fought them. You beat them.'

'Ferius . . . um . . . had something to do with it as well.'

'I wish I could be as brave as you.'

'You are,' I said. 'You would've—'

She spun back to me and her eyes were angry and filling with tears. 'Don't. I'm not brave, Kellen, so don't say I am.'

Lacking anything either clever or reassuring to say, I simply said, 'I don't understand.'

'Just . . . Just let me say this.' She wiped the tears from her eyes and wiped her hands against her dress. 'It's not the same for girls, Kellen. The masters hardly ever want to teach us the high magics. They think we shouldn't be allowed to learn anything except healing and—'

'Then make them teach you,' I said. 'My sister doesn't take no for an answer. She—'

'I'm not Shalla!' she whispered fiercely.

Several of the initiates looked over and for a second I was afraid they might think I'd done something to hurt Nephenia.

'I'm not Shalla,' she repeated, this time more quietly. 'I'm not powerful the way she is. The masters teach her, because if they didn't everyone would know it's because she's a girl. But me? They can just keep putting me at the back of the class. I have to beg and plead and stand behind the boys on tiptoes to try to see the spells they're being shown. If some of the other students didn't spend time with me after class, I'd never be able to pass my trials.'

Other students. Like who? I wondered.

'I need those people to help me, Kellen. I don't want to end up like my mother, married to a man who treats her like a Sha'Tep. Who uses her like a servant and expects her to . . . I have to earn my mage name.'

A part of me knew that I should be listening – really listening – to the things she was telling me. I should have been more sympathetic. I should have been able to understand that Nephenia was just trying to survive in the world the same as I was. But I'd just spent the past several hours being told by everyone who'd ever pretended to be my friend that I was diseased and would never have any power. I guess it kind of stuck. 'Why are you telling me this, Nephenia? Is all this just an excuse so that you can feel better for siding with the others?' I rose this time, partly because I was so angry and partly because this was probably going to be the last time I got to be near her. 'You didn't come over here to tell me how brave I am. You came to say goodbye.'

'Not because I want to,' she said desperately, as if that made any difference in the world. 'Maybe someday—'

'Maybe if I suddenly become a powerful mage? Then you'll talk to me? Then you'll want to . . . ?'

I was close enough to see her lower lip starting to tremble. 'I'm sorry, Kellen. I'm just so sorry,' she said, and turned away from me.

I said a few things as she walked back to the others, things that no brave, heroic young mage would say about a girl who was crying. I said them quietly though, under my breath, like a coward, and so figured no one had heard.

'You kiss your mother with that mouth?' a voice asked from behind me.

I spun around to see Ferius Parfax sitting cross-legged against one of the colonnades, holding a large card in one hand and a paintbrush delicately in the other. An open leather case lay next to her, filled with more brushes and tiny pots and jars. 'What are you doing?' I asked, surprising myself with how angry I sounded.

'Painting a card, obviously.'

The dowager magus's question of the night before came back to me. 'Of what?'

Ferius stared at the card in her hand. 'None of your business.'

The glib answer irritated me. 'You snuck up on me.'

'Wasn't hard,' she replied, dipping the brush in something clear before wrapping it in a cloth and placing it back in the leather case. 'Maybe next time you and your little girlfriend should try casting a "pay attention to the world around you" spell.'

'She's not my . . . She's not anything. I don't want to talk about it.'

'Me neither,' Ferius said, and reached into her waistcoat and pulled out a smoking reed and stuck it between her teeth. From inside the leather case she took two cloth pouches and then a tiny pinch of powder from each. When she tossed them against each other, they erupted into a tiny burst of flame that lit the reed.

'What are those powders?' I asked.

'Stuff I use for paints,' she replied, taking a puff of her smoking reed. 'Not a good idea to mix them.'

119

She blew a ring of smoke in the air that drifted towards me. The act seemed oddly accusatory. 'Nephenia walked away from me because I have no magic,' I said, now realising I *did* want to talk about it. 'One day I had promise and she seemed to like me, the next I didn't and I guess she decided I wasn't worth the trouble.'

If I was expecting sympathy, which I was, I didn't get any. 'You know what I'm wondering?' Ferius asked. I didn't respond, but that didn't matter because she went on anyway. 'I'm asking myself if that girl stopped being quite so pretty tomorrow, well, if you'd notice her at all.'

She gave me all of three seconds to come up with a reply before she laughed. 'You crack me up, kid. You know that?'

'Shut up, Ferius,' I said. The sun was getting lower in the sky and Master Osia'phest was shuffling off down the street. Evidently the lesson was over. 'Are you a Daroman spy? Did you do something to make Tennat and the others sick?'

'Nope.' She gave me a sidelong glance. 'Did you?'

'Don't be stupid.'

'Says the kid who just asked a suspected spy to reveal herself.'

'If you're not a spy then what are you?' I asked. 'Because I don't believe some Argosi wanderer would still be hanging around here after what happened last night.'

'I'm a *woman*, kid. You probably haven't met one before, coming as you do from this backward place, but it's like a man only smarter and with bigger balls.'

It occurred to me that she'd just insulted my mother, my sister and every other female in my clan. But something else was bothering me. 'Aren't you worried that Ra'fan and Ra'dir and Tennat might come after you again?'

She got to her feet and walked over to sit down on the bench next to me. 'What, those morons from last night?'

'Them or someone else. Don't think the same tricks will work again. Next time they might—'

'Next time I'll use a different trick.'

All I could see in her face was her usual smug self-assurance, but I still remembered the genuine fear in her eyes the night before. 'They've seen your smoke and your steel cards. What happens when you run out of tricks? What happens if more powerful mages decide to attack you and they—'

She shrugged. 'Guess we'll find out when it happens.' She took another drag of her smoking reed. 'But let's deal with more pressing concerns. Like that little lady you seem to fancy so much but just treated like dirt.'

A whole town full of mages, half of whom probably wanted to see her dead, and she wanted to talk about my love life. 'Look, unless you have a spell to make her like me despite how much of a loser I am, just keep your thoughts to yourself. Besides, it's like she said – she's not special.'

Ferius looked at me and let out a long breath, the smoke filling the air between us like fog on an early spring morning. 'Okay, kid, you did me a favour last night, so I'm going to do you one in return.'

I turned away from her. 'If you're going to make a joke about teaching me spells again, then don't bother.' I was tired of the way Ferius made fun of magic as if it was all a game.

I felt her hand on my shoulder and nearly pulled away in surprise, but her grip was too strong. 'I *am* going to teach you a spell, kid, not because you want it but because you need it.' She leaned over and whispered a string of words in my ear.

121

It was, like always, just another of her stupid tricks – Ferius pretending that things that weren't real spells were just as important as true magic. I could have just forgotten it and gone home, but the truth was, I felt pretty awful about how I'd acted towards Nephenia. So when I noticed her lagging behind the other initiates leaving the oasis, I ran quietly up to her.

She turned and saw me and I saw the fear in her eyes. Fear that I was going to yell at her or say terrible, angry things to her. Fear that I was going to reject her. *The way you rejected me.* I shook the thought from my head. If I was going to make a fool of myself, I'd at least do it properly. *Calm*, I reminded myself. *First comes the calm.* I closed my eyes for just a second, envisioning the spell doing its work, and then I spoke the incantation, exactly as Ferius had said it to me. 'You said you weren't special, Nephenia, but you're wrong. One day you're going to figure that out for yourself, but in the meantime, just know that you're special to me.'

For a long while she stood there as if every part of her was trapped in a binding spell. Then I watched a single tear-drop begin to form in her right eye. Just before it began rolling down her cheek she threw her arms around me. 'Thank you, Kellen,' was all she said.

She didn't kiss me or apologise, or promise to stay friends with me. She didn't give me some keepsake or secret code. I knew that tomorrow she'd have to do just what she'd said – go along with the others, because that's what you do when you don't feel powerful enough on your own.

But for those few seconds while I had my arms around her and felt her face pressed into my shoulder, my cheek buried in the soft curls of her hair, I didn't mind.

Okay, so it wasn't magic.

But it felt awfully close.

I returned to my bench between the columns, intent on making a few clever remarks to Ferius about her spell – only to find her gone and Shalla sitting there in her place. She looked paler than usual. Tired.

'Where's Ferius?' I asked.

Shalla shrugged. 'She left. I don't think she likes me. Then again, she's some kind of Daroman spy so—'

'She's not a spy,' I said.

'Then what is she?'

A woman. It's like a man only smarter and with bigger balls. No, that was not going to make me sound clever. 'Who knows? Probably just what Father said: an Argosi wanderer.'

Shalla started to say something but then coughed. I was going to ask her what was wrong when she nodded towards the street where Nephenia had gone. 'What was *that* all about?'

I glanced back just in case Nephenia was still there, but the street was empty. 'Nothing. I was just—'

'I don't know why you waste time with Mouse Girl,' Shalla said. 'Her family isn't powerful, she's not that pretty and she's never going to be much of a mage.'

A dozen angry retorts arrayed themselves in my mind, organised from nastiest to least likely to get me in a worse mess than I was already in. I tossed them all out. 'She thinks you're amazing.'

Shalla's mouth opened and then closed again. *Now there's a magic spell if ever there was one.* It didn't last of course. 'You know these people aren't your family, right? Panahsi, Nephenia, that crazy Ferius woman? None of them are family.'

'So what?' I asked, the anger rising in my throat despite my attempts to stay calm. Shalla really is smarter than I am. Somehow she always knows just how to dig down into me. 'What has my family ever done for me? All those hours Mother and Father spent doing spells on me to bring out my magic? All they did was make me feel sick and weak and horrible. Do you think they'll even let me sleep upstairs any more once I'm stuck being a Sha'Tep for the rest of my life? Will you even call me your brother when I'm coming to serve your dinner or scrub your floors?'

I expected Shalla to launch into a tirade, but she just smiled and took both my hands in hers. Then, as if that were somehow insufficient, she let go of my hands and reached over to hug me. 'None of that matters, Kellen. You're always going to be my brother.'

Of all the shocks I'd had in my life recently, that was the biggest. Was my sister really going to tell me that it didn't matter if I became Sha'Tep? That she'd love me no matter what? I guess that's why I was doubly surprised when she whispered in my ear, 'Because I've figured out a way to fix your magic.'

14

The Snake

'It was your idea really,' Shalla said as we crept along the path.

'What was my idea?' I asked, shouldering the pack she'd brought with her and now expected me to carry. 'You still haven't told me what this is all about. And what are we doing on the Snake, anyway?'

The Snake was the second of the intertwining routes that ran north–south through the Jan'Tep lands, so called because of the way it wound itself around the nearly five hundred miles of caravan track called the Staff. Daroman military engineers had carved out the Staff from the surrounding forest hundreds of years ago in order to facilitate trade, travel and, in times of war, moving an invading army into our lands. The Snake was a much older road whose proper name was the Path of Spirits. It was said to be occupied by the ghosts of our ancestors who waged a never-ending war with those of our ancient enemies, the Mahdek. It was also the place where Jan'Tep mages went on vision quests when seeking out the high magics.

'When you were duelling Tennat the other day,' Shalla said, 'you spoke to that falcon flying overhead.'

I nearly dropped the pack to the ground. 'Shalla, that was just a trick. I was just pretending so that I could—'

'Scare Tennat. I know. But you haven't thought about the reason *why* it scared him. It's because a mage with a power animal can channel magic even if their bands are still in place.'

'So?'

'So what if you really *did* have a power animal?'

It was a stupid hypothetical question. The kind of impossible thought experiment that appealed to ageing spellmasters, my annoying sister, and pretty much no one else. 'Well, we're never going to find out, are we? Since you need actual magic to summon a power animal, which, in case you hadn't noticed, I don't have any more.'

'But I do.'

I stopped right there. 'Father's allowing you to continue your trials? I thought he was going to make you wait because you . . .' *almost killed your own brother.*

I supposed he had to let her finish. If the council was considering the strength of the bloodline, then my father's only hope of becoming clan prince was for Shalla to make an impression on the lords magi. She wouldn't receive her mage name until she was sixteen, but by passing her trials three years early she could prove the strength of our house. Not that any of that would help me. 'Shalla, hardly anyone bonds with power animals any more. They're too risky. Why would . . . ?'

She looked down at her feet. 'Mother helped me convince father that a familiar might . . . temper my behaviour somewhat.'

Fat chance, I thought. While it made sense in theory that when a mage and their familiar bond there's a kind of fusing of personalities, I doubted some cat or duck was going to teach my sister humility.

Shalla coughed and I noticed again how pale she looked. 'What's wrong with you?' I asked. 'You look worse than Tennat, and he nearly got his neck sliced by Ferius last night.'

'It's just a cold,' she said, and started down the path again. 'I'm not going to let it get in the way.'

'So what does any of this have to do with me?' I asked.

'I convinced Father to let you be my watcher. You're going to protect me.'

I nearly broke out laughing. 'You expect me to guard you from evil Mahdek spirits on the Snake? With what? My winning personality?'

'Don't be stupid, Kellen. Nobody's seen any Mahdek for decades. Besides, I've got my own warding spells and no doubt Mother will have cast a scrying spell to watch over me. All I need you to do is keep any bugs or sick animals from trying to bond with me while I'm under the calling spell.'

'So I get to watch you become even more powerful, and in exchange I get what?'

She smiled as if she was about to reveal that she was the one who invented the wheel. 'I've got a plan. Once I've got my falcon—'

'What makes you think you'll get a falcon?' I interrupted. Falcons were bold creatures who seldom allowed themselves to be commanded by humans and so were the rarest of power animals to respond to a summoning. 'You're more likely to spend the rest of your life bonded to a mouse or a tree frog.'

Shalla rolled her eyes at me. 'Kellen, please. Can you imagine me with something that weak? I'd rather just die and come back and try again in the next life.'

'Fine,' I said. 'If you get a falcon . . .'

'*When* I get my falcon – I've figured out a way to keep the summoning spell going even once the bonding has taken place. I'll use a sympathy spell to channel my will through the falcon to summon one of its fellows. If there's another one anywhere within ten miles of here I'll make it come and then it will try to bond with me, but I'll already be bonded to my one.'

'So the bird will have no choice but to bond with me?' I tried to imbue the words with as much incredulity as possible, but the thought of getting my own power animal was beyond tantalising. A falcon. A *falcon*. Not only would I have a way to channel my magic past the damned bands on my forearms, but I'd be able to pass the final two tests. Also, pretty much everyone else in town would be lining up for my attention. A *falcon*. 'But . . . how can that work? I mean, it makes sense, but why hasn't somebody else tried it?'

Shalla smiled. 'Because regular mages get so lost in the moment of bonding that they forget everything else. People are stupid and sappy that way, but I'm not. I'll keep my focus and I'll keep the spell going, and you, my brother, will have your own power animal.'

I looked at my sister, struggling not to drop to my knees, throw my arms around her waist and promise to for ever more be the best brother the world had ever seen. There were a hundred reasons to doubt both Shalla's motivations and her ability to pull this off. But if she could? If it were at all possible? A *falcon*.

Hours later I sat with my back against a tree, staring up at the sky through the forest canopy as the moon reached its zenith. I kept the small cooking fire we'd made using a simple fire spell (well, Shalla had made) at my back so that I wouldn't lose the night vision I needed to keep an eye on my sister, who was meditating in her spell circle some thirty yards away. She'd insisted that I keep my distance so that the sound of my breathing wouldn't distract her, but I knew it was really because she didn't want to risk my presence tainting her spell.

Like a lot of mind spells – what my people call silk magic – the calling is basically invisible to the eye. If I looked very, very carefully, I could almost imagine a subtle shimmer around Shalla – a soft expansion of the air as the spell pushed outwards into the forest, summoning a power animal to her.

It was kind of remarkable that any of this was happening. Most initiates spend days trying to cast it, only to fail from exhaustion and have to try again another time. Shalla, despite obviously being at less than her best, of course got the spell to work on the very first try. As petty as it sounds, part of me wished that nothing, not even a cockroach, would come near her.

My job as watcher was relatively simple. If an insect or a sick animal tried to approach Shalla, I had to chase it away. Insects are unsuitable as familiars. I'm not entirely sure why, but I think it has something to do with their brains being too simple, incapable of proper communication with a mage. So bonding with one would be kind of a waste and it would keep other animals from answering the summons.

Sick animals were more dangerous. A sick animal would try to bond with the mage in a desperate attempt to prolong its life. But the illness inside the animal would infect the mage, crippling their magic for years. Even after the animal died, the sickness remained. It wasn't a death sentence for a mage, but it was close.

I suppose I should have been at least a little proud that Shalla trusted me with something so important. But by then I was fairly sure of two things. First, she had almost certainly lied about having our parents' permission to summon a power animal. Being Shalla, she probably figured that once it was done and she'd shown how wonderfully things had turned out, everyone would forgive her.

The second reason why she likely felt safe with me as her watcher was that she probably didn't need one. A perfectly formed calling spell has two parts, one to summon the right type of creature, and a second to warn off the wrong ones. So chances were that any sick animal would just avoid her. So really there wasn't much for me to do except sit and wait and hope that she could really do what she promised.

That thought kept me occupied for the first few hours of the night, but as the chill began to set into my bones, so too did my doubts whether Shalla would really summon a familiar for me. I glanced over at her again, looking for some sign of duplicity. She looked as still and serene and arrogantly self-assured as ever. Did she even need me there at all? Or was I just an audience to witness her upcoming triumph?

Shalla loved to chide me for being lazy and acted as if all I needed in order to become a powerful mage was to really apply myself, but I knew she took no end of pleasure in having more power than I did. Would she really risk giving that up? Or would she back out on the deal once she had what she wanted?

I tried copying her cross-legged pose, my arms in front of me, bent at the elbows, my right hand facing outwards with the ring and little finger touching the palm – the sign of reaching out. My left palm faced inwards with the second and third fingers touching, forming the sign of summoning. Using the silent breath that Master Osia'phest had taught us since childhood, I repeated the simple four-syllable incantation over and over. *Te-me'en-ka. Te-me'en-ka.*

I closed my eyes, not because the spell required it but because staring at the unsparked tattooed bands on my forearms wasn't going to help my confidence any. Inside my mind and my heart I shaped my will and thought about falcons. *You are summoned. We are meant to be together. We are meant to be soul-bonded. You are summoned. You will come.*

I kept on, over and over, doing my best to ignore the growing pain in my head from the constant recitation of the spell, concentrating on the somatic forms, the silent verbal incantation and the inner shape of my will all at once. *Te-me'en-ka. Te-me'en-ka.*

I kept it up for what felt like hours but was probably only a minute or two. The breeze rustled my hair, sending strands of it tickling my face. Drops of sweat stung my left eye. Blinking away the tears did nothing for the pain but broke my concentration completely. I wiped the sweat from my brow and realised I was nearly soaked in it. Nothing had changed. The fire still crackled, Shalla still sat in her circle thirty yards away from me. It was as if the entire world had ignored my efforts.

Oh ancestors, I'll forgive you for every lousy thing you've ever done to me if you'll just give me a power animal. I promise I'll be good to it. I'll feed it whatever it wants and keep it from harm. I'll give it as long and happy a life as I possibly can. Just don't leave me like this. Don't leave me alone.

It was only then that I realised I'd mistaken the crunching of dried leaves for the crackling of the fire. Something had been hiding in the darkness, and it was coming for me.

131

15

The Masks

There was a brief instant where, in my dazed state, I managed to convince myself that somehow, despite the bands on my forearms and the weakness of my will, the spell had worked. A power animal was coming to me. Okay, so it was running along the ground, which meant it wasn't a falcon, but still . . .

The fantasy was soon shattered. Not even the most ardent self-deception will let your brain miss the heavy footsteps of men approaching for long.

My first thought was that it would be Ra'fan and Ra'dir, but there was no way Ra'meth would risk having his family connected to a direct attack on the House of Ke. Three men were coming, obscured by the shadows of the trees. Their dark travelling clothes gave no clue as to who they were or even what country they might be from. As they crept forward I could make out the masks covering their faces. Black-and-red lacquer, shaped like grinning monsters, with assorted fangs and horns and tusks adorning their features. *Mahdek*, I thought, suddenly unable to breathe. They used to wear masks like these when performing their vile demonic rituals. I scrambled to my feet. *They've come back. The Mahdek have come back.*

'You'll stay away if you know what's good for you!' I shouted, trying to speak in the commanding tones of my father. The words sounded a lot more threatening in my head than they did carried into the night air on my trembling, high-pitched voice. 'I have dark and terrible magics!' I added, which managed to sound even more ridiculous. *Ancestors,* I thought, *if you have to send the Mahdek to torment me, couldn't you at least give me something clever to say?* I looked over at Shalla for help but she was still lost in her spell, oblivious to the danger.

The men in their masks crept closer and my memory conjured up the shiny, metallic ink drawings on the old scrolls that the masters would sometimes pull out to frighten us. Terrifying images that would haunt our nightmares. 'Who among you would fight the ancient enemy?' Master Osia'phest would demand when we acted above ourselves. 'Which of you would face the Mahdek wizard wearing his ritual death mask?'

Not me, that's for sure.

The tallest of the three men stepped forward. His mask had two pairs of curved horns, one red, one black, on either side of his temples. 'Take him,' he said to the others.

A wide-set man whose mask had a third eye in the middle ran for me so quickly that in my rush to get away I backed into a tree. My head slammed against the hard bark and floating yellow lights filled my vision. My attacker would have got his arms around me were it not for my knees having already buckled, dropping me low to the forest floor where I scrambled around the tree.

Just as I got my feet under me I felt him grab at the back of my shirt. But now fear was replaced by something else:

desperation. Desperation is a lot like fear only more useful. The big man spun me around and slammed me into the tree, but as he reached for me a second time I pulled out the metal card Ferius had given me the night before and slashed out with it, slicing the skin of his palm. His scream prompted me to attack again, this time at the other hand. I caught him on the wrist and the razor-sharp edge sent blood spitting into the air as he fell backwards out of the way.

A third man, this one with long, curved tusks extending up from the lower half of his mask, started towards me. I had a brief moment in which I could have escaped, but I hesitated. Even if I got away, then what? I was too far from town to get help. If my mother was scrying to watch over Shalla, then she and my father would be on their way already. But they wouldn't get here in time to save my sister if I ran.

Not knowing what else to do, I braced myself against the tree behind me and kicked out at the second attacker. *Too soon, damn it.* He was still too far, so when my foot connected with his stomach it barely brushed him. In desperation I threw the card at his face. *No, idiot! Not the face.* Despite my poor throw the card lodged itself in the forehead of his mask and I heard him yelp in surprise. But it didn't bite deep enough to wound him. Had I thrown it at any other part of his body I might have cut him, slowed him down. Instead he grabbed me by the neck with both hands, his grip so strong that I was instantly unable to breathe. 'Nasty little bastard,' he said, his voice a deep, guttural growl. He took one hand away and used it to pull the card out of his mask. 'Let's see how you like getting cut.'

'Don't,' the leader said, the horns on his mask glinting in the light of my small fire as he came forward. 'Bind him.'

Tusks shoved me back, hitting my head hard against the tree trunk a second time to stun me. At first I assumed they'd cast a binding spell on me, but instead the man unwound a length of rope from his waist and used it to tie me to the tree. It struck me as odd that none of these men had attempted to use a spell. *I thought the Mahdek were supposed to be dark wizards. Focus, damn it!* 'Shalla!' I shouted. 'Wake up! You've got to wake up!'

The leader pushed Tusks out of the way and stood only inches away from me, as if he wanted me to see every inch of his hideous mask. 'Scream all you want. She's lost in her little spell, waiting for her darling power animal to come to her.'

'My mother is scrying for us!' I said. 'My father will come for us when he—'

'Of course they're coming. Maybe they can even see us now.' He looked up at the sky. 'Can you see me, mighty Ke'heops? Do you know what I'm going to do to your precious child? Come on. Send down a bolt of lightning to strike me!' He turned back to me and laughed. 'You see? Even if they are watching, they're still too far away.'

'Who are you? Why are you doing this?' I said, my voice pleading.

Horns ignored me and went back into the trees for a moment, returning with a large brown sack in his hand. 'Make sure he's properly tied. He's a slippery one.' Tusks walked behind the tree and checked the ropes, tightening them even more and making me groan at the pain in my wrists.

'He's not going anywhere,' Tusks said.

The leader nodded and reached into the sack. What was in there? I had visions of wickedly curved knives or vials of

135

poison. The sack wriggled a bit and I thought, *Snake – he's brought a snake that's going to bite me and fill my veins with its venom.* But when the man's hand came out of the sack it wasn't holding a knife or poison or a snake. It was holding a small white animal, its patchy fur revealing red, oozing sores. Its eyes were wet and blurry as if it couldn't see properly. It was a dog. A sick animal barely holding on to life.

The leader set the diseased animal down on the forest floor a little ways from Shalla and immediately it began to stumble slowly, awkwardly, painfully towards her. That was when I understood what they were going to do to my sister. That was when I really screamed.

16

The Creature

The more I shouted, the more I begged them to stop, the more the men in masks laughed at me.

'Look at him,' Tusks said as he wrapped a bandage around Third-Eye's wrist where I'd slashed it with the metal card. 'We're not even doing anything to him and he's still losing his little Jan'Tep mind.'

My eyes were focused on the sickly little dog that would take a step towards Shalla, pulled in by her magic, then stop and sit for a moment, licking at a wound on its paw.

'It's taking too long,' Third-Eye complained. 'Just pick up the damn pup and throw it at her.'

'That's not how the magic works, you fool. The dog has to answer the summons. It has to want to bond with her. She can't refuse it, but the dog has to come to her.'

'Get away!' I shouted at the dog. Why wasn't her own magic working? The defensive aspect of her summoning spell should have kept sick animals away.

The men laughed and Tusks said, 'Shout all you want, boy. The puppy's deaf – one of the many unfortunate symptoms of the disease we gave it.' He turned to the other two. 'I wonder if the girl will become deaf when she bonds with it. Won't that be interesting to find out?'

'Why are you hurting her?' I cried.

'We're not hurting her,' Horns replied. 'She came seeking a familiar, and that's what she's going to get.' He came over and put a gloved hand against my jaw. 'They think so grandly of themselves, your clan, your family, don't they? And she's the worst of them all. So convinced she's going to become the greatest mage of her people. And who knows? Maybe she could've been.' He nodded to Tusks, who walked over to the dog and gave it a gentle push. It started ambling towards Shalla again. 'But I'm betting once she's bonded to this little thing she won't be nearly so high and mighty any more.'

'Please don't do this,' I said. 'It's not too late. Just take the dog back and we can talk. There must be something you want!'

Without warning, the back of his hand slapped me across the face. 'I want to enjoy this. That's what I want.'

Third-Eye laughed appreciatively. 'These Jan'Tep. Take away their little magics and they become like lost babes in the woods.'

'We've never done anything to you!' I shouted, pulling against the rope that held my wrists. 'The war between the Jan'Tep and the Mahdek happened three hundred years ago!'

'Ah,' the leader said, his voice almost a whisper, 'but the effects of that war? They just keep going on and on, don't they?'

The little dog, the poor creature drawn by Shalla's power, was only inches away from her now, sniffing in the air as though it could smell her magic. Within moments it would touch her and the bonding would take place. It would be over for Shalla. She'd be weak and sick for her whole life.

138

I convinced Father to let you be my watcher. You're going to protect me.

This was my fault. I was the watcher. I was supposed to keep this from happening. *Damn you, spirits of our ancestors. Damn you all. How could you let me fail again?* In hopeless agony I reached out with my will as I'd been doing before. If there was another animal nearby, maybe it could . . . I didn't know what it could do, but I was desperate. All I could do was try. I concentrated again on the summoning. *Te-me'en-ka. Te-me'en-ka.*

'It's taking too long,' Third-Eye said. 'If the parents really were scrying, then they'll be close now.'

'Almost there now,' Horns whispered. 'Almost there.'

Despite my efforts to focus, I couldn't help but open my eyes. The sick little dog was extending a scabby paw towards Shalla.

'No,' I said, pleading. 'Please, no.'

Horns nodded. 'Let it happen, Kellen, just let it—'

Before I could ask how the man knew my name, he was cut off by the sound of something in the branches high above us. I looked up, but whatever it was ran too fast for me to make out anything other than the briefest glimpses of brown fur. It ran along the branches on four legs and I guessed its body to be about two feet long. It was hard to be sure though, because the colour and lines of its coat were so much like the tree bark it seemed to melt into the branches.

'Ancestors protect us . . .' Tusks said.

Suddenly the creature flew down at us, the claws of its back legs raking the back of Tusks' mask as it swooped past him. Even before Tusks could try to swipe at it with his knife, the monstrous thing had glided away, slamming into the small dog that was now only inches from Shalla, rolling with it on the ground. When the creature came back up, it had the sad little dog's neck in its jaws.

'Hells,' Horns said. 'What is that thing?'

Even now, with the creature barely fifteen feet away, it was hard to make out its shape against the forest floor. The fur that I had first thought to be the brown of the trees above was actually darker, almost as black as the shadows themselves. It shook its head once, twice, a third time. On the final shake I heard the crunching sound of the dog's neck breaking, ending its suffering. The killer let the body drop to the ground and turned to face us. At first I thought it might have been another dog, but this wasn't like any dog I'd ever seen. Its face was almost like that of a cat, only wider and thicker, with a flat snout. Its fur bristled, and now I could make out dark stripes along its sides and its thick tail. Its eyes reflected the blood red of the flickering firelight.

'Weapons at the ready,' Horns told the others.

The creature looked down at the dead puppy at its feet, then rose up on its haunches and opened its mouth wide to let out a growl of such rage and ferocity I would have turned and run had my arms not been bound. *It's angry. It's angry because it had to kill the dog.* I don't know how I knew that, but something in the creature's face, in the growls and chitters that came from its mouth, convinced me that I was right.

The creature began moving closer to us. That was when I saw the dark furred webbing that stretched from its front paws to its rear – that must have been how it had seemed to fly at us even though it had no wings. The front paws that tore at the ground as it approached didn't resemble those

140

of a dog or a cat; they were more like black fingers with sharp claws.

'*Nekhek*,' one of the men whispered. 'A demon's familiar has come for us!'

Nekhek. The word meant 'herald of the darkness'. A creature so foul it was said to be the Mahdek's favourite weapon against my people, its bite stealing our magic and poisoning our spirits. I struggled uselessly against my bonds, desperate to get away. Tusks and Third-Eye ran immediately.

Even through my fear, a question rose in my mind. If these men were Mahdek, then why were they terrified by their own weapon?

Horns hesitated. 'Pray the creature takes her, Kellen,' he said to me. 'The world would be better for it.' Then he too turned and raced out of the clearing and into the night.

For a long while the monster just stared at me, making odd sniffing sounds punctuated by chitters and growls. Then it started coming towards me, its movements unnatural to my eyes, especially the way it would stop sometimes and wipe at its face with those eerie paws that looked almost like hands.

'What are you?' I asked stupidly. 'Did I . . . ? Did I summon you somehow?'

Oh ancestors . . . send me a spirit to chase this monster away.

The nekhek came closer and sniffed at my feet, then moved up my leg. Its snout snuffled over to my hand. I kept expecting to hear a voice in my head demanding a blood price for killing the dog. 'You saved my sister,' I said. 'If . . . If that means there's a debt to be paid, then I'll pay it.'

I could feel its nose sniffing around my fingers. Its tongue reached out and licked at my skin for a moment, then the

141

creature opened its mouth and I felt its teeth on the edge of my hand. Was this what destiny had in store for me? Was a nekhek going to devour me as I remained tied to a tree?

Just as I felt the teeth beginning to bite down, the nekhek suddenly flew through the air as if hurled by a great hand. The creature slammed against the trunk of a tree and fell to the ground unconscious. 'Got it!' my father said, emerging from the path behind me with my mother and several others.

'The men who attacked us,' I said, trying to keep my wits about me. 'They went west, deeper into the forest.'

'Go,' my father said, and four men ran past me.

My mother came into the clearing, glancing at me only briefly before she went to Shalla and began the sequence of spells needed to ease my sister out of the summoning.

'There were three of them, Father. They wore masks. Like the Mahdek ones from the pictures.'

I felt him working at the rope binding my hands behind the tree. 'I know. Your mother saw them in the scrying. We should never have allowed this foolishness. I knew what Shalla was up to. I'd hoped you would have more sense than to help her in such an unwise endeavour.'

The rope gave way and my hands came free. I began rubbing at my wrists, trying to get feeling back into them. 'Shalla told me she had permission. She said –'

My father came from around the tree and I saw the grave expression on his face. 'Did you believe her?'

I found my eyes wandering down to the leaves on the forest floor. 'I wanted to,' I said.

'A Jan'Tep can't allow his desires to overcome his sense nor the needs of his family. A Jan'Tep must be . . .' He stopped then, and after a moment let out a long breath. 'Mahdek on the Path of Spirits, and with a nekhek servant. Ancestors above and below, these are dark signs.'

I looked over at the nekhek. I could see its sides rising and falling with shallow breaths as two men warily began to bind it with the rope that my father had removed from my arms. 'I don't understand. Those men were as scared of the creature as I was.' I reached down and retrieved Ferius's steel card from where Tusks had dropped it. 'Weren't the Mahdek supposed to be—'

My father cut me off. 'Leave those men to your elders.' He turned to the men binding the nekhek. 'Make sure it can't open its jaws. It will try to bite once it wakes, to infect us with its poison.'

My father started to walk away from me but I grabbed at his arm. He turned and looked at me with surprise. I don't think I'd ever done that before. 'The nek . . . the animal. I don't think it was working for those men. I think it saved Shalla's life.'

My father's eyes narrowed. 'Kellen, whatever you think you saw, whatever that demon creature was doing, it wasn't trying to save Shalla. The nekhek is a creature of shadow and deceit. They were trained during the wars to chew poison weeds and bite Jan'Tep mages to paralyse their magic. They are our enemies as much as the Mahdek themselves.' He clapped me on the shoulder. 'But we have one now, in part thanks to you, so this night has not all gone ill.'

'I don't understand. You're going to kill it?' Somehow the thought troubled me. Despite the stories I'd heard as a child, this animal had saved me from those men and Shalla from a fate that she would have considered worse than death.

My father shook his head. 'Not yet. Where there is one

143

nekhek there will be others, and that is the greater threat. We will cage the creature and use pain spells to break its spirit.' He glanced over at where Shalla was being cared for by my mother. 'It was clever of your sister to conceive of the means to use sympathy to bind the kin of another creature. We can use blood magic to draw other nekhek to this one so that we can kill them all before they become a threat.'

He walked over and lifted Shalla up in his arms. 'It's time to bring your sister home.'

'I don't understand,' I said. 'That creature killed the diseased dog those men were using to infect Shalla. It *saved* her. How can you –'

He cut me off with a look. 'You've had a shock. You were terrified of those men and you saw what some frightened part of you wanted to see. I don't fault you for it, Kellen. But now you have to be a man and come to accept the things a man must do to protect his family. A Jan'tep must be strong.' His expression changed a little, becoming . . . I couldn't tell. *Proud?* 'When the time comes, Kellen, I want you to be the one to put the blade in the monster's heart.'

Before I could even think of an objection, the sound of wings flapping caught my attention. I looked up to see a bird slowing its descent as it flew towards us, moving with a heartbreaking grace and elegance. Without thinking, I reached a hand out to it, but the bird evaded me and landed on Shalla's unconscious form. For just an instant, it blinked, its eyes turning from a dark brown to blue then to gold. It settled there, on my sister's shoulder, as my mother and father looked at each other and smiled.

Shalla had found her falcon.

144

17

The Nekhek

The next day saw a flurry of activity that began with my being something of a hero and ended with me becoming a traitor.

'She's still asleep,' my mother said, noticing me poking my head into Shalla's room. 'An interrupted summoning spell is hard on anyone and doubly so on someone as young as your sister.' Her tone was calm on the surface but full of barely contained accusations underneath. The falcon, sitting on the edge of Shalla's bed, turned its head to gaze at me with similar menace.

'It was Shalla's idea,' I said. 'Why am I to blame?'

'I didn't say you were, but since you chose to bring it up, why in all the world did you agree to such a thing?'

I reached for a sensible, believable reply. I found none. 'She said she was ready.'

'She's thirteen!'

'And she's more powerful than half the mages in this city.'

'Not last night, she wasn't.' My mother came to stand in front of me and placed her hands on my cheeks as she examined me. 'Look at you, still bruised from getting into fights, and now this.'

'I'm fine,' I said.

She ran a finger along the hollow of my left eye the way she always did when I got hurt. I still had a cut there. When she seemed satisfied I wasn't dying she said, 'Couldn't you see how weak Shalla was?'

I went to sit down on the reading chair next to my sister's bed. The events of the previous day started to replay themselves in my mind. 'She said she had a cold.'

'Well, it's not a cold.'

'Bene'maat,' my father said from the doorway. It was rare for him to use my mother's name in front of us.

'Don't try to gentle me like some barnyard animal, Ke'heops,' she said, her tone a warning that I recognised. 'Our daughter could have been killed, or worse.'

My father put his hands in front of him. 'I'm not, but Shalla was the instigator of this nonsense. Children her age have been sneaking onto the Path of Spirits trying to find their power animals since long before you or I were born, and none has ever come back with anything worse than a headache and the sniffles.' He paused and looked over at me with something like pride on his face. 'Kellen did everything he could to protect his sister.'

'Those men—'

'We'll find the Mahdek who attacked her.'

Something about that bothered me. 'I don't think they were Mahdek, Father. I think they were ordinary men sent by Ra'meth.'

'Ra'meth and his sons already submitted to interrogation by the lords magi. We used silk magic to discern the truth of their words. They were neither there nor had any knowledge of or involvement in the attack.'

146

What was it Ferius had said the other night? That if there's a spell for everything then there's probably a spell to counter it. 'Maybe they found a way around the interrogation.'

'Oh?' my father said, his expression suddenly irritated. 'And what exactly is your expertise in these matters?'

I closed my eyes, thinking back to the way the men who'd attacked us had been dressed, the way they talked. 'Maybe the masks had something to do with it? Besides, the Mahdek were supposed to be wizards. Why didn't these men use any spells?'

'The Mahdek are deceivers,' my mother said. 'They use tricks and traps and, yes, dark magics to do their will. But magic can be traced. These Mahdek wanted to hurt us without being tracked down.'

I wasn't sure I was convinced, but I let it drop. 'What's wrong with Shalla?' I asked. 'You said it wasn't a cold but—'

'We're not sure,' my father replied. 'But her magic's been weakening steadily for the past three days.'

Three days? Why three days? Unless . . . 'She fought me three days ago. In the oasis.'

I looked over to my father and saw his steady gaze. He nodded, but there was something else . . . something he wasn't telling me. Then I remembered that Tennat was sick too. 'Spirits of our ancestors . . . Osia'phest was right. They're going to blame me.'

'Who is going to blame you, Kellen?' my mother asked. 'And blame you for what?'

'Tennat duelled me and he got sick. Shalla fought me next and now she's sick too. People are going to think I poisoned them or that I'm diseased and they got sick because of me.'

'No,' said my father.

147

'I'm going to be exiled. Ra'meth will convince the council to—'

'No,' he repeated. 'I will deal with the council and I will deal with Ra'meth. Whatever has happened is either coincidence or, more likely, caused by the presence of the Mahdek and their nekhek servants nearby.'

'But I told you, when the nekhek showed up those men ran.'

'They were running from your mother and myself, not from their own servant.'

'But they—'

'Enough, Kellen. You've brought us a lifetime's worth of foolishness these past few days. Now you will obey your parents. You will do what your mother and I tell you to do and say what we tell you to say.' He came over to where I sat and knelt down so we were eye to eye. 'Later today you will accompany me to the oasis. Our people need to see the nekhek and be reassured that there is no danger. If anyone asks you, you will tell them that the creature was in service to the Mahdek raiders who attacked your sister. Do you understand?'

'I . . .' what was I supposed to say? This was my father. The head of my family. I was his son and my duty was to obey. Besides, even if this particular nekhek *wasn't* working for these particular Mahdek, it was still a creature of deceit and darkness, as my father had said. It had torn that little dog's throat out without a second thought. As much as my people had feared the Mahdek, we probably feared the nekhek more.

So why has this one come to me?

At my father's insistence I accompanied him to the oasis, so that no one could accuse him of hiding the one person who'd seen everything that had happened. Hiding, though, was exactly what I most wanted to do. The crowd was densely packed, the smell of sweat and fear and anticipation so thick that I found it hard to breathe. The hum and buzz of muttering was like a swarm threatening to envelop the city. A lesser man than my father would have found it impossible to speak over it.

'Our Jan'Tep ancestors gave us magic so that we could protect each other,' he said, standing four feet above the ground atop the cloth-covered cage, his voice silencing the crowd. 'So that when danger came, we would face it together, not cower under our beds or wail in prayer.'

A few murmurs arose from those near me, some voicing concern but most supporting my father's sentiment. I'd never seen that many people in the oasis at one time before. Bodies were crammed into every square inch and spilling out onto the surrounding streets.

'You people throw the oddest parties,' Ferius Parfax said from behind me.

'Why do you keep sneaking up on me like that?' I asked, irritated.

'Why is it you never pay attention to anything around you?'

She gave me a grin to take the sting out of the words and I felt a stab of guilt over not telling her that the dowager magus had asked me to spy on her. 'Ferius . . .'

'Later, kid,' she said, looking past me. 'Your father's talking.'

Ke'heops went on about courage and honour and how the council and every mage in the clan would protect the town. He told the story of what had taken place on the Snake the previous night and assured them that he'd already sent word

149

to other Jan'Tep cities. Some of the council members took turns reciting poems and stories about how we'd overcome nekhek infestations before and reminded us all that there was a reason why the Jan'Tep thrived, when the Mahdek were all but gone from the world.

'Let us see the enemy!' an old man shouted from nearby.

Other voices rose up in agreement. Speeches were fine, but few had ever seen a nekhek in their lifetime. My father looked annoyed but finally jumped off the cage and down to the sand. 'Very well,' he said, and pulled the cloth from the cage.

As the creature inside was revealed, its jaws opened wide and it growled at the crowd. Its paws scratched at the bars and lock on the front of the cage, probing for the means to escape. The onlookers in the oasis shrank back, hands covering their mouths as if they could catch a disease simply by breathing the same air as the nekhek.

There was no shouting, no screaming. Only the awed silence of a people come face to face with the creature that has stalked their nightmares. That, and the sound of one woman laughing.

'Have you lost your mind?' I hissed angrily to Ferius Parfax. 'Stop laughing!'

A figure wearing a robe of red-and-white silk pushed through the crowds towards us. It was Ra'meth. 'Of course,' he said, a sneer on his face. 'The Daroman spy and her little Sha'Tep ally from the House of Ke take joy at the presence of a creature bred to draw the power from Jan'Tep mages and the life from our children!'

Ra'meth's words very nearly echoed my father's own as to why the other initiates had been getting sick. *Except nobody's complained of being bitten by a demonic shadow creature, and it doesn't seem like the kind of thing you forget.*

'Kellen was the one who faced down the Mahdek,' shouted someone. It was one of the mages who'd accompanied my father the night before. 'Without him we never would have caught the nekhek and it would still be out there.'

'So he would have us believe,' remarked Ra'meth.

'So I say,' my father replied, coming towards us. People parted before him, showing him even more respect than usual. You could see on their faces that the prospect of Mahdek assassins had reminded them that it mattered who became clan prince. They wanted strength in all its forms. Strength was what my father offered.

When he reached us he stopped in front of Ferius. 'Would you mind telling us what's so funny?'

She put up a hand. 'Sorry, sorry. It's just that . . . well, is that –' and here she pointed at the creature in the cage. 'Is that really the dreaded *nekhek*? Bane of the Jan'Tep people? Corruptor of mages and warriors and –' she giggled like a child – 'mercy killer of sick puppy dogs?'

'It is a plague animal,' Ra'meth said. 'Bred to chew weak-weed that mixes with the creature's saliva. A single bite can paralyse a mage's power, making us defenceless. It brings disease and ill luck. It is a creature of darkness and death, and its kind has wrought more destruction upon the Jan'Tep than the Mahdek ever did.'

For some reason that sent Ferius into an uncontrollable flurry of laughter, and if it hadn't been for a warning look from my father, I'm pretty sure Ra'meth would have lit her up with fire magic right then and there.

It was true that in the light of day the nekhek didn't look quite so fierce. Its fur wasn't as dark as I'd remembered, more a tan colour like the sand around the oasis. Its claws and

151

teeth looked sharp, but were no longer nor sharper than those of a wild cat. But I still remembered the speed with which it moved, the way it had snapped the neck of the sick animal that the men in Mahdek masks had tried to use against my sister, and when I looked at the glinting black irises staring back at us, I didn't doubt for a second that it could have torn out my throat just as easily as the dog's. 'It's a lot more dangerous than it looks,' I said.

'Oh, I'm sure it is,' Ferius said. 'Positively deadly. It's just that, well, in Darome and most other places, they're mostly known for rooting through bins and occasionally stealing food. See, the rest of the civilised world wouldn't call that animal in there a "*nekhek*".'

'What do you call them?' my father asked.

'Oh, they have many names, mighty Ke'heops. The Berabesq call them *senhebi*, "wind leapers". The Daromans call them *felidus arborica*, "forest gliders". But most folks on the frontier just call them squirrel cats.'

'Squirrel cats?' I asked.

Ferius, her eyes filled with tears from laughing so much, barely held back her chortling long enough to say, 'Your ancient enemy is basically just a really, really big squirrel.'

18

The Red Deck

'You're really starting to annoy people around here, you know that?' Ferius and I were walking down an alley towards the seedy little guest house where she was staying. There were nicer ones in town, but apparently this was the only one willing to rent her a room. *The Jan'Tep do not hold grudges.* That sentence was really starting to sound hollow in my ears.

'Can't help it, kid,' she said. 'You people have endless ways of amusing me.'

'Well, *you're* not amusing anyone.'

It had taken stern words from my father to keep half a dozen people from challenging Ferius. She'd thanked him politely but told the crowd they were more than welcome to set up appointments at her guest house, where she'd happily kick their asses one a day for as long as they wanted to keep it up. Finally the council had ordered everyone to leave the oasis and to stay away until further notice. It probably would have made more sense to keep the nekhek locked up somewhere inside, but both my father and the council were of the view that the oasis had the best magical wards and would make it much easier to use sympathy spells to draw any other nekhek later on. The crowd hadn't needed much incentive to disperse after that. Fear of the creature's poison and disease was enough to keep them away.

My guilt over not telling Ferius about the dowager magus's interest in her faded as my irritation with her grew. 'You're wrong, you know,' I told her.

'I'm wrong about lots of things. Which one in particular is bothering you today?'

'The nekhek. It's a lot more dangerous than—'

'Squirrel cat, kid. It's just a big damned flying squirrel. Might as well learn what a thing is if you're going to kill it.'

'Whatever. I've seen pictures of all kinds of animals in books, and that thing doesn't look like a squirrel to me. Besides, squirrels aren't even native to this part of the continent.'

'Neither are you.'

'What's that supposed to mean?'

She tapped a finger against my forehead. 'Look how pale your skin is, kid. You reckon a climate like this breeds people who burn so easy under the sun?'

I looked around and saw a couple walking down the street and pointed them out. 'There are plenty of Jan'Tep with dark skin. There are Jan'Tep with different shape and colour eyes too.'

'Exactly. You Jan'Tep aren't a race, you're just a collection of different families. Mages who came from all over the continent to fight over the oases across this territory. Sometimes you waged war over them, other times you just merged with other tribes who'd come for the same reason. I bet not one of you has a drop of blood from the original people that lived here.'

154

'So what?'

'So maybe the squirrel cats were drawn here for the same reason. Maybe they like magic too.'

I felt as if I was losing the argument, but I wasn't sure how. 'My people belong here. We need the oasis to give us the strength to protect ourselves from those who'd hunt us down or enslave us for our magic.'

Ferius snorted. 'Enslave you? That's rich.'

'What do you mean? And what does any of this have to do with our right to protect ourselves from the nekhek?'

Ferius stopped and put a gloved hand over my eyes.

'Hey!'

'Stop squirming, kid. Just picture the animals you saw in your books. Can you do that?'

Focusing on an image, making it crystal clear in the mind's eye, is something mages are trained to do from their first lessons. 'Of course I can,' I said.

'Good. Now think about the animal back there in the square.'

'I am.'

She slapped the back of my head. 'Not the monster in your stories. Not the thing everyone tells you to see. I want you to picture the actual creature trapped inside that cage.'

It's hard comparing a drawing made from pen and inks to a real thing you've seen, but I did my best to envision them side by side in my mind. 'Fine. I'm doing it.'

'Well? Can you really tell me that those two things aren't related?'

'I . . .'

The truth was, I couldn't. While they didn't look exactly alike, it was probably just because I'd always pictured the animals in books as . . . I don't know, further away? I'd seen the nekhek up close. I'd seen what it could do. I'd felt its rage. 'I still don't think it's the same thing.'

Ferius removed her hand from my eyes and started back down the alley. 'Of course not, kid. The creature you've captured, why, that's the dreaded *nekhek*! Demon slayer of Jan'Tep mages! Also, rampant eater of other people's rubbish, and hoarder of nuts.'

'You're wrong,' I said. 'Maybe it looks like a . . .' I felt so stupid I couldn't even say the thing's name out loud. 'Look, I've seen how vicious that creature is. Wait until the council uses it to reel in all the other nekhek in the area and kill them. Wait until you see what a pack of them looks like. Then maybe you'll understand.'

'And what are you going to do while they're torturing that animal?' she asked, stopping in her tracks.

Something sharp in her voice surprised me. I had to walk ahead of her and turn back round to see her face. There was no humour there. No jokes. Her eyes were deadly serious.

'What do you mean? What do I have to do with this?'

'You said that animal saved your sister.'

'I said it killed a sick dog before it could bond with her. That's not the same thing. Maybe the nekhek just likes to kill other animals.' I was lying to myself though. I could still see the look on the creature's face after it had snapped the diseased dog's neck. If anything, the nekhek had looked enraged at having to do it.

Ferius reached into her waistcoat and pulled out a deck of her cards. These weren't the regular ones like she'd given me, nor were they the sharp metal ones she'd used as weapons. The backs of these cards were the darkest red I'd ever seen, almost black. She fanned them and held them out to me. 'Pick a card, kid.'

'What's this about?'

'You said those men were trying to hurt your sister. You were begging anyone or anything to save her, and that squirrel cat came along and you got what you wanted. Isn't that right?'

'You're distorting the facts,' I said. 'You're making it sound like—'

'Pick a card, Kellen.'

I looked around, suddenly realising how dark it had become. 'Not until you tell me what this is about.'

'It's about you deciding whether or not you're going to be a man.'

'You keep going on about me having to be a man. You keep insulting my people's magic and my family's –'

'The world's got plenty of mages, Kellen. What it needs are *men* and *women*.' She made the words sound different than the way people usually say them. Important, somehow.

I hated the way she spoke about magic as if it were a joke, as if my people were no different than children playing with toys. More than anything I hated the way she kept holding the fanned cards out to me, challenging me to take one.

'Look, I'm not—'

'Shut up and pick a card. Pick a card or turn around and walk away and don't ever look back. The world is a big and dangerous place and there's more darkness filling it than you'll ever know. Only one thing fights that – men and women who don't walk away from their debts. Pick a card now, Kellen, because I won't ask again.'

I was so sick of her tricks and her games. For every little thing she taught me, there was some test or trap, each one

157

forcing me to do things I didn't want to do. But even though I'd only known Ferius Parfax for all of three days, I knew without the slightest doubt that while this might be a trick, it wasn't any kind of joke. If I didn't take the card I would never see her again. I don't know why, but the thought scared me. I took a card from the middle.

'Three of hearts,' I said, my eyes captured by the dark crimson hearts set against the beige background, the calligraphy of the number three written in the same red-black ink as the back of the card. 'What does it mean?'

She closed the deck and slipped it back into her waistcoat. 'The card you pick doesn't matter.'

'Then I don't get it,' I said, holding the card up. 'What am I supposed to do with this?'

She sidestepped around me and headed further down the alley. 'How should I know? Just do the right thing. Maybe just look that animal in the eyes before you consign it to death. Do what you think the man you want to be would do. Then I'd suggest you get rid of that card real quick.'

I looked down at the thing as if it might burst into flames. 'What did you just make me take? Is this some kind of curse?'

'Life's a curse, kid. Love is the cure.'

I started running after her but stopped myself when I realised how stupid I must look. 'I don't know what that means!'

'It's your debt, Kellen. You figure out how to pay it. Reckon I saved your life, so now that's one less debt for me.'

I wanted to tear the card up and toss it on the ground and stomp on it until it was crushed into dust. Damned Ferius Parfax with her stupid jokes and her tricks and her mysterious remarks. I looked back at her and saw that she was almost at the door of the guest house. 'Wait! If the card is supposed to represent some kind of debt, then what are you doing with a whole deck of them?'

She held up something in her hand and I heard coins tinkling. 'Getting really, really drunk,' she said, and walked through the open door.

I was halfway home and walking through a narrow alleyway that usually provided a convenient shortcut when I found myself face to face with a palace guardsman. He looked oddly out of place in the dirt and dust of the alley.

'You startled me,' I said, trying to recover my breath.

He gave no reply, but instead held out a roll of parchment. Even in the dim light I could make out the black wax seal of the dowager magus. I cracked the seal and opened it, careful not to let the anticipated gold disc fall out. However, the parchment was empty, save for a single, hastily scrawled message. 'At your convenience,' it said.

I looked down at the ground, wondering if perhaps the disc had fallen without my noticing. Without it, Osia'phest wouldn't allow me to attempt the third trial alongside the other initiates. 'Was there anything else with the message?' I asked the guard.

Again he remained silent.

I noticed he also made no move to leave, or to let me walk past him. 'So when she says, "At your convenience," what she really means is . . .'

The guard gave me a slight smile for the first time. 'Now,' he said.

My second meeting with the dowager magus was just as odd as the first, though vastly more uncomfortable.

'Just how stupid is your father?' Mer'esan asked, hands across her lap as she sat in her chair looking up at me.

I worked my way through a rather long list of possible replies, trying to find one that would perfectly articulate my anger at this slight against my family's honour while also protecting me from a death sentence. 'Forgive me, Mer'esan, I don't understand the question.'

'Yes, you do. Your father believes the Mahdek have come back from the dead to attack our people, that they decided to target your sister, and that bringing a nekhek to our city is a good idea.' She wrinkled her nose. 'Disgusting little monsters.'

'Ferius . . .' I hesitated.

'Speak,' Mer'esan commanded.

'She says the animal is called a squirrel cat – that it's not a demon at all.'

'And what do you believe?'

Again I searched for a reply that wouldn't get me into trouble. 'Lord Magus Ke'heops,' I began, using my father's formal title, 'believes that some of the Mahdek must have survived, perhaps growing their numbers in secret. He believes they intend to use the nekhek to—'

'No, he only *says* he believes this foolishness.' Her eyes narrowed. 'Apparently you think he's even more of an idiot than I do. He hopes to take advantage of this opportunity to show how *his* strength is what our people need now that my husband is dead.'

A thought occurred to me then, like a fist clenched around my stomach. 'Do you intend to resist my father's election as clan prince?'

'I couldn't care less who becomes the next clan prince, child.'

160

The next words came out of my mouth far too fast for my own good. 'Then what exactly *do* you care about, Mer'esan?'

The sudden stare she gave me convinced me that I'd gone too far. She rose to her feet and began walking around me as if I were a poorly made sculpture she were examining. 'You fought your own friends to save the Argosi woman. Why?'

I considered my reply. If Mer'esan had decided that Ferius was, in fact, some kind of spy or wished us ill, it wouldn't be hard to interpret my actions as treason against my own people. 'You commanded me to maintain her interest in me, Dowager Magus.'

She stopped in front of me and held up a hand. Once again I could see the web of coloured tendrils of energy weaving under her skin. 'It takes almost every ounce of magic I have to keep myself alive, Kellen, but I assure you the minuscule amount that remains is more than enough to beat the truth from you.'

I thought up a dozen other reasons, plausible explanations for my actions. I'm a reasonably accomplished liar most days. But the dowager magus seemed to be better at detecting dishonesty than I was at conjuring it. 'I like her,' I said.

'You *like* her?'

I nodded.

'Is she particularly pretty? Do you desire this woman? Do you hope she might –' Mer'esan waved a finger in the direction of my trousers – 'teach you things?'

I felt my cheeks flush and started fumbling for words, then stopped myself. *It's a game. Mer'esan knows I wasn't referring to some misplaced teenage lust. She's testing me again.*

'Ah,' the dowager magus said, tapping my forehead. 'Clever.

161

Good.' She resumed her slow walk around me. 'Show me more.'

'You don't believe the Mahdek have returned,' I said.

'That much is obvious.'

'But you think there *is* a threat,' I added.

'Again, obvious.'

I thought about how angry she was over my father's assumptions. 'You believe the men in masks are a distraction.'

She quickened her pace. 'Obvious. Obvious. Obvious. Ask me a question worthy of an answer.'

I tried to imagine who might be working against us. The Daroman kings had a long history of seeking control over the Jan'Tep. That was why people were so quick to believe Ferius must be a spy. The Mahdek – if there were any left – had sworn blood oaths to destroy us, which explained my father's convictions. The Berabesq considered our magic to be a blasphemy against their six-faced god ... We had no end of enemies – that was precisely why magic was so vital to our society, why the trials were so harsh. It was why Jan'Tep and Sha'Tep were not allowed to marry – for fear that such unions would weaken the bloodlines.

'Speak,' Mer'esan said, still pacing around me. 'I'm growing impatient of watching you stand there.'

'A moment,' I said.

Despite the avarice of our enemies, we had never been subjugated. Our magic had always been too strong. So why was Mer'esan – the oldest and most knowledgeable person in our clan – suddenly so concerned?

'Ask the question,' she demanded, her sandals slapping against the wooden floor.

'What is the one foe that magic cannot withstand?' I asked.

She stopped, and patted me on the arm. 'Good,' she said, her voice suddenly weary. 'This is the question that men like your father, like those pompous fools on the council, cannot think to ask. The very possibility of a threat that magic cannot solve is utterly foreign to them.'

Whereas for me, the possibility of using magic to solve anything is fading fast.

'The second trial comes to an end and you have failed it,' she said, without a trace of sympathy in her voice. 'Now you fear you will fail the third as well.'

'How can I create a spell using two disciplines when I can't break even one of my bands?'

'I told you once before: do not ask questions to which you already know the answer.'

'Then . . . it's over. My sixteenth birthday is in a few days. I'm never going to become a mage. I'm going to be Sha'Tep.'

I felt myself becoming dizzy, as if just saying the words out loud had drained the strength from my limbs. Mer'esan held my arms. 'You will never be a Jan'Tep mage like your father and mother. Whether you become a servant like your uncle is up to you.'

Like a child I held out my forearms, the metallic ink of the bands almost glistening in the cottage's soft light. 'Can't you help me? You have the power, I know you do. Can't you—'

'I cannot,' she said simply.

'Why?' I asked, tears sliding down my cheeks. 'Why is this happening to me? Why won't anyone help me?'

She didn't answer, but simply led me by the hand to the door of the cottage. 'These are the questions of a child, Kellen. You already found the one that matters, the one that binds all of our fates together. Ask it again.'

She had ushered me outside. 'What is the foe that can't be defeated by magic?'

Mer'esan looked at me, her face so full of sadness that for the first time she looked every one of her years. 'The truth,' she replied.

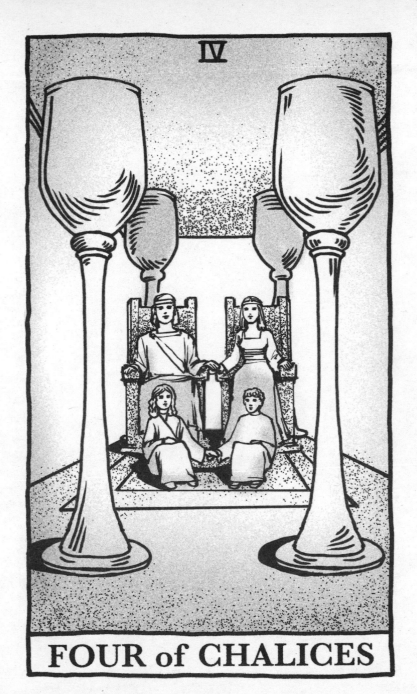

IV

FOUR of CHALICES

THE THIRD TRIAL

To rely on those spells already known is to allow the enemy to know your weapons. Our magic cannot be stagnant, but must adapt and change to protect our people against those who would take it from us. Only those who can demonstrate the ability to devise new spells can truly be called Jan'Tep and earn a mage's name.

19

Blood Magic

The coarse sand on the path leading to the village square scratched at the skin of my bare feet as I crept along, as quietly as I could, cursing the way the food I'd stolen from the kitchen bounced awkwardly inside the cloth sack against my back. I'd been a fool to bring so much. If anyone caught me near the nekhek's cage I'd have a tough time convincing them I was there for a midnight picnic.

Go back, part of me commanded. *There are probably things worse than becoming a Sha'Tep, and if you get caught you're going to find out exactly what they are.*

I couldn't just go back though. I'd spent hours sitting in my room in the darkness, trying to think of some way to spark my bands, to prove Mer'esan wrong. It got me nowhere. Through all of it I just kept finding myself staring at the blood-red markings on the card Ferius had given me and thinking about the animal that had saved my sister's life, sitting in a cage, waiting to die.

I shifted the bag to redistribute its weight across my shoulders. Would the nekhek even want any of the food I'd brought? What did they eat, anyway, when they weren't supposedly feasting on the soft flesh of Jan'Tep babies?

The sound of a door opening stopped me in my tracks. I held my breath and crouched in the shadows as a man with limp grey hair stumbled out of the house barely five feet from me. He pulled down the front of his trousers and let out a loud belch. The sickly-sweet smell of his breath reached me a second before the stench of his urine. I held my breath, praying he'd stop before the urge to wretch overcame me.

The old man looked down, admiring the stream of his piss as it went on and on, the puddle it formed on the ground leaking back down the slope towards me. A few seconds later I began to feel the trickle of urine work its way between my toes. The steady hiss finally stuttered to an end, followed by a deep sigh and then a cough. The old man didn't even bother hoisting his pants back up. He just stood there, looking up at the moon reaching his right hand back to lean against the side of the house while the other idly scratched his hip.

My legs were beginning to burn from crouching so long and again I considered turning on my heels and running, but if I left now I didn't think I'd have the courage to try again later. Damn Ferius Parfax and her stupid cards and her idiotic frontier philosophy. *Do what you think the man you want to be would do.*

Fine, Ferius. I'd look the nekhek in the eyes. I'd even give it something to eat. Out of all the different foods I'd stuffed in the bag, there must be something that would appeal to the little monster. Maybe it would gorge itself and choke to death and save everyone a good deal of trouble.

'What are you doing, standing there in the dark like an idiot?' a voice called out.

Hells, I've been seen. I tried to tense the muscles in my legs

170

and almost cried out from the pain of pins and needles. *Move, damn you! Don't just sit here waiting for him to grab you!*

I had just managed to push my way to a standing position when the old man said, 'I'm just enjoying a little fresh air. Go back to bed.'

It's just someone inside the house talking. I haven't been spotted.

The person in the house said something else but I didn't hear it. The old man replied with a grunt that turned into another bout of coughing. Then he turned and limped back into the house, his pants still halfway down his thighs.

I let out my breath and shifted the bag of food again before stepping out from the shadows, rubbing my thigh with my free hand and doing my best to step around the little puddles of urine as I headed down towards the oasis, cursing Ferius Parfax all the way.

It took only a few minutes more to reach the edge of the seven columns. I stopped to gather up what little courage I could find in myself. I realised suddenly that I was standing under a glow-glass lantern hanging from a pole and felt a flicker of panic that it might light up, making me visible to anyone walking along one of the adjoining paths. I needn't have worried; the lantern was completely dark. I looked up and, like a fool, reached out with my will and tried as hard as I could to make the glow-glass spark. Nothing happened. There just wasn't enough magic inside me to bring it to light. I was useless. For once in my life that turned out to be a good thing though, because I soon realised that there were already people at the oasis.

'Do it again!' Someone had whispered so loudly that the sound carried the entire distance from the centre of the oasis to the column where I crouched. *Tennat!* I shuddered at the thought of what he might do to me now that he knew I had no magic to fight back with. He was supposed to be sick, like me. *What's he doing here?*

'Shut up,' cautioned a deeper and less nasal voice. It was my former friend, Panahsi. 'Osia'phest will skin us alive if he finds out we've been practising blood sympathies.'

'No one's going to care, Pan,' Tennat replied, sounding too excited to be cowed. 'The council said they were going to use sympathy on the beast anyway.'

'Yes, but the council will use silk spells to spread it to the other nekhek,' a soft female voice replied. Hearing Nephenia speak made me shift from my position so that I could see around the corner. Soft light from the small lantern at her feet cast a glow on her pale blue dress. She stood over the boys, who were kneeling in front of the four-foot brass cage the mages had warded hours before.

Inside, the creature that had sent three armed men fleeing for their lives growled its outrage.

I don't care how innocent Ferius thinks that thing is, I thought. *Nekhek or squirrel cat . . . it looks as if it would tear my face off if I tried to feed it.*

The three of them continued their conversation, unaware that I was listening. 'The point of the sympathy is to make the other nekhek in the hills feel this one's pain,' Panahsi said. 'Then they'll be forced to come here, and Ke'heops and the other master mages can rid us of them all at once. It's the only way to protect the clan.'

'Doesn't mean we can't try out a few of our own spells on the creature first, right?' Tennat argued. 'Look, if we want to pass the third test, then we need to be able to show a new spell that combines two disciplines, or at least construct a variation of one of the usual ones. No initiate has ever devised a spell incorporating blood sympathy. We'll have the pick of apprenticeships if we can make it work. When are we ever going to get a chance like this again?'

Panahsi and Nephenia exchanged a hesitant look, but a moment later, they nodded to each other in agreement.

I felt oddly betrayed that my one friend and the girl I never stopped thinking about were here, even after everything that had happened between us. But I shouldn't have been surprised. It was one thing to know the theory behind blood sympathies, but actually getting to test them was something else entirely. Blood magic was far too risky to try out on humans or even pets. But something insidious like a nekhek, a creature you didn't have to feel sorry for, who wouldn't want a chance to try out magic like this?

'Here, watch this,' Nephenia said. They were nearly a hundred feet away from me so I had to squint to make out what was happening. The animal was reaching out with its paws between the bars, no doubt trying to claw at Nephenia. She made a somatic gesture with her left hand, the little finger touching the thumb, and then reached the index finger of her right hand to touch one of the bars. Blue light flickered in and out and the nekhek suddenly flew back from the bars to thump against the back of the cage.

'How did you do that?' Tennat asked. 'That was beautiful!'

'Lightning,' she said, looking down as if she were a little embarrassed by his praise. 'I can't make much but it's enough to conduct through the iron bars.'

The nekhek scurried back into the far corner of the cage, away from Nephenia. I took a quiet step back from the edge of the square. I'd seen enough to know that I didn't want to stick around. It sickened me to watch the way the three of them acted like children, egging each other on as they tormented the nekhek. I'd believed Nephenia and Panahsi were better than that.

While I'd been ready to risk getting bitten by that little monster, I wasn't going to take a chance on the humiliation of getting caught by Tennat. Perhaps he would just blackmail me into giving him one of my few personal possessions, but he could just as easily decide to tell his father that they'd caught me bringing food to the nekhek. Of course, since it looked as if he'd fully recovered from his earlier weakness, if I were really unlucky he might use this opportunity to impress Nephenia by working a blood sympathy spell on me. I wasn't going to let that happen. I'd tried my best to do what Ferius had asked, but sometimes life didn't work out the way you hoped. The nekhek probably already knew that. If not, it would figure it out soon enough.

I was about to turn and trudge home when I heard a sound that drove a spike into me. The cry wasn't human, but it filled me with feelings I didn't like. Shame. Disgust.

'That's amazing!' I heard Tennat cheer. 'How are you doing that?'

Despite my fears I returned to my spot and looked back into the square. What I saw made my insides wither. Within the cage, the nekhek was spasming again and again, its muscles clenching so hard its whole body jerked uncontrollably into the air and then back down to slam against the floor of the cage. The creature twisted and turned, clawing at its belly.

Panahsi was holding a long piece of string in his hands, dangling and shaking it. 'It's the string,' he told the others.

174

'I've used sympathy to bind it to the little monster's intestines.' He began winding the string around one of his fingers. 'So when I give it a little twist . . .'

The animal gave another screech that sounded almost human to me. It set my teeth on edge and started a pounding in my skull.

'Show me how to do it,' Tennat said, sounding like a gleeful toddler.

Panahsi shook his head, his eyes focused in deep concentration. 'It's not as easy as it looks. Blood sympathy takes a lot of preparation. I had to spend most of the day meditating just to get ready.' He smiled up at Nephenia. 'Worth it though, wouldn't you say?' He whipped the string out hard and I saw the nekhek's body lift inside the cage, all four limbs extended, the furred webbing between them stretched unnaturally. The animal screamed once more and then fell to the floor of the cage, shivering.

'That's probably enough, Panahsi,' she said, favouring him with a nervous smile. 'We're not supposed to kill it. Let's go back before we—'

'Let me try something,' Tennat interrupted, pushing the other two away from the front of the cage. 'My brother found this in a book Osia'phest was keeping hidden in the masters' library.' From his pocket he brought out what looked like a short, thin tube and began whispering.

'Is something supposed to be happening?' Nephenia asked.

'Just a second.'

I didn't recognise the spell he was casting, but I had a feeling I knew what he was going to do with it. There was a part of me that wanted to rush out and yell at them to stop. No matter how vile the creature inside the cage, there was

175

something wrong with this. It wasn't just that I resented the way they were taking turns showing off for each other, it was the way Tennat giggled when the nekhek cried out.

I wasn't gullible enough to believe the nekheks really stole human babies and fed them to their young – at least, if they did, I'd never heard of it happening in my lifetime. But I also knew they carried disease that could kill even a master Jan'Tep mage. They were a threat to our safety and had to be eliminated. But it's not as if it was their fault, was it? Can something really be evil just for being what it is?

I shook my head. Ferius and all her stupid talk were confusing me.

Tennat had stopped whispering his spell. 'Watch this,' he said.

I couldn't bring myself to look away as he reached down and picked up a handful of sand from the ground. He started pouring it from his closed fist down into the hollow tube. At first nothing seemed to be happening, but then the nekhek jumped up from the floor of the cage. Its mouth was open wide as if it were desperately trying to suck in air. I felt sick.

'You've linked the tube to its throat. Not bad,' Panahsi said, a trace of admiration in his voice.

The nekhek made raw, almost gurgling sounds. It was going to die now, I knew. The three of them were swept up in the thrill of magic, the sensations of power, of accomplishment, of all the things I would never feel. They were too far gone to stop now. The creature knew it too. It turned its head desperately as if looking for someone to save it. For just an instant its face turned to where I knelt in the shadows. The moon was high in the sky and the light glinted off the animal's eyes. They were like small shiny black marbles surrounded by black fur. I could see its pain so clearly in that moment. The anger. The fear. And I finally saw what Ferius had wanted me to see.

I saw myself.

I saw who I was and I saw the man I wanted to be.

I finally understood how that man was different from my friends and from my family, from my people. And I knew precisely what that man would do.

It was something very, very stupid.

20

Jailbreak

'Stop it,' I called out.

'Kellen?' Nephenia asked, her eyes fixed on me as I walked to the centre of the oasis, the rock hidden in my hand.

'What are you doing here?' Tennat said irritably, his concentration slipping and the link between the tube and the nekhek's throat fading. The creature fell back in the cage panting. 'Now I have to start all over again! It figures you'd want to ruin everything.'

'Stop it, Tennat,' I repeated, getting steadily closer to them and still not having a clue what I was going to do when I got there.

Their faces were practically glistening. You could see it in their eyes. Joy. Excitement. Desire. Surprise and annoyance that I'd interrupted them, and something else too: a tiny sliver of concern. *They're worried that I'm going to tell on them,* I thought. As if anyone in the village would really punish them for what they were doing. Maybe they *would* have got into a little trouble. My father would be angered over the potential delay in his plans to deal with the remaining nekhek in the hills, our teacher Osia'phest would certainly mete out some modest punishment for casting spells without proper supervision, but everyone else would probably quietly cheer them for being bold and brave, for once again demonstrating that although the Daroman had military might, it was the Jan'Tep who controlled magic. But only true Jan'Tep, of course.

I hate my people, I realised, with the clarity that comes from an idea you've never dared to consider before. *I hate all of them. I even hate my family, because one day they're going to think I'm just as worthless and vile as the animal in that cage.*

'Did you . . . want to try?' Nephenia asked gently.

'Great,' Tennat said. 'Let's have the spy-lover Kellen waste our time with yet another failed spell.'

Nephenia gave me a look of pity and then slapped the back of Tennat's head. 'Don't be cruel. If Kellen wants to try . . .'

The hells with you, Tennat. The hells with you, Panahsi, even you, Nephenia. The hells with Mother and Father and everyone else.

'You've got to be reasonable, Kellen,' Panahsi said, his tone a remarkably poor impression of a sympathetic adult. 'This is blood magic. It's beyond . . .'

'It's beyond you, Kellen.' At least have the courage to say it.

Panahsi was right of course. The three of them could already work spells I'd never be able to cast, not for as long as I lived. Inside the cage, the nekhek lay on its side, still moaning in pain. *You can't stop them from doing this. They'll only hurt you as well if you try.*

'Maybe if you let yourself go,' Nephenia said, reaching out a hand. 'I mean, concentrate on the spell, but let go of the fear of doing it wrong. You worry too much, Kellen.'

I almost laughed. Fear. Sure, that was all it was. I looked again at the nekhek trapped behind the bars, terrified out of its mind.

Then I realised that she was right. Fear was the answer. Fear held its own kind of magic, if you could harness it.

'Don't waste your time, Neph,' Tennat said. 'We could stand here all night waiting and Kellen wouldn't spark a glow-glass bulb. Besides, I've got something really cool I want to—'

'There's one spell I can do,' I muttered, more to myself than to him.

'Yeah? What spell is that? The running-away spell?' He scrunched his face tight. 'Or maybe the trying-so-hard-you-wet-your-own-pants spell? I hear you're good at that one.'

'Tennat!' Nephenia said.

'All right, all right,' Tennat said, his hands up in mock submission. 'It's just a fact. Some people can't work magic. Maybe when you join the servants we can still—'

'You can't either, Tennat,' I said. 'Not when you're afraid. Even the masters can't cast spells when they're afraid, when they can't concentrate. But I've got one that works no matter how scared I am.'

Tennat gave a snort and stepped in front of Panahsi and Nephenia to give me a shove. 'Your friend with the razor blades isn't here, Kellen. You think I'm afraid of some sickly, magic-less—'

I swung the rock hard and slammed it into the side of his head. Tennat's eyes went wide with surprise and he hung there for an instant. Then his body worked out what had happened, his legs gave out from under him and he fell to the ground.

'What the hells—' Panahsi started, but I didn't give him a chance. I swung the rock again and got a glancing hit against his lips and front teeth. He stumbled back out of the way. I didn't give him a chance to recover. Panahsi was smart. He

180

only needed to get away from me for a moment and calm himself long enough to cast a spell. I couldn't give him that chance. Pain works as well as fear to break concentration, so I kicked him in the knee. He let out a scream and went down next to Tennat.

Nephenia, her eyes full of shock and confusion, was already forming a knot spell with her left hand that would have me writhing on the ground in another second. 'Kel . . .' She hesitated for just a second. So did I. This was the girl I'd wanted ever since I was twelve years old, for whom I'd written dozens of stupid, lovesick poems. I still kept them in a box buried in the garden behind my home. I knew I'd never show them to her, that I'd be humiliated if my sister or anyone else found them, but I'd kept them all the same. I'd tried to draw pictures of her too, and if there'd been an ounce of magic in me I swear I would have used it up on every charm spell ever devised. I guess you could say I was in love with her.

Maybe that was why, when I punched her in the face, it was with the hand that wasn't holding the rock.

'Stop him,' Panahsi said, clutching his leg. I could see him trying to concentrate but the pain was too much.

I had to keep them all off balance. My people aren't used to physical pain. We're not violent. Or rather, we don't usually like to get our own hands dirty. A Jan'Tep man is supposed to be calm and collected, reserved and, when he speaks, full of brilliant insights and wit. I was screaming like a lunatic at all of them, at the very world around us. 'How do you like my magic now?' I shouted. 'How do you like it now, you bastard –'

Something struck me hard on the back of the legs. Panahsi had found a stick and had hit me with it even as he lay on his side. I went down, but twisted away just in time to avoid the stick landing on my head. Someone kicked me in the ribs. It was Tennat. He kicked me again. I tried to kick him back, but I was stuck like an overturned turtle. At first I couldn't get a solid connection, but when I did I pushed back with both feet, sliding myself back along the sand towards the cage. I felt something grab at my hair and thought the nekhek might be clawing at me, so I pulled my head away. It would serve me right if, after throwing my life away for it, the little monster ended up killing me.

Glancing back, I realised it was trying to grab at the latch of the cage. There was a lock that kept it from opening, but I still had the rock in my hand. I rolled around and got my knees under me, taking a kick in the middle of my back from Tennat in order to have my chance. I slammed the rock down hard on the lock. Once, twice. On the third try it broke, and the door swung open.

The others were all on their feet now, coming towards me. Nephenia, bless her heart, actually had a hand on Panahsi's arm as he limped towards me, as if she might hold him back. They all stopped in their tracks when they saw the nekhek emerge. *No, not a nekhek. It's called a squirrel cat.*

The creature growled, a thin, almost feathery sound that was full of rage. Panahsi and Tennat stumbled back from it. I looked at the little monster, its furry face only a foot away from my own. It moved closer, its eyes catching mine. For a second I thought it might be trying to protect me. *It understands*, I thought. *It knows what I did.*

Two things happened just then, both of which I guess I deserved. The first was, the squirrel cat bit my hand so hard it drew blood. The second was that the little monster ran away, out past the edge of the colonnades and away from the oasis, leaving me with the three people I'd just assaulted in order to free it.

'A bind!' Panahsi shouted. 'Someone use a binding spell on the damned nekhek!'

'The creature's too far away,' Tennat replied.

'Then go after it!' Panahsi punctuated his words with a kick to my stomach.

I saw Tennat run past me after it, but he came back a moment later. 'It's gone. It's too damned fast.'

I felt another kick to the gut. I grabbed at the leg, wrestling it and using it to pull myself into a sitting position. I should have stayed down. Panahsi grasped my hair with one hand and drove his fist into my face with the other. Blood exploded from my nose, the droplets falling slowly and glowing in the soft light, like the petals from summer blossoms picked up by the wind. *It's like a magic spell*, I thought, the idea striking me as incredibly funny despite the ensuing waves of pain.

'You think this was a joke?' Tennat said, kicking me in the side while Panahsi held my head up by its hair. 'You think you're going to laugh your way out of this?'

'Stop it! Just stop it!' Nephenia cried.

I looked up to see her face full of tears and uncertain anger. Why was she so angry with me? *Maybe because you punched her in the face, idiot.* And yet here she was, trying to pull Panahsi away from me. Twin bruises were forming around the eyes of my one-time friend, painting dark, uneven circles. *You'd make an ugly squirrel cat, Panahsi*, I thought absently.

'Stop laughing,' he said, slapping me across the face. It seemed like a sissy thing to do, but then I realised his hand must be hurting from punching me. That sent me into more spasms of laughter.

Tennat kicked me again. I heard something crack. 'What's so funny, you stupid, magic-less piece of crap?'

'Don't you get it?' I asked. 'I *do* have magic. I just made a squirrel cat disappear.'

I don't know if anyone but me thought that was funny, because at this point Panahsi and Tennat were taking turns kicking me and then someone's foot connected with my head, snapping it back so that it collided with the corner of the cage.

The light of the moon winked in and out, the world alternating between harsh reality and perfect, peaceful darkness, blacker than any shadow.

'Ancestors!' Panahsi said. 'What is that?'

I thought he was looking at me and wondered just how much blood was leaking out of my head, but as my vision came back I followed the line of his sight towards the other side of the colonnade. A shadowy form was scurrying along the ground towards us. No, not *a* shadow. *Many* shadows.

As the dark shapes came closer, throwing up sand as they raced towards us, the light from the lantern revealed colours ranging from every shade of brown to the deepest black, their fur almost matching the darkness around them. *Nekheks*, I thought, absurdly still not sure what to call them even as I felt myself start to panic at the sight of more than a dozen of the creatures. Finally they stopped, half encircling Tennat and the others, growling and chittering furiously. One of the creatures, which I recognised as the one I'd freed from the cage, the one that had bitten my hand so hard it was bleeding even now, rose up on its haunches. It growled

184

and chittered too, only something about the noises he made was different.

I could understand them.

He – and I suddenly knew it was a he because of the tone of his voice – glanced at me for a second before turning to Tennat and the others, baring his teeth and saying, 'All right, you hairless skinbag sons of bitches. Which one of you wants it first?'

21

The Squirrel Cats

The oasis was so quiet that I wondered if perhaps the disturbing image before me was the result of one too many blows to the head. The squirrel cats – though now the word *nekhek* seemed more appropriate – held their ground, the muscles of their furry bodies twitching, almost quivering in anticipation. Panahsi, Nephenia and Tennat were more still, each one struggling to find the inner calm required to cast Jan'Tep magic. I found myself counting the seconds down, as if I were about to witness a mage's duel. I could almost hear old Osia'phest: *'Seven . . . six . . . five . . .'*

'Damn it,' Panahsi said, fingers twitching as they ran through the somatic forms for a conflagration spell. He'd incinerate the animals if he could cast the ember magic wide enough, but his face was glistening with sweat and his chest was still pumping from his prior exertions. He couldn't draw the magic inside himself yet, but he still kept his eyes on the squirrel cats. Panahsi knew full well that he was more powerful than Nephenia and Tennat. He'd see it as his job to protect the others. He really was a pretty admirable person when he wasn't kicking you half to death.

I had no idea what the squirrel cats were thinking. The

fur of the thin, flat skin between their front and hind legs rippled in the soft late-night breeze. It was like watching waves on the surface of a lake, if that lake happened to be made of pure unbridled rage and the promise of imminent bloodshed.

'We should back away,' Nephenia suggested without taking her eyes off the creatures. 'Then we can call for help.'

Panahsi's hands were still running through the somatic forms, but he said, 'We can't. The quieting spell is still active. No one can hear us.'

So that's why I didn't hear you until I was near the ring of the columns. It made sense of course. With the little monster screaming under their blood spells, someone would have been bound to hear eventually. But none of them, not even Panahsi, had the experience to cast a hush that could cover the whole oasis. Somebody must have helped them do it – maybe Tennat's brother or his father?

'No backing away,' Tennat said, his voice soft, almost reassuring. 'We kill them. Every last one of them.'

Apparently he wasn't as good at bluffing as he thought, because a couple of the squirrel cats started growling and I could see them shifting, muscles bunching in preparation to attack.

The lead animal chittered back at them, 'Nobody attacks until I give the damned order.' Some of the others hissed and growled, but I had no idea what they'd said until the leader snapped back, 'Well, I'm in charge now, so shut up and wait.'

The little chitters and grunts and growls he made were so clearly speech to my ears that I kept thinking Panahsi, Tennat and Nephenia must be able to understand them too. None

187

of them showed any sign of it, though Nephenia looked conflicted. She glanced over at me, her face full of fear and anger and . . . I don't know what. Maybe regret? *Or maybe you just want to see that because then it might not be over between you. Like maybe you just think you suddenly learned to speak Nekhek because maybe that would justify betraying your own people.*

'They haven't attacked us yet,' Nephenia said. 'Maybe if we just leave—'

'No,' Tennat said, his voice more forceful now. 'We'll be heroes for this, Neph. You'll be able to choose any path of study you want and the masters will support you. We can set our entire futures right now if we wipe this lot out. When Pan casts the fire river, be ready to support his spell. Then we can watch these little monsters dance to their own death.'

The sickening excitement in Tennat's voice at the thought of burning these animals alive set my stomach churning, but it also felt oddly reassuring to know that he was just as rotten a human being as I'd always suspected. *Is it wrong that I kind of like hating him this much?*

Slowly and quietly, I began shifting my weight, preparing to get my feet under me.

I didn't know what to think about the creatures who were now only seconds from their deaths. Were they the vicious nekhek as I'd always believed? Evil spirits that had long ago served the same Mahdek bastards who had waged war on my people in centuries past and may have come back to kill my sister just two days ago? Or were they just what Ferius claimed – squirrel cats – animals trying to protect themselves as any of us would when attacked?

The leader bared his teeth and growled something that

would've got me in a good deal of trouble if my parents had ever heard me utter it. Who knew animals had such foul mouths?

'I think I'm ready,' Panahsi said. His chubby fingers once again twitched through the somatic pattern for the river of fire. It wasn't quite perfect, but probably close enough to work. I was going to have to make a decision now: watch as he killed the entire pack of squirrel cats, or take one more step into treason against my own people.

'Don't do it, Pan,' I said. 'Just back off and let them go.'

'Shut up, Kellen,' he replied.

Nephenia reached out but stopped short of touching him. 'Maybe Kellen's right. They're not attacking. We can—'

'Good,' Tennat said, his voice still sounding as if he were soothing a nervous horse. 'By the time Panahsi casts the spell it'll be too late for any of them to get away.'

I had my arms under me now. With a solid push I could get to my feet and make a run at Panahsi before he got the spell off. Just as I was about to move, the lead squirrel cat turned and chittered at me. 'Hey, kid, tell the fat one a couple of things for me.'

I froze. First, because it's weird to have an animal turn and speak to you, and second, because I was kind of annoyed that he'd called me *kid*.

'What do you want me to say?' I asked.

'Say you're sorry for being a traitor,' Tennat replied, assuming I was talking to them. 'Or just keep cowering there. Either way, your turn is coming.'

The squirrel cats were still waiting, as if they were somehow prevented from attacking. Panahsi was breathing easier now, calmer. The lids of his eyes half closed and his lips were moving as he rehearsed the spell. Fire spells are tricky – make one mistake and you get all the flame you asked for but not on the right target.

'Come on, Panahsi,' Tennat urged. 'Light them up.'

'Just a second. I'm almost ready.'

The squirrel cat gave an odd noise then, a kind of 'huh-huh-huh' sound that I was suddenly quite sure was his way of laughing. 'Kid, you listening?' he asked.

'Uhh . . . yes?'

'Tell fatty that just because he doesn't understand me, doesn't mean I don't understand him. Oh, and tell him to look behind him.'

I looked over to where the animal was nodding. There wasn't any light behind Panahsi, so at first all I saw was a rock in the shadows, only I didn't remember there being a rock there before. The shape moved and I suddenly figured out what it was, and why the squirrel cats had waited. While everyone was standing around staring at each other, one of the pack had snuck around the long way to get behind Pan.

'Panahsi, stop! Look behind you!' I called out.

He ignored me. I guess he figured I was probably just trying to distract him. The first syllables of the fire river started flowing from his mouth – a deep baritone that vibrated on the precise resonances called for by the spell. *Hells, he's doing it.*

The lead squirrel cat evidently understood. He let out a new sound, this one a sort of 'heff' that I interpreted as a sigh. 'All right then, skinbags. You asked for it!' He gave a short, sharp snarl and the black shape of the animal behind Pan flew into the air, going straight for the back of his head and digging its paws into his thick hair. The creature wrapped its front paws around his head, the furry webbing between its limbs covering his face while it used its long, cat-like hind paws to kick at the skin at the back of his neck. The other squirrel cats scattered, moving quickly even though they never took their eyes off the source of the flames.

'Aim, you fat idiot!' Tennat shouted.

I saw Nephenia extend her arms, touching the thumb and middle finger of each hand together as she spoke three words into the night air. It was a kind of shielding spell that kept the other squirrel cats from jumping onto Panahsi.

'Nice!' Tennat said. 'Keep it up a little while longer.' He brought his own hands together, fingers forming an attack spell. Predictably it was another gut sword. He aimed at the lead squirrel cat, who skittered in a zigzag pattern as if trying to dodge someone throwing rocks. That wasn't going to work against a gut sword though, which didn't require perfect aim, only a clear line of sight. I got to my feet and charged at Tennat, but at the last second he turned on me and his expression shifted to a grin. Pain exploded in my abdomen – worse by far than anything I'd felt during our duel the other day. Whatever illness Tennat had been suffering lately was clearly healed now, because I was pretty sure he was about to kill me.

'Tennat, don't!' Nephenia screamed.

Hey, maybe she doesn't hate me, I thought, as my insides started crushing in on themselves.

She let go of her shielding spell and grabbed Tennat by the shoulder, but he just shrugged her off. He said something to me which I couldn't possibly hear in all the noise, but I guessed must be along the lines of, 'I'm going to kill you now, Kellen, because, as you long suspected, I am a huge moron whose only ambition has been to make your life hell until I could find an excuse to end it.'

Panahsi screamed. One of the squirrel cats had just bitten a tiny chunk of flesh out of his arm. Nephenia, evidently making a quick calculation about whose life was more important at that exact moment, turned back to start the shield spell again.

I tried to roll away, to get somewhere out of Tennat's line of sight, but to no avail. It didn't look as if I was going to get much help from the squirrel cats either. They were focusing all their attention on Panahsi, throwing themselves at the shield Nephenia was putting up, some of them getting through as she struggled to maintain her focus. Pan managed to reach back and grab the one on his neck. The flames of his fire spell danced around his fingertips, setting the creature's fur alight, as he hurled the thing away, into the centre of the oasis. Two of its fellows raced towards it. The poor creature rolled on the sand in obvious agony as its fur began to burn. When the other two reached it, they turned around and kicked their back paws in the silver sand, half burying the burning creature to smother the flames. The injured creature got back up, hobbling back towards the fight, though I could see part of the thin membrane that allowed them to glide was burned away.

For a brief instant Tennat turned to the others, giving me a moment of reprieve from the gut sword. 'Get it together. Burn these things to ash before they try to escape!'

But Pan's spell was starting to fade. His concentration, which had been phenomenal considering the situation, was finally breaking. There were lines of blood on his face and hands and belly from where the squirrel cats had leaped on him.

192

Nephenia was exhausted too, from trying to keep a shield around him. I saw her eyes as she turned to plead with Tennat to stop attacking me and help protect Panahsi. I guess I must not have looked too good because she started screaming at Tennat.

He didn't care. He'd found a moment and an excuse to rid himself of the monster he hated most, which turned out to be me. In my entire life I'd never been in this much pain. My inner organs were being compressed and twisted – things which weren't going to be repairable. I looked up into his face, ready to plead with him. He liked it when people begged. *Maybe if I* . . .

Suddenly Tennat's eyes went wide and then his mouth opened as if he were about to say, 'Oh.' He dropped to his knees and behind him stood Nephenia, holding the stick that Pan had used to hit me. Tears were flowing down her cheeks. She'd just betrayed the people whose support she needed most so that she could save me. She didn't look happy about it.

I tried to stand up, to reach out to her, but my legs wouldn't support me. It was all I could do to kneel there on my hands and knees and see the battle come to its conclusion. Panahsi was done. The combination of our fight earlier and the pain from his wounds had left him unable to concentrate enough to cast another spell. Six of the squirrel cats surrounded him, ready to pounce and tear him to shreds. A few others crept around Tennat's prone body, sniffing at it and baring their teeth, the stripes of their fur an angry black against the pale silver sand of the oasis. The rest were stalking towards Nephenia.

'Stop!' I called out. 'Leave her alone.'

'Stay where you are, kid,' warned the squirrel cat whom I had, in my infinite wisdom, freed from his cage earlier, setting off this entire disaster.

I crawled on my hands and knees towards where Nephenia stood, shaking, terrified by the creatures in front of her whose entire bodies seemed to vibrate as they waited for the moment to attack. One of them turned suddenly, rearing on its hind legs so that its eyes were at the same level as my own. It opened its mouth wide and let out a growl that carried the scent of blood and an overabundance of rage. There was no doubt in my mind that these animals were fully capable of killing us.

'Back away, kid,' the lead squirrel cat chittered. 'I owe you a debt for springing me out of that cage, but you're on your own if you get between us and our prey.'

'She didn't attack you, she just—'

'The bitch shocked my insides with her lightning,' he said. 'She's going to get what she deserves.'

Nephenia was staring at me, no doubt wondering why I was talking to dumb, angry animals who just chittered and growled in reply. Panahsi looked as if he was having trouble staying on his feet. Tennat had woken up but wasn't moving. I saw the first creep of a smile on his face and saw something reflected in his eye. A light. I glanced behind me and saw lanterns come to life in one of the houses off the square. Evidently the quieting spell had started to fade and someone had heard the ruckus, or else they'd woken up and seen the glow from Panahsi's fire spell. It wouldn't be long before people came to check on what was happening.

'There are people coming,' I said to the squirrel cat. 'As soon as they're close enough to see you they'll summon the master mages. You'll all be killed!' I did my best to emphasise the importance of that last word.

The leader made his little huh-huh-huh laugh and started towards Tennat. 'Don't worry. We'll be done with these three long before anyone gets here.'

Whatever else the creature was, he wasn't very nice. *I suppose I might not be either if I'd just been tortured.*

As scared as Tennat was of the squirrel cats, he reserved his anger for me. 'You're a traitor, Kellen. Everyone is going to hear –'

He was interrupted by a voice from the darkness behind us. 'If you're going to concoct a story, always best to make it one folks will believe.'

I swivelled my head to see who'd spoken, my brains being too addled at that moment to make it out. At first all I could see was a dot of red light floating in the darkness. Then I made out the tiny trail of grey-white smoke rising from it. The figure stepped forward out of the shadows and Ferius Parfax came into view, a smoking reed sticking out of the side of her mouth.

'Well now,' she said, her customary smirk firmly in place, 'you must be just about the cutest little bunch of critters I ever laid eyes on.'

22

The Deal

The squirrel cats growled and pawed at the sand as Ferius approached. With every step she took I thought for sure they would attack. She, on the other hand, had no such doubts. She just swaggered towards us. 'Kellen, would you do me a favour and tell the little buggers that I'm not the enemy?'

The animal in the lead chittered furiously. 'Tell the Daroman bitch to take a walk if she wants to keep her eyeballs.' He sniffed the air. 'If she really is a Daroman, that is.'

Ferius looked over at me. 'Let me guess, he threatened to rip off my ears?'

'Your eyeballs, actually.'

She shook her head. 'It's always something with their kind. Ears, eyeballs, tongues. They're never happy unless they're threatening to rip something off of you.'

'Kellen, what's going on?' Nephenia asked. She and Panahsi and Tennat were backed up against each other, trying to stay as far away from the surrounding creatures as possible.

Bad enough I can barely keep from crumpling to the ground. Now I have to explain this? 'Just give me a second.'

'You tell his fuzzy little lordship,' Ferius declared, sounding more than a little annoyed, 'that there are wars and there are *wars*, and that he's one wrong move away from starting the kind that never ends well for anybody.'

'Yeah?' the squirrel cat countered. 'Well, maybe that's—'

Even if Ferius couldn't understand the words coming out of the little chitters and growls, she got the intent.

'These three are cubs to their kind,' she said. 'You kill them, and this whole place is going to go . . . Ah, hell.' She stopped and pulled something from her waistcoat. With a flick of the wrist a card spun through the air, landing in the sand a few inches from the animal's face. He hissed at it for a moment, then crept forward and stared at it with black beady eyes.

'Ask him if he knows what it is,' Ferius said.

The squirrel cat reached forward and picked the card up in its paws. From my vantage point I could see that it was one of the dark red ones she'd shown me that morning. It was a seven of diamonds, though I had no idea if that had any significance. The squirrel cat looked at the card, then at Ferius. He ambled over, walking on his hind legs with the card in his paws, and dropped it in front of me. 'Tell her the deal is acceptable.'

'What deal?' I asked.

He just stared back at me with no discernible change in his expression. I was fairly sure he was trying to communicate that I was an idiot.

'He's agreeing to the deal,' I told Ferius.

She gave a nod. 'Good. Pass me back the card.'

I did, and watched as she held it in her hand for a moment, as if memorising the intricate illustration on its surface. When she put it back in her waistcoat she seemed a little more . . . I don't know, tired? Finally she looked over at the animals. 'Well? Go on then, critters. Get out of here.' When the lead squirrel cat opened his mouth to speak, she stopped him. 'Tell the little bugger to save any last speeches or posturing for somebody who cares.'

The animal grunted, then chittered to the others. As one, they turned and ran out of the oasis and into the deep shadows of the night, away from the city and towards the mountains. I'd kind of expected him to stop and say something to me. It bothered me a little that he didn't.

Ferius sighed and then glanced towards the lights of lanterns coming towards us. 'All right, children. Let's get back to that song we're all going to sing.'

'Yours will be sung in screams,' Tennat said from where he still lay on the ground. I thought it was a pretty good retort, all things considered. His hands started moving, preparing a somatic shape. 'Once my father learns what happened here he's going to use spells that will tear the skin from your flesh, the blood from your—'

Ferius looked over at me and grinned. 'Now where have I heard that kind of threat before? You think he's part squirrel cat?' Then she put the heel of her boot on Tennat's right wrist. 'You know, boy, since it's obvious to me now that your only aim in this life is to become the most heartless, vicious thing you can, maybe you should keep quiet until your bite is as dangerous as your bark. The only thing your precious daddy and his fellow mages are going to care about is the fact that there's a tribe of nekhek close to their city who aren't afraid to fight. They aren't going to be too impressed by the fact that you and your little friends came here to torture the one they'd captured, only you were so stupid that even a weakling like Kellen here –' she pointed at me, which didn't make me feel any better at all – 'managed to beat the

198

three of you senseless long enough to set the little monster free.' She knelt down on one knee and got right up in his face. 'Third, you don't know for sure that Kellen's father isn't going to come and do you serious harm if he finds out what you tried to do to his son, "mage's council" or not.'

'But we have to tell people what happened,' Panahsi said, standing sturdier now, though his eyes were still a little unfocused.

'That's simple,' Ferius replied. 'The four of you, good friends that you are, were taking a late-night stroll to do some innocent astronomy work outside the city when you saw that herd of nekhek here freeing their fellow. Being brave souls, you all tried to stop them, but you got overwhelmed. All of your injuries –' she looked over and winced at the sight of me. *Still not helping* – 'came from the nekhek.'

Nephenia shook her head. 'But, Lady Ferius, no one's going to believe that we—'

'Of course they won't believe you,' Ferius interrupted. 'They'll know you're lying, especially since one of you obviously paid the guards to take a break. But people will think it's because you were coming here to show you weren't afraid of the nekhek. See, we give them the obvious lie so they don't look for the bigger one.'

You wouldn't think that people who had done the kinds of things to each other that we'd just done would be able to let it go so quickly, but my people are pragmatic. Nephenia didn't want the conflict to escalate. Panahsi was so tired he just wanted it to be over for now, and Tennat, well, Tennat probably figured he could use this against me – or the others – somehow. Or both. In the end, Ferius just seemed to know how to pull each person's strings and convince

199

them that, for now at least, her solution was in everyone's best interests.

By the time the first five or six men and women entered the oasis, glow-glass lanterns in hand, the deal had been struck. People were asking me questions, but I really had no way of answering. Once the fight had ended, whatever mixture of fear and shock had been keeping me going started to slip away. I was fading in and out of consciousness until Ferius declared that she needed to get me to my parents and the others should get home too.

The last thing I remember is Nephenia looking down at me just before she turned to leave. 'You hit me, Kellen,' she said.

23

Injuries

When you're fifteen years old and nearly a man, waking up repeatedly to find yourself being carried home is kind of embarrassing. This time it was Ferius doing the carrying, which made it worse.

'You're strong for a girl,' I said, cringing as the words came out of my mouth. Lately I was discovering that the more beaten up I got, the dumber my thoughts became.

'Strong for a girl, I suppose, but just about average for a woman.'

'I don't know many women who can carry me,' I insisted. 'I'm not that skinny.' Somehow it was important to win this point.

Ferius let out a little puff of air in a 'pfft' sound, which I gathered was meant to be dismissive. 'Kid, the only women you have around here are born and bred to do their little magic spells and be pretty to look at. Kind of like what passes for men.'

I was fairly sure that was an insult to all my people but I wasn't quite sure which part to argue against, so I just tried to focus my eyes on the street ahead of us. It was pitch black for the most part, families long having gone to sleep. We were halfway to my house, and normally the glow-glass lanterns on every corner would have illuminated our way, but Ferius didn't have the magic required to light them and I wasn't in the mood to try, so we proceeded in darkness. I wondered if this was what it was like for all the Sha'Tep servants who had to start their work day before dawn, shambling to whatever shops or households where they would perform their assigned duties in the dark. Did they carry torches? Ferius seemed to have pretty good eyesight because she walked sure as can be along the street towards my home.

'What are you going to tell my parents?' I asked.

'The truth. I found you like this in the oasis with your three idiot friends and about a dozen squirrel cats.'

'They aren't my friends any more,' I said reflexively. *Ugh. I sound like a child.*

Ferius glanced down at my face, which I gathered didn't look very good, because she said, 'Yeah, kid, I'm inclined to agree.'

'I . . .' I hesitated. There was something I wanted to say, or rather, something I wanted Ferius to say, but I wasn't sure how to bring it up. 'You haven't said anything about what I did,' I said finally.

'Was there something you *wanted* me to say about it?'

'No, I just thought . . .' The truth was, I kept expecting her to say that it was brave of me to free the squirrel cat, that she was . . . I don't know, impressed or maybe proud of me. I'm not sure why I cared what a Daroman wanderer thought when my parents were going to be furious with me, but it seemed unfair that I'd got so badly beaten up and wrecked my life and wasn't even going to get complimented.

'You want me to tell you that you did the right thing,'

202

Ferius said as we turned a corner. My family's home was down the next block.

'Well, did I?'

She stopped, her eyes still focused on the street ahead of us, not looking at me. 'I don't know, kid.' She let out a long, slow breath before she spoke again. 'When you see the world outside your home town, outside the walls of what you were brought up to see, then you discover that you almost never know if you're doing the right thing. One action, brave and true, leads to war and destruction. Another, craven and greedy, leads to peace and prosperity.' She let the words hang in the air a while, then seemed to come back to herself. 'I'll tell you one thing for free though.' I could hear the smile in her voice even before she looked down at me. 'You did what you did like a man.'

I felt my chest tighten a little, probably because my injuries were starting to flare up again. 'You talk about being a man a lot,' I said.

Ferius laughed. 'I guess I do, kid.' She resumed walking towards my home.

We were a few doors away when the pain from my various injuries really started to bother me. My ribs felt like they were breaking into bits, the inside of my mouth ached from where I'd been punched in the jaw, and even the skin on my right arm where I'd slid along the ground itched like seven hells. I scratched at it, which only made it worse. 'Ouch,' I said.

She looked down at me and laughed. 'Ouch? "Ouch"? Is that what you were saying while they were punching and kicking you? "Ouch"?'

'Shut up. It hurts.'

She ignored me and went on. 'I mean, is it like one of

203

those Jan'Tep magic words? "Ouch, I say to thee – nothing shall penetrate my magical Ouch shield!"'

'Stop it,' I said, still scratching at my arm, preferring the pain to the itching, but then it hurt so bad I yelped out loud.

'Quit scratching, kid, you're going to make yourself bleed and the cut'll get infected.'

I held up my forearm to look for blood, but saw none, just the dirt and grit from the ground outside the oasis. I knew every twist and turn in the tattooed sigils of those bands, had spent countless hours and days begging for them to spark. Even in the darkness of the street, I sensed something had changed. The silver inks of the first band no longer lay flat and lifeless. They moved, a tiny, subtle movement, a delicate dance of magic beneath the skin.

'Kid?' Ferius asked.

I blinked, trying to see better, desperate to prove to myself I wasn't imagining it. *Oh please*, I begged my ancestors. *Please don't let this be a trick.* As I'd done thousands of times before, I set my will upon the band.

Nothing happened, and I saw that the sigils weren't really moving at all. I felt such a deep, biting sense of disappointment that my eyes filled with stupid, childish tears. Even though I tried to hold it back, a sob escaped my lips.

'Relax, kid,' Ferius said.

'You don't understand! You never did! This is all I've—'

'No, I mean it. Shut up and relax.'

All of a sudden I understood what she meant. When I'd first seen the change in the band on my forearm, I'd become elated, but you can't exert your will on the fundamental forces of magic when you're excited, just like you can't when you're crying like a baby. It takes calm. Control. Command.

I closed my eyes to stop myself from paying attention to the band itself and instead sent my focus inwards, calling forth the power that would attach to the silver sigils, willing the tiny tattooed links between them to break apart, freeing the magic inside me. I didn't rush, didn't think about how long it was taking or the fact that Ferius was still holding me in her arms or that I had no friends any more or that if I failed I'd become . . . I let it all go. I stopped asking myself if I had the magic of my people. I was done asking.

'Hey, kid, look.'

'I know,' I said, my eyes still closed. I didn't need to look at the sigils because I already knew they were glowing with magical force.

'Which one is that?' Ferius asked.

I opened my eyes, and then drew clean, beautiful air into my lungs before I said the single, awestruck word: 'Breath!'

Ferius was looking down at me, not smiling exactly, but at least she wasn't making any stupid jokes. I let myself stare at the silver sigils of the breath band, the tiny, beautiful symbols shining like stars on the canvas of my skin, each one representing a different form of breath magic I could now cast.

I had sparked a band.

I reached out with my other hand towards one of the glow-glass lanterns above us and pushed at it with my will. A soft light began to emerge, slowly pushing back against the darkness around us. It wasn't much, in fact it was barely anything at all, but it was there. It was real.

I wasn't Sha'Tep.

I wasn't broken.

I had magic.

As the glow of the lantern began to warm my skin, I caught Ferius's eye and was surprised by what I found there. She was staring at my face. 'Aw, kid, no . . .'

I knew I probably looked a mess. I'd taken a beating that was so bad I could barely feel my cheeks or open my eyes from the bruising. But I still resented her for not having the decency to at least pretend to share my happiness. To the hells with her Argosi ways and her spite for my people. Still, I was feeling generous. 'I know it looks bad,' I said. 'Guess even with magic I'm going to need you to teach me how to fight.'

Ferius opened her mouth but then closed it again. She hoicked me back up, the muscles of her face tensing as if I'd just got a whole lot heavier. 'No, kid, now I'm going to have to teach you how to run.'

24

The Mark

'Why won't you tell me what's wrong?' I asked again.

We had finally reached the first of the seven wide marble steps that led up to the entrance of my family home. I felt my sense of elation over breaking the breath band fade a little as the thought of the punishment awaiting me behind those thick double doors ahead of us sank in. I had snuck out of my father's house without permission, set free one of the creatures my people most feared and despised and struck my fellow students. *When did I become such a terrible son?*

'I can stand on my own,' I muttered.

'Take three deep breaths, kid,' Ferius said as she set me down.

'What good will that do?'

'It'll keep your voice from sounding thin and whiny when you talk to your parents.'

As if that'll make any difference. Why hadn't I just run to find one of the city guards when I'd come upon Tennat, Panahsi and Nephenia torturing the squirrel cat? That would have put a stop to it without setting the little monster free and ruining my life. There was a knot in my stomach. Back at the square I'd thought I was doing the right thing, but now I had to explain it to my parents without sounding completely insane, and all I could think was that maybe I *was* insane. Mages don't attack other mages to save a creature whose favourite food was probably Jan'Tep babies. But if I hadn't saved the animal, if I hadn't fought against my friends, would the breath band have broken? Would my parents balance out my crime against the rewards to our family?

'Stand straight, kid,' said Ferius at the sound of footsteps from inside the house. Someone was coming to the door. 'If you can't *be* tough, *look* tough.'

I thrust my shoulders back and immediately felt like an idiot. The problem with Ferius was that she confused things that mattered – like being able to cast a shield spell – with things that didn't, like standing up straight. Who cared if I *looked* confident? I'd already brought shame on my father when my magic had failed, and now I'd compounded it by helping the nekhek escape. Even if Panahsi and Nephenia stuck to the story, Tennat would tell his father and Ra'meth would demand that I be prosecuted for my actions. My father was going to have to humiliate himself in front of the council and invoke his prerogative as a master mage to have the punishment lessened. Saving me was going to hurt his chances of becoming clan prince. Against that, how much would it matter to him that I'd sparked a single band?

I glanced over at Ferius, searching for something clever to say that would let her know just how badly she'd screwed up my life, but her eyes were still fixed on the doors to my house. 'You sure about this, Kellen?' she asked.

It was one of the few times she'd ever used my name. 'What do you mean?'

Ferius turned and knelt down a fraction so that we were eye-to-eye. She was only an inch or two taller than me, so it annoyed me that she'd bothered. 'My horse is tethered about a mile from here. She can carry both of us a ways, and there's a place a few miles down the road where I can get us another. Say the word, kid, and I'll get us out of here.'

'Are you joking? I just sparked my first band! I'm going to be a Jan'Tep mage like my father! Why would I ever . . .'

The doors creaked open; light from inside cut through the night. Ferius nudged me over a few feet. 'Stay in that patch of shadow,' she said.

Spirits of our ancestors, I thought. *I must really look terrible.*

It would only get worse. Chances are I was facing house arrest coupled with a public flogging. The latter wouldn't be so bad so long as my mother was allowed to heal the wounds right away. But if I was stuck inside, how was I going to take my mage's trials? For the first time I had an actual chance of passing them for real.

My mother's face appeared, lit from behind like one of the goddesses our ancestors used to worship. Even with the look of concern on her face she was beautiful. *And powerful*, I thought, feeling the soft movement in the air from the magical energy crackling around her.

'Kellen, is that you?' she asked, her eyes not yet adjusted to the darkness. She looked around but I was in the shadows. Her eyes fell on Ferius.

'Lady Ferius, where is—'

'I'm here, Mother,' I said, trying to step out but Ferius put a hand on me and kept me where I was.

'Oh, thank the ancestors,' she said, turning back for a moment to shout into the house. 'Ke'heops! Kellen has returned!'

A moment later my father emerged from the house, his silver-and-blue robes shimmering from the light behind him. He was holding a small scrying mirror in his hand, and when he caught sight of me he placed it into one of the pockets of his robes. 'Where is she?' he demanded.

At first I thought he must be referring to Ferius and had somehow missed her standing a few feet away. 'It's not her fault, Father. It was my idea to . . .' I couldn't finish the sentence. *Of course it's her fault, you idiot. Ferius is the one who convinced you to help the squirrel cat.*

His eyes narrowed and then he glanced over at Ferius before setting his gaze back on me. 'I don't care about the Argosi card player. What have you done with your sister?'

My father's face was a mask of anger and frustration that scared me more than the hideous black-and-red lacquer ones worn by the men who'd attacked Shalla and me in the forest.

'Father, I swear, I haven't done anything with Shalla. I haven't even seen her since—'

'Oh,' my mother said, her voice equal parts frustration and fearful resignation. I knew that tone, or at least a small part of it. She'd been scrying for hours, trying to find my sister. The spells used for scrying are dangerous, draining a mage's power as their mind searches further and further afield. My mother looked exhausted. How far had she pushed herself?

I started towards the stairs, but Ferius put a hand on my shoulder again and stopped me. 'When was the last time you saw the girl?'

My father's jaw clenched and I knew he was rightfully outraged. This was our household's business, and to have an outsider ask the question was unseemly. My mother answered.

'Shalla woke up hours ago, largely unharmed, but ... her falcon was dead. It had sickened in the night and nothing we did helped it. Her spells wouldn't work. She was terrified that she might be like ...' She hesitated as she glanced over at where I stood in the shadows. 'We told her it was far too soon to fear a permanent loss of her magic, but Shalla just became more and more agitated. She was inconsolable and eventually I had to give her a light sedative to calm her. She should have slept for hours, but—'

'Shalla snuck out sometime this afternoon,' my father said, his voice grim. 'We thought she must be with you, Kellen, that the pair of you had hatched some further foolishness to restore your magic.'

I felt suddenly disgusted with myself. While I was busy bringing yet more shame to my family, something terrible had happened to my sister. I was almost too ashamed to show my parents that I'd sparked the breath band.

My father rubbed the back of his hand against his forehead, looking more tired than I'd seen him in a very long time. 'We must attempt the scrying again.' He turned to my mother. 'I do not have the magic of silk, Bene'maat. We must risk more of your strength if we are to find her.'

My mother returned his gaze. 'Husband ... I will try, but—'

'Or you could just go look for the girl,' Ferius said. The casual, almost dismissive tone of her voice instantly angered me. I turned to say something, but stopped when I saw her kneeling on the cobbled street, the fingers of one gloved hand tracing patterns in the dirt and dust. 'I could track her,' she said, then looked up at my father. 'I can do it quiet too, since I reckon the reason you haven't gone yourself is that you don't want the wrong folks knowing your daughter's missing.'

I tried to imagine how you could search for someone without using scrying spells. It seemed preposterous. But my parents' panic was beginning to infect me. 'Can you really do it, Ferius? Can you find my sis—'

'Be silent, Kellen.' My father's voice brooked no dissent. He started down the stairs, slowly, methodically, until finally he stood towering over Ferius. 'And what will it cost me, Argosi?'

He made the word *Argosi* sound like something mean and dirty. 'Father, Ferius is my friend. She would never—'

Before I could finish, Ferius Parfax replied: 'A pardon.'

Everything went still. My father looked confused at first, but then he crossed his arms across his broad chest. 'A pardon for whom, Argosi? For your Daroman king?' It wasn't the first time someone had accused Ferius of being a spy rather than a simple trader, but it surprised me that my father would believe such a ridiculous rumour. Ferius was . . . well, nothing like how I imagined a spy would be.

But Ferius didn't answer, and so my father went on. 'Perhaps your fat king wishes for absolution for some new crime he has committed against the Jan'Tep? Has he betrayed us once again to one of his allies and now fears our retribution?' My father let the allegation hang in the air, his eyes never leaving Ferius, as if he expected her to crack at any moment under his scrutiny. Again she said nothing and again my father probed with more questions. 'Or perhaps you wish to purchase this pardon for yourself. Perhaps you've betrayed your masters in the capital and hope to find sanctuary here, in the only place the Daroman army fears to tread.'

Despite my father's ominous words and overwhelming presence, Ferius seemed unruffled, but I noticed she pretended to brush dust from her waistcoat. When she was done one of the pockets was open. *She wants to make sure she can reach her weapons*, I realised. When she finally spoke, her voice was colder than the ice spell used to preserve the bodies of the dead for burial under the hot sun. 'No need to be so coy, master mage. If you want to accuse me of something, why don't you go ahead and see where it leads you?'

'Would you threaten me, woman?'

'Long past time somebody did,' she replied.

Flat-soled sandals clacked against the marble steps as my mother ran towards them. 'Stop this!' she commanded. 'My daughter is missing! She may have been taken!' My mother knelt down in front of Ferius and placed her hands on the other woman's boots. 'Please . . . I know something of the Argosi ways . . . I know you don't mean to be like this.'

Ferius knelt down until her face was at the same height as my mother's – the same way she'd done to me earlier. 'Sister, the fact that you're on your knees tells me you don't know spit about the Argosi.'

'Please, Lady Ferius, Shalla is my—'

'I'm still not a lady,' Ferius said, cutting her off, 'and that won't change no matter how many times you . . .' She broke off and shook her head. 'Ah, forget it, sister.' She rose up and pulled my mother to her feet. 'I'll find your little girl for you.'

'And the fee?' my father insisted. 'To whom must I grant this pardon?'

'To Kellen,' Ferius replied.

I felt a stab of shame. Ferius was trying to purchase my safety at the cost of threatening to leave my sister out there alone. 'No,' I said. 'I won't—'

'Don't move,' Ferius warned. I hadn't even realised I'd started towards them.

My father looked over to where I still stood in the shadows. 'What shameful acts have you brought upon our house now, Kellen?'

'I . . .' *I lied to you. I freed our enemy. I fought my own people. I hit the girl I love.* Suddenly I was too ashamed to speak.

My father started to walk towards me, but Ferius grabbed his wrist. 'It don't matter what he's done. You want me to find the girl, you grant him your pardon right now. When I get back, if he wants, he comes with me. Out of this town and out of your hair. But either way, you give him your pardon.'

Even in the unlit street, I swear I could see my father's blue eyes burning the darkness away. I thought for sure Ferius had pushed him too far. My mother must have thought so too, because she got between them and put a hand on his chest. 'Our daughter is out there, Ke'heops. Our Shalla. Alone. The men who attacked her could be hunting her even now while we stand here arguing.'

My father didn't even bother to turn to look at me when he said, 'Fine. I pardon you, Kellen.' He made it sound like a verdict. Then he turned back to Ferius. 'Now go, Daroman. Show us these tracking skills you Argosi claim to have.'

'I want to help find Shalla,' I said.

'Sorry, kid,' Ferius said, her eyes still on my father. 'You're too injured and I need to move too fast.'

'Injured?' my mother asked. 'Kellen, what's happened to you? Come here now!'

I obeyed, feeling like an idiot. My sister might be in danger, but my mother was going to fuss over a few bruises. As I walked into the light streaming from the doorway, I held up my right arm in a desperate bid to win a moment of my father's approval. 'Look. I broke the breath band.'

214

'By the ancestors . . . what is that on his face?' my father demanded.

'It's just blood,' I said. 'I got hurt, all right? It's not—'

The forefinger of my father's right hand gave the slightest twitch. The glow-glass lanterns all around us flared bright as the sun, banishing every shadow, except one that I couldn't see.

'No!' My father's shout split the night in half.

My mother ran towards me and started rubbing at my left eye, making the bruise on my cheek hurt even worse. 'It's all right, mother. It's just—'

I hadn't even seen my father move, but now his strong hands lifted my mother out of the way and set her down behind him. He reached out with his left hand and took hold of my jaw so hard I could feel my gums squeezing against my teeth. He leaned over, staring into my left eye.

'I can see fine,' I said. 'It's not damaged or anything.'

My father didn't reply until my mother tried to take his arm. He shrugged her off. 'This cannot be wished away,' he told her.

I tried to pull away from his grip. 'I already said it's just a little blood and dirt.'

With his free hand, my father reached into the pocket of his robes and pulled out the small round scrying mirror. He held it up in front of me. There, in the mirror, I saw my face. As expected, I was bruised and battered, with blood caked on my swollen cheeks and forehead. At first I was so focused on my wounds that I almost didn't notice the thin black lines curving around the outside of my left eye. They looked like twisting vines, almost like an illustration drawn by a master artist. You might almost have called them pretty if you'd

215

.

never seen them before, in the picture books meant to scare children and the manuscripts old Osia'phest kept to show initiates the perils of dark magic.

All at once I understood why Ferius had kept me standing in the shadows, why she'd forced my father to forgive me before she'd agreed to look for Shalla. Ferius had been trying to protect me. *What a stupid thing to do*, I thought. *Everybody knows there are some things you can't protect against.* I just kept staring into that mirror, horrified by what I saw, because in those creeping black lines around my eye I finally saw what was wrong with me.

I had the shadowblack.

25

Family

Of all the tales my people tell, of all the great myths of heroic mages casting the most daring and dangerous of spells to save their clans from monsters both devious and diabolical, the very best ones – the most thrilling and terrifying stories of all – are always about the shadowblack.

When the Mahdek sorcerers performed their foulest spells, committing atrocity upon atrocity in order to spill forth perfect pitch-black hatred upon the world, they pierced the thin veil that separates our world from the hundred hells beneath. Some of those sorcerers, their mouths split wide with manic glee, discovered that by emptying their souls of any shred of goodness they created a void contrary to all the laws of magic and nature. Such an emptiness could not last of course, and it was slowly, inexorably filled by something worse than mere evil. A mage who descended those final steps into darkness found the inky marks around some part of their body – an arm, a torso or, perhaps, an eye. Those marks were the sign of the shadowblack taking over.

'Come with me, Kellen,' my father repeated. How many times had he said it before he grabbed me by the shoulders and pulled me from the street, up the marble stairs and through the wide double doors into our house?

His shout had carried down the street. Already we could hear people coming from their homes, looking to find out what was going on.

'Into the study,' my mother said, her voice calm, steady, in control. I couldn't say the same for myself.

'You've got to fix me, Mother,' I pleaded. 'Please . . . I didn't do anything! I didn't ask for—'

She placed one hand on each of my cheeks and gripped me hard, locking my head in place. 'Listen to me now. You're scared. You're hurt. You are still my son.'

You are still my son.

It wasn't relief that I felt exactly, as she let go of my face and put an arm around me, but it was *something*. '*Family*,' my father had always said, '*is the strong stone on which we stand. It is the beginning and the end of what we are.*' I knew at that moment that he must be right, because what I wanted more than anything in the world was to know that I still had a family.

'You'll find my child,' he said to Ferius, blocking her from entering the house after us. It wasn't a question.

I saw her hesitate, but finally she nodded. 'Make sure you honour our deal, master mage. This isn't the boy's fault.'

My father gave the slightest hint of a laugh, but it held no mirth, only a desolate pain bigger than any desert. 'There is no one to blame for this, Argosi, any more than one can blame the lightning when it sets fire to the village.'

I expected some clever reply from her, but none came. I think maybe I blinked from sweat dripping into my eye and then she was gone and my father closed the door and turned to us.

'I don't understand,' I said absently, one finger still tracing

218

the line of my glyphs across my forearm. 'I only just sparked my breath band and now I have the shadowblack? Why is this happening to me?'

My mother was ushering me into the room when my father abruptly caught her in his arms, holding her close and hiding his eyes in her shoulder. 'All is not yet lost,' my mother said to him. 'With the favour of the gods, the Argosi woman will find our daughter swiftly and safely.'

But what about me?

A few minutes later I was sitting on the silk settee in my mother's study, my back straight and hands on my knees – as if somehow good posture was going to save me – while she used a small brush to apply a wet, sticky substance around my left eye. 'Will this stop the spread of it?' I asked.

'It's only mesdet, silly boy,' she replied. 'It's what I use around my own eyes. It will hide the markings for now, in case someone sees you.'

She put down the brush and went to her tall cabinets, filled with tiny drawers and shelves lined with jars and pots and instruments.

'How long will it take?' I asked.

She held up a small vial and examined its contents. 'How long will what take?'

'For the shadowblack to consume me.'

In the stories, an afflicted mage didn't become a demon all at once. At first he was no different than before, save for the black markings. But over time the pattern would grow, and slowly the mage would commit worse and worse acts of evil until finally his soul was ready for possession by the demon spirit.

219

'Let the concerns of the present be our focus,' my father said, standing behind her. 'And let us not paint the future before its canvas appears to us.' He leaned in to peer at my eye for just a moment as my mother went back to her jars. 'Perhaps things are not quite as bad as they seem.'

I was so tired and hurt and confused that his words almost made me giggle. The man who, minutes before, had screamed as if he'd watched a thousand devils descend upon the world, was now telling me that maybe things weren't 'quite as bad as they seem'.

Outside of stories, I didn't really know much about the shadowblack, other than what any initiate is taught in his first year of training. Of the fundamental forms of magic, six can be safely wielded by a Jan'Tep mage: iron and ember, breath and blood, sand and silk. The seventh, shadow, cannot. It is the void, the emptiness. It is the absence of living magic and the place where only demonic energies thrive. No Jan'Tep would ever study or seek out its power any more than one would willingly contract the red plague or lung rot. The shadowblack was a terrible disease that only came to terrible people.

People like me.

I remembered back to what my parents had said about my grandmother. Could the disease be passed down from parent to child? Perhaps, like some conditions, it skipped a generation. *Why me? I've never had enough magic to make a dent in the sand, and now this?*

A darker thought entered my mind, like a silk spell, or a snake that slithered under the bedsheets while you slept. *It should have been Shalla.*

I tried to push the vile feeling away, wondering if, even

now, the shadowblack was taking me over. *None of the shadow-black mages in the stories were teenagers,* I thought desperately. My grandmother had to have been old before it had taken her, so maybe I had years. *Maybe I can still have a bit of a life before I become a monster.*

'It is a type of curse,' my father said, jolting me back to the present.

'It is a disease,' my mother corrected.

My parents stared at each other for a moment. It seemed to be part of some longstanding debate between them. But it wasn't theoretical for me. 'Well? Which is it? What's going to happen to me?'

My mother turned back to her instruments and passed a hand over a small brass brazier, carefully raising the forefinger of her right hand until the flame was at the exact height she desired.

'Your mother is correct, in her way,' my father said. 'And I am right in mine.' He sat down next to me on the settee – an unusually comforting sort of act for him that only made me more uncomfortable. 'The shadowblack *is* a kind of disease, but one of magic, not nature. It was brought down on us as a final curse by the Mahdek after we defeated them in the last war between our peoples. It is their corrupting magic that gives it power over us.'

'The Mahdek are supposed to be dead,' I insisted. 'All the masters say so.' *Except you saw a group of them in their demon masks just two days ago.* 'Could they really have come back?'

My father's eyebrows rose in the centre of his forehead – a sign of despair I'd seen on plenty of people before, just never on Ke'heops. 'I don't know, Kellen. Better and truer mages than I have tried to purge this world of the last vestiges of

Mahdek magic. If someone out there is trying to strengthen it . . .' He let the words trail off. Then, because men like my father don't shy away from the truth, he said, 'Some of the greatest mages of my parents' generation were lost to the shadowblack. It worked its way into their souls slowly but inexorably, twisting their hearts even as the black markings twisted along the lines of their skin. Once the demons took them, all the powers those great men and women had used to protect their people had been turned against us. We nearly lost the clan.'

'Enough, Ke'heops,' my mother said from her worktable. 'Don't scare the boy any further.' She came back to us with a glass vial held between her hands. 'There are a few records of mages who showed the signs of the shadowblack one day only to have it disappear the next, never to return.'

I reached up a hand and traced the black markings around my left eye, feeling my way from the cold sensation they brought to my fingertip. 'It's not fair. I only just broke my first band. How did I get cursed with a disease that strikes master mages?'

'I don't know,' my father said.

I don't know. Three words I'd never thought to hear him say. He put a hand on my shoulder. 'But perhaps in that weakness lies our one hope, Kellen. If the shadowblack truly feeds on a mage's magic, then the absence in you might prevent the disease from thriving.'

I tried to take some comfort from those words. Perhaps whatever had been weakening my magical ability *could* enable my mother and father to remove the shadowblack from me. Then maybe, just maybe, I could then build up my power and pass my tests. I hung on to that slim thread of hope the

222

way a drowning man docs the last shred of river grass he can reach. *Please, all you gods of sun and sky, of sea and earth, please stop making my life so damned rotten.*

'Drink,' my mother said, holding out the vial.

I looked inside. A blue-and-green mixture swirled around of its own volition. 'What will it do to me?' I asked.

My mother's eyes narrowed even as she gave me a faint smile. 'A lifetime of mastering medicinal spells and now I must answer to you?' She reached out a hand and tousled my hair. 'It's to heal those horrible cuts and bruises, all of which will, I promise you, be a topic of further discussion once the present crisis is over.'

The fact that I was going to be in trouble later was oddly reassuring. Having to face a flogging and house arrest – hells, even having to become a Sha'Tep – didn't seem so bad any more.

'You'll need to be strong, Kellen,' my father said, rising to stand by my mother. 'You'll need to be brave.'

I looked up at my parents. They looked like the painted portraits of the heroic mages of our past, when our people were feared and admired throughout the civilised world. *You need to be strong. You need to be brave.* I took the vial and drank it down. 'I can do that,' I said.

Both the words and the potion made me feel a little better. I was still young, and the shadowblack marks had only just appeared. My mother was brilliant, my father one of the most powerful mages in our clan. I could tell just by looking at them that they had a plan to fix this. Things were going to be okay.

The first tear slid lazily down my mother's cheek, and with a sleepy impulse I reached out as though I could wipe it away. My father's eyes were dark, stricken but hard. I watched the world grow hazy and felt my head become far too heavy to hold up. That was when I knew that things *weren't* going to be okay.

My mother had drugged me.

26

The Bands

I woke up screaming.

My body was slick with sweat, every part of me on fire. I had dreamed that I'd been strapped down on a table as vile Mahdek mages with black lacquer masks drove red-hot needles into my skin, burning the shadowblack into my face, down my shoulders and arms. I had awoken at the moment when they'd begun piercing the skin around my forearms.

It was just a dream, you idiot, I told myself. *Stop screaming.*

The concoction my mother had tricked me into drinking had left my mind in a daze. I couldn't seem to move, even to open my eyes. After a few moments I realised that the reason I kept screaming was because the pain I felt in my forearms was real. *The bands. Something's happening to the bands . . .*

Instinctively I tried to raise my arms, but I couldn't. Despite the thick fog in my skull, I managed to shout for my parents and force my eyes open. That was when things got worse.

I was no longer in my mother's study lying on her settee. This was my father's private chamber. I was bound onto his worktable, thick leather straps holding my wrists and ankles. My father stood over me, one hand pressing down on my chest as the other pushed something sharp into my forearm.

225

'Father? What are you doing? Why does this hurt so much?'

He withdrew the needle then, but didn't answer me. He just moved his hand and dipped the needle into a tiny metal cauldron sitting atop a brazier that burned with a fierce heat. When the needle came back out, it held a single drop of molten silver. I saw then that there were other dishes sitting on top of other braziers, each one a different colour, holding a different molten metal. *Copper, brass, gold, iron . . .* They were the metal inks used to tattoo the bands on Jan'Tep initiates as children, to connect us with the fundamental forces of magic. But when I looked down at the band for ember, I saw the reverse sigils burning there, dark and ugly, forever severing my connection to the magic of fire, of lightning, of energy.

'Father, please, stop! Don't counter-band me!'

When a child is banded, it's done with only the tiniest amounts of the ink – so small you can barely see the drops on the needles. But my father was using much, much more. He was doing to me what he'd threatened to do to Shalla: counter-banding me permanently. Once he completed the process, I would never again be able to wield my people's magics, not even the feeble cantrips that a Sha'Tep servant can still perform near the oasis. He might as well cut off my hands and tear out my eyes.

'Don't do this, Father,' I begged. 'I'll do anything you ask, but please don't—'

'Stay calm, Kellen,' he said, and pressed the needle into my arm, drawing forth another scream from me.

When I could again catch my breath, I tried shouting for my mother. Bene'maat was a gentler soul who loved Shalla and me more than anything. She would make Ke'heops see sense.

'You have to trust your father,' she said, her voice far closer than I had expected. I felt her hands pressing on the sides of my head, pulling it back down to the hard surface of the table. She was standing behind me. She'd been helping him do this to me.

'There has to be another way,' I begged. 'Please, just try—'

'We have tried everything else,' my father said. 'We have tried your whole life to—'

'Ke'heops,' my mother warned.

Whatever words she was going to say next disappeared into sobs. Her tears dripped onto my forehead, one by one, as my father continued to dip the needle into the metal inks and then drive it into the skin of my forearms. 'You are my son,' he said, his words sounding like those of a man confessing to a crime. 'You are my responsibility.'

They had lied to me. They had let me believe that there was hope so that they could put me to sleep and strap me to this table. Nothing I said, no reasoned arguments or passionate vows, stopped them. My father just kept dipping the needle into the molten inks and then driving them deep into my flesh, sealing away my magic, making me a prisoner for life.

'I'm your son!' I screamed, pulling in vain at the restraints. 'How can you do this to your own son? Why would you—' For an instant I felt as if I were back in Mer'esan's cottage, with the dowager magus giving me that look of hers. '*Do not ask questions to which you already know the answer.*'

Pieces of my life broke apart in my mind, twisting and turning as they took new form. How often had I been in this room, my mother and father casting the spells they said were to heal my magic? How many times had my mother traced an invisible line with her finger, going around my eye, always

227

my left eye, looking at me so closely, telling me I was going to be fine? 'You knew,' I said. 'You knew I was going to get the shadowblack one day. All those times you said you were trying to help me develop my magical ability . . . you weren't, were you? You were weakening me.'

My mother tried to hold my hand. I clenched it into a fist to resist. 'It was your grandmother,' she said.

'I inherited the disease from her? But why me? Why not—'

'You did not inherit the shadowblack from my mother,' my father said. 'When you were a child, we found her with you, here, in this room. She had taken one of my banding needles and she was drawing the void from the marks around her own eye, using it to . . .'

He stopped speaking, apparently unable to say the words that came so easily from my own mouth. 'Grandmother banded me in shadow.'

No one contradicted me.

'She must have hated me,' I said.

'Seren'tia loved you, Kellen,' my mother said. 'But her mind was lost. When your father saw her, standing over you, piercing your skin with the ink of shadow . . .'

My father's voice was hard. 'I thought I stopped her in time. I thought I'd saved you.'

My mother reached out her hand to touch him. The intimate gesture made me feel sick and alone. 'There were signs,' she said to me. 'Even as a child I could sometimes see the pattern begin to form around your left eye. We thought that the magic of shadow fed on the other six. We hoped that by suppressing your magic, we could starve the disease. It seemed to work for a time, but then the markings would come back. We didn't realise . . .'

'We were wrong,' my father finished, his voice just as sure and strong as ever.

'You only masked the symptom, didn't you?' I asked, not expecting, or waiting, for an answer. 'By weakening my magic you allowed the disease to progress that much faster. You took away my life, piece by piece, and now—'

'We had no choice!' he shouted, his composure breaking for the first time, even as the needle stabbed into the skin of my forearm. 'We never knew if the disease might spread on its own, if Shalla . . .'

And there it was. Of course. Shalla. The hope of our family. The most promising mage our house had ever produced. She had to be protected at all costs. 'Because you love her,' I said.

He became furious. 'I am doing what is right for our family! For our house. For our people. If the shadowblack takes you fully and your magic recovers, you'll become a threat to our clan, as my mother was! I cannot let that happen. I *will not* let that happen.' He pushed the next drop of ink into my arm. Even enraged as he was, the motion was careful, precise. Controlled.

A thought occurred to me then – the sort of desperate, futile sliver of an idea that you think up when you're so frenzied that your mind can't understand that you've already lost. 'You swore!' I said. 'You told Ferius Parfax that you would pardon me! You gave your word.'

My father stopped then, just for a moment. His eyes were full of guilt and sorrow when he looked at me. He leaned over and kissed me on the forehead. 'I have pardoned you, Kellen, for shaming our family this way, for bringing this darkness into our house.' Then he turned back and dipped the needle into the molten ink. 'Now it is your turn to forgive me.'

27

The Truth

It takes six nights to band a Jan'Tep child, one for each of the disciplines of iron, ember, silk, sand, blood and breath. First you must secure the ores from the mines that run deep beneath the oasis. Close proximity to the mines sickens mages, so Sha'Tep are employed for this task. The ores must be quickly transmuted with chemicals and fire into the liquid form used for the inks before separation from the ground renders them toxic. Each banding ink has its own special process, its own complexities and dangers that require the mage preparing them to do so slowly, methodically, without hesitation. Without remorse.

During the daytime I would lie strapped to the table, my mind drifting in a fog from the drugs my mother forced me to drink. I knew they released the straps to bathe me sometimes, because the table underneath me was clean even though I was sure I'd soiled myself several times. At night, with the light of the moon glimmering in through the window, they would renew the work of counter-banding me. I too would begin my work fresh each night, screaming in outrage, begging for mercy. My father and mother would try to make me understand that this was for the best – for our family, our clan and our people. I would call them liars and monsters, and swear vengeance on the world as if the demon had already claimed me.

None of it made any difference. Like a steady water clock we all just kept dripping away the hours. Slowly but surely my father finished one band, then the next. I was fairly sure that the gold band for sand magic was complete, forever denying me the spells for seeing afar or uncovering secret knowledge. The iron band too was done. I would never cast a shield spell to protect myself or anyone else. They progressed one by one, from the strongest form of magic to the weakest. Soon my father would counter-band the silver, taking away forever the breath magic that had been mine for only a few precious moments.

When my voice failed I would lie there listening to the flames of the braziers, punctuated by the tap-tap of my father's needles as he dipped them into the tiny cauldrons. Sometimes I heard my mother crying over me. One time I think it was my father.

I kept wanting to ask about Shalla and whether Ferius had returned with her. I knew she hadn't though, because while I hated everyone and everything in the world I somehow knew without the slightest shred of a doubt that if Ferius Parfax had known what was being done to me she would have knocked the door down and set the place on fire. She would have stood there with a smoking reed in her mouth and those razor-sharp steel cards of hers in hand. 'Kicking down doors and asses is just what a woman does when a kid's being tortured,' she would have said.

That was why I knew it wasn't her coming to save me when I heard the polite, almost tentative knock at the door.

'Do not disturb us,' my father said.

The knock was repeated, followed by the turning of the handle.

231

'Away!' my father commanded. 'The door is locked for a reason.'

A voice on the other side called out, but from where I lay strapped to the table the words were muffled, incoherent. My father and mother ignored them.

Then something odd happened. I heard the sound of something heavy battering at the door. My father looked up, his eyes narrowed in annoyance, then the noise came again. The third time I saw the hinges weaken and my father got to his feet. The fourth time they gave way completely and the door flew open.

'By the crying souls of our ancestors,' my uncle Abydos said, 'it's true. You're counter-banding your own son!'

'Remove yourself from this room, Abydos,' my father warned. 'What happens here is of no concern to the Sha'Tep.' His use of my uncle's status was intentional – a reminder that he was family by blood but not by rank.

'Don't do this, Keo,' my uncle pleaded. 'You don't know that this is truly the shadowblack. There are tests you could—'

My father carefully set the needle down on the table. 'No one has called me "Keo" for a very long time.' He walked over to face my uncle. I don't think I'd ever seen them stand quite like that, almost as equals. 'I am Ke'heops now, a mage of the Jan'Tep and the head of this house. You would do well to remember that fact, and as you do, to remember your own place in the scheme of things.'

My mother stood. 'Please, both of you, stop. This isn't helping.'

When the Sha'Tep are addressed by their Jan'Tep betters, they almost always look away. In fact, I was fairly sure that I'd never even noticed the colour of my uncle's eyes because he was always looking down or to the side when one of us

232

spoke to him. He didn't do that now. 'Kellen is my nephew, Bene'maat. I won't allow you to—'

Out of nowhere my father's hand rose, the movement far too fast to be a spell. I heard a loud crack and only then realised he'd slapped my uncle in the face. 'You won't *allow*? It is not your place to *allow* anything, Abydos. You are a member of this household, not this family.'

'Ke'heops, please, you're tired,' my mother began. 'This is . . . it's hard on all of us. Perhaps if you explained to Abydos why—'

My father's hand rose up again, cutting off the discussion. 'The head of a Jan'Tep house does not explain himself to a Sha'Tep servant.'

'Hit me again, Keo,' my uncle said, his voice almost inviting. 'Better yet, set aside your great and grand magic. Fight me the way we did in the days before our paths separated. Show me what kind of man you are when you aren't hiding behind the mantle of a mage.'

My father's fists clenched. Abydos didn't move an inch. For the first time, I wondered what my father had been like as a boy. Had he been like me, small and scrawny, trying to survive as best he could as he waited for his powers to emerge? It was hard for me to imagine, and yet here, now, he seemed somehow smaller than Abydos.

I felt my mother shift a little from where she stood behind me. The silk of her sleeves made a soft sound as she brought her hands out in front of her and I knew she was preparing a spell. 'Would you fight me as well, Abydos?' she asked. 'Shall I set my magic aside and you can strike me with the resentment I see burning in your eyes?'

My uncle looked so shocked it was as if my mother had

struck him twice as hard as my father had. 'Bene'maat . . . Kellen is your son. Surely there is some other way to—'

'There is only one other way,' my father said. He looked back at me. 'Either I finish banding Kellen, sealing in his magic so that the shadowblack can never feed on it, knowing that I must then send him into exile forever, to wander alone far away from those who would recognise the disease and try to hunt him down, or I can kill my boy with my own two hands in order to protect our people.' He turned back to Abydos. 'Which would you have me do, brother?'

My uncle hesitated for a moment, and I saw all his rebellious strength drift away. His eyes returned to the floor, where they remained when he next spoke. 'I will prepare something to eat. Kellen will need to regain his strength after you're done for the night.'

For the third time, Abydos was going to break the rule regarding meals being eaten at the family table. This was, in its own small way, my uncle's last line of resistance.

As though nothing had happened, as if order and civility had somehow returned to the world, my father said, 'That would be most welcome, Abydos. Thank you.'

Then he returned to the worktable, where I lay held down by leather straps that bit into my skin whenever I struggled against them, and continued the careful, methodical destruction of my future.

Sometime the next morning I woke groggily to sunlight streaming through the window, and a voice floating up from the gardens below.

'Kellen?'

The voice was female. *Ferius?* I thought. No, too young.

234

Shalla? No, not nearly arrogant enough. Since there really weren't very many women in my life, I should have figured it out sooner, but in my defence I was quite heavily drugged and, really, who would have thought she'd ever speak to me again?

'Nephenia?' I asked, my voice a raspy wheeze that probably hadn't carried as far as my teeth, never mind the fifteen feet below the window to where she must have been standing. I tried again but still couldn't produce anything so grand as a moan, never mind a shout.

'Kellen, it's . . . me.'

There was a lot of weight in that 'me', I thought. I had no clue what it meant of course, but it was somehow nice to feel that I warranted that long a pause just for such a simple word.

'Kellen, I know you're angry, but . . .'

I think she said something else but I got stuck at 'you're angry'. What was I supposed to be angry about? Had Nephenia drugged me and then tied me down to a table in my mother's study only to start jabbing me with needles night after night?

Copper. The word came out of nowhere. *Copper for ember. Copper for fire spells, for lightning.* Last night my father had finished the copper band around my left forearm, forever cutting me off from one more form of magic.

'. . . Ferius,' Nephenia said.

What about Ferius?

I tried to concentrate on what she'd been saying during the time I'd been ruminating about copper magic.

'. . . masks, but no one is . . .'

Someone had seen Ferius attacked by a group of men in

235

masks outside the city – that was what it was. Unless I had just made that up? Damn it. Why couldn't I think straight?

Mother's potions, stupid. You can't think straight, so stop trying.

'. . . Two days since . . .'

Okay, no focusing, no thinking straight. What did that leave? *Think sideways.* Nephenia was outside my window. She wouldn't be there if she knew about the shadowblack, so my parents had kept that quiet. She was calling from outside, in the garden, which meant she must have already tried to visit me but had been turned away from the front door.

'. . . when are you and Shalla going to . . .'

Damn it, what had she just said about Shalla? Something about Shalla and myself, which meant Nephenia thought she must be here, so my parents must have told Osia'phest that they were keeping us both home from our lessons.

Unless Shalla really is back?

No, no way that was possible. She would have come to see me somehow. Even if she agreed with my parents' decision to counter-band me, she'd have found a way to sneak in and tell me this was all my fault and I just needed to try harder somehow.

Okay, what have we got?

Shalla was still missing and my parents had kept it secret, just like they'd kept secret both the fact that I had the shadowblack and that they were counter-banding me. Somebody had reported seeing Ferius attacked and taken away by men in masks, which had to be connected to the men who'd attacked Shalla and me in the forest when we'd tried to summon familiars.

Not bad for someone who's completely dazed and drugged, I thought. *Not bad at all.*

236

Except that I was also pretty sure that nobody would be looking for Ferius and nobody would care that she'd been captured.

'Nephenia?' I called out, my voice a little stronger now.

No answer came, which struck me as very rude until I noticed that the bright yellow sunlight was gone, replaced by the purple-grey of dusk.

Hours had gone by. I had nodded off. Darkness felt like a blanket being pulled over me. Soon my parents would come back into the room and start on the next band. Would it be blood magic this time? Or maybe breath? Were they down to the last and weakest band already?

Despite the dull thud of the drugs that kept me docile and the leather straps that held me down, I felt an overwhelming desire to do something, anything, to hurt my parents. Lacking the ability to *actually* commit any act of violence, I started crying, and in between my feeble sobs I said, 'You aren't my father any more, Ke'heops. You aren't my mother, Bene'maat. You're just two horrible people who strapped me down and took my life from me. I'm going to kill you both one day. I'm going to kill everybody in this stupid rotten town.'

Even as I spoke the words, I knew this was nothing more than the wasted utterance of a child lashing out at everyone around him. That was why I was so surprised when a fuzzy brown-and-black face suddenly appeared at the edge of my window and, in a chittering, growling little voice, said, 'Kill everybody in town? Now you're talking my language, kid.'

28

The Negotiation

There was a moment when the squirrel cat had first appeared at the window when I'd thought I might be hallucinating. I was still drugged, after all, and I'd been strapped down to that table for several days.

'Are you simple, kid?' the creature asked.

'Simple?'

'Slow. Dumb. Thick. Stupi—'

'I get it,' I said. 'The answer is no.'

The animal reached a paw into the narrow three-inch gap that separated the two wood-framed horizontal panes of glass. They were secured in position by a lever that required a small key to unlock it. When I was younger I used to try for hours to find a way to get it open, with everything from thin steel pins to a mallet. 'You won't be able to open it,' I informed the animal as he floundered at it with his paw. 'The only way is if you have —'

The lock slid off the lever and down onto the floor. The two halves of the window swung open and the squirrel cat clambered onto the sill and settled on his haunches.

'How did you do that?' I asked.

'Do what?'

'Undo the lock.'

He looked at me with a quizzical expression on his furry muzzle, his head tilted to one side. 'I thought you said you weren't simple.'

The sound of another chittering voice came from outside. It seemed to irritate him. He turned his head towards the open window. 'It was a joke,' he said. 'I'm being friendly.'

'You brought another . . .' It occurred to me that I wasn't sure how to refer to the animal. Did they prefer being called squirrel cats or nekheks?

'She insisted on coming,' he said, turning back to me. He raised his shoulders towards his ears and dropped them again. I took this to be a shrug. 'Females! Am I right?'

I had absolutely no idea what he meant. 'Yeah, females,' I said, then feeling particularly awkward, I asked, 'Do you have a name?'

He chittered something at me, then, seeing the confusion on my face, repeated it.

'*Reichis?*' I asked.

'Close enough.' He hopped off the windowsill and onto the table, then crawled onto my chest, his claws tapping against the fabric of my shirt. I had to stop myself from trying to shake him off. I'd seen what those claws could do. 'So,' he said, peering at me with those black beady eyes, 'we should probably get the negotiations started.'

'Negotiations?'

He let out a breath that I caught full in the nostrils. It was disgusting. 'You sure you ain't—'

'I'm not simple,' I said, irritation temporarily overcoming my anxiousness. 'I've just never . . . negotiated with a squirrel cat, that's all.'

'You don't say.' He sat back on my chest, leaning on his haunches as he glanced around my father's study, his eyes pausing on every shiny bauble and metal instrument. 'Nice place you have here,' he said. He brought his paws up to just below his whiskers and starting clacking his claws together as his thick bushy tail twitched excitedly.

'Why are you doing that?' I asked, suddenly suspicious.

Reichis seemed surprised. 'Doing what? I'm not doing—'

'You're tapping your paws together.'

'No, I'm not,' he said, and immediately brought them back down.

'Yes, you were. I saw you. What does it mean?'

He hesitated. 'It's . . . It's something my people do when we're, you know, intimidated by a superior intellect.' He looked down at me. 'That's why I'm going to free you in exchange for only four . . . five of these little trinkets you have here.'

'Five?' I'm not sure why the number bothered me. None of the items in the room belonged to me anyway, but I had the feeling he was trying to con me.

'It's a good deal, kid. Trust me.' He started blinking his eyes at me in a strange repetitive pattern. 'You want this deal, kid. You want to say yes.'

My experience with squirrel cats was admittedly limited, but there was a connection between us that made me recognise what he was doing. 'Are you trying to mesmerise me?' I asked.

'What? No.' He stopped the blinking. 'I don't even know what that is. Mesmerising? Never heard of it.'

'You're a terrible liar,' I said.

That seemed to genuinely offend him. 'I'm an excellent liar,' he growled, baring his teeth at me. 'You tell anyone otherwise and I'll—'

He was interrupted again by the chittering from outside.

'Gods damn it, leave me alone,' he muttered.

Squirrel cats have gods?

He started chittering back to the other animal out the window, too quickly for me to follow what he was saying. Then he turned back to me and grunted. 'Fine. Look, kid, since technically you set me free from those other skinbags, I'll get you out of your current predicament for free.' He turned back to chitter out the open window. 'Even though I saved his stupid sister from bonding with that sick mutt, which is how I got nabbed in the first place.'

The sounds of movement in the house drew our attention. I realised then that the moon was coming up fast, and soon my parents would be coming in to begin on the next band. *Oh spirits of the first mages*, I prayed, *please don't let them do it to me again.*

'Hey, kid,' Reichis said, suddenly sniffing around my face. 'Put a dam in that river. We've got work to do.'

'I'm not crying,' I said.

He gave his little huh-huh-huh laughing sound. 'Now who's a terrible liar?'

Before I could reply he crawled over to the strap holding my right wrist. He started working at it with his teeth, pulling for a few seconds on one side, then moving to the other, the whiskers on his face tickling my wrist even as the hairs on his tail got in my nose. I was afraid I'd start giggling like an idiot, but in less than a minute he had the first strap off. 'Think you can do the other one?' he asked. 'I'll get going on your ankles.'

I reached over and started undoing the strap over my left wrist. I was a little embarrassed that it took me longer than it had taken him.

'Okay,' he said, when all four restraints were off me and he'd jumped back onto the windowsill. 'You're free, kid.' When I didn't move, he started making a waving motion with one paw. 'Go on, little bird. Fly away. Fly away now.'

Squirrel cats, it turns out, are sarcastic assholes.

As quietly as I could, I swung my legs off the table and got to my feet. It turned out to be a bad idea, because a second later I was face-flat on the floor.

Chittering resumed from outside the window.

'I forgot, all right?' Reichis chittered back. He hopped down onto the floor next to me. 'You're still pretty drugged, kid, and they've had you tied down for a couple of days so you're bound to be a little out of it.'

'A little?' The only reason I hadn't yelled out when I'd hit the floor was that I could barely feel my face. Slowly and awkwardly I got to my hands and knees. There was no way I was going to be able to climb out the window.

'Don't worry,' Reichis said, seeing my discomfort. 'I brought something to help with that.' He opened his mouth and reached in with one paw to pull something small and green from inside one cheek. 'It's lightning weed. It'll perk you right up.'

'You want me to eat something you've been carrying around in your mouth?'

He gestured with a paw to his body. 'You see any pockets here?' The thin lips of his mouth pulled back in what I assumed was a grin. 'Of course, there was one other place I could've stored it.'

Ech. 'This is fine. Thanks.' I reached for the piece of green leaf in his paw but was distracted by the sounds of arguing from outside the room.

242

My mother's voice was faint, weary. 'We must rest another day, Ke'heops. You can barely stand as it is. The effort is too much.'

'No,' he replied. I don't think I'd ever heard my father sound so tired. 'I will finish this. I just need . . . a moment.' A key was scratching at the lock, as if he kept missing the keyhole.

'Ah, crap,' Reichis said, pulling the weed away from me.

'What are you doing?' I whispered. 'In about one minute my parents are going to come through that door.'

'That's the problem, kid. Even if you swallow the lightning weed, it'll take longer than that to go through your stomach and into your blood.'

The thought of being discovered by my parents, of being tied back down to the table, this time with stronger restraints that meant I'd never escape, drove me half mad with fear. I started trying to clamber up to the window, but I couldn't. In desperation I turned to Reichis. 'Help me,' I said. 'Please, I can't . . .' That was when I noticed he had stuck the leaf back in his mouth and was chewing it. 'What are you doing?'

'Give me your arm,' he said, his mouth now full of foaming green muck.

'What? Why –'

He growled and then reached out with his paws and grabbed hold of my right wrist. Before I knew what was happening he bit down on it hard, his teeth piercing the skin and sinking deep into the flesh. I was about to scream from the shock and pain when something changed inside me. It felt like a flame running up the length of my arm, into my chest and down through the rest of my body. The room lit up, every colour brighter, clearer. I could think clearly again. More importantly, I could feel the strength return to my limbs.

243

'Works best when it goes straight into the blood,' Reichis explained, leaping up onto the windowsill. He looked around longingly at the jars and instruments in my mother's study. 'If you want to bring any souvenirs, kid, I'd do it now. I doubt you'll want to come back here anytime soon.'

I couldn't imagine anything I'd want from my parents ever again, but then I saw the deck of cards Ferius had given me sitting on a little shelf near the table, the razor-thin steel one and the dark red card on top. I grabbed them and stuffed them into the pocket of my trousers. 'Let's go,' I said as I climbed out the window and into the night air. 'I've got everything I'll ever need from this place.'

29

The Hideout

I scaled the wooden trellis that ran down the side of the house to the garden. On a normal good day it would have taken me ten minutes to do it without breaking my neck, but with the lightning weed in me I got down in less than one.

'How do you skinbags ever escape from predators when you move that slowly?' Reichis asked from where he was still perched outside the window. He sprang, spreading his arms and legs wide. The furry membrane between his limbs billowed as it caught the air, and he glided down effortlessly, swooping past my head to land several yards ahead of me. Without pausing he bounded out of the garden and on to the street. I followed as fast as I could, which turned out to be pretty fast considering I was barefoot.

We ran down the streets and alleyways of my neighbourhood, staying in the shadows, avoiding places where people congregated. I tried as hard as possible not to think about the black markings around my left eye, about the pain that still laced my forearms where my own parents had tried to permanently counter-band me, and the fact that the life I had always envisioned for myself was now truly gone.

Shalla and Ferius are out there somewhere. Focus on that.

Reichis seemed to have a remarkable knowledge of the town, leading us through small paths between houses, into other people's gardens that just happened to lead out onto darkened alleys.

'How do you know the town so well?' I asked, running close behind.

'I'm a professional, kid. I've been casing your place for days. I worked this route out the first night.'

Squirrel cats have professions?

Reichis and the other squirrel cat kept up the pace, making it hard for me to catch my breath. It wasn't until we found ourselves outside a burnt-out single-storey building near the edge of the Sha-Tep district that he allowed us to stop. 'You can go vomit in there if you want,' he said, pointing with his snout towards the blackened door hanging off one hinge that led inside.

'I don't need to vomit. Why would you think that?' I asked.

Reichis walked up to me and sniffed. 'You're definitely going to puke, kid.'

A sudden wave of nausea overwhelmed me. I ran inside the building and dropped to my knees, green, foamy bile pouring from my mouth as I coughed uncontrollably.

'Yeah,' the squirrel cat chittered quietly behind me. 'I probably should have mentioned that lightning weed has a few unpleasant side effects.'

'You think?' I asked, wiping my mouth with my sleeve only to be overcome once again. I knelt there, unable to do anything but shiver as my guts churned. A light rain started outside, rare for this time of year. It pattered against the slat wood roof, dripping through the gaps to land on the back of my head and neck as I heaved over and over onto the dirt floor. *Kill me*, I thought. *Just kill me right here and now.*

Reichis sauntered over and sat on his haunches. 'Can't you . . . you know?' He made an odd circular motion with one paw.

'What?'

'Do some magic or something. Aren't your people supposed to be good at that?'

A chittering noise from just outside followed by a soft growl drew our attention, but Reichis didn't seem concerned. 'Oh, right,' he said, turning back to me. 'You're an invalid or something.'

'I'm not an invalid. I'm just . . .' *Just what?* I stared down at my forearms where my parents had tattooed counter-sigils into five of the six bands. Iron, ember, sand, silk, blood . . . the metal inks my father had tattooed onto me were thick and perfectly formed as though they were shackles melted into my skin. *But shackles can be broken. These can't.* All that was left was the band for breath, weakest of the six.

'Hey, kid,' the squirrel cat said. 'You're leaking again.'

'I'm not crying.'

He gave a little snort. 'Sure. Must just be your Jan'Tep magic summoning rain from your eyeballs.'

'You make a lousy familiar, you know that?'

That got me a growl. His fur bristled, and I swear it looked darker all of a sudden; I could see fierce silver-grey stripes along his flanks. 'My people are the apex predators of the world, got it? When devils want to scare their young into obedience, do you know what they do?'

'I didn't know devils had children.'

'They threaten to let the squirrel cats in to eat their eyeballs, that's what! We ain't nobody's familiars. What do I look like

247

to you anyway? Some kind of weak-willed, feeble-minded falcon who's going to bring you field mice to nibble on while you sit on your ass all day?'

'That's not what familiars do.'

He looked away and waved a paw in the air. 'Whatever. Clean yourself up, would you? You look like you've got rabies.'

I wiped the last flecks of green foam from my mouth onto the sleeve of my shirt. 'So I guess all the stories about your kind serving the Mahdek were just myths?'

'The Mahdek didn't have familiars,' he replied. 'We were more like . . . business partners.'

'Business partners?'

He looked back at me and cocked his head. 'Let's just say that we and the Mahdek shared a few mutual enemies. Your people, mostly.'

'So why are you helping me?'

The squirrel cat sauntered over to the door leading outside and chittered loudly. 'Good question. Why *am* I helping him?'

A series of chitters and growls followed, none of which I understood. When Reichis looked back at me he just grunted, 'Females.'

'How come I can understand you but not any of the other squirrel cats?' I asked.

Reichis glanced up at me. 'Do you speak our language?'

'Not so far as I know.'

'Then there's your answer.'

I couldn't see how that explained anything, but I got the sense he wasn't interested in discussing it futher. The nausea having mostly passed, I started to push myself up. With the effects of the lightning weed wearing off, I found I was exhausted and the soles of my bare feet hurt like seven hells. After a few false starts, I managed to stand. Barely.

'Looking good, kid,' Reichis said unconvincingly.

Suddenly the other squirrel cat leaped into the building and growled. 'Great,' Reichis said. He turned to me. 'Okay, turns out this wasn't the best hiding place.'

'What? Why?'

'Somebody's tracked you here.' The other squirrel cat chittered for a moment, then Reichis added, 'A bunch of somebodies.'

Most tracking spells use a combination of silk and iron magic – silk to bind to the subject's mind, and iron to create the pull, drawing the mage ever closer to the target. There were any number of people who might be using those spells on me now. My parents for starters. Tennat and his insane brothers. Bloodthirsty Mahdek assassins. I was starting to wonder who *wasn't* determined to kill or cripple me.

'How close are they?' I asked.

Reichis ran to the door and sniffed the air. 'Hard to say. This whole city stinks of skinbags.' He sniffed again. 'There's one that's nearly here though. Female.' His ears went slightly flat as the sides of his mouth twitched up to reveal his teeth. 'And soon to be dead.'

'Wait . . . What?'

Reichis didn't reply. Instead he crouched down low, the muscles of his haunches tensing, preparing to pounce, his tail twitching. I could still hear the sound of the rain outside, and beneath it the sound of light footsteps approaching.

'Oh, this is gonna be fun,' Reichis snarled.

I sidled up to the door, my back against the adjoining wall. I slid my hand in my pocket and drew the one steel card Ferius had given me.

'Kellen?' a voice called from outside. 'Are you in there?'

Nephenia.

She appeared in the doorway, the fingers of her right hand tracing the form for the spell she'd used to find me. 'Kellen, you've got to get out of here! There are people coming to –'

Too late she saw Reichis and the other squirrel cat. I'd caught the motion from the corner of my eye and, in what was certainly one of the dumber moves in my life, I stepped in front of Nephenia, arms wide. 'Reichis, don't.'

If you've never had a squirrel cat launch itself at you, jaws wide, claws out, gliding membranes extended and eyes absolutely crazy with rage, well, I don't recommend it.

'Reichis, stop!' I barely got my arm up in time for him to sink his teeth into it. For a second he held on, claws trying to grab for me. I'm pretty sure the little monster would have torn my arm off if the other squirrel cat hadn't leaped on him and taken him by the neck. Reichis let go almost instantly, landing neatly on the floor and turning his rage on the other animal. 'Mine!' he growled.

She growled right back.

Nephenia stood close behind me. 'Kellen, what's happening? What are they doing?'

Reichis started chittering and growling almost incoherently. It took me a moment to make any sense of what he was saying. 'I don't care what scent she's giving off!' he shouted. 'She and the other skinbags tried to kill me!'

The other animal's reply wasn't nearly as loud. In fact it

250

was quiet... like a whisper. Whatever it was, it took the fight out of Reichis. He looked, well, I guessed it was frightened. He knelt down low, his chin on the ground. 'Fine, let her talk,' he mumbled. 'I'm still going to kill her later.'

'Kellen?' Nephenia asked.

I turned, and saw that she was drenched from the rain and not dressed for it. Her hair clung to her face and she looked absolutely terrified. I wanted so badly in that moment to hold her, to reassure her, but I just wasn't sure I could trust her. 'What are you doing here, Nephenia?' I asked.

She looked down at Reichis. 'Is that . . . ? Is that the one we . . . ?'

'Tortured?' he growled. 'Used filthy Jan'Tep magic on?'

'He looks different,' she said. 'Not like the monsters we were told about at all.'

I wasn't sure what to say to that, given he looked pretty much the same as when she'd tortured him, so I settled for, 'His name is Reichis.'

For some reason that set tears streaming down her cheeks. 'I'm so sorry,' she cried. 'I don't know why we . . . I wanted so badly to prove myself to the others. I wanted to show I could do the high magics.' She turned to look at me, all the composure drained out of her face, replaced with misery. 'Will you tell him I'm sorry?'

'He can hear you,' I replied.

She turned and, with what I thought was remarkable bravery, knelt down in front of Reichis. The hackle of his fur rose as he bared his teeth at her and growled something I couldn't make out. 'I'm sorry,' she said. 'I know there's no excuse for what I did.'

251

When Reichis didn't respond, Nephenia looked up to me. 'Does he understand? He's not—'

'Tell the bitch I'm going to sneak into her house one night very soon. I'm going to climb up onto her face and rip off her ears and then I'm going to eat her eyeballs right in front of her.'

There was so much rage radiating from him it practically made the rain dripping through the roof steam off his fur. I guess I couldn't really blame him. 'She thought you were a monster, Reichis. She didn't understand.'

'If I could take it back, I swear I would,' Nephenia said, practically begging him now. It made for an odd sight.

He bristled. 'Fine,' he growled. 'Tell her to pick her favourite eye. She can keep one.' He looked up at me and snarled. 'The other one, I'm eating.'

'What did he say?' Nephenia asked.

'He said . . .' I locked eyes with Reichis and did my best not to flinch. 'He said he understands. He says we all do stupid things sometimes. He says he forgives you.'

Reichis was not impressed. 'Oh, that's it. Now I'm going for your eyeballs too, you lousy—'

He was cut off by the other squirrel cat, who nipped his ear. Reichis growled back at her. 'Being around you is like having thorns in all four paws, you know that?'

Nephenia rose to her feet. 'We have to get you out of here, Kellen. Tennat and his brothers are looking for you. They're using tracking spells.'

'Like you did,' I said.

She nodded. 'I found you first. The spell is stronger when there's an emotional . . . I just found you first, that's all.' She shook her head. 'Everyone's gone mad, Kellen. Tennat's been

252

strutting around like his father's already the clan prince. The council says they're going to hold the election tonight, even though it wasn't supposed to happen for weeks yet.'

'I don't understand. I thought they wanted to use the initiates' trials as a way to see which house has the best bloodlines?'

'That's just it – they're putting the initiates through the trials tonight, one after another. Everybody is scrambling, trying to make sure they have a secret to sell for the fourth test. Panahsi won't even talk to me. He just keeps practising spells inside his family's sanctum.'

The other squirrel cat sniffed the air and chittered something. Reichis translated. 'More headed this way.' He looked up at me. 'Four of them, all mages from the stink.'

Nephenia closed her eyes for a moment. 'It's Tennat. He's using the same spell I am . . . there's a kind of tension between the two.' She opened her eyes. 'Kellen, you've got to get out of here. Now.'

'How? They'll just keep tracking me.'

'I sparked the band for silk magic yesterday. There's something I can try that will confuse them, make them follow me instead of you. I'll use distortion spells to keep them off my trail, and if they do find me, they'll just think Tennat messed up his spell.'

'And what if he doesn't? What if he figures out—'

'He won't. Tennat thinks I'm just a silly girl who plays at being a mage.'

'Time's running out,' Reichis chittered. 'I can hear them fumbling around inside one of the houses on the other side of the street.'

Nephenia took my hands. 'Kellen, I've heard people talking,

253

saying that the Mahdek are the ones who took your sister. They say that Daroman woman, Ferius Parfax, was looking for her and then she got taken, too.'

Reichis shuffled up to the door. 'Make up your mind, kid. Either way, I'm out of here.'

I caught Nephenia's eyes. 'Are you sure you can do this?'

She nodded. 'Find your sister, Kellen. If she goes to the mage trials tonight, there's still a chance that your father will be elected instead of Ra'meth.' When I hesitated she said, 'Let me do this, Kellen. Let me do the brave thing for once in my life.'

How the hells am I suppose to make these kinds of choices? 'What do we have to do?' I asked.

She closed her eyes and formed somatic shapes with both hands, two simple cantrips, one for attracting, one for shunning, each the reverse of the other bound into a single spell, then interlacing the syllables of the evocations back. It was clever actually. Then she put her arms around me and hugged me. 'I need to strengthen the connection between us. It'll make it easier to fool Tennat's tracking spell.'

We stood like that for a while before she let go, but she didn't step away. 'I think . . . I think it's working,' she said. I wasn't sure how to reply, all I could think about was the fact that my lips had never been this close to hers.

Reichis snorted. 'You do remember you were puking up green foam a few minutes ago, right?'

Hells. 'I'd better go,' I said.

'No,' Nephenia said. 'You stay here. I'll go first and draw Tennat and the others away. Wait until after I'm gone, and then go find Shalla.'

Before I could stop her, she started out the door. 'Wait,' I said. 'Why are you doing this?'

254

Nephenia paused at the door. 'Back at the oasis you told me that one day I'd figure out I was special.' She turned and looked back at me, a silhouette framed by the doorway, rain pouring down all around her, ready to risk her life for mine. 'I'm done waiting.'

30

The Prisoner

Those next few minutes nearly drove me insane. Every sound I heard – every drop of rain dripping onto the floor through the leaky roof, the steps outside of Sha'Tep returning to their homes after their day's labours, running, stumbling to get out of the wet – I jumped at all of them. I kept wondering when the next noise would be Tennat and his brothers shouting for me, or Nephenia screaming.

'You know,' Reichis said, 'I kind of like that human. Maybe I'll let her keep both eyes.'

'That's decent of you.'

'I'm still going to eat one of her ears.'

After another minute, he went to the door and sniffed the air outside. I couldn't help but wonder, given how arrogant the little bastard was, whether his sense of smell could really be as good as he claimed it. 'They're gone,' he said, then added, 'Guess this is where we part ways.' He started out the door.

'Wait! Stop!'

The squirrel cat peeked a head back in. 'What?'

'I thought you were going to help me!' I replied, immediately wishing the words hadn't come out sounding so desperate.

Reichis gave a passable imitation of a shrug. 'I did help you. I freed you from your parents before they finished . . . whatever it was they were doing to you. I gave you lightning weed and got you out of the house, and now you're here, in this lovely hideout where you can lay low for a while.'

'My sister's in danger! So is Ferius. I need you to help me—'

'*You* need?' the squirrel cat repeated. 'You *need* a lot of things, kid. What's in it for me?' He shuffled over and started pawing at the pockets of my trousers. 'Don't suppose you've got anything to trade?'

'Stop that,' I said, pushing him away. If I'd been smarter I would have brought something from my father's study to bargain with. In my defence, I'd never had to put the lives of people I cared about in the hands of overgrown avaricious part-feline rodents before. 'You said . . . You said there was a tradition between your people and the Mahdek. You said sometimes you worked together.'

'So?'

'So, be my business partner.'

The other squirrel cat chittered.

Reichis gave what sounded like a loud, stuttering cough. It took me a moment to realise he was laughing. 'Him? What's he got to offer?' He started walking around me like a merchant inspecting defective wares. 'He doesn't own anything, he can't fight worth a damn and from what I've seen so far, he doesn't have any magic. Why in the world would I—'

The other animal was on him again. This time Reichis resisted, but within seconds she landed him flat on his back with her teeth around his neck, shaking him. 'Fine!' he growled. 'Gods damn it. I'll do it.'

The female gave one more shake and then let him go. With

as much dignity as anyone could muster in the situation, Reichis righted himself and snarled at her. 'You're a terrible mother, you know that?'

'That's your *mother*?'

He looked up. 'Of course she's my mother. Can't you see the resemblance?' Without waiting for a reply he ambled back to me. 'All right. We'll *try* this thing. One time. I'll help you find your sister and the Argosi and in return you help get me something I want. But I'm not your familiar, understand? I'm not your pet and I'm not your friend. If you can't hold up your end of the bargain, I'm gone. Got it?'

'I guess that's fair,' I replied, my eyes still on the other squirrel cat, who now looked as placid as still water.

'Hold out your hand,' Reichis said.

Great. He's going to bite me again. I figured this must be part of the ritual and, not being in a position to refuse, I did as he asked. Sure enough, he sunk his teeth into my palm. It hurt worse than the other two times. 'Do your people have any traditions that *don't* involve biting?' I asked.

Reichis started for the door. 'That wasn't for any tradition. You just piss me off.'

With the effects of the lightning weed having worn off, it was even harder for me to keep up with Reichis and his mother. The pair of them led me down the pre-dawn streets and alleys on such a winding path that I soon lost my bearings entirely. It wasn't until we stopped in front of a long, vine-covered wall over ten feet high that I realised where we were. 'What are we doing behind the palace?'

'Climbing,' Reichis replied, leaping up to swiftly ascend all

258

the way to the top of the wall. He turned and looked back down at me. 'Quietly, if you can manage it.'

It took me forever to make the climb. It didn't help having Reichis sniggering at me all the while. By the time I got to the top I could barely get in enough breath to speak. 'I don't understand. Is my sister here?'

I heard a soft rustle as Reichis's mother climbed up effortlessly behind me. She chittered something I couldn't understand. 'We don't know where your sister is, kid,' Reichis replied. 'That's why we're here. We need to talk to the prisoner.'

I looked out over the endless gardens within the walls, my eyes settling on the dark shape of its lone cottage. I felt ill. I'd thought the dowager magus had been trying to help me, or at least wasn't part of whatever conspiracy was trying to tear down the clan. 'Who is Mer'esan keeping prisoner?'

Reichis looked up and tilted his head. 'You really don't know anything, do you? The old lady isn't keeping anyone prisoner. *She's* the prisoner.'

31

The Cell

'I suppose this was inevitable,' Mer'esan said as she opened the door to the cottage. She caught sight of the markings around my eye and something like sympathy flickered in her expression. 'Come inside. We'll need to cover that up before someone sees you.'

As I entered, Mer'esan noticed the two squirrel cats following behind and her upper lip curled. 'Hideous little monsters, aren't they?'

Reichis sauntered past her. 'You're no prize yourself, you rancid old prune.' He clambered onto the lone chair in the room, then hopped up onto a shelf and began examining the various trinkets adorning it.

'Foul-mouthed too,' Mer'esan said, motioning for me to stand beneath a lantern.

'Wait . . . You can understand them?'

'I'm three hundred years old, Kellen. You think I haven't the magic to follow their simple little minds?' She gave me a look of disdain that was remarkably like the ones Reichis kept giving me. I decided not to mention the similarity.

From within the folds of her garments, Mer'esan pulled out a small jar. She opened it and dipped a finger inside,

260

then spread a small quantity of lotion over the markings around my left eye. *She knew*, I realised. *Not just that I had the shadowblack, but that I'd end up back here.*

'There,' she said, once she was done. She handed me the jar. 'Keep this with you. The paste blends well enough with your natural skin colour, but you'll need to put more on as it wears away over the course of the day.' She grabbed my jaw and forced me to lock eyes with her. 'This won't protect you, you understand? Mages who know the spells will be able to track you if they want to. Believe me, son of the House of Ke, they will want to.'

'Is there a cure? Can you—'

The dowager magus took a seat in her customary chair. 'What did I tell you about asking questions to which you already know the answer?'

My heart sank. She was right – I already knew the answer. My parents had already confessed to me that they'd long feared I would contract the condition. They must have searched everywhere for a cure, if only so I didn't embarrass our house and hurt my father's bid to become clan prince. *Was there ever a time, even just a moment, where they saw me as their son and not as some danger to our house that had to be dealt with?*

'Great,' Reichis chittered, peering down at me from his perch on the shelf. 'He's crying again.'

'I'm not—'

'They are simple creatures,' Mer'esan said. 'For all their cunning, they do not comprehend the notion of sympathy.'

Reichis's mother stepped forward and gave a low growl. The dowager magus bowed her head in reply. 'I suppose you have a point, little mother. I stand corrected.'

261

'What did she say?' I asked.

'She reminded me that our people sometimes suffer from the same deficiency.'

'So it's true? You're locked in here?' I started looking around the small one-room cottage, at the walls where they met the floor and the bottom edge of the door. I could find no signs of anything that might be used to hold a mage captive.

'I can leave anytime I want,' Mer'esan replied.

'Then you aren't a prisoner?'

'We're all prisoners in our own way, Kellen.'

'Yes, but . . .' I stopped, noticing the odd expression on her face and sensing that nothing I said or asked would get her to answer what I wanted to know. That, in and of itself, provided the explanation. 'A mind chain,' I whispered, awed that such a thing was even possible against a mage of Mer'esan's power.

She said nothing in reply, merely leaned back in her chair, looking placidly at the wall in front of her as if it were a peaceful vista. The spells lighting up her skin beneath the silken fabrics she wore shifted and shimmered, her features changing back and forth, sometimes young and beautiful, almost innocent. Other times she looked as old as every one of her three hundred years.

A sudden anger overtook me. Who would chain her like this? Who would have the strength? Mer'esan was vastly more powerful than Ra'meth or even my father. Maybe if the whole council of lords magi were working in concert, but the chances of that were slim. That left only . . . *Oh* . . . 'Your husband. The clan prince did this to you, didn't he?'

Again there was no reply, as if she hadn't heard my question. *The mind chain keeps her from saying or doing anything that would impede its control over her.* Underneath the calm exterior, I saw a deep sense of sorrow in her eyes. Sorrow, and betrayal.

Reichis's mother walked over and clambered up onto the old woman's lap. It was an oddly intimate gesture. 'Disgusting creature,' the dowager magus said, but then proceeded to stroke her fur.

'What if we took you out of here?' I asked. 'Would the chain still—'

'I like this old place,' Mer'esan said before I could finish. 'I'm used to it. It's like my own little . . .' she seemed to struggle with the next word before finally saying, 'oasis.'

This is her power source. This was why she never left the cottage: only here did she have the strength required to maintain the spells holding her body together. 'All these years . . . keeping yourself alive . . .' Had she been waiting so long for the clan prince to finally die and for his spell to fade?

'The things we build in life often outlast us,' she said absently.

I took this to mean that the mind chain was too powerful. Even with her husband in the ground, she was still bound by it.

So then what? She figures out she'll never be able to break the spell, that she's going to go on like this, never able to reveal the truth, until she dies. All that left was waiting for an opportunity – for someone who might ask the right questions to unlock the chain. 'That's why you summoned me that first day,' I said, knowing she wouldn't reply. 'You didn't care if I passed my trials; you were looking for someone who might figure out your secret. That's why you were so interested in Ferius. You thought that maybe an Argosi like her might

263

uncover it . . . perhaps she could help you reveal it.' But then why not just have someone bring Ferius here? *Because that would be too direct. The mind chain would never allow it.*

Mer'esan, the most powerful living mage of my people, had been left only with the hope that, by some combination of outside events and subtle manipulations, her secret could be discerned by the very weakest mage in our clan: me.

Okay, then do it. Figure out the secret that's binding her.

I tried to think of ways of getting round the chain – some roundabout way of asking the question that might enable her to answer. But a spell this strong, cast by the clan prince himself – probably when he was at the height of his power – wasn't going to be broken by some clever turn of phrase. No query, no riddle, no guessing game would uncover what was locked inside her. *So think of something else. Change the game somehow.*

'What's the plan, kid?' Reichis asked.

There was a small table in the corner of the room. I dragged it in front of Mer'esan and reached into the pocket of my trousers for the deck of cards Ferius had given me. I laid them out on the table, face up. Four suits, each one with its little symbols: white seven-pointed stars we call septagrams, to represent the suit of spells and the Jan'Tep people, golden shields for the Daroman empire, silver chalices for the Berabesq, and black leaves for the Mahdek.

'I would think someone with all your troubles would have better uses for his time than to play cards with an old woman,' Mer'esan commented.

'Just one game.' I ran my fingertips across the surface of the cards. Each suit had the same numbers, but the names at the bottom were different. The highest card of the Daroman

264

suit was the king, but for the Berabesq it was called 'Grand Vizier', and for the Jan'Tep, of course, 'Clan Prince'. The cards went on like this, down to the lowest numbers, each one depicting people in various settings, like actors waiting to deliver their performance.

'And what game do you wish to play?' Mer'esan asked.

I caught her stare and tried to see in her eyes whether she understood – whether my ruse would enable her to navigate around the mind chain. I picked up one of the cards, a seven of leaves, representing something called a Mahdek shaman. I tossed it on the table in front of her. 'Let's make our own game,' I replied.

Her eyes narrowed, but she gave me a small smile. 'Clever,' she said, and then reached to pick up the rest of the deck. 'What shall we call this game of ours?'

'Let's name it after the one foe that can't be defeated by magic,' I replied. 'The truth.'

32

The Card Game

The game we played made no sense, its rules inconsistent and certainly unknowable. It didn't matter. All that concerned me was the story that Mer'esan so desperately wanted to tell – the story that had been locked inside her for centuries.

We sat across the table from each other. She shuffled the deck and dealt each of us thirteen cards, face up, laid out across two rows. Somehow every one of her cards featured scenes with figures bearing seven-pointed stars. Whether through guile or magic, she had given herself the entire suit of spells – the suit of the Jan'Tep.

I looked down at my cards. Each of the figures painted on their surface carried or wore a number of black leaves. *So I'm to play the Mahdek.*

Mer'esan fanned out the rest of the deck into three circles. The largest she placed at the centre of the table between us, face down so that the backs of the cards showed. 'The oasis,' she said, then laid down two smaller circles of cards, one on the right and the other on the left.

It took me a moment to figure out what they represented. 'Duelling circles?'

She nodded and placed one of her cards inside her circle,

face up, showing a young woman with outstretched hands above which floated seven septagrams. 'Your turn,' she said.

I was about to reach for one of my cards when I suddenly understood what this was. 'You're . . . enacting the duels from the final war between the Jan'Tep and the Mahdek. But why?'

'It is only a game,' she replied. 'Now make your choice.'

The last war had taken place nearly three centuries ago, when Mer'esan would have been a young woman. We had nearly been wiped out in that conflict. The Mahdek had used the magic of shadow – of the void – to unleash demons, attacking Jan'Tep children in their sleep so as to distract even our most powerful mages. My ancestors had fought back, drawing on the other six fundamental forms of magic: iron and ember, sand and silk, breath and blood.

Not knowing the rules, I made the simplest choice I could. I selected one of my cards. It was named 'The Warden of Leaves' and showed an archer shooting eight arrows into the air, the fletching of each one made from a black leaf. I placed it inside my circle.

'Wrong!' Mer'esan declared, and took my card away.

'I don't understand. My card was an eight of leaves and yours only a seven of spells. Shouldn't mine—'

'This card cannot defend itself,' she said. 'It is in grief.'

'In grief? What does that mean?'

She pointed to the two rows of cards laid out in front of me. Two of them had somehow ended up face down. 'Those cards are taken. They bind your warden of leaves in grief.'

I looked under the two cards. They were both low numbers, a two and a three. Each of them depicted a child.

'Now choose your next attacker,' Mer'esan commanded.

Confused and shaken, I placed another face card, this one was a nine – the shaman of leaves.

'No!' Mer'esan said, and took that one away too.

'Let me guess, it's "in grief" too?'

Her eyes blazed angrily. 'Yes.'

I glanced back down at my remaining cards and saw another had been flipped over without my noticing, this one a five. 'This is wrong,' I said, finally understanding her intent. 'The Mahdek attacked our families, not the other way around. They were the ones who—'

'Play the game!'

Frustrated, I took three of my cards at once, including the highest numbered card, the speaker of leaves, and placed them in my circle.

'Grief.' Mer'esan ripped the card from the circle and tossed it into a growing discard pile next to her. She grabbed the second and the third. 'Grief and more grief. You cannot win this way.'

My circle was empty again. Moreover, almost all the cards on my side of the table had somehow been flipped over, like rows of corpses strewn across a battlefield. 'This isn't what happened! The Jan'Tep duelled the Mahdek demon summoners, not their children.' I rose from my seat. 'Why are you lying to me?'

Mer'esan wouldn't meet my eyes. 'Sit down,' she said. 'The game isn't done yet.'

'Then what is my move?' I demanded. 'Every time I try to play a card you tell me it can't fight back!'

'You have no cards left to play,' she replied. 'All you can do now is watch.'

Reluctantly I took my seat. Mer'esan placed one of her cards, the clan prince of spells, inside the oasis. Her hands were shaking, and I couldn't tell if this was because she was fighting the mind chain or from some deeper agony that came with the memories.

She reached a fingernail under one of the cards making up the fanned-out circle of the oasis and turned it over, sending all the other cards flipping over in sequence until at last they were all face up. Every one of them was a septagram. The oasis had been taken by the Jan'Tep. 'You are defeated,' she said.

'I don't understand. What spell did the clan prince cast?'

'The only spell that matters. The one that lets you win the game.'

I followed her gaze to the Mahdek cards laid out in front of me. They were all face up as well. Each of the leaves depicting their suit was now blood red in colour.

'This makes no sense,' I insisted. *It makes perfect sense. You just don't want to believe it.* My people lived in beautiful cities, but had no great architects. Our magic came from the oases in the centre of those cities, yet we did not have the means to create new ones. Always we told ourselves it was our great ancestors who had devised these things for us and that our duty was to protect them from being taken away by our enemies.

But the Mahdek had never tried to take the oasis from us.

We had stolen it from them.

They hadn't launched a war between our peoples.

We had simply massacred them in their sleep, beginning with their families, their children.

We had looted their future for ourselves.

'How could this happen?' I asked.

Mer'esan, tears streaming down her face, turned one of the

269

cards in the circle back over, sending the others flipping face down again. The pattern on the back of the cards was gone, replaced by solid black, the colour of shadow. There was only one kind of spell that called on the power of the void.

'That's not possible,' I said. 'The Mahdek were demon summoners, our people would never—'

A sob escaped Mer'esan's lips, the last links of the mind chain slowly breaking apart. 'Do you propose to tell me the rules of the game?'

I looked at the cards representing the ancestors I had venerated my whole life, the ancestors whom I now knew had summoned horrors with which to murder the children of our enemies, in order to weaken their mages. 'Then . . . that's how the war ended? Through assassination and dark magic?'

'Ended?' She picked up the cards from the oasis and held them in her hand. 'No, Kellen of the House of Ke. Once a game like this has begun, it is never ended.' She placed the cards face up on the table, one on top of the other, with increasing speed. The illustrations went by so fast that I had trouble making out which cards they represented, but I thought I saw something . . .

'Stop!' I said. 'I can't see what's happening.'

'You never can,' she said, stopping at last as she placed one final card on top of the stack.

A young man stood surrounded by six books, each one displaying a septagram. The card was called 'The Initiate of Spells', and I had seen it before, both when Ferius had shown me her deck and when Mer'esan had played it during the game. Only now something had changed.

The figure facing us bore the same studious expression as

before, but now I saw black markings twisting around one of his eyes. *Just like mine.*

'This can't be . . . What are you telling me, Mer'esan?'

She flipped over the card so that it was face down. The back had returned to the unremarkable pattern I'd seen before. 'I have said nothing, son of Ke. We are merely playing at cards.'

My fingers trembled as they rose up to meet the cold skin around my left eye. 'The shadowblack . . . When our ancestors found they didn't have the power to defeat the Mahdek, they . . . we . . . called forth demons to destroy them. First we attacked their families to break their spirits, then we killed their mages.'

Mer'esan's expression was flat, though the tears still flowed down her cheeks. 'That would be a sound strategy, if you were trying to win the game at all costs.'

'But that's just it . . . the cost . . . The Mahdek didn't curse us with the shadowblack; we infected ourselves when we used the magic of the void to summon demons.'

Mer'esan let out a long, deep breath that sounded like a sigh and wiped the tears from her eyes. The mind chain was broken. 'History is written by the victors,' she said, 'but the truth has a way of revealing itself.'

I heard a low growl and looked down to see Reichis's mother glaring up at the dowager.

'What did she say?' I asked Reichis.

It was Mer'esan who answered. 'She says that it is not in the proper way of things that a parent should let their child suffer for crimes they had no part in.'

I felt something hard and cold in my stomach. 'Tell her she doesn't understand the Jan'Tep then.'

Slowly and carefully, Mer'esan picked up the cards from

271

the table and handed them to me. 'Every society has atrocities in its past, Kellen. Do you think the Daroman empire was built on nothing but courage and military brilliance? Or that the Berabesq viziers worship their six-faced god with nothing more than prayers and celebrations?'

'How can you be so calm?' I demanded. 'Your own husband cast the spell that kept you from revealing what he and the others had done in the name of our people!'

'He wasn't an evil man,' she said. 'He looked at what lay ahead for our people – from the Daroman empire reaching out from the east to the Berabesq in the south who would happily commit genocide against us for what they saw as our devil magic. To survive we needed to strengthen our spells and train more young mages than ever before. The Mahdek knew the secrets of creating the oases within their cities, making their spells more powerful and enabling their young to learn the ways of magic more easily.'

'Would the Mahdek have destroyed us?'

'It didn't matter. We couldn't take the chance. We had to take the oasis in this city from them, as we had to take all the others.' She rose from her chair and walked away from me. 'Those are the rules of the game, Kellen.'

'Wait . . . Where are you going?'

She stopped, just for a moment, her hand on the door. 'The chains that have bound me for almost three hundred years are gone. I think I would like to go outside now.'

When I joined Mer'esan in the cool night air she was staring into the darkness blanketing the gardens. I wondered how long ago they'd been planted here, and who tended them, and whether the dowager magus had ever even seen them up close before. None of these questions though were the ones that mattered.

Just past the gardens, the great palace stood proudly before us. The seat of our clan's governance. A place we hadn't even built ourselves. 'Did we create nothing of our own?' I asked.

Mer'esan gave a small, bitter laugh. 'Of course we did. The Mahdek were always few in number. This city, for example, is far too small to house our entire clan. So we built—'

'The slums,' I said. 'The Sha'Tep slums.' Ill-made structures of rough wood and unshaped sandstone. 'Three hundred years, and all we made ourselves were hovels.'

'Our people never set out to be architects or builders, Kellen. Magic is our vocation, the one endeavour we prize above all others.'

I thought about the illness that had overtaken some of the other initiates, and of Shalla. 'I have to find my sister,' I said. 'Someone is trying to hurt our people the same way we hurt the Mahdek. They're destroying children so that—'

Mer'esan cut me off. 'Is that what they're doing? *Destroying* children?'

I wished for once that she wouldn't turn everything into an enigmatic question, but then I realised I already knew the answer. When the men in Mahdek masks had attacked us the night we were trying to summon familiars, they hadn't attempted to kill Shalla, they'd tried to make her bond with a sick animal. They had simply tried to permanently weaken her magic. *Which is exactly what's happening to the other initiates.*

'Who would want our people to survive, but to lessen our magic?' I asked.

273

Mer'esan shrugged. 'A reasonable question, but not the right one.'

I closed my eyes, trying to envision all the pieces of the puzzle, arranging them in my mind the way I would the complex geometries of a spell. 'You said before the war, we didn't have as many Jan'Tep mages as we do now, and they weren't as powerful as the ones today.'

'Yeah,' Reichis said, giving a snort. 'We call those "the good old days".'

I'd got so used to *not* thinking of him as a nekhek that I'd forgotten that the squirrel cats saw us as enemies.

'Hey, don't look at me,' he said, catching my stare. 'If my people were after yours we'd just sneak into your rooms at night and rip out your—'

'Eyeballs. Yes, I get it.'

Mer'esan tapped me on the forehead. 'Focus.'

'So the real question is, who has the most to gain by our mages being weaker?' *No, that's still not it.* This was just like casting a spell – you had to get every element exactly right for it to work.

All of a sudden, I had it. 'Who suffers most when those with magic become too powerful?'

Mer'esan smiled. 'Good. Clever. Now that you have the question, I believe you also have the answer.'

I did too. How many times had I sat in my room, panicking over what would happen if I couldn't spark my bands . . . getting more and more resentful every time Shalla or one of the others became more powerful? *Because I knew they'd lord it over me that much more, laugh at me, expect me to be their servant. Because that's what you do to people who don't have magic of their own.*

'Those who suffer most when magic becomes too powerful

274

are those without it,' I said. 'The Sha'Tep are the ones attacking us.'

Mer'esan nodded. 'As our magic grows, the gap between us becomes wider and wider. Every generation the Sha'Tep become more like slaves.'

'What's a slave?' asked Reichis. The other squirrel cat chittered at him, and after a few moments he looked up at me. 'Humans are disgusting.'

'Go,' Mer'esan said. 'If we are correct and the conspirators are Sha'Tep, then they will have taken your sister and the Argosi to the place that gives us our magic but where we ourselves cannot tread.'

'The oasis? But we go there all the time. It's where we learn to work our magic in the first place!'

'Is it the wellspring, or merely the fountain?'

'Stop testing me!' I said. 'My sister and my friend are in danger!' I looked down at the bands on my forearms, wishing I'd broken the silk band that might let me perform scrying spells before my parents had counter-banded it. *Only Mother said she'd already tried to find Shalla that way and couldn't. The wellspring or the fountain* . . . 'The mines . . . You're talking about the mines. The oasis is the source, but it's the ore from the mines that lets us create the inks for our bands.'

'So what?' Reichis asked.

'Mages can't enter the mines without getting sick from the raw ore. That's why the Sha'Tep have to extract it for us so that we can be banded with the six fundamental magics.'

Mer'esan reached out a finger and touched the top of my cheek just below my left eye. The sensation felt odd . . . like the vibration in the air when lightning is in the sky. 'Seven. There are seven magics, Kellen.'

275

In all the excitement of helping the dowager magus break the mind chain, and in the revelation of what my ancestors had done to the Mahdek, I had managed to forget the shadowblack that banded my eye and marked me forever, placed there by my own grandmother. 'Why did she do this to me?'

'Who can say? Perhaps it was madness, perhaps the disease had eaten away at her mind.'

The words came out before I could stop myself. 'I'm glad my father killed her. She deserved to die.'

Mer'esan withdrew her hand. 'The Seren'tia I knew was a wise woman, a mage of great skill and subtlety.'

'Until she went insane.'

The dowager magus looked at me, her expression not so much disapproving as . . . sad. 'We must make a choice, you and I. We must decide whether to hate the madwoman who tried to destroy you, or whether to believe that some part of your grandmother's soul remained, and perhaps she understood something that we do not. Magic is neither good nor evil; it is how we use it that dictates its purpose.'

'What purpose then? Why would my grandmother want me to have the shadowblack?'

'Only time will tell, and only if you survive long enough to walk the path before you.' She turned away from us and started walking deeper into the garden. 'My path leads me elsewhere.'

'Wait!' I called out. 'We have to stop the Sha'Tep conspirators! You have to help me –'

She paused, just for a moment. 'I have given three hundred years to our people, Kellen, most of those spent bound in a spell cast by the man I loved, and who loved me. I have been chained by magic, and now I am sick of it, and of the past.

The future belongs to you and to your generation. Only one task remains to me now.'

'What?' I demanded. 'What could possibly be more important than the future of our people?'

'I want to go for a walk in my garden,' she said, and began walking towards the wide beds of flowers and vines, her hands outstretched, reaching for them. With every step, the spells shimmering beneath her silken garments flickered. Soon they began to fade, and the skin beneath the cloth, and the muscles and bones beneath the skin, crumbled in on themselves. Before she'd touched a single petal, the dowager magus had become dust.

33

The Mine

The entrance to the mines was marked by weather-worn pillars covered in an unpleasant grey moss that gave off an eerie glow in the darkness. I crouched behind a nearby tree, expecting palace guards to come chasing after us at any moment. The forest all around was silent for the most part, the notable exception being my laboured breathing.

Without any more of the lightning weed, and compounded by everything else I'd been through over the last few days, it was all I could do to keep up with the damned squirrel cat.

Reichis seemed less than impressed with my stamina. 'Your people really can't—'

'Enough,' I said, holding on to my knees as I bent over to catch my breath. 'I get it. Humans are useless. Squirrel cats are the greatest hunters, trackers, runners, fighters . . . Did I miss anything? Poets, maybe?'

He gave a little snorting sound. 'You know I can understand sarcasm, right?'

I kept expecting his mother to give him a well-deserved bite as she seemed prone to doing, but somewhere along the road she'd left us. No doubt to return to the rest of the pack.

I glanced back the way we'd come at a barn about thirty yards behind us. We'd made a quick search of it, finding it empty except for a mottled black-and-grey horse that I was pretty sure belonged to Ferius.

Okay. So if Ferius was in the mine, there was a good chance Shalla was too. Which meant all I had to do was sneak through what had to be miles of tunnels, find Ferius and Shalla, free them and get them back out without being seen. Easy.

I glanced down at my forearms, just in case the silk band had sparked so that I could use mind clouding spells to mask our presence. It hadn't. Of course it hadn't, nor would it ever, now that my father had counter-banded me from ever wielding silk magic. *Okay, so not easy.*

I'd thought about trying to go for help, but Tennat and his brothers were still hunting me. Ra'fan would have me in a chain spell long before I reached the centre of town. Besides, even if I made it home, I'd no doubt end up strapped back down on that table with my father finishing the counter-banding. He wasn't likely to pay any attention to my incoherent screams about how the dowager magus had revealed to me that our people had cravenly massacred the Mahdek and now somehow the Sha'Tep – who nobody believed were capable of so much as talking back to a mage – had somehow hatched a plot to weaken the magic of Jan'Tep children.

No wonder Reichis hated us so much. It turned out we were pretty rotten.

Which is why it might not be such a good idea to place my life in the hands . . . or paws rather . . . of a creature that despises anything that walks on two legs. 'Do you really hate our kind?' I asked him.

'I don't hate *all* humans,' Reichis replied. 'The Mahdek were pretty much the most peaceful types you'd ever meet. Your people, on the other hand?' He gave a dismissive snort. 'Basically giant walking turds that try to ruin everything around them.'

'How would you know what the Mahdek were like? They all died before you were born.'

He tapped a paw against the side of his head. 'Squirrel cats have excellent tribal memory.'

I started to object and then realised I was coming perilously close to entering into a debate with a creature who most likely greeted other members of his species by sniffing their backsides.

'Enough talking,' he growled, and took off at a run for the mine entrance. 'Let's go save the Argosi and make the world a better place by killing off a few Jan'Tep.'

It was the smell that hit me first. I'd always imagined mines smelled like . . . well, nothing, really, but this one had the stale, rotten stench of stagnant water. Every time I opened my mouth to take in a breath I could practically taste the rancid air and dust all around us. How could anyone stand to work down here, day after day, extracting the ore to make banding inks that only served others?

And how could we make members of our own families live like this?

Reichis was right. My people really are horrible.

I'd have felt more guilty about my own complicity, but right then I was preoccupied with the small dank tunnel surrounding me. I'd never been this far underground before – which is how I'd managed to reach the age of fifteen before discovering that I was terrified of being trapped in small spaces.

'You okay, kid?' Reichis asked. 'You look worse than usual.'

'Shh!' I hissed fiercely. 'You want them to hear you?'

'I'm a squirrel cat, idiot. The only things other humans hear from me are animal noises.' He pointed with a paw up at what appeared to be a family of rats skittering along a groove inside the wall above us. 'There are always lots of those around, in case you hadn't noticed.'

In fact, I hadn't, but I wasn't about to admit that to him.

Reichis led the way, deeper and deeper into the mine, periodically stopping to sniff at the floor or the walls. He seemed to do it an awful lot, which made me wonder if his sense of smell was really as good as he claimed.

The tunnels were a more worrying concern though. We hadn't brought a light source with us, but thick patches of the glowing grey moss revealed just how rotten the wooden beams were that supported the sides and girded the roof above us. More than once we had to turn back because a passage was blocked by a cave-in.

We had another problem too.

'You sure you're all right, kid?' Reichis asked. 'You look—'

'Don't say it.'

He ambled over to me and sniffed. 'No, I'm serious. I think you might be sick or something.'

'Just tired,' I said, leaning a hand against the wall to support myself. The sudden wave of nausea was so strong that I had to force myself not to throw up. I couldn't remember ever feeling this awful, and I had a lot of experience with feeling awful. I looked down at the palm of my hand and saw red blisters beginning to form. When I looked back at the spot where I'd put my hand, I saw a thin vein of ore running like a crack in the wall.

'We must be getting close to the centre of the mine,' I whispered. 'Jan'Tep mages get sick down here. Master Osia'phest said the more powerful the mage, the worse it is in the mines.'

'So what do we do?' Reichis asked.

Ancestors . . . If it's bad for me, Shalla must be dying down here.

'We keep going.' I set off down the tunnel. 'I'm not much of a mage. Let's hope that's a good thing for once.'

It took us about twenty minutes to find out where they were holding Shalla and Ferius, and for me to discover that feeling nauseous was going to be the least of my problems.

'Three men,' Reichis said, scampering back to where I waited around the corner. 'They're wearing masks like those morons I chased away last time.'

'And you're sure Ferius and Shalla are there?' I kept my voice as low as I could, barely even a whisper.

He nodded, which looked disturbingly odd in a squirrel cat. 'The Argosi is there for sure, tied to some kind of post. There's a second human female on the ground, unconscious. I got a decent sniff off her from the air outside the room. She smells young, definitely Jan'Tep. Also, really arrogant if you ask me.'

'You can *smell* arrogance?'

He tilted his head at me. 'You can't?'

I couldn't tell whether he was making fun of me. Reichis seemed to have an entirely inappropriate sense of timing when it came to cracking jokes and being in mortal danger.

I got down on my hands and knees and crawled as silently

as I could to the end of the passage so I could peer around the corner.

There wasn't much to see in the dim light – their oil lanterns didn't add much illumination to what was already provided by the patches of grey moss. The men in the carved-out room didn't seem concerned about being discovered either. Two of them sat on chairs, laughing to each other, while a third appeared to be cooking something with several small braziers and metal pots. All three wore elaborate black lacquer masks like the ones I'd seen the night Shalla and I were attacked.

Ferius Parfax hung limply from one of the support beams, ropes at her wrists forcing her arms above her head. A second figure lay unconscious on the ground. I couldn't make her out in the shadows, but I was sure it was my sister.

'Well?' Reichis asked.

I crawled back around the corner and tried to think up a way to get Ferius and Shalla out of there. 'I'm thinking.'

'What's to think about? We go in there, kill the people we don't like and rescue the people we do. Simple.'

'There are three strong men in there, probably with weapons. What are we supposed to do with them?'

'Eat their tongues?' he suggested. 'Two for me, one for you?'

It was rapidly becoming apparent to me that, whatever his virtues, Reichis had a lousy sense of self-preservation. On the other hand, there was something oddly infectious about the little monster's excitement at the prospect of getting into a fight. Also, I was acutely aware that he was trying to greedily ensure more guards for himself.

What's wrong with me? When did I start looking for fights?

I realised then that something was changing inside me.

Maybe it had been for a while now. It could have been an after-effect of the lightning weed, or the strange connection I was forming with the squirrel cat. Maybe it was just because I now knew without a doubt that I was never again going to feel like a part of my clan or my family. My entire life I'd just assumed that, because of my parents, I was destined to be a great mage – a Jan'Tep hero like the ones in the stories I'd grown up on. Only I wasn't a hero. I wasn't special.

I was just really, really angry.

'Come on, kid,' Reichis chittered. 'Those sons of bitches aren't going to eat themselves.'

Sure, I thought. *No problem. Well, one problem.* 'I don't have a weapon,' I whispered.

'Just use your teeth,' was Reichis's remarkably unhelpful advice.

As we crept towards the room, I reached down and picked up a fist-sized rock from the tunnel floor.

Stick with what you know, I guess.

34

The Rescue

There are, if you believe the old stories, dozens of excellent ways for a lone hero and his faithful familiar to outwit and defeat superior numbers of enemies in his quest to save the captured princess. Unfortunately, all those methods require magic – a lot more of it than I could work with my meagre breath band. Also, I didn't exactly have a familiar. I had a . . . what was it Reichis had called it earlier? A business partner. It turns out that a 'business partner' is a lot like a familiar, only it doesn't do any of the things you ask it to do.

'We should create a distraction,' I whispered, looking around for something we could use for that purpose.

'No problem,' Reichis chittered. 'I can handle that.'

Without any warning, the squirrel cat leaped into the room, screeching and growling like a rabid creature gone mad. Apparently he hadn't understood that the point of the distraction was *not*, in fact, to spectacularly announce our presence to our enemies. With no other options left, I gripped the rock tighter and ran in after him.

I recognised the grotesque black lacquered masks on two of our opponents as the same as the ones worn by the men who'd attacked us when we'd tried to summon power animals. One had a pair of misshapen tusks and a wide-mouthed frown carved onto its surface, and the second had a terrifyingly angry third eye at its centre.

The third man here had a mask I hadn't seen before, mostly notable for long twisting ears on its sides. I briefly wondered if he felt bad at having been given the least intimidating mask, then noticed the long knife in his hand and decided that if he did, then he'd found a way to compensate.

Reichis went straight for Tusks, the biggest of the three, jumping high in the air to land on a narrow shelf carved into the tunnel wall, then using it as a platform to launch himself onto the big man's head. It seemed like a poor strategy given the lacquer mask would protect the man's face, but Reichis clambered over the top and dug his hind claws into the eye sockets. I heard a terrified shout as the man realised what was about to happen and tried to knock Reichis away. The squirrel cat jumped off, tearing a chunk of hair and scalp from the unprotected back of the man's head in the process.

'Nekhek!' Ears screamed.

'Don't be an idiot,' Third-Eye said, his knife held out as he faced off with the squirrel cat. 'Didn't you hear? They're not demons at all. Probably just some kind of ugly dog.'

Reichis growled in response, so incoherently furious that I had no idea what he was saying.

'Come here, mutt,' Third-Eye said, getting ready to grab at Reichis while Tusks recovered enough to pick up a heavy club. They were moving to corner the squirrel cat.

Neither of them had noticed me yet, so I ran up and brained Tusks with the rock. His head was harder than I'd hoped, and as he spun around he elbowed me in the chest, pinning me against the wall. Having no better ideas, I decided to follow Reichis's general approach and just kept hitting him with the rock again and again. I missed the side of his head, but caught him in the jaw, breaking off a piece of the lacquer mask and drawing a pained shout from him.

The third man, Ears, caught me around the middle and slammed me against the wall. I felt the air go out of me, but by a mixture of luck and instinct I managed to smash the rock down on his back while driving my knee as high as I could. I caught him in the chin, but I swear the pain that shot through my kneecap from the impact with his mask was worse than whatever I gave him.

I heard a loud grunt and turned to see Tusks kick Reichis, the toe of his boot hitting the squirrel cat full on and sending him flying backwards. I gave a scream and ran for Tusks, rock held high. He backed away from me so fast that his head hit the wall behind him and he looked as if he'd stunned himself. I turned back to the others only to see Third-Eye coming at me again, running past the post where they'd tied Ferius. At the last instant she stuck out her leg and he tripped over it.

Third-Eye landed face first on the hard, rocky floor. He wrapped a strong hand around my ankle and started pulling me down with him. I leaned over to try and knock him out with my rock, but Reichis beat me to it, leaping onto the man's back and clawing through his linen shirt and into his skin. Apparently this was just as painful as it looked, because within seconds Third-Eye had released my ankle. He scrambled on hands and knees and fled the room, desperately trying to dislodge Reichis, who kept chittering, 'Who's the mutt now, bitch? Who's the mutt now?'

'Reichis, get back here!' I shouted, even as I turned back

to face the other attackers. Fortunately Tusks was on the ground, unconscious, while Ears was on his hands and knees, still stunned from my earlier efforts with the rock. He raised his knife and swiped, trying to slash at my legs. I saw Ferius, still hanging from the post, raise one booted heel and then kick Ears in the side of the head. He went down hard and stayed there.

'Hey, kid,' she said, eyes barely able to focus on me. Even in the dim light I could see the bruises on her face and angry red welts around her neck. 'This your idea of a rescue?'

'It's not like I've had a lot of practice,' I countered. I was shaking, barely able to keep hold of the rock, which now felt slick with blood. 'How am I doing so far?'

She gave a hoarse chuckle. 'Untie these ropes and help me get your sister out of this damned mine and into some fresh air so I can have a smoke – then I'll let you know.'

I was in the process of doing just that when Reichis came racing back into the room. 'We have a problem.'

'What now?' I asked, using Third-Eye's abandoned knife to cut at the ropes holding Ferius's wrists.

Reichis looked oddly embarrassed. 'Turns out I was wrong when I said there was only three of them down here.'

35

The Tunnels

With Ferius free and Shalla now in my arms, we ran as fast as we could through the tunnels. That proved not to be very fast at all. It turned out I wasn't as strong as I'd always assumed, and it was all I could do to keep from dropping Shalla or falling flat on my face.

'Let me take her,' Ferius said. 'You're barely holding on.'

'And you're barely conscious,' I said.

She shook her head. 'Damned drugs. They forced something down my throat when they caught me. It's making me dizzy.'

I kept us moving, trying to listen for which tunnels might be clear. I could already hear the echoes of our pursuers' boots striking the rocky ground of the mine as they came after us. 'How many more men?' I asked.

'Five,' Reichis chittered.

'Six,' Ferius said. She glanced down at the squirrel cat. 'How many did he say?'

The next few seconds of running were punctuated by Ferius and Reichis arguing over who had the better hearing. It would have been less annoying if they didn't need me to translate. For my part, I didn't care who was right, but since I had no idea how well squirrel cats could count, I went with the higher number.

We hit another intersection, the narrowing tunnels splitting off in three separate directions, each equally dark, dank and menacing. Which way out?' I asked.

Ferius peered each way, eyes narrowed as she tried to fight off the dizziness from the drugs. 'About thirty yards straight ahead and then we turn right,' she said.

Reichis ran ahead then turned back. 'Can't go this way,' he said, and raced back past us.

Over the next few terrifying minutes we fell into a pattern, making turns or doubling back every time we heard the men in masks getting too close. Ferius would figure out the most likely path and Reichis would scout ahead, checking to see if it led out of the mine or into more danger.

The problem was, however good Ferius's guesses were, she'd only been in these tunnels once, and the men in masks knew them a lot better than we did. Every time we thought we were getting close to the exit, they managed to cut us off and we were forced to turn again.

'They're herding us deeper into the mine,' Reichis grumbled.

'Yeah,' Ferius agreed, once I translated. 'Reckon that's the point.'

With no other options, we just kept moving. I had to stop more frequently now, kneeling down to rest Shalla on my thighs to give my arms a moment's rest. I tried to wake her up, hoping she could run on her own, but the veins of ore in the tunnel walls that were making me feel sick must have been infinitely worse for someone with Shalla's magical ability.

We were slowing down, and our pursuers knew it. The

echoes of their footsteps were accompanied by laughter. The hyenas had almost run down their prey.

'You go, kid,' Ferius said, leaning against the wall. 'Me and the squirrel cat will slow them down while you—'

'I'm not leaving you here!'

'And when did I volunteer to die down here just so two lousy humans could live?' chittered Reichis.

'As it turns out,' a voice called from the tunnel behind us, 'no one is leaving here.'

Without a word, Ferius and I lifted Shalla from the floor, each taking one arm across our shoulders as we half ran, half stumbled down the passageway, driven by nothing more than panic and a last burst of strength.

The sounds of pursuit followed, but they slowed, becoming almost leisurely. We reached the end of the tunnel and hit a dead end.

'Sha'Tep miners have to spend most of their lives learning these tunnels,' the voice called out, closer than he'd been before. 'One wrong turn and you fall into a sinkhole, or wind up lost in the miles of empty passages. You could die in a cave-in and your corpse would rot for years before anyone discovered it. Do you even have any idea how lost you are right now?'

We turned and saw six figures in black lacquer masks coming towards us, each one unique, with its own horrible features. The one in front bore twin curved horns, one red, one black. He'd been the leader of the three who'd attacked us in the forest.

'I'm sorry it's come to this, Kellen,' he said, the mask muffling his words even as the reverberations along the cave walls lent them a frightening, other-worldly quality. Even with

291

all of that, I wondered why I hadn't recognised his voice before.

As gently as I could, I took Shalla's other arm from Ferius and set her down on the cavern floor. When I rose again, I balled my hands into fists and turned to face the leader of the Sha'Tep conspiracy. 'Hello, Uncle Abydos,' I replied.

NINE of LEAVES

THE FOURTH TRIAL

The most powerful magics are those kept most secret. A Jan'Tep mage must be able to uncover hidden lore, but equally he must be able to discover the secrets of his enemies. Only then has he truly earned his mage's name.

36

The Traitor

'I should have known it would be you who figured it out,' Abydos said. He removed his mask and handed it to one of his men. 'You always were smarter than your parents or your teachers gave you credit for.'

I'm also good at bluffing, Uncle. I relaxed my hands and held them out in front of me, my fingers taking the shape of a particularly nasty ember spell. 'I'd rather not set your intestines on fire, since we're related, so you'd better stay back.'

All things considered, I sounded remarkably calm and confident. *I think I might be getting better at this lying-all-the-time thing.*

Several of the men in masks laughed. One of them pointed at me. 'Look there, the little mage thinks he's going to use spells on us! Here, in the mines!'

Abydos spoke more gently. 'Jan'Tep magic is much harder to work down here, Kellen, that's why your sister is faring so poorly.'

I whispered to Ferius. 'Don't suppose you have your razor-sharp steel cards?'

She shook her head. 'They took my waistcoat when they

captured me.' She shouted down the tunnel at them. 'Along with my damned smoking reeds!'

Tusks came barrelling towards us. 'That's not all we'll take, you lousy Argosi—'

My uncle put a restraining hand on his shoulder. 'Stop. I told you before, this woman saved my nephew's life. Let's have no more violence than is absolutely necessary.'

I felt the impulse to explain that he'd already done plenty of harm, but Ferius took a step forward, fists up as if she meant to challenge them all. 'Well, I hate to disappoint you, but unless you and your little masked theatre group let us pass, I predict there's going to be a whole lot of violence in the near future for you.'

Abydos ignored her, walking towards us, eyes on me. Reichis clambered up my back to sit on my shoulder. His growl sounded surprisingly loud in the cramped tunnel. 'Just give me the word, kid, and I'll rip this one's face off and make my own mask with it.'

I decided to translate for my uncle. He didn't seem nearly as scared as I would've hoped. He just stood right in front of me and said, 'Don't do this, Kellen. We're not your enemies. We're your people, your true family.'

'You kidnapped my sister and attacked my friend. I'd say that makes us enemies.'

One of the other men drew his knife. 'Stop wasting time. We can't take a chance on—'

'Be quiet,' Abydos said, and for the first time in my life I heard my father's commanding tone coming from my uncle's lips. 'Listen carefully, Kellen. You and the others are going to come with us now. You can carry Shalla if you like, or my men will carry her for you.'

298

'You're not touching my sister ever again.'

'She's not your sister, Kellen, not in any way that matters. She's Jan'Tep. She's one of them.'

The strength in his voice, the raw confidence that I'd never had in myself, made me feel so weak I could barely stand. 'Why can't you just let us go?' I hadn't meant it to sound like begging, but it did.

'Because the world doesn't work that way, Kellen, and this isn't just about you and me. I'm taking you somewhere now, for your own good. If you try to run, or if any of you attack, I'll kill the animal. Do you understand? I'll kill the Argosi. I'll even kill my niece if I have to.' He locked eyes with me. 'Do you believe me, Kellen?'

I tried to look away, but I couldn't. I felt trapped in the unwavering certainty of his gaze. My entire life I'd ignored my uncle, always seeing him as a pale shadow of the man my father was. Now I understood that I'd had it wrong the whole time. 'I believe you.'

'Good,' he said, and turned to walk back down the tunnel, not even bothering to make sure we followed. 'You always were the smart one.'

Abydos led us on a winding journey further into the mine. Despite my earlier defiance that I wouldn't let anyone touch Shalla, my arms finally gave out. When my uncle saw that I was lagging behind, he ordered his men to carry her. I didn't have the strength to resist.

At first the tunnels we passed through were very much like the ones we'd been running through before – shabby, worn, the rotten timber supporting the ceiling looking as if it could give out at any moment. After a few minutes, though, we entered a different part of the mine. It was like leaving a Sha'Tep hovel and entering the marble and limestone sanctum of a lord magus. The tunnel walls were perfectly smooth, almost polished. Every few yards a pair of thick columns, almost like those that ringed the oasis, supported the ceiling above us. I looked up and saw symbols etched in metallic inks, which after a while I realised represented the stars we could see above the city at night.

'Impressive, isn't it?' Abydos asked.

Reichis gave a little chitter on my shoulder. 'What's the point? If you want to see stars, just look outside.'

'How long has all this been here?' I asked.

My uncle shook his head. 'Who can say? Centuries, certainly.' He ran a hand along one of the smooth walls. 'The Mahdek had a flair for architecture.'

I tried to hide my surprise. It didn't work.

My uncle chuckled. 'Yes, Kellen, we know the truth about the Mahdek, about the oasis, about all of it.'

How could they know? Mer'esan had been the only one who knew the secret, and she'd been bound in a mind chain for centuries to keep her from revealing it.

'Ha, just look at him,' one of the other men said from behind his black lacquer mask. 'His little mind is breaking apart trying to imagine how the Sha'Tep could know something the mages don't.'

'It wasn't through some elaborate deduction, if that makes you feel any better,' Abydos said. He stopped and motioned down one of the side tunnels, where rockfall separated this section of the mine from the shabbier parts. 'We didn't know these tunnels existed until recently.'

One of Abydos's men gave a loud cough, then said, 'The

Jan'Tep always want more and more ore, to make more ink, to tattoo their precious bands. They don't give a damn about the men and women who have to get it for them. We have to keep digging deeper and deeper, but we don't have the means to reinforce the tunnels properly. Every year, more cave-ins. Every year, more Sha'Tep killed. Wasted lives and wasted deaths!' There was a terrible anger and grief beneath his words.

Abydos put a hand on the man's shoulder. 'One life wasn't wasted though, Paetep. Her loss revealed the original mine, the one with the richest veins of ore. The one the Jan'Tep ancestors collapsed so no one would ever enter it again.'

The richer veins of ore explained why I was feeling weaker all the time. I could see Shalla in the hands of one of my uncle's men. Her skin was a sickly pale grey. I had to figure out a way to get her out of here before it was too late. 'Why would our ancestors have closed the mine? We need the ore.'

'Most likely because they hadn't known they'd need the banding until after they'd taken the oasis. The magics of this land don't come as naturally to the Jan'Tep as they did to the Mahdek. So it was only after they'd brought down the mine that they realised they still needed the ore.'

Paetep stopped and stood in front of me, his big chest rising and falling, barely restrained rage showing in every twitch of his limbs. 'Our whole lives they lie to us, making us believe they were the ones who created the city we live in and the oasis that protects us. It's our role to serve them so they can serve the clan, that's what we're told.' I could smell the heat of his breath. 'Liars. Every one of them.' He kept clenching and unclenching his fists.

301

'Take a step back, friend,' Ferius said. 'I'm just starting to like the kid.'

Two of the other men started moving towards her. Even with masks covering their faces, I could sense how wound up they were.

Reichis hopped from my shoulder to Ferius's. 'Oh, please, tell me the talking is over and I can start with the eyeballs.'

Ferius, even if she didn't understand his words, caught his meaning. She gave a little chuckle. 'See, boys, that crap you shoved down my throat is starting to wear off now. Me and the squirrel cat are itching for a fight, so if you want to take a swing at me, go ahead.'

Even though her voice was calm, there was something reckless in her eyes. She looked angrier than I'd ever seen her. I actually felt relief when Abydos called his men off. 'This gets us nowhere,' he said, pushing them along the tunnel. 'The Jan'Tep that rule now aren't even to blame for what's been done to us. They've been repeating a lie told to them for so long that they don't even know it's a lie any more.'

'But you reckon you got it all figured out, Aby?' Ferius asked.

'Not at first,' he admitted. Then he pointed to the end of the passageway where an arched marble entranceway led into darkness. 'But then we found the mausoleum.'

37

The Chamber

The space we entered was the largest we'd seen in the mines, over thirty feet across, the ceiling almost as high. The effort to carve it out, to lay the foundations and put in supports, must have been staggering, and yet it was the shape of the space that took my breath away.

What Abydos had called the 'mausoleum' was seven-sided, and each wall was covered with intricate sigils, some of which I recognised, most of which I was sure weren't in any book or scroll or even in the mind of any Jan'Tep spellmaster in any of our cities. I stood facing one of the walls and held up my right forearm with its sparked breath band. There were nine sigils on my band, each one a different form of breath magic from which spells might be constructed, if I had the power. The wall opposite me had dozens.

'It's an arcanum,' I said, but no one even noticed. Of the people there, only Shalla would have cared, and she was unconscious.

'Put the girl down there,' Abydos told his men. 'On the altar.'

Towards the middle of the room, a set of stairs descended from each of the seven walls, leading to a recessed area at the very centre that reflected the shape of the room itself but was only large enough for a simple stone table.

'Why are they putting Shalla on the altar?' I asked.

'Better than the floor,' Abydos replied.

Reichis hopped off my shoulder and started sniffing around. 'Lot of dead people in here.'

He was right. I'd been so focused on the inscriptions of spells that I hadn't noticed the dozens of three-foot-square openings carved into the lower sections of the walls. Inside each one lay a body, wrapped over and over in thick strips of linen, the covered heads facing out towards us. This wasn't part of the funerary practices of my people; nor were the black lacquer masks covering the faces of the dead.

'Funeral masks,' Abydos said, removing one and handing it to me. His casual treatment of the deceased felt wrong to me, but my uncle seemed untroubled. 'It took me weeks of sitting here, staring at these things, to figure out that the Mahdek had never worshipped demons at all. They feared them.'

'Then why the masks?' I asked.

'Superstition, or possibly just tradition. I suspect they believed the mask would frighten off any demons that came for them in the eternal darkness.'

'And you desecrate the dead, without a second thought,' Ferius said. 'Wearing the masks to scare your own people. You sure are a brave bunch.'

'They aren't *our* people!' Tusks shouted, tearing the mask off his face. He was younger than I expected, with sandy brown hair and soft features. I doubted he was more than a couple of years older than me. 'My people are treated like servants. We can't choose our own work, we can't marry without permission. We can't even . . .' He stopped, looking as if all the air had gone out of him.

'The Sha'Tep are forbidden from having children,' Abydos said. He nodded to where Shalla lay on the table in the lower section of the room. 'The great houses want only more mages like her.' He reached out a hand to my cheek. 'If the lords magi had their way, those like you and me would—'

'I'm not Sha'Tep,' I said, pushing his hand away.

'That's what we all tell ourselves,' Abydos said. '"It's just temporary . . . My magic will come back if I just wish it hard enough."'

A man older than my uncle removed his mask. 'It wasn't always this way. Once we were soldiers as often as servants. Some of us trained as scholars and diplomats. We even had our own seats on the council. But year after year, generation after generation, people like your father take away more and more of our rights.'

'Why didn't you speak up?' I asked, as ashamed as I was angered by their words. 'Why not demand your rights?'

'Our grandfathers and grandmothers tried,' said a woman, her face hidden beneath a horrific fanged mask. 'Just like their grandmothers and grandfathers before them. Each time they were punished. Pain spells. Mind chains. *Magic.*' She said the word as if it were something filthy and disgusting.

I looked up at Abydos, my uncle, who I'd spent my whole life believing was the mild, contented fellow who happily brought us our food and took care of our home. 'Father would have listened,' I said. 'He would never—'

'Ke'heops is the worst of them all,' he said, cutting me off even as he turned away from me. 'When we were children . . . you could never have found two boys more alike. We

305

were best friends. We did everything together: laughing, looking out for each other, finishing each other's thoughts. Then one morning he began sparking his bands.' Abydos held up his arms, the lines of the sigils so faint they just looked like old scars. 'I didn't, and from that day forth the brother that I'd loved, that I'd protected, treated me like little more than a useful pet.'

'Sounds like a hard life,' Ferius said. 'A brave man might stand up and fight to change it. He just wouldn't do it by hurting children.'

Abydos strode towards her, his face as much a mask of rage as any of the black lacquer ones worn by his followers. For a moment I thought he might strike her, but he calmed himself and his voice was almost pleading. 'Don't you understand? I'm doing this for Kellen!'

'For me? What are you talking about?'

'When the others first approached me with their plan, I refused. I said I loved my family.' He turned to me. 'What good is my love if all I do is stand by while your parents destroy the magic inside you that you long for so much, even more than Ke'heops ever did.'

'They thought I had the shadowblack,' I said. 'They were trying to protect me.' The words sounded utterly unconvincing even to me.

'They were protecting *her*,' Abydos said. He walked down the stairs to where she lay unconscious on the table. 'Shalla – who has none of her mother's kindness, and all of her father's arrogance. Shalla, who would one day become a monster worse than any of them, if we gave her the chance.'

I started after him, but two of the men grabbed me before I took a step. 'Uncle, what are you doing?'

He bent down to the floor and lifted up a narrow tray, which he set down next to her on the table. I saw the flames of six small braziers. Above each one rested a tiny clay jar bearing a symbol representing the liquefied metal within. A piece of loosely wrapped silk sat on the right side of the tray, the kind that might be used to hold writing implements, but which I knew contained a set of long, thin needles, one for each jar.

'I'm doing this for you, Kellen. I couldn't stop Ke'heops from denying you your magic, but you and I can make him pay for what he's done to you. We can do it together.'

He looked back up at me, a terrible love in his eyes that held me more than any binding spell, more than the men who gripped my arms. 'You . . .' My voice was barely a whisper. I was so desperate not to say the words but somehow unable to stop myself. 'You're counter-banding Shalla for me.'

How many times had I resented Shalla for the luck she'd never earned, for the way magic came to her so easily. How many times had I secretly wished she would fail, that her bands wouldn't spark. How many times, lying there strapped to that table over the past days, had I wished my parents would burn the counter-sigils into her skin instead of mine, and take the magic away from her forever.

'Shalla had nothing to do with any of this,' I said, to myself as much as to Abydos. 'She tried to help me find my magic.'

'Shalla is the worst of all of them.' Abydos's voice was soft, almost regretful. 'I tried . . . in my own small way I've tried to get her to change, but she is a perfect replica of Ke'heops in female form, only she will be stronger than he ever was, when she comes into her power. She'll be the worst tyrant our people have ever seen.' He shook his head and looked back up at me. 'She will treat you as a pet at best and a slave at worst, Kellen.'

'You don't know the future,' Ferius Parfax said. 'Even the wisest of us doesn't know that.'

'Perhaps not, Argosi.' To me he said, 'Look in your heart and tell me I'm wrong, Kellen. Tell me that Shalla will still call you brother the day after you're made Sha'Tep.'

I wanted to. I wanted to call him a liar and say he didn't understand Shalla, that underneath the arrogance she was different. I wanted to tell him that she'd always love me as her brother, but I couldn't. I couldn't be sure it was true.

Abydos picked up one of the needles and dipped it into one of the heated ceramic jars. 'Did you know that it's easier for a Sha'Tep to inscribe the counter-sigils than for one of the Jan'Tep? The very magic that courses through their veins rebels against the act, as though it were a kind of desecration.'

'How did you learn the counter-sigils? Only the lords magi know their forms.'

'Your father of course. I don't think he meant to leave them unlocked in his study, but he was distracted while stealing your future from you.' He held up the needle. A single drop of liquid copper dangled from its end. 'I will show you how. We can do this together.'

'You'll show me how . . .' The Jan'Tep were monsters, as cruel to their own Sha'Tep brothers and sisters today as they had been to the Mahdek they'd massacred three hundred years ago. My father spoke of honour and doing what was best for our house, but that had only meant doing what was best for him. My uncle . . . My uncle had suffered in silence my entire life until I'd set off this chain of events, from cheating at my duel with Tennat, to Shalla nearly killing me, to my father unwittingly revealing how he'd suppressed my magic my whole life. Now my uncle had finally found a way to help me get back at the world.

'*We can do this together.*'

'Uncle Abydos?' I said.

He put down the needle. 'Yes, Kellen?'

'I'm ready now. Tell your men to let me go.'

He nodded and the men on either side of me released my arms.

'I'm going to come down there and take my sister,' I said. 'Then Ferius and Reichis and I are going to carry her out of here, back up to the surface, where I'm going to put her on the horse in the barn and take her home.'

'I can't let you do that,' he said, the expression on his face so sad and lonely that I genuinely felt as if I were disappointing him.

'If you try to stop me, Uncle, I'll kill you.'

38

The Bluff

Abydos set the needle down on the tray and began walking up the stairs towards me. Out of the corner of my eye I saw his men readying their weapons. Ferius shifted her weight, no doubt preparing some manoeuvre to give her an edge when the fight began.

Reichis clambered up my leg and back onto my shoulder. 'Finally. Which one do I get to kill first?'

'I think the animal's going to attack,' the young sandy-haired man warned, his knife at the ready. He moved into position next to Abydos.

The deep rage that had led me to threaten my uncle dissipated far faster than I would have thought possible, replaced by the cold, hard reality of our situation. There were just too many of them. Ferius, for all her taunts, was still groggy from the drugs they'd given her to fight them off. I'd used up what little strength the mine hadn't already sapped by carrying Shalla further than my arms could handle. Even Reichis, for all his posturing, seemed to know that we couldn't win this fight.

'This would be a good time for a really powerful spell,' he chittered in my ear.

'I've got one that channels a light breeze,' I said, ignoring the confused looks of my uncle and his followers. 'Think that'll work?'

Reichis gave a sigh. 'Why did I ever agree to partner up with a magic-less skinbag?'

'I think because your mother ordered you to.'

'That's dirty fighting.'

Okay, so we can't win this with magic, and we can't win it with weapons. What I really needed was some kind of ingenious ruse. Didn't I used to be good at that? I'd tricked Tennat into beating himself in our initiates' duel. *Problem is, one gullible bully is easier to bluff than six deadly serious men and women.* What I needed was a way to reduce their numbers so that Ferius, Reichis and I could make a move. *Okay, so what weakness does a conspiracy have?* The answer hit me like a blast of ember magic. *Trust.* 'There's something you failed to consider about this great rebellion of yours, Uncle.'

He gave a low chuckle, and smiled to the other Sha'Tep. 'You see what I told you? Always some trick or scheme rolling around in his head. Never lets anyone see when he's scared. Never backs down.'

'This whole plan of yours is vulnerable – it relies on the Sha'Tep who live and work in the great houses poisoning the initiates from those families.'

'It's not poison,' one of the women said defensively. 'It just lessens their connection to the power of the oasis.'

'Which will make the lords magi believe the bloodlines are weakening,' I said, following the train of logic.

The young man with the sandy hair nodded, apparently excited that I'd worked it out. 'With the clan prince dead, the council are terrified that the Berabesq will try to take advantage of our weakness to once again try to destroy us, or that the Daroman military will come to conquer us.'

The big man who'd worn the tusked mask spoke up. 'When they see barely a handful of initiates becoming mages, they'll realise how much they need the Sha'Tep. The mages don't have the strength to pick up weapons. They don't know how to fight or what it feels like to ache from hard labour.'

'Exactly,' Abydos said. 'The Jan'Tep will finally understand that they need us, not as servants, but as equals.'

I shook my head in disgust. 'Ancestors! No wonder there's never been a Sha'Tep conspiracy before. You people are terrible at this.'

'Don't,' Abydos warned. 'Don't mock these people and the risk they take.'

Okay, time to see how gullible you are, Uncle. 'One of them has betrayed you.'

'What? Who?' the older man asked.

'No one,' Abydos said. 'He's just trying to stall.'

I took a chance and pushed back. 'How can you be so stupid? Of course I was bluffing before – I was hoping Shalla would wake. But then I realised just how careless you've all been.' Now that I thought about it, they really *had* been careless, which made it all the more easy to make my ploy sound believable. 'Ra'meth knows! You haven't launched some grand rebellion. All you've done is to turn over power to our family's greatest enemy!'

'What are you talking about?'

I started to weave recent events into my story. 'The day after Tennat and his brothers attacked Ferius, Tennat showed up at the oasis and his magic was weakened. He couldn't cast any spells.'

312

'We got to him just like we got to the others,' the big man said proudly.

'Except that the next night he was casting blood sympathy spells! And just hours ago he was using silk and iron magic to track me! Don't you see? Ra'meth figured out what you were doing and caught the Sha'Tep who was poisoning Tennat.'

'Don't be ridiculous,' Abydos said. 'Sephan here –' he indicated the young man with the sandy hair – 'is Ra'meth's personal servant. He'd know if anyone in the House of Ra had found out.'

I leaned back against the wall, letting my exhaustion show through. 'You know, Uncle, all my life I thought that the main difference between you and my father was that you didn't have magic. Now I know it's that you're incredibly dumb.' I pointed to Sephan. 'Ra'meth put a mind chain on him. His will is bound and he can't even do anything that would let you see that he's been caught.'

My uncle and the others looked over at Sephan, who looked back at them in confusion. 'I don't know what he's talking about. I'm fine. I couldn't get any more of the compound into Tennat's food that night. Everything will be fine.'

'Except you'd have no choice but to say that if you were mind-chained,' the big man pointed out.

I had to hold back my sigh of relief. I'd given, I thought, an excellent performance. The fear and then the anger on my face had been believable, and my lie was just credible enough to create doubt in their minds.

My deception had only one flaw, which had already started to squirm around in the back of my mind. There was a reason why my story was so convincing.

313

It turned out to be true.

'Well, well, well,' a voice said from down the corridor in the mausoleum. 'This all sounds positively dire.'

It was Ra'meth.

39

The Hero

It says something about how much I hated and feared Ra'meth that my first reaction was to try to hit him with a spell.

'Breath magic?' He looked amused. 'That's really the best we can hope for from the son of the great Ke'heops?' He made a tiny gesture with one hand and whispered a single syllable. I found myself paralysed. The lord magus turned as he gazed at each of the walls in the mausoleum. 'Absolutely remarkable. This will make my ascension as clan prince an even more memorable accomplishment for our people.'

Reichis sprang into the air, only to collide with something invisible before falling to the ground. The squirrel cat growled, rearing up to launch himself at the mage, but Ra'meth uttered a second spell and Reichis fell unconscious. 'I really thought we'd killed all those filthy creatures centuries ago.'

'How is this possible?' one of the Sha'Tep conspirators asked, straining against invisible bonds. 'Mages can't work spells here in the mines.'

The corners of Ra'meth's mouth rose in a jackal's grin. 'I won't lie to you. It's not as easy as it looks. The compounds I had to drink have some rather unpleasant intestinal side effects. Nonetheless, they do counteract the effects of close proximity to the ore.' The lord magus brought his palms together as if in prayer, then turned them so the backs faced each other before intertwining the fingers together. Suddenly we were all falling, tumbling as if the entire chamber were spinning at great speed. I felt myself hit one of the walls and stuck there as if dozens of hands were holding my limbs immobile.

'You see,' Ra'meth said to Abydos and his followers, 'the reason mages do not mine the ore ourselves is not that it's impossible for us, simply that it's beneath us.'

'Jan'Tep bastard!' Tusks shouted, but for all his anger and size, he was trapped like a fly inside an invisible web.

The trick to resisting a binding spell isn't pulling against it on a physical level, you have to set your mind against it, willing it to break apart. With every fibre of my being I commanded the spell to shatter, but I might as well have been trying to crush an ocean with my bare hands.

Ra'meth seemed to find my exertions amusing. 'I've seen your father breach much stronger shackles many times, you know. It's not that hard – just a matter of will.' He approached me without a trace of fear that I would break the spell. 'Come, Kellen of the House of Ke. Are you not your father's son? Show me the strength of your bloodline.'

'Leave the boy alone,' Abydos said, struggling against his own bonds. 'Kellen has nothing to do with this.'

Ra'meth stopped. 'Nothing? You do the boy a disservice. None of this would have been possible without him.' He reached down and took hold of my wrist. To me it felt as if thick iron manacles held it against the wall, but Ra'meth lifted it up effortlessly to scrutinise the bands on my forearms. 'Ke'heops does excellent work. Very precise. I doubt a hundred mages working in concert could break these counter-sigils.'

He looked up at me. 'Your father must have risked a great deal of his strength in order to so utterly bind you.'

Well, I thought, fighting off the bitterness that threatened to engulf me, *it's not hard to see where Tennat gets his shining personality.*

'I warn you, do not harm him!' Abydos shouted, straining so hard I could see the veins in his neck sticking out.

A flicker of pain passed over Ra'meth's features. 'That is a remarkable calibre of will you have, Abydos. I don't think I've ever felt someone push so hard against a binding spell. You would have made a powerful mage had you been able to spark your bands.'

'I don't need your magic,' Abydos said, pulling against the invisible shackles holding him to the wall. 'I don't need any filthy Jan'Tep spells to deal with you. I'm a man! Do you hear me? A man!'

Again Ra'meth flinched, tensing the muscles of his right hand to draw more of the iron magic through his band. 'Will you stop that? You're giving me a headache.'

As my uncle tried to fight back against Ra'meth's binding spell, I racked my brain to see some kind of way out of this. Shalla was still unconscious, Reichis had passed out on the floor and Ferius was as trapped as I was. My experience of life thus far led me not to expect people to miraculously come to save me, so all that was left was to try to talk my way out of this. 'You're not seeing the whole picture, Lord Magus,' I began.

'Oh, do shut up, boy.' He made a twisting motion with the thumb and middle fingers of his left hand and suddenly I couldn't speak.

Guess that leaves hoping for some kind of miracle. My people aren't religious by nature, having left such superstitions behind generations ago. *So probably no miracles either.*

'Don't you dare silence him,' Abydos said. 'Or are you afraid of words now, you coward?'

'You can be quiet too,' Ra'meth replied, and cast the same spell on Abydos.

It's incredibly difficult to keep multiple spells working at once, so I supposed one hope was that Ra'meth would over-extend himself and one of us could attack. He glanced around the room. 'Now, if you don't mind, I need to figure out how it all happened.'

Ra'meth turned to the man who'd worn the one-eyed mask. 'Right. You were doing something . . . unseemly to poor Shalla when, in a burst of desperation, she broke through the terrible drugs you gave her and hit you with a –' he looked over at me – 'lightning spell? Does that sound like something your sister might do? Never mind.' He turned back to Paetep, the man who'd lost his wife in a cave-in. 'Everyone likes a good lightning spell.' With a snap of the thumb and little finger of both hands he sent a bolt of white-and-yellow light that struck the man through the chest.

Static crackled, accompanied by the smell of charred flesh. Paetep was dead.

Breaking through the silencing spell, Abydos unleashed a bellow of pure rage.

'You really are a strong fellow,' Ra'meth said, momentarily touching a hand to his brow. 'Now, what's next?' He turned to Sephan. 'Right. You, my fine and loyal servant, died during an act of sublime courage. Realising you'd done wrong by your house, you tried to stop Abydos from wreaking more havoc on our people. Alas, he strangled you.'

Ra'meth touched the fingers of both hands to his lips and then reached out with them. Sephan writhed, his body sliding slowly up the wall, legs shaking and jerking beneath him. Ra'meth closed his hands into fists and I heard a cracking sound as Sephan's neck broke.

'You bastard,' Abydos said, once again defying the silencing spell. Once more he set himself against the invisible shackles of Ra'meth's binding spell. With an inner strength I could scarcely fathom, he took a step forward.

'Stop,' Ra'meth commanded.

Abydos took a second step. 'You shouldn't have come here alone, Lord Magus.' The air was practically shivering around him, as if the wind itself were trying to hold him still, but Abydos wouldn't stop. 'But what mage ever thinks he might need help to kill a Sha'Tep?' A third step.

'You will not come closer,' Ra'meth said, pouring more of his will into the spell. He'd made a mistake though, by binding so many of us; he didn't have the focus to cast defensive spells.

Step by step, inch by inch, Abydos pushed forward.

'How is this possible?' Ra'meth asked, struggling now. 'You have no magic.'

'No magic,' Abydos repeated. Blood began to seep from the corners of his mouth, then his ears, and finally from his mouth. This was killing him, and yet he kept going, his arms now outstretched, reaching for Ra'meth's throat. 'Just a man. One Sha-Tep man who is tired of your coward's magic.'

'No!' Ra'meth said, trying to move away even as my uncle's hands wrapped around his neck.

Suddenly the shackles were gone, from all of us. The binding spells that had continued holding up the bodies of the dead

319

men fell away, and they slumped to the ground. Now that I could move and speak again, I rushed to help Abydos.

My uncle's eyes were now filled with blood and I knew he couldn't see me, but as he squeezed the life from Ra'meth, he smiled. His face beamed with so much pride that he looked like the statue of an ancient hero come to life. That smile was still on his face as Ra'meth's own eyes closed. It was still there too as a half-dozen knives, flying through the air like a flock of birds, struck Abydos in the back, lifted him in the air and carried him away from Ra'meth.

I shouted my uncle's name and tried to run to him, but a new binding spell was upon me. For a moment he hung suspended. His eyes blinked away the blood. He turned his head to me and said, 'If I'd had a son . . .'

I tried to reach for him but my limbs wouldn't respond. All I could do was watch in horror as the blades slipped out of Abydos's body and he fell to the ground, eyes staring up at the ceiling. One by one the knives drove down, impaling each of his hands, his feet and finally his chest.

I screamed then, and kept screaming even after a silencing spell prevented any sound from escaping my lips.

For most of my life I had thought my uncle a simple, contented servant, then a vicious traitor to our people. Only in the final seconds of his life had I seen him for the complicated, indomitable man he really was.

A man in blue robes entered the room, ahead of another mage in white. 'Are you injured, Lord Magus?' he asked.

Ra'meth rose to his feet, his hand rubbing at his neck. 'A little bruised, but wiser for it.' He looked down at my uncle's broken body. 'You were right, Abydos. It would have been terribly arrogant for me to come here alone.'

40

Floating

I was floating in the air, my body slowly drifting through the winding tunnels of the mine like a twig caught in the current of a slow-moving stream. I lifted my head and looked behind me to see Ferius, Shalla and Reichis all floating along with me, but they appeared to be asleep. It felt so much like flying that I wondered if I might be sleeping too, until I heard the mage in blue ask, 'Where would you like them, Lord Magus?'

I turned my head and saw Ra'meth leading us outside. He pointed to a barn down the path. 'In there should do nicely.' He looked over at me and nodded. 'Ah, good. Let's finish our story, shall we?'

'What have you done to the others?'

'Your sister will be sick for some time, I'm afraid. She spent far too long in the mines. As for the Argosi and the nekhek, they were beginning to annoy me so I put them to sleep.' He patted me on the shoulder. 'But let's talk about you. Brave and brilliant lad that you are, you tracked your filthy uncle and his co-conspirators to this place where you uncovered their nefarious plot.'

We neared the barn and he motioned for the mage in white to open the doors. 'Alas, they captured you, and, Sha'Tep being rather vicious when given the chance, they . . .' He paused, then looked to the other two mages. 'Any recommendations?'

'Fire, Lord Magus?' the one in white suggested.

'Ah, fire! Excellent.'

The mage in blue sent Shalla's body floating into the barn, where it drifted down to the ground, followed by Ferius and then Reichis. 'Do you know why the Sha'Tep love fire so much?' Ra'meth asked as I floated past him. 'It's because it's the closest they'll ever come to wielding true magic. That's why they locked you all in here and set fire to the barn.'

One of Ra'meth's men presented him with an unlit torch. The lord magus closed his eyes, formed a set of somatic shapes and then spoke a single word. The torch ignited instantly. He made a second gesture and the flames were reduced to a red glow, perfectly controlled by Ra'meth's will. 'You probably haven't learned the spell for thirstfire, have you?' His man tossed the torch into the barn, where Ferius's horse stood tethered to a post, already rearing and bucking in fear. 'You can try putting it out if you like.'

They shut the door and I heard it being barred from the outside. I got to my feet and started pounding on it, screaming for them to let us out. Once Ra'meth unleashed the thirstfire, nothing would stop it until everything inside the barn was burnt to ashes.

'What's with all the shouting, kid?' Reichis said. He took a few wobbling steps towards me. 'Gods-damned Jan'Tep magic. Just give me a minute and I'll rip that skinbag's throat out.'

'Remarkable,' Ra'meth said, from the other side of the door. 'The nekhek has already broken the sleep binding. Let's see if he's equally resistant to fire, shall we?'

'The lords magi will find out what you did,' I shouted, still banging on the thick wooden wall between us. 'You'll never become clan prince!'

'Really? But I'm a hero, don't you see? I'm the one who found you in the burning wreckage of this barn. Too late to save you, alas, far too late. In a rage, I risked my own life to enter the mines to confront the man who murdered you. Imagine my horror when I discovered the culprit was your own flesh and blood. In an act of righteous vengeance, I killed the traitors who had slaughtered you and your sister.'

'My father will kill you for this,' I yelled. 'Unless my mother gets to you first!'

Ra'meth laughed, a soft, musical sound, neither angry nor fearful. 'You are quite correct, Kellen. My whole life I've never been as strong as your father, or your mother for that matter.'

He went silent for several seconds. I kept expecting the torch to burst into unquenchable flame, but it remained with its tightly controlled crimson glow. Ra'meth, it seemed, wasn't done tormenting me yet.

'If I'm being completely honest,' he said, 'I'd come to believe that I would never dare set my magic against theirs. But then something remarkable happened. You, a weakling boy, mere weeks from being declared Sha'Tep, bested my own son Tennat. Not through any strength of yours, mind you, but by using his against him. That was when I saw my path to victory. I would defeat your father exactly as you defeated my son.'

'Except that my father's not an idiot,' I shouted, looking around the barn for something I could use to prise open the door.

'No? He just spent the last several days exhausting his magic in order to bind yours. He's weak as a child now. I can almost see him sitting there, trying to rise, seeking to summon his strength, only now sensing what is to come. Ke'heops has used his own power against himself, and now I'm going to kill him. I have one small task ahead of me first, one last act of courage, a great gift for our people. Then I will go before the council and set before them all the ignominy of your house. I will lay such slander against your father, against your mother, that Ke'heops will choke on my words. He will call me a liar. When I challenge him to a duel, he will have no choice but to accept. In his weakened state, I *will* kill him this time.'

'Why?' I shouted at the heavy door of the barn. It made no sense. No amount of competition, of feuding, could justify the raw venom inside him. 'How can you be this way?'

I thought he'd gone and that my question would go unanswered, but a few moments later I heard him speak again, his mouth close to the door, almost whispering. 'My whole life I've watched as your father paraded himself like the paragon of Jan'Tep society. Always looking down on me. Always believing I was less than he was.' There was a brief pause, and then he said, 'You can't imagine what that feels like.'

The torch burst back into flame.

41

The Barn

The first lick of flame slithered away from the torch and began climbing the barn's southern wall. Reichis raced over and leaped onto my shoulder, his entire body thrumming with anger and fear. 'Put it out! Quick! This entire place is catching fire!'

He needn't have bothered pointing that out. I was already trying to extinguish the torch. I grabbed a half-full bucket next to the horses' watering trough and threw it on the torch. As if in answer, the flames hissed and spat, but showed no sign of quenching.

The squirrel cat scrambled down to the ground, running a mad route between my legs. 'It's not going out! Why won't it go out?'

'It's *thirstfire*,' I shouted, refilling the bucket and dumping it out on the torch again. 'It won't go out by natural means.' The flames were already spreading out across the walls. Within minutes the entire barn would be engulfed in flame.

'Stamp it out, Kellen! We're going to burn alive in here!'

'It won't do any good,' I said. 'Stepping on the flames will just set my clothes on fire.'

'Then banish the spell! Do *something*.'

I envisioned my will taking dominion over the flame, and chanted the words old Osia'phest had taught us. When nothing happened, I reached further inside myself and redoubled my efforts. As if in answer, the counter-banded ember sigils on my forearm seemed to tighten, to strangle the vessels underneath my skin. *Spark, damn you. I refuse to die just because of some stupid tattoos.*

There's this hope you have, deep down, that when you most need it – in that instant where everything suddenly matters because now it's life and death – you'll be able to overcome whatever it is that's held you back your whole life and find your true strength. That was how it worked in all the old stories: the young Jan'Tep mage, face to face with the demons who have been tormenting his village, finally casts the great spell of banishment that had eluded him for so long.

'Are you doing anything?' Reichis asked. 'Because it just looks like you're constipated.'

It turns out all those stories are lies. *Or maybe you're not the young Jan'Tep hero in the story. Maybe you're the demon that gets destroyed.*

The flames were spreading, slowly but surely, making their way around the wooden walls of the barn. Already my eyes were watering from the smoke. Blind panic overtook me and I ran back to the door and hurled myself against it over and over. I got nothing for my efforts but a shooting pain through my shoulder.

'Hit it harder,' the squirrel cat chittered.

'I can't,' I said, gasping from the pain of my exertions. 'I'm not strong enough to break the door.'

'Then just—'

'Shut up,' I said, trying to concentrate. I focused all my attention on the door, looking for a weakness in it, finding none. The only weakness I could find was in myself. Reichis could see it too.

'Damn it all,' he chittered frantically. 'If I was going to take on an idiot human as a business partner, why didn't I pick Ra'meth? At least he has enough magic to dismiss a fire spell!'

My throat tightened under the growing strain of frustration and terror. 'Well, if I'm going to die in this burning barn with nobody but a stupid *nekhek* to give my eulogy, I'd rather you found something nice to say.'

'Well, let me see,' Reichis growled back. 'You're weak, you're a coward and you seem to be pretty much the only member of your race who doesn't have any magic. But on the other hand . . .'

He stopped chittering. I glanced around to see what he was looking at, but all I saw were the burning walls. 'What?' I asked.

'Nothing. I can't think of one good thing about you, Kellen. You're the most useless member of a useless species I've ever seen and now we're going to die because of it.'

The flames crackled as they travelled up the wooden beams to the hay that was stored on the second level of the barn. Smoke was filling the room. Soon it would be hard to breathe. 'I'm trying,' I said, dragging first Shalla's body and then Ferius's to the water trough. I splashed some of the remaining water on each of them, not sure what good it would do but having no better ideas. I glanced around the barn again, searching for something, anything, that might help. If there had been enough horses I could've hoped that they might stampede and smash through the walls. All we had was Ferius's horse though, and though it was growing more and more agitated, I knew it wouldn't be enough. *Sorry, whatever your name is. It's not fair that you have to die without knowing the reason.*

The heat was overwhelming and whatever moisture I had left in me was sweating out from every pore. We didn't have much time. Unlike the horse, Reichis understood what was happening, but his instinctive fear of fire was making him frantic. He tried to climb one of the walls, but there was too much fire and smoke now. The squirrel cat made it halfway up before tumbling down to the ground, coughing and shaking. I felt a strange empathy for the little monster. As terrified as I was, it must be worse for an animal covered in fur, for whom fire wasn't a normal part of life. I knelt down to try and pick him up. He bit me.

'Get away from me, human,' he growled. He got on his feet and shook himself. The shock of falling seemed to have brought him back. His eyes were a little clearer and he looked as if he'd mastered his fear. I wished I could say the same for myself.

'I was trying to help,' I said.

He looked up at me and gave a little snort. 'If you're going to cry, go do it over the torch. Maybe you can put it out that way.'

'I'm not crying, damn it. I'm sweating from the heat.'

'Sure.'

I moved to the centre of the barn where the smoke wasn't as thick and reached into one of Ferius's saddlebags, which were on the floor. I was looking for a cloth to wrap around my nose and mouth. What I found was the little pouch of red powder she'd shown me when she was painting her card. I rummaged around and found the pouch of black powder.

Hells, I thought, remembering what she said about them exploding on contact with each other. *No need to worry about burning to death. I'll just blow us all up instead.* I thought about tossing them to opposite sides of the room to keep them separated, but then had a better idea. Well, not a better one, but it was the best I had. I ran to the barn door.

'What is it?' Reichis asked, following behind me.

'These powders. They make an explosion on contact with each other.'

'What's an explosion?'

I almost laughed. But when would a squirrel cat have ever seen anything explode? Careful to use only my left hand, I scooped out a small handful of black powder and dropped it by the door. Part of me expected it to catch fire right away, but it didn't. Whatever it was made from stayed inert until it met with the opposing chemical. With my right hand I pulled out a small handful of the red powder. 'Stay back,' I said to Reichis. I took a few steps back myself and then tossed the red powder towards the black. They exploded in a small ball of flame and, just for a second, I felt a surge of hope that the door might give way. It didn't.

'Do it again,' Reichis said. 'Use more this time.'

'I used half of each bag.'

'Then—'

'It doesn't work that way,' I shouted in frustration. 'It needs to be contained somehow. It needs something to direct the force. Damn it, I can't think!'

The horse had broken its tether and was now running around the barn in circles, futilely searching for an escape. The noise and the chaos were making it impossible for me to concentrate.

329

I shut my eyes tight and clamped my hands around my ears so that I could focus. I turned my thoughts back to the powders sitting in their pouches on the ground. The first try had accomplished nothing but to feed the flames even more. A second wouldn't do any better. *The powder is the answer. Somehow. I just need a way to control the explosion so it doesn't dissipate. Why couldn't you have broken the damned ember band?* Only . . . what I needed wasn't actually ember magic. That was for *creating* energy, not focusing it.

I removed my hands from my ears and looked down at them, my eyes fixating on the specks of powder stuck to my fingertips. Master Osia'phest had told me at the oasis that the *carath* spell didn't generate wind; it channelled whatever force was at the precise point of the spell. If the only energy present was a light breeze, then it channelled that breeze in the direction of the spell. If something more powerful was present . . .

'Reichis, I've got an—'

'Kellen, look out!' he shouted.

I turned just in time to see a raging mass of hoofs and muscle rearing down at me. The horse, its mouth frothing as the sides of its coat smouldered from contact with the burning walls, was going mad, stomping on everything in its path. I jumped out of the way just in time to watch its hoofs smash into the dirt floor. The pouch containing the red powder tipped over and its contents began spreading towards the one with the black. I tried to reach in to pick them up, but the horse reared once more and again brought its hoofs down, and this time the pouch with the black powder tipped precariously. If the black one fell too . . .

'He's afraid of the fire,' Reichis said, as if I might not already be aware of that fact.

330

I reached out and tried to gentle the horse, but it snapped its teeth at me. 'Damn it, you're going to get us killed, you stupid beast! Reichis, the powder!'

'I'm on it,' Reichis chittered. I turned to see him bounding from the other side of the barn. At first I thought he was going to run to the pouch of black powder to snatch it out of the way. Instead he leaped in quick progression from the floor up to a barrel and onto a shelf that held grooming equipment. From there he launched himself and spread his limbs wide, gliding onto the horse's neck. The beast reared up, trying to shake him off, but the little squirrel cat held firm on to its mane and climbed up closer to its head. I watched in awe as Reichis, still hanging from the mane with one paw, used the other to grab the horse's ear. I thought he was about to bite into it, but instead he started chittering furiously. The horse reared and shook once more, then its hoofs landed on the ground and it stopped moving.

'His hide is starting to burn, Kellen,' Reichis said, still sitting atop the horse's head.

I grabbed a blanket folded over one of the stalls and used it to tamp down the horse's sides. It took the treatment with surprising stillness. 'What did you do?' I asked, looking into the horse's eyes. The fear was still there.

'Horses are terrified of fire,' the squirrel cat said. 'It drives them mad.'

'I know that. So how did—'

'There are still one or two things that scare them worse than fire,' Reichis said, looking down at the horse's eyes. 'I let him know which ones I could do to him before we burned alive.'

Ancestors save me from my new business partner. 'All right. Stay back,' I said.

331

'What are you doing?'

Something that's probably just going to get my hands blown off before I burn to death. I knelt down and with my right hand carefully scooped up some of the red powder from the ground. With my left I grabbed a roughly equal amount of the black.

I let the powders slip slowly away until I was left with just a pinch between the forefinger and thumb of each hand. It probably wasn't enough to do more than burn the hells out of my fingers, but if I could make it work without killing myself then maybe I could try the spell again with more. *I hope you knew what you were talking about, Osia'phest.* I coughed again and realised this was probably my only chance. I'd have to aim for the point where the door met the wall. Maybe if I hit it just right, there would be enough force to make it buckle. Of course, for all I knew, Ra'meth's mages would be waiting for us. *The hells with it. Let the squirrel cat deal with that problem.*

I had one shot at this. One spell that I wasn't complete rubbish at, using breath – the one form of magic I'd sparked and the only one my father hadn't counter-banded. *If I failed this time . . .*

'Kellen, if you're just going to piss about . . .'

I let out what breath was left in my lungs, said a brief prayer to my ancestors that, if I had to be reincarnated, I wouldn't come back as a squirrel cat, and tossed the powders into the air in front of me. My hands formed the somatic shape for the spell: bottom two fingers of each one pressed into the palm, the sign of restraint; fore and middle fingers pointed straight out, the sign of flight; and thumbs pointing to the heavens, the sign of, well, somebody up there, help me, please.

The powders met and exploded in front of me – a split second of red and black fury that bulged out as if it were trying to reach up and grab my face. Then something – the spell, I guess – took hold of the fire and shot it straight out away from me. *Please hit the edge of the door*, I prayed.

Smoke and heat blew into my face and I stumbled backwards, losing my footing and experiencing a brief feeling of release – of floating – before I hit the ground. *Don't pass out*, I told myself. *Whatever you do, don't . . .*

Something cool and furry was on my left cheek. It went away only to return again a second later. The pattern continued for a few brief moments until I opened my eyes. Two beady black eyes set back from a whiskered snout looked down at me. The squirrel cat was sitting on my chest tapping my face with his paw.

'What the hells are you doing?' I asked.

'I'm slapping you. I've seen humans do this when one goes unconscious. Is it helping?' He pulled his paw back again. 'Should I use my claws?'

'Stop it,' I said, pushing him off my chest.

I tried to rise too quickly and things started to go black again. I took in a breath close to the floor and then pushed myself up more carefully. The smoke seemed less thick. 'Did I hit the door?' But if I had, wouldn't Ra'meth's men be in here already, sticking something sharp in my belly?

'Not even close,' Reichis said.

'Damn it,' I said, getting my feet under me and doing my best to shake off the effects of the blast. 'I can try again . . . I can . . .'

'Don't bother,' Reichis said.

I followed the line of his paw towards the other side of

the barn. The fire was still raging around us and I could hear wooden beams beginning to crack. The smoke cleared just enough for me to see what I'd done. I'd missed the door by a good six feet. It didn't matter. Where the wall had been there was now a huge gaping hole; slats of charred wood blown through and supports falling over. I took one teetering step towards what was left of the wall. Two bodies lay partially buried under the debris where Ra'meth's mages had stood guard. I didn't bother to check whether they'd survived. I assumed you needed a torso to live.

I heard something shambling behind me and a moment later felt Reichis's paw on my leg. 'Kellen?'

'Yeah?'

'I think maybe I've found something about you that I like.'

I stared at the wreckage, the bits of burning wood and red-hot metal. I'd never seen destruction like that. Even the thirstfire torch had been blasted to pieces. A breeze was rushing into the now three-sided barn, feeding the flames but giving me a taste of fresh air I'd never expected to breathe again.

I knelt down and carefully picked up the pouches of black and red powder, putting one in each pocket before I went to drag Shalla and Ferius out of the barn. 'Yeah,' I said. 'I think I've found something about myself that I like too.'

42

The Hunting Party

It took a little while for me to get my strength back. By then
Ferius was already regaining consciousness. Shalla was still
out of it. I suspected it would be a while before the effects
of the mine wore off.

'Something bothering you, kid?' Ferius asked.

I looked behind me to see her barely holding on to the
reins of her horse, listing from side to side as the animal
navigated the uneven forest terrain. She was so beaten up
that the only thing keeping her conscious was Reichis periodically clambering up onto her shoulder to slap her around
the face with his paw. The squirrel cat seemed to find this
tremendously entertaining.

'Nothing much,' I replied, turning back to make sure the
horse I'd taken from one of Ra'meth's men wasn't leading us
off the edge of the narrow path. Below lay a steep-sided gorge
that I was using to guide us back towards the northern edge
of town. Shalla lay unconscious across my saddle, her breathing
still so slow and shallow that I couldn't stop myself from
repeatedly checking her pulse.

Ferius gave a chuckle. 'You're a terrible liar, kid.'

'Guess I'd better start practising then.' My own uncle had

335

conspired against our people. My parents had been secretly weakening my magic all these years because they'd known since I was a child that I was going to develop the shadow-black. And it turned out my clan had never fought a war against the Mahdek people. We'd murdered them in their sleep and stolen their cities – and their magic. 'No one is who they say they are,' I said.

'First thing you learn wandering the long roads, kid. Everyone thinks they're the hero of their own story.'

'Somebody's out there,' Reichis chittered suddenly, beady black eyes glimmering from his perch on Ferius's shoulder.

I looked all around and saw only trees and rocks and thick underbrush. 'Where are they?'

The squirrel cat's whiskers twitched in annoyance. 'I don't know – they must be hiding. But I'm telling you: this place stinks of Jan'Tep.'

'What's the little bugger saying?' Ferius asked, a hand reaching back into her waistcoat for her razor-sharp steel cards. 'Maybe we'd better—'

Whatever she was going to say was cut off by a sound like the screeching of a thousand nails dragged across a chalkboard. Reflexively my hands formed the somatic shapes for the shield spell I'd been taught to practise every day since I'd started school. *'Senhathet!'* I shouted. It accomplished nothing of course. I couldn't spark the tattooed iron band around my forearm that would have given me access to that form of magic. Also, I wasn't the target.

Reichis leaped away from Ferius an instant before she went flying from her horse. There was no sign of any weapon, but instead a shifting purplish light that moved like water through the air, pooling around her, holding her aloft even as patches of it extended into long black tentacles and began to strike her over and over. A *lightshaper*, I thought, looking around for the source but still unable to see who was casting the spell.

I rolled Shalla forward on the horse's back and jumped off to try to help Ferius. Her mount reared wildly, desperately trying to stamp at the strange light surrounding its mistress. The glowing shape seemed to take notice, and suddenly three of its tentacles bunched together and drove themselves deep into the animal's belly, only to split apart again, tearing the horse's insides out. The horse's screams became a terrifying counterpoint to the gleeful shrieks of encouragement I heard from somewhere in the shadows.

I reached my hands into the pouches inside my pockets. *Lightshapes can be blown apart*, I thought. But how was I going to hit the shape without burning Ferius?

'Enough,' a voice called out. The sound was muffled . . . distorted. *Someone's using a misting spell . . . That's why I can't see them, and why I can't recognise who's speaking.*

A moment later the purple lightform dissipated and Ferius fell heavily to the ground. I ran to her and found she was still breathing. But her face and arms looked as if a dozen men had been kicking and beating her all night. Her right eye was already swollen shut, but the left flickered open. 'Hey, kid? How come you keep pissing people off and I'm the one who takes the beatings?'

'Step away from the Daroman spy, Kellen,' the voice called out again.

I recognised it this time, and turned to see the misting spell had been dismissed. 'Panahsi?'

My oldest friend shook his head. 'Not any more. I passed my mage's trial this morning. My name is Pan'erath now.'

337

'You're a lightshaper,' I said, not quite able to keep the awe out of my voice.

He gave me a smile that was proud and dismissive at the same time. 'Been practising since the trials started. Since you betrayed us that first time, helping a Daroman spy against your own people.'

'She's not a spy, Pan! She's just a—'

Tennat appeared from the darkness with his brothers close behind. 'Go on, Kellen. Tell us how she's nothing more than an innocent Argosi who just happened to arrive right before your treasonous uncle and his Sha'Tep allies came up with a plan to destroy our clan.'

Ra'dir sent out a blast of fire into the air, lighting up the forest. 'Where's the nekhek?'

'Ran away, no doubt,' Ra'fan said, his hands already preparing one of the binding shapes I knew he'd use on Reichis the second he spotted him.

Ra'fan was a chaincaster and Ra'dir a war mage, so neither of them had been the one to cast the misting spell. 'So I guess you're the sightbinder of this hunting party, Tennat?' I asked.

'My name is Ra'ennat now,' he replied.

Great. Everybody has a mage's name except me.

I felt Ferius reach out to grip my arm. There was no strength to it. 'Kid, soon as I make my move, grab your sister and run. I'll keep them—'

'You're half dead and flat on your back,' I whispered back. 'What kind of "move" are you planning to make?'

She sounded oddly offended. 'I've still got moves.'

'Come on, Kellen,' Panahsi – *no, he's Pan'erath now* – called out. 'Step away from the Daroman and don't make this worse

338

than it needs to be. We know all about the conspiracy. We know how she and your uncle plotted to use the nekhek to destroy our clan's magic.'

'It makes sense if you think about it,' Tennat said. I had no intention of calling him Ra'ennat. 'If our clan lost its magic, you wouldn't really be a cripple any more, would you?'

I rose to my feet. 'You're a liar, Tennat. Your family knew what was going on and you –'

I was interrupted by a groaning sound and turned to see Shalla, still draped across the horse's back, her body shivering and convulsing. I started towards her. 'I've got to get her home to—'

I was knocked off my feet by a blast of force. 'You stay away from her!' Pan'erath shouted. When I looked up at him his face was full of righteous anger. *He thinks he's protecting her. From me.*

I finally understood what was going through Pan's mind. He wasn't ganging up against his friend. He was facing off against the classic villains of all our childhood stories: the foreigner spy, come to tear apart the clan; the nekhek monster, foul teeth hungry to pierce the flesh of Jan'Tep mages and destroy their magic. *And the most nefarious of all: the traitor Sha'Tep, who would deliver his own sister to his clan's enemies out of bitterness and envy.* Pan'erath was the hero – the young mage who'd assembled a coven to save the helpless princess. It all had such perfect symmetry. 'You're an idiot,' I told him.

Ra'fan uttered a word and my arms pinned themselves against my sides, crushing my own ribs.

'Don't,' Pan'erath said. 'Save the spell for the nekhek.'

I don't think Ra'fan liked being ordered around by someone who'd only been made adept a few hours before, but he complied and I felt the crushing grip fade away. 'The monster's probably already fled back to its lair,' he said dismissively. 'We should just—'

'We do this my way,' Pan'erath said, taking a step towards me. 'Surrender, Kellen. I promise I'll speak for you to the council. I don't want to see you hurt.' Winding tendrils of light, red this time, formed around his hands as his fingers traced tiny symbols at his sides in preparation. 'Or we can duel, and I'll do my best not to kill you.'

He's so proud of his lightshaping spells, I thought. *He won't be able to resist the urge to show them off.* But Pan hadn't seen me use the powders and he didn't know what I could do with them. Fire could burn through his lightshapes. If I was fast enough, I could end the fight in one shot. Our people's most ancient laws would demand that the others let us go.

Of course, one look at the way Tennat, Ra'fan and Ra'dir were glancing at each other told me they had no intention of honouring the terms of any duel. *So there's no way my one spell is going to get me out of this alive.*

'That's a really tempting offer, Pan,' I said as I walked very slowly to kneel beside Ferius. I closed her waistcoat against the cool night air. 'But you shouldn't have attacked my friends.'

'Kid, this is a terrible plan,' she whispered.

'Quit calling me kid,' I said, palming the deck of steel cards I'd taken from her.

I stood back up and turned to face the four of them. 'No more duels, Pan. No more rules. No more games. I'm giving you one chance, because . . .' *Because we were friends once. Because you waited a whole year to take your tests just so I wouldn't be alone with people like Tennat.* It seemed hard to believe that he'd once valued my friendship so highly. All that was gone now. 'Get these three morons out of here and help me clean up the mess Tennat's father made before our whole clan really is in danger.'

The early crest of Pan's lightshaper magic slithered and grew around his hands. 'I'd rather see our people disappear from the world than take orders from a Sha'Tep weakling.'

For a moment I tried to think of something to say, some way to break down the wall between us, but there wasn't one. Pan'erath was a Jan'Tep mage. I was a Sha'Tep traitor. That was all there was to it. I looked out into the tops of the trees, still not seeing Reichis but having no choice but to hope he was somewhere up there. *Wonder what he'll charge me for this.* 'In that case, gentlemen, I rescind my offer. I'm going to kick all your asses and then I'm going to save our people myself.'

When you've only got one good spell it's hard to resist the urge to use it. After all, the powder magic was the most powerful weapon I had, and neither Pan nor the others had seen it before. With any luck, I could take them by surprise and maybe even knock one or two of them out of the fight at the outset. Even more though, I so badly wanted to show them that I had my own magic, that I was as good as they were. *And then what?* There was no way I could hit them all fast enough. Ra'dir's war-mage training meant he'd be prepared for surprises, and Ra'fan would use one of his chaincaster spells to bind me the second I fired off the spell. *Fine*, I thought. *Card tricks it is.*

'Don't do this,' Pan said, a look of genuine concern on his face for the first time.

I guess it's one thing to make threats against an enemy and another to realise you're about five seconds away from killing your childhood friend. 'Don't worry,' I said. 'I'll try to be gentle.'

The way I had it figured, my one chance was to stop thinking like a Jan'Tep and start thinking like an Argosi, the way Ferius did when she kept tricking them. All Pan and the others understood was magic – who had what spells and when to use them. They didn't notice the uneven terrain and the shifting darkness around us. They didn't consider how close together the four of them were standing, or that I might not be alone in this. All they saw was a good old-fashioned Jan'Tep tale of good versus evil, where good always wins. What I saw was a card game with a half-dozen different decks in play. *Ancestors save me*, I thought. *I really am turning into an Argosi.*

'Come on,' Tennat urged. 'Make your move, coward.'

I almost laughed. Even now, after everything that had happened, with us ready to maim or even kill each other, Tennat was still using the same old taunts he'd tossed at me our whole lives. I ignored him and turned my mind to solving the first of my very real problems: Ra'dir. If he hit me with the flames or lightning from a war spell, I'd be dead before the fight even started. Then again, if Ra'fan got one of his chain spells around me, I'd be helpless. I needed a way to get both of them off balance at the outset. I glanced up at Tennat and smiled. 'Hey, remember that time I nearly got you to crush your intestines with your own spell? How much do you want to bet I can make you blind yourself?'

He took a step forward. 'I can't wait to get you in a small room away from prying eyes, weakling.' He spread his arms wide apart – the opening of the strongest of the blinding spells. Once he set his intention and uttered the words, he'd bring them together and it'd be like a curtain closing over me. The second he opened his mouth, I flung one of Ferius's steel cards straight for him.

Ra'dir and Ra'fan were more experienced and knew not to flinch, but Tennat suddenly fell back – right into them. 'Get out of the way, you idiot,' Ra'dir shouted, trying to shove him aside to get a line on me.

I dived to my right, rolling awkwardly over my shoulder but managing not to drop the cards or slice my own palm on them. As I came up on one knee, I flung two more. One sailed harmlessly off into the darkness, but the other caught Ra'fan in the leg. He gave out a yell and stumbled forward into Pan'erath.

A burning sensation passed my left ear as one of Ra'dir's spells flew by. If I hadn't still been in motion, he'd have set me ablaze instead of the tree behind me. I kept moving as fast as I could. *This isn't going to work for long*, I reminded myself. *War mages train to hit moving targets.*

I ran behind the trees, flinging cards as I went, trying to keep the group close together and prevent any one of them from getting a line on me. A lucky throw sent another card spinning into Ra'fan's left hand, a thread of blood appearing where his palm was cut open. He wouldn't be casting any chain spells for a few minutes. *It's working!* I thought. Then a shape of almost black light enveloped me and I found myself pinned against a tree. Pan'erath had finally cast his own spell.

I'd known this was coming of course. If I'd prepared pinches of powder instead of the cards I could have blasted the shadows apart, but that wasn't my plan. *I guess now I find out just how reliable squirrel cats are.* 'Reichis, now!'

For a second nothing happened. The others had just started to relax when a chittering voice said, 'Okay, but you're really going to owe me for this.' A dark shape swooped down from the treetops onto Pan's head. I watched in sick fascination as Reichis covered Pan's face with the furry webbing that stretched between his front and back limbs while his rear claws drew gashes into the back of Pan's neck, causing him to stumble back, screaming in pain.

I felt the shadow release me and flung two more cards to keep the others from grabbing Reichis.

'Get him off me!' Pan shouted.

'Lousy torturing skinbag,' Reichis growled. 'Let's see how well your blood magic works once I've ripped your eyes out.'

'Reichis, don't!' I screamed.

Fire flared in Ra'dir's hands as he prepared to blast the squirrel cat out of existence. I wondered if he cared that he was probably going to kill Pan at the same time. Reichis didn't take any notice, his complete commitment to revenge outweighing any sensible fear he might have. I launched the remaining cards at our enemies, desperately trying to distract them. I missed them all, except for Ra'fan, for whom I was seriously starting to feel some sympathy, since I'd now hit him for the third time, this card lodging deep into the muscle of his shoulder. 'Damn it!' he screamed. 'Blind him, Tennat!'

'My name is Ra'ennat,' his brother insisted, but in the chaos and confusion he couldn't summon the concentration to make the spell work. *Still haven't learned that you can't cast spells when you're scared.*

Ra'dir had a lot more training and composure though. He fired his spell, eyes on Reichis. The squirrel cat leaped off Pan's face, but his left side still got caught in the blast and his fur caught fire. I took off at a run and by some small miracle caught the squirrel cat mid-air. I curled into a ball and tumbled forward to roll on the ground, smothering the flames with my body. From the burning sensation on my torso, I guessed I wouldn't be growing any chest hair for a while.

Reichis got out from under me and ran back into the forest. I felt a twinge of resentment at his utter lack of gratitude, but I forgave him a few seconds later when he emerged from the trees behind our opponents and gave Ra'dir a deep gash in the back of the leg before disappearing back into the underbrush.

'Get the nekhek,' Pan'erath ordered, rising up from the ground, blood on his forehead and iron in his eyes. 'I'll deal with the Sha'Tep.'

The shifting blackness around his hands grew and slithered out towards me, reaching for me. *Okay, this is it*, I thought, as I dug my hands into my pockets and brought out generous pinches of the red and black powders. '*Carath*,' I said, uttering the simple breath spell as I flung the powders into the air towards each other. My fingers took on the somatic shapes, aiming the resulting explosion into Pan's lightform. It blew apart and he fell to the ground, winded.

'How . . . ?' he began, looking up at me.

'I told you before, Pan. I'll never be Sha'Tep.'

'You'll never be Jan'Tep either,' Ra'fan said, his bleeding hand outstretched towards me. Somehow he pushed through the pain and shock of his wounds and cast a chain spell that wrapped itself around me, paralysing me where I stood.

Reichis appeared again from the underbrush and raced for Ra'fan, but this time Ra'dir was ready for him. He fired off another blast and the squirrel cat had to pull up short to keep from running right into it.

'Reichis, run!' I shouted.

He hesitated as if he might stay, but I think he realised the odds had turned sour on us. 'Sorry, kid,' he chittered, turning back into the darkness before Ra'dir could try again.

Ra'fan gritted his teeth and beads of sweat appeared on his forehead as he clenched his fists. *Damn . . . he's not just trying to bind me any more.* Every part of my body was being squeezed, crushed by the force of his will. I was sure I heard my ribs creaking as the invisible chains tightened around them. 'You're done, Sha'Tep. I'm killing you. Now.'

'I'm afraid I still have some need of him,' Ferius Parfax said. In the periphery of my vision I saw her struggling to stay on her feet as she flung one of her steel cards straight for Ra'fan's eyes.

It flew in a perfect line, only to disappear into the watery light emanating from Pan'erath's hands. 'This is your fault, Daroman.' I'd never heard his voice sound so cold, so hard. 'You ruined everything.'

The tendrils of light set themselves upon Ferius, pulling at her hair, her hands, bending her fingers back too far. I tried desperately to reach into my pockets for more powders. If nothing else, I might be able to create some kind of distracting flash.

'I don't think so,' Ra'fan said. The squeezing around my ribs grew tighter and I couldn't take in a breath any more.

Tennat, evidently having finally overcome his fears, started walking towards me. 'It's over now, Kellen. You played all your dirty little tricks and now it's time to say goodnight to the world.'

346

He spread his arms, uttered a word, and in an instant I was completely blind.

I heard Ra'dir say, 'Keep an eye out for the nekhek. It's still dangerous.'

Tennat practically giggled. 'No, it isn't. My blinding spell covered all of them. The moment the creature shows up, we burn him.'

Something dropped heavily to the ground a few feet away from me. *Pan must have dropped Ferius*, I thought.

'It's enough,' he said. There was a weariness to his voice. 'Let's bring them back to the council. They'll stand trial for what they've done.'

'No,' Tennat said.

'We agreed—'

The sound of footsteps accompanied Tennat's voice as he walked the last steps towards me. 'You may have agreed, Pan, but the rest of us have different plans.' My eyelids closed reflexively as thumbs began pressing against them.

'Tennat, no!' Pan called out.

'Look!' Tennat said, scraping with his thumbnails at the paste covering the markings around my left eye. 'Look at the marks. It's like my father said: Kellen is a shadowblack.'

The forest went silent. I heard the sound of more footsteps coming closer, so close I could feel breath on my face. 'So it's true,' Pan said. Something wet hit my cheek just below my eye. Pan had spat on me.

'We take him to the council,' he said. 'They need to see what he's become.'

'They can see from his corpse,' Tennat said, and I felt him gripping the sides of my head again.

'No. I said—'

A brief sound of scuffling ended when Ra'dir said, 'You're still new at this, Pan'erath. You don't understand how wars are fought. Think of this as the fifth test – the one every war mage has to pass.'

Tennat's thumbs pressed ever so slowly against my eyes. I would have screamed, but the chain spell wound its way over my mouth and Ra'fan squeezed what little air was left in my lungs. *This is it*, I realised. *I'm going to die now. For real. Forever.*

Tennat's voice crept into my ears. 'You deserve this, Kellen. For being a liar and a cheat. For all of—'

He screamed so loud I went deaf for a second.

Another shout of pain, this one I think from Ra'dir. More screams. More shouts. Chaos penetrated the darkness of my world. I had no idea what was happening, but then I realised the blinding spell was gone. I opened my eyes just in time to watch a white-gold light smash into Ra'fan so hard it flung him deep into the darkness of the forest. A dull thud echoed in the air.

With Ra'fan unconscious, his chain spell dispersed and I fell to the ground. I looked up to see Pan standing alone, his eyes full of tears.

At first I thought he'd changed his mind – that once he saw what the others were doing, he had turned on them to save my life. But then the white-gold light shimmered again, and Pan's body lifted up high above the ground. He spun in the air, slowly, almost gracefully, as if he were underwater. Finally his body settled some seven feet up, his arms and legs splayed out as if he were tied to four horses pulling him apart. He was still conscious. He said, 'But I did it for you . . . I saved you.'

My head turned, following the line of his sorrowful gaze,

and I saw Shalla leaning unsteadily against a tree. Her arms were outstretched in front of her. One by one the links holding back the coloured bands on her arms began shattering like thin rings of glass exploding to the vibrations of a perfect note. The last constraints on her abilities fell before the raw force of her magic. Shalla's eyes, usually a piercing blue, gleamed pure gold, like the light of her spell. She turned her palms up and Pan's body rose even higher into the air, then she closed them into fists, and he crashed to the ground.

'Nobody touches my brother,' she said.

43

Pan'erath

I rose to my feet slowly, unsure whether I was looking at my little sister standing there or one of those gleaming gods of vengeance the Berabesq write about in their holy books. 'Shalla?' I asked.

She took no notice of me. Pure, radiant magic cascaded around her hands again, building to a crest that would destroy Pan and the others along with half the forest.

'Shalla, don't!' I shouted.

She turned to look at me. At first she didn't seem to recognise me, but then the gold in her eyes gave way to blue. 'Kellen?' she asked. 'You look terrible.' Her hands slumped by her sides and all of a sudden her knees gave out. She fell back against the tree and slid to the ground with surprising elegance.

'I swear, that kid's too pretty for her own good,' Ferius said, grunting with effort as she stood up. 'Too damned powerful for anyone else's.'

I knelt beside Shalla. 'She's not breathing right. What's wrong with her?'

'The human body's not meant to move that much energy. I reckon she'll be all right, but she needs healing.'

'Can you—'

Ferius shook her head. 'I don't deal in that kind of medicine. She'll need your mother's help.' She knelt down and reached under Shalla's shoulders. 'Come on, help me get her onto the horse.'

Sounds of movement in the brush drew our gaze, and a moment later Reichis emerged. He looked just about as beaten up as the rest of us and the fur down his left side was singed. 'Sons of bitches,' he swore. 'Nearly knocked me halfway up the damned mountain.' His beady eyes looked around at the unconscious mages on the ground, then up at us. 'You didn't leave any for me?'

I translated for Ferius as we lifted Shalla onto the horse's back. She laughed, then groaned. 'Tell the little bugger to stop making jokes. My ribs hurt.'

Reichis ambled over and skittered up a tree before hopping onto my shoulder and starting to pick at the burnt parts of his fur. 'Who says I'm joking?'

Ferius and I spent the next few minutes tying up the others with copper binding wire I'd found in Panahsi's bag. *No, his name's Pan'erath,* I reminded myself. *That's who he is now. Jan'Tep through and through.*

When I looked down at him, I saw the same pudgy face I'd known most of my life, his otherwise handsome features still too soft and pockmarked from a life-long fondness for lemoncakes and other sweets. But there was something else there, too. Anger. Determination. Something inside him was now as hard and sharp as the cards in Ferius's steel deck.

How many times had Panahsi stuck by me these past couple of years while his magic got stronger and mine just weakened?

351

How many times had the other initiates urged him to stay away from me? To shun me? Pan could have run his mage's tests ages ago. He could already be a powerful mage, apprenticed to one of the masters, maybe even being groomed to join the lords magi on the council one day. Instead, he'd stuck by me.

We'll never be friends again. The thought put a sick, empty feeling in my chest. There was no apology that either of us could offer that would ever tear down the wall between us. We'd done things to the other that neither would ever forgive. Each of us had made choices the other would never really understand or condone. 'We're done here,' I said, as I finished binding his hands behind a tree trunk. I didn't bother promising to send someone from town to free him and the others. If Pan'erath didn't already assume I would, then it's not like he'd believe me just because I said so.

'You sure we shouldn't kill him?' Reichis asked, looking down from a tree branch.

'Of course I'm sure,' I snapped.

For once, the squirrel cat didn't seem offended. He just looked down at me with something that, in a less homicidal creature, might have been sympathy. 'He'll never let go of this, kid. You can smell it on him.'

'I'm not going to smell him, Reichis.'

The squirrel cat hopped down to the ground and sniffed at Pan's face. 'Too bad, because if you did, even dumb as you are, you'd sink your teeth in this one's throat before you ever turned your back on him.'

'Time to get moving, kid,' Ferius called out.

I looked around and saw the way she was wiping sweat from her brow, the way her hands shook. Exhaustion and injury were taking their toll. Pan had killed her horse, leaving us with only mine. 'Take the horse,' I said. 'Bring Shalla to my parents. My mother can heal both of you.'

'I'll be fine, kid. I just—'

'You're not fine!' I shouted. 'Nobody's fine. Shalla's barely breathing and you can barely stand. So take the damned horse and get my sister to safety.'

'Okay, kid. Okay.' She locked eyes with me. 'And what about you?'

I set about picking up as many of the steel cards as I could find. 'I'll come soon.'

'You're going after Ra'meth,' she said. It wasn't a question.

Reichis crawled up my side to sit on my shoulder. 'Damned straight *we're* going after him. If I can't taste the flesh of these skinbags, then I want the guy responsible for all of this.'

Ferius cocked an eye at the squirrel cat. 'Is he bragging again? His kind do that a lot, you know.'

'Tell the stupid Argosi to—'

'Shut up,' I said.

The two of them looked at me, startled. Contrary to what they both thought, I wasn't even the least bit interested in pursuing Ra'meth. I'd learned my lesson. I wasn't the young Jan'Tep hero going off to defeat his enemy in a glorious battle. Ra'meth was one of the lords magi of our clan. He was vastly more powerful than Pan or Ra'dir or the others. He was also smarter. He'd managed to outwit my uncle and the Sha'Tep and everybody else, all so he could line things up perfectly to make himself clan prince. Now all he had left to do was to stand before the council and tell his lies and cast the blame at my father's feet. *Would that be enough though?* My father had a lot of supporters on the council. Could Ra'meth really be sure they would all elect him then and there? Or would

353

he need something else? *One more act of courage*, he'd told me. *A great gift for our people.*

It didn't matter. None of it mattered – not my fear, not even Ra'meth's plans. I couldn't let him become clan prince. I had to stop him before he got to the council chambers. I turned to Ferius. 'I need you to do this for me,' I said. 'I need you to get Shalla to my parents. They'll believe her, and that will give them time to prepare for whatever comes next.'

She reached out a hand and gripped my shoulder. 'You're tough, kid. You've proven that. But you can't go after a mage like Ra'meth by yourself.'

'Leave the skinbag to me,' Reichis growled.

I translated. Ferius, surprisingly, didn't crack a joke. Instead she bowed her head to the squirrel cat. 'Anyone can see that you are a fierce warrior, a skilled hunter and a wise scavenger,' she said, with an odd formality to her voice. 'But the skinbag in question will have other mages with him. They are too many, and you are too few.'

Reichis gave a little snort in reply. There's something really disturbing about a squirrel cat snorting dismissively. 'Too few?' He sprang off my shoulder onto her back and then started running down the path. 'Come on, kid. Let's go get the rest of my people. Then we're going to really tear those hairless sons of bitches apart.'

The squirrel cat kept up a furious pace as we raced along the forest paths, skirting thick copses of trees and running across clearings where the terrain suddenly dipped wildly. Reichis moved like water flowing down a winding stream – his feet finding the perfect route under fallen trees and over rocky outgrowths. I couldn't keep up.

354

'Stop,' I gasped, knocking my shoulder against a tree as I slid to an awkward halt.

The squirrel cat turned to look back at me. 'What? Why?'

Sweat was dripping down my face, stinging my eyes. I'd accumulated a dozen more bruises and scrapes in the past half-hour. 'I'm going to be dead before Ra'meth even gets the chance to blast me, that's what. Give me a minute.'

'We're almost there. Just tough it out.'

'No,' I insisted, still trying to get my heart to slow down.

Reichis cocked his head. 'You know, I really wonder some days why my people ever feared yours. It seems to me you can barely get your arses out of bed without having a heart attack.'

'Just . . .' *Why can't I catch my damned breath?* 'Just give me a second.'

The simple truth is, my people aren't especially strong physically. Most things that matter we do with magic. Even the Sha'Tep use objects spelled by clan mages to ease their labours. *We're really not a very tough people, I guess.*

'Listen, kid,' Reichis said, sitting back on his haunches to scratch at the fur under his chin, 'when we get to my people, let me do the talking.'

'Since I don't speak squirrel cat, how was I supposed to do it in the first place?'

He gave a little chortle. 'Yeah, but my people aren't dumb like yours, so even if you can't understand what they're saying, they'll understand you just fine. So when negotiations start—'

'Negotiations? You mean to tell me the rest of your pack are going to want to get *paid*?'

Reichis looked up at me as if I were dim. 'Kid, everything comes at a price. We're squirrel cats, not dogs. We don't work for bones and a pat on the head. Think it through, would you?'

'Fine,' I said. 'So what are they going to expect in return for helping us?'

The thin line of his lips twitched a bit and I realised I'd just stepped into a trap. He launched into a remarkably complete list of every shiny, valuable object in my house and, in fact, half the other houses around town – things I'd never even seen. According to Reichis, squirrel cats spend quite a bit of time 'casing' locations.

'You realise I can't promise things I don't own,' I said, when he was finally finished.

'Oh, that's okay.' He held up a reassuring paw. 'You can just help us get access to the stuff. Or you can find us other things of equal value later.'

Later. It almost made me laugh that he thought there would be any kind of 'later' for me. Once this was done, I was going to be exiled if I was lucky, executed if I wasn't. A smarter person would have left all this behind the moment he'd realised he had no future among his people. *Is that what an Argosi would do?* I wondered. *Just walk away?* But I wasn't Argosi. I wasn't Jan'Tep or Sha'Tep or anything else. I was just a guy with one spell, a squirrel cat and a complete inability to stomach the thought of Ra'meth winning or what he might do to Shalla if he became clan prince. 'All right,' I said finally. 'If all this goes smoothly, I'll get you what you want.'

He gave me the squirrel cat equivalent of a grin. 'Great. That's really . . .' I think he must have noticed that I was watching him clack his claws together again because he stopped abruptly.

'What is it?' I asked.

Reichis lifted his snout. I noticed then that the breeze had shifted and brought with it a strange smell. Fire . . . and something thick and acrid that made me feel sick to my stomach. *Burning flesh.*

One last act of courage, Ra'meth had told me. *A great gift for our people.*

Reichis took off like an arrow and I followed as quickly as I could, ignoring the pain and exhaustion, my muscles fuelled by the scent of death, and pulled inexorably towards the sound of flames and the most horrible screams I'd ever heard.

44

The Flames

The first glimmers of the flames lit the gaps between trees more than a hundred yards ahead of us. By then the smoke was already choking me, making it even harder to keep up with Reichis, until finally it was only his fear of fire that slowed him down enough for me to catch up. The flames formed a wall that seemed to stretch forever before curving round to form a circle enclosing the glade. Reichis raced back and forth along it, desperately looking for an opening. 'They've ringed the whole area with fire,' he chittered frantically. 'My people are trapped!'

'How did he even find them?' I asked. 'I thought –'

The squirrel cat growled. 'My stupid mother. She told the tribe to gather here.' He turned and glared at me, the flames giving his eyes a hateful glow. 'She wanted them ready to help you, to protect you and that damned Argosi –'

More screams cut us off – this time, though, the voices were those of Ra'meth's men.

'What's happening?' I asked, trying to get closer, but the heat was too much for me.

'My people are killing yours,' he said, still running along the wall of flames. 'As it should be. As it always should have been.'

I watched in horror as he got too close and his own fur caught fire almost instantly. 'Stop!' I shouted. Without thinking, I threw myself over him again, wrapping my entire body around him. I felt the rest of my shirt burning and had to keep rolling to put out the flames. Reichis was less than grateful.

'Get off me!' he snarled, crawling out from under me. 'I have to go help them!'

I reached over to grab him by the scruff of his neck. 'You'll be dead before you get near them.'

He bit me until I let him go. 'Then get us in there! You're supposed to be a damned mage. Use that –' he waved his paws in the air – 'spell thing of yours.'

There were probably a dozen different spells that could bring down a fire wall, either by removing the original spell or cooling the air around it. None of them were ones I could perform of course.

I started coughing again, struggling for air. 'Wait . . .' Air was the problem. Air was feeding the fire. That gave me two possibilities – one of which didn't risk blowing my hands off, so I decided to try that one first.

I stepped back from the wall. Breath spells manipulate the movement of air, and one spell in particular can draw air towards the caster. I ran through the somatic forms a couple of times – both hands extending outward, then making the fingers touch the palm in a smooth sequence, alternating the right hand with the left, moving like the air itself. The movement was simple enough, but it had to be performed with perfect fluidity.

'What are you doing?' Reichis asked.

'Just a minute.' The second part was the visualisation.

Concentrating on air is harder than you'd expect. You have to specifically *avoid* thinking about the things air moves, such as leaves or dust, and focus on the air itself. Once I had that, all that was left was the verbalisation. This one was tricky though – it had to be voiced entirely on an inhalation. Even harder, you had to keep repeating it throughout the entire spell.

'*An-ahl-ha-teht,*' I whispered.

Nothing.

I kept going. Osia'phest always used to say that with magic you had to focus on performance, not outcome. '*An-ahl-ha-teht . . . an-ahl-ha-teht . . .*'

'Keep it up,' Reichis urged. 'Something's happening.'

I continued the spell and watched as the wall began to bend, the six-foot flames losing their strength, slowly starving for oxygen.

'It's working, keep going!' Reichis said.

'*An-ahl-ha—*'

My voice was cut off as the smoke filled my lungs. My stomach seized and I crouched over, coughing uncontrollably. 'Can't . . .' I said. 'Can't breathe through the smoke.' I looked up to see the flames had regained their full strength.

'Then throw me!' Reichis said.

I tried to stand up straight and clear my vision. 'Throw you?'

'The treetops are on fire so I can't climb up them to glide down. Throw me over the flames!'

'No,' I said. 'Even if I could, you'd be alone in there!'

'My people are alone, right now, dying!'

'Give me a second,' I said, still trying to calm my breathing. My second plan was the eminently worse option, but still

360

better than what Reichis proposed. I walked back about ten feet from the wall of flames and took a pinch of powder from each of my pockets. 'Come here,' I told Reichis, as I tried to figure out the timing that was going to be required for this to work.

'What are you doing?'

I nodded towards the flames. 'The second I start running, you run with me. At my speed. Don't get ahead of me and don't fall behind. Understand?'

I looked at the heavy pinches of red and black powders held between my fingers and took a last clean breath.

Reichis clued in to what I had planned. 'Are you out of your—'

'Just do it,' I said, and started running, heading straight for the wall of fire. The instant my right foot hit the ground, I tossed the powders into the air two feet in front of me. As my second step landed and the first spark ignited between the grains of powder, I formed the somatic shape with my hands and spoke the word. '*Carath!*'

The blast shook the ground in front of us, at the edge of the wall of flames, just as Reichis and I leaped in the air. For one brief instant, the explosion drove back the fire and we passed through unscathed. We landed awkwardly on the other side and I found myself rolling head over heels until I finally landed hard on my back. The squirrel cat looked down at me. 'Not bad. Now get up and help me kill that mage.'

I staggered to my feet to witness the wreckage of burnt trees all around us. Pockets of fire rose from the underbrush as though a mad priest had lit dozens of braziers around a fallen temple. Bodies littered the ground, human and squirrel cat. A bloody fight had been fought here between tooth and blade, between claw and spell. Only one figure still stood, his arms outstretched as if he were dancing alone among the flames. *Ra'meth*.

I didn't wait for him to notice me. I didn't make threats or demands. I didn't even think twice. Instead I dug deep into my pockets and tossed enough powder into the air to shatter stone. With the word and the gesture, I unleashed the explosion straight at his heart. The blast cracked the night sky and the resulting flames engulfed him. A moment later they faded away as if they'd been nothing more than a faint spark of a worn-out piece of flint.

Ra'meth turned to me. 'Hello, Kellen.'

45

The Voice of Fire

The next thing that happened was that Reichis went berserk. The sight of his fellow squirrel cats dead all around the clearing tipped his crazy-but-controlled ferocity into a heedless rage that swept over him so completely that I swear I nearly got caught up in it too.

'Reichis . . .' I warned, seeing the muscles bunching in his haunches as he prepared to attack. 'Wait. We need to—'

Whatever he growled at me then was too primal. It didn't have any human equivalent so I couldn't understand it. I tried to grab at him but he was too fast, kicking up dirt and brush behind him as he raced towards Ra'meth. There was a moment when I thought he might have a chance – his speed and rage propelled him at his enemy like a spell. If he just got his teeth into the mage's neck before he could raise his arms, he could – but no. Even as the squirrel cat leaped into the air, Ra'meth turned and uttered a single word. Reichis froze, his body swaying in the air as if he were hanging from a rope. 'They really are fierce little vermin, aren't they?' Ra'meth flicked his fingers and the squirrel cat flew through the air before his body crashed into a tree. I heard the sounds of bones snapping.

I should have run. I should have taken off and hidden and tried to come up with some plan to survive this. I simply couldn't. The sound of Reichis's broken growls of pain echoed over and over in my ears, deafening me to the sound of the flames, of the trees creaking as they fell, of everything but his pain and my heart beating faster and faster and faster. Finally another sound broke through – a growl that came from my own lips. I dug my hands into my pockets and pulled out more powders than I'd used the other times I'd cast the carath spell. I flung them into the air and made the somatic forms and spoke the word. The explosion lit up the night sky, surrounding Ra'meth in a perfect sphere of fire. It raged on for a second, then another, but finally it faded away. The mage was unharmed. 'Fascinating,' he said, taking a step towards me. 'Do it again.'

There was no fear in him, only in me. There was also no point in holding anything back. I used even more powder this time – so much that I felt it burn the skin on my fingers even before I spoke the word. The explosion followed the line of my index and forefingers right for Ra'meth's heart. Again my spell struck true, again he shrugged it off.

'Remarkable,' he said, as the last trickle of flame faded. '*And* you escaped the thirstfire in the barn. Impressive all round. I take it since you're here that you also dealt with my sons. Did you kill Tennat?'

'I figured having you for a father was punishment enough.'

He gave a good-natured laugh. I took advantage of the moment's distraction to fire the spell again. Even with only a tiny shred of his focus, he could keep the shield up. I wondered for the first time whether maybe Ra'meth had been wrong all these years. Maybe he was more powerful than my father, he'd just never had the courage to challenge him to a duel.

'That little spell of yours, Kellen,' he said, head tilted as he looked across the fire-strewn ground at me, 'it's just the first-form breath spell channelling the explosion from some sort of chemical powders, isn't it? Truly ingenious. It reminds me of those old spellslingers who wandered around, combining a few little spells with other tricks to make their way through the world. Quite a romantic notion, don't you think?' He cast his own spell then – a minor pain cantrip that ought to do little more than cause an itch.

It felt as if my insides had turned to ice and I screamed.

'The problem is, however, that there's a difference between a boy with a spell and a real mage. The true Jan'Tep is complete. He can attack but also defend. He knows how to weaken his opponent's power while enhancing his own.' He cast another spell, and this time I was thrown backwards through the air until my back struck the same tree as Reichis had and I found myself on the ground next to him.

I gasped for air, tasting blood in my mouth. Ra'meth ignored my moans. 'I don't hate you,' he said, turning to survey his handiwork. 'In fact, I admire your daring. You're a better man than your father, I'll give you that. All he's ever done is treat magic like a little castle he builds around himself, brick by brick, hoping to climb its pathetic walls to become clan prince. And for what purpose? None. He would sit back and have us live here like frightened animals, hoping the real predators pass us by in search of better prey.' He turned, pointing south. 'I would see us be a great power again, Kellen. I would see the Daroman king begging at our feet.'

I don't know if he was waiting for some sort of clever retort

365

from me, but given I could barely breathe, he was going to be waiting a long time.

Finally he turned away again. 'We were meant to be the rulers of this world, Kellen.'

I looked around and noticed a large outcropping of rock a few feet away. Reaching down, I took hold of Reichis as gently as I could. He groaned from the pain of his broken ribs. *At least he's alive. Now keep him that way.* I crawled, slowly, quietly, towards the rocks.

'I wish my sons were more like you,' Ra'meth said. 'For all I've given them, they are little more than dull-witted bullies. They giggle and preen like complacent fools, content for others to be weak rather than making the sacrifice to become powerful themselves.' He turned and fired another spell that struck me in the side. Suddenly I was rolling on the ground, trying to protect Reichis. When the force dissipated, I continued my pathetic, almost instinctive effort to reach the dubious safety of the rocks.

'I could make something of you, you know,' he called out as I cowered behind them. 'You've earned that opportunity, with your cleverness and your daring. Besides, our people always love a good story about the brave young orphan boy taken in by the master of a great house. We just need to make you an orphan first.'

How about I make your sons orphans instead? I removed my pack and reached inside for Ferius's deck of steel cards. Every shield spell has gaps. Maybe if I flung the cards fast enough, at different parts of the shield, one might slip through. The odds weren't good of course, but I was all out of ideas.

'I know I should kill you, Kellen. It's always better to wipe every last trace of your enemy off the face of the earth. We

366

should have done that with the Mahdek centuries ago. Now we jump in our beds at every mention of their name, fearing that somewhere out there lurks one more, waiting for their chance.'

I laid the cards out in front of me. I'd have to time things perfectly. *Even then, will it do any good?* Ra'meth could just keep his shield spell up until I ran out of cards.

'But damn it all, boy, I really think you and I could make a go of it. I need an enforcer for my house. Ra'fan hides behind the work of others. Ra'dir has the stomach for violence but not the intellect, and Tennat . . . well, let's just say that if you feel you must kill him in order to accept my offer, it wouldn't be a deal-breaker.'

Who talks about their children this way? I was in serious danger of sympathising with Tennat.

A creeping motion from the shadows caught my eye and I saw a squirrel cat – not Reichis – crawling on its belly towards us. The creature was bleeding from wounds all over its body, and its fur was charred by fire. *The poor thing is looking for a place to die,* I thought, and picked up one of the cards. Did I have the nerve to give it a quick death? The squirrel cat got close to me and I recognised her as Reichis's mother.

I reached out a hand to help her reach the protection of the rocks, only to have her sink her teeth into my forearm. 'Damn it!' I swore. I was getting tired of being bitten.

'Forgive me,' she said in a mix of chitters and desperate gasps for air.

I can understand her, I realised. Maybe it was through breaking the skin, getting their saliva into your bloodstream, that the squirrel cats created whatever bond allowed communication with a human.

367

'My name is Chitra,' she said, and slunk a little closer to Reichis. I understood without her having to tell me that she was using her last moments of life so that she could die next to her son.

'Well, Kellen?' Ra'meth called out. 'What do you think? Let's do this: you kill your father for me, and I'll kill Tennat for you. We both win, and the world will be a better place for it.'

Chitra gave a cough that sent blood dripping down her chin. 'Humans . . .' she said as she dragged herself a little closer, '. . . are something of a disappointment, at times.'

I reached out to her. 'What can I do?'

She nuzzled my hand. 'Take what I have to give.'

My hand came away bloody. 'I . . . I don't understand.'

'The red powder,' she said. 'Mix my blood in it.'

I pulled the pouches out from my pockets and reached into the one with the red powder. 'What will this do?'

Chitra ignored the question, instead collapsing next to Reichis. She extended a paw and placed it on his muzzle. 'He will be so full of anger, this one. You must be his caution, as he will be your courage. You will teach him when to flee and he will teach you when to fight.'

'I . . .' What could I say to her? We were about to die, and Reichis could barely tolerate me. 'I will,' I said finally. 'I promise.'

She gave a strange little cough, and more blood dripped from her mouth. It took me a moment to realise she'd laughed. 'Perhaps you should have him teach you how to lie too. You don't seem to be very good at it.' The sides of her mouth pulled up a little bit, making a weary smile. 'You must be firm nego-tiating with him. He will steal the rest from you, anyway.'

Reichis's eyes blinked open for a moment, the little black orbs finally seeming to understand what he saw. He let out a moan then, so full of pain and sorrow it pulled me into it, drowning me. I had never known love, I realised then, and now could only watch as it slipped away.

'Keep him from extortion and blackmail, if you can,' Chitra went on, her chitters almost inaudible over the crackling of the flames around us. 'He has many bad habits, this one.' She lay her muzzle down on his. 'But every once in a while he makes his mother so very proud.'

My hand wouldn't stop shaking, even as I tried to mix her blood in with the red powder. 'I don't understand,' I said, blinded by the tears filling my eyes as I watched the life fade from her. 'What am I supposed to do?'

'The Mahdek believed that magic should be used to give voice to the spirits of the world,' she said, barely a whisper now. 'Let yours speak for me.' Chitra let out one last sigh, in which everything that was left of her settled upon the dying earth. Inside the pouch at my side, the red powder glistened and smouldered with a heat that threatened to set it aflame.

A blast of fire lit the air above my head. 'I don't believe you're taking my offer seriously, Kellen.'

'No, really, I'm considering it,' I said. I was lying of course, but so was Ra'meth. This was all a game for him – one last little piece to take from Ke'heops. When he killed my father, he wanted to be able to look down at him and say, 'See? Your son betrayed you. He was willing to murder you in your own house in exchange for a room in mine.'

I looked down to where Reichis still lay on the ground next to his dead mother. His own breathing was shallow, his eyes flat as they looked up at me.

'I suppose you're right to refuse,' Ra'meth called out, even though I hadn't said anything. 'An arrangement like ours would be unlikely to last.' He sent a blast of flame that lit up the outcrop of rock where I hid. 'Come then. Stand and face me one last time – one final act of courage before you die. When you enter the grey passage, stand tall before our ancestors and tell them you faced death without fear. This is the greatest gift I can give you, Kellen. A clean death. A Jan'Tep death.'

I reached my hands into the pouches, still feeling the stickiness of Chitra's blood on the fingers of my right hand. 'I'm coming,' I said.

I rose, very slowly, and faced Ra'meth. He glowed with red, swirling magic all around him, an endless ocean cresting and crashing and cresting again. It was like watching a painting of one of the first lords magi come to life. He nodded to me, not unkindly. 'Good. Good. It's better this way. You weren't meant for this world, Kellen. You were meant for—'

My hands came up into the air, the powders floating, glimmering for an instant in the light of Ra'meth's own magic. I waited, for just an instant, letting the first sparks ignite as the grains of black and blood-red powder collided against each other, then I formed the somatic shapes with my hands and said the words, slowly and deliberately, wanting them to ring out into the night sky. '*Carath Chitra.*'

Ra'meth brought his own hands up, fingers shaping the shield that had so effortlessly protected him from my earlier attacks. He looked disappointed.

The explosion flew at him, the flames ragged, like claws grasping at the invisible barrier of his shield. 'I told you, boy,' he said, 'there's more to magic than –'

His words were cut off as the two spells collided. The air

370

all around him turned into red and black cinders as if his shield had begun to burn from the inside out. Then another rush, as it collapsed completely, and the fire of Chitra's life and death raged all around him, the blood-red flames biting at his clothes, his flesh. I heard Ra'meth scream once, then he fell silent in a heap on the ground.

Chitra's blood had given voice to the rage of her people.

I looked down at where Ra'meth lay on the forest floor. There was an almost perfect circle around him where the shield had kept out most of the blast until right before it collapsed. I waited until I saw the rise and fall of his chest to make sure he was still alive, then I reached into the pouches in my pocket for more powder to finish the job.

Something was wrong with my vision. The forest, or what remained of it, was still right there in front of me. Burnt trees and the charred corpses of men and squirrel cats littered the ground. Nothing moved, and yet, when I closed my right eye and gazed out through my left – the one with the shadowblack marks around it – the violence came to life. Screams of pain, of rage, of dying echoed in my ears. I shuddered, not because the sights made me sick, but because they made me feel good.

'Intoxicating, isn't it, kid?' I turned to see Ferius Parfax walking towards me, leading two horses with her.

'I don't know what you're talking about,' I replied, and turned my attention back to Ra'meth.

'Your sister's going to be fine, in case you're wondering,' Ferius said. 'Squirrel cat's alive too.'

It felt as if the marks around my left eye were moving, writhing under the skin, cold and yet burning at the same time. It made me feel alive. Powerful. 'What about you?' I asked. The words sounded as if they were coming from someone else. Someone weak and stupid. Someone who was in danger of forgetting that his enemy was at his feet, his life in his hands. My fingertips brushed the powders in my pockets. In a few seconds I was going to end Ra'meth for all time. I wouldn't fear him ever again.

Ferius rolled her shoulders back, then tilted her head from side to side. 'I'm a little sore. Nothing I ain't used to.' She walked over to stand close to me. Too close. 'Come on, kid. You proved you're the big man. Time to go do something real.'

Something real? She still didn't know when to stop mocking people. I looked down at the man who'd murdered my uncle, who'd tried to take over my clan and tried to kill my sister. 'I have to end him.'

I felt Ferius's hand on my arm. 'You *want* to end him. It's not the same thing. Look at him, Kellen.'

I did. Scorched hair and skin showed through the burnt patches in Ra'meth's robes where the explosion had broken through his shields. He was still unconscious, but I thought I heard him groan.

'Wait long enough and maybe he'll wake up,' Ferius said, practically whispering in my ear. 'If you're real lucky he'll reach out a hand, maybe twitch a finger. You can tell yourself that he was about to cast another spell.'

'He might.'

Her hand squeezed my arm. 'No, he won't. Not with those injuries. It'll be months before he can work a spell again, and you know it.'

'Shut up, Ferius,' I said, my eyes still on the form of the man at my feet. *Say something,* I begged him. *Make a move.*

'You'd be within your rights,' Ferius said. 'I've travelled the length and breadth of this continent and there ain't a court anywhere that would condemn you for what you're about to do.'

'Then why are you talking me to death?'

She spun me around to face her. 'Because the Argosi don't got no country, kid. But we got our own ways, and this ain't one of them. You have to decide now which road you want to walk.'

'It's the shadowblack,' I pleaded, wishing she would get away from me. I had to force my hands to stay in my pockets even as they itched to come out and toss the powders into the air and put an end to her annoying, self-important, incessant philosophising.

'The shadowblack?' She laughed. It was a strange sound, and I knew something about her in that laugh. Ferius wasn't laughing because she thought this was funny. She wasn't even laughing because she wanted to. She was laughing because this was how Ferius Parfax told the world she refused to be afraid of it. 'Imagine if you could just go and catch a disease that meant you could do whatever you wanted, kill whoever you wanted. No guilt, no accountability. Now, wouldn't that be just fine?'

'I'm not imagining this!' I shouted, wishing I could make her leave before I did something I'd hate myself for. 'The shadowblack is real. It's in me!'

She grabbed me by the neck with her other hand, squeezing. Damn, but she had a strong grip. 'We all got ugliness inside us, Kellen. Yours is worse? Then fight harder. Figure it out. But don't you ever pretend you don't have a choice.'

My fists clenched and I felt the powder rubbing against the skin of my palms. 'You don't understand! He killed

Reichis's people. He tried to kill my sister. You can't know what that's like. You can't –'

Suddenly she squeezed harder and I was having trouble drawing breath. 'I can't understand? Is that right, Kellen, son of Ke'heops, child of the Jan'Tep?'

She'd never referred to me in such a formal way. She'd said it the same way she said everything, as if it were all some mildly curious, sardonic observation about the world around her, as if nothing really mattered. The darkness in her eyes told a different story. I knew now, finally, the secret she'd kept hidden behind her smirks and jokes. Somehow, in that knowing, I felt the dark rage inside me slip away.

Ever since she'd shown up, I'd wondered who Ferius Parfax really was – *what* she really was. Despite all her claims about being a simple Argosi wanderer, her denials about being a Daroman spy were so feeble that all it did was persuade everyone – me included – that she probably *was* working for their king. I always wondered why somebody so clever, so full of tricks, did such a bad job of convincing people she wasn't a spy. Now I knew. 'You aren't Daroman,' I said.

'Never claimed to be.'

'And you're not just an Argosi either.'

'Sure I am, kid.' She reached into her waistcoat and fanned out a deck of cards. 'See?'

'Show me,' I said.

She tilted her head. 'Show you what?'

'Show me *your* card. The real one.'

Without her hand moving at all, one of the cards slowly slid up from the others. I took it and turned it over. It was a jack, just like others I'd seen in the deck, but not a septagram for the Jan'Tep or a sword for the Daromans or even a chalice for the Berabesq. This one depicted a black leaf on the top-right corner. 'You're Mahdek,' I said.

'Now that's just silly, kid. Everybody knows there ain't no more Mahdek.'

'Because my people massacred them. Only . . . no one can massacre an entire people, can they? Some have to escape. Some wouldn't have been in the cities when the attacks came.'

Ferius took the card back and packed the deck back into her waistcoat. 'Oh, they got rid of us all right. There isn't enough Mahdek blood in the world to bring my people back. What's left are just . . . ghosts, I guess you could say.'

'Did you . . . ?' I hesitated to ask the question, not sure I could live with the answer. Ferius had changed my life. She'd given me so much, I couldn't bear to think that she was just as cold and mean as everyone else in the world had turned out to be. 'Did you come to get revenge? Is that why you're here? To kill my people for what they did to yours?'

She leaned back against the side of one of the horses and pulled out a smoking reed from inside her waistcoat. 'Toss a little of that powder together, would you, kid?'

Not knowing what else to do, I did. It created a tiny burst of flame in the air. With the speed of a whip cracking she reached out the reed and the end caught fire. 'When I was a girl,' she said, taking in a breath of the smoke, 'my grandma and grandpa – my folks had died a while before – anyway, they made me swear the same oath they'd taken, the same one my folks had taken and every one of us had taken since the days when that old clan prince of yours and his mages killed off my people.'

'You swore revenge,' I said, almost surprised to find there

375

actually was one paranoid fear my people held that turned out to be true.

Ferius nodded, sending twin puffs of smoke from her nostrils. 'That's just the way it is sometimes.' She motioned towards Ra'meth. 'Blood for blood.'

'So all of this . . . saving my life—'

She cut me off. 'My grandparents died when I was still too young to fend for myself. We're not a long-lived people, I guess. Life without a land of your own is hard. I wandered the long desert roads for a while, not knowing what I was doing. Pretty soon I was at the end of my rope. Starving, dying of thirst, covered in a dozen wounds from one scrape or another. I was pretty much done for.'

I tried to imagine what that would be like – to be completely alone in the world. 'The Argosi,' I said. 'They took you in.'

She chuckled. 'What a bunch of weirdos. Everything is cards with them. Cards for this, cards for that. But they saved me that day. Kept saving me too, every time I'd run off and nearly get myself killed. Every time they did –' she reached into her waistcoat and pulled out her deck of blood-red cards – 'they made me take one of these.'

'They're debts? For saving your life?'

She nodded. 'Every one of these is a life I have to pay back.'

I reached into my own trousers and pulled out the dark red card she'd forced me to take the day she'd gone on about debts. 'And this is a life I have to pay back.'

'Yep.'

'So . . . you just gave up on revenge for your people?'

Ferius looked up at the night sky, where the flames still burning around us lit up her face, making her suddenly terrifying. 'No, kid, I just figured out that no matter how

376

many Jan'Tep I killed, I'd never be able to bring my own people back.' She dropped the smoking reed and stamped it out with the heel of her boot. 'The Argosi believe that the world hangs on a delicate balance. Some things – like the way your people abuse magic, like the way the Daroman roll over the rest of the world with their empire – those things bring us closer to destruction. Other things, sometimes just little things, they help push us the other way. Reckon if I can't bring my people back, least I can do is save the world.' She reached out a hand and held my arm, just for a moment. 'Feel like helping?'

I reeled back, as much from her words as her unusual gentleness. How could anyone live that kind of life? How could she sit back and let the people who had murdered her tribe just keep living in the same cities they'd stolen from them? I looked down at Ra'meth and remembered the look on my uncle's face as the bolt of fire had burst through his chest. 'I don't think I'm like you, Ferius.'

'Never asked you to be.' She walked over to where Reichis lay on the ground and very gently scooped him up and placed him in a bag that she slung over her shoulder. 'Tough little bastard, isn't he?' She looked over to me. 'You've got a decision to make, kid. There's a little shack a few miles out of town. Fella there knows some healing ways. Figure he can help the squirrel cat. He also brews up some kind of drink that makes a sane person's head spin round and round. It's a safe bet that I'll be there a few hours. If you want to learn the Argosi path, come find me.' She put a foot into the stirrup and got up on the horse. 'If not, well, then I reckon that's one less card I have to worry about.'

She started turning the horse around and I was struck by

377

the thought that I might never see her again. 'Wait,' I said, struggling to find some excuse to make her slow down. 'The card I saw you painting at the oasis ... the dowager magus thought you were here because there was something that you believed could make civilisations rise or fall. Was she right?'

She turned back. 'Canny old bird, wasn't she?' Ferius reached a hand carefully across her chest so as not to disturb Reichis and pulled a card from her waistcoat. 'Finished this while I was waiting to make sure your sister would be okay.' She flipped the card through the air at me and I caught it in my hand.

'You're giving this to me?'

'Depends. If all you're planning on doing with your life is killing Ra'meth, then you might as well tear it up for all I care.'

'What if ... ? What if I don't kill him? What if I come find you?'

She grinned. 'Then make sure to bring the card with you, kid, cos I'll need it for my deck.'

'Why?'

She kicked her horse and started down the path. 'Because that card might just change the world.'

As Ferius disappeared from view I turned the card over and finally saw what she'd been painting ever since she'd come to town. It was, as Mer'esan had predicted, one of the discordances. The inscription at the bottom said 'Spellslinger'. It was a painting of a young man standing in front of an open road with a squirrel cat sitting on his shoulder and fire in his hands. The figure looked just like me.

46

The Mage's Trial

An hour later I was dragging Ra'meth's unconscious body up the sandy street that led to the court of the lords magi. My horse had developed a limp in his step a quarter-mile back and, figuring enough people and animals had already died for me, I slung Ferius's pack on my shoulder and walked the rest of the way. Now I had a limp.

One of the guards out front caught sight of me about twenty feet from the steps to the oasis. They were crowded with families each awaiting their child's turn to face the court and learn the verdict of their mage's trial. 'Stop where you are,' the guard called out. He was a big man, I guessed in his forties. As he ran towards me he kept his hands at his sides, fingers forming the shapes that told me he was probably a chaincaster. I was getting sick of those.

I stopped, still looking past him at the families on the steps. I recognised several of the initiates from my class. They recognised me too, and turned away. The slight didn't bother me. I was more baffled by the fact that, despite our clan very nearly having been taken over by rebellion and conspiracy, Jan'Tep life still revolved around deciding who would get to be a mage and who would become a servant.

379

'Just dropping something off,' I told the guard, and let go of the collar of Ra'meth's robes. I rubbed at my shoulder, partly to show I wasn't about to attempt any spells and partly because, well, my shoulder hurt.

The people on the steps started shuffling towards us, peering down at the unconscious form next to me. It took only a few seconds before they realised who it was, and about two seconds more before they started coming for me.

'Stay back!' The cold determination in my mother's voice surprised me. I turned to see her striding towards us, the long flowing fabric of her dress dancing in the night breeze. 'Are you all right?' she asked me, her eyes still on the guards trying to approach.

'He's attacked one of the lords magi,' the guard in front of me said.

I thought that was a little unfair. After all, how did they know I hadn't just *saved* Ra'meth from somebody else? It didn't really matter though, because when my mother turned to face the guards, she looked a good deal scarier than I did. 'Kellen stopped a murderer from taking over our clan,' she said, then turned to me, and I guessed from her expression that Ferius must have told her what had happened. 'He saved my daughter.'

The gratitude in her smile was so pure, so genuine, that I don't think she could possibly have understood that the other side of that coin was how obvious it was that she saw me not as a son, but as a kind of treasured servant. I had done my duty, which was to protect Shalla.

I decided I could live with that. 'Is she all right?'

'She is disoriented, but recovers quickly. She wanted to come but we felt—'

'It's better she not be here,' I said, not wanting to know any more about my parents' feelings than was necessary.

My mother looked down at Ra'meth. 'You let him live.'

'I did,' I said.

She held my gaze a long time before turning to the court guards. 'Take Ra'meth prisoner. Bind him with copper and silver. He will be made to answer for his crimes.'

I suppose I'd never really thought about just how powerful a mage my mother was. For all her strength, she'd always deferred to my father. I wondered now, seeing how the others reacted to her, why she let him stand as the head of our family. *I guess I really don't understand my own people all that well.*

There was a certain amount of confused shuffling about as the guards did as my mother commanded. She had no formal authority over them, but I doubt they wanted to risk angering a woman whose magic was practically making the air ripple around her.

'The council will want the boy taken into custody,' the leader of the guards told her, motioning to me.

I caught just enough of a flash of uncertainty in my mother's expression that I decided to answer before she could. 'Tell the lords magi that I'll be with them momentarily,' I said. 'I feel like sitting down for a minute.'

My mother nodded. 'I will inform the council that you will see them when you're ready.' She squeezed my shoulder. 'I know you'll do what's right.'

Her last sentence echoed in my head like one of the fundamental spells we used to practise as children, uttering each syllable a dozen different ways, trying to find its perfect articulation, then how it related to the next syllable, until

381

we could comprehend the full meaning. *I know you'll do what's right.*

I walked over to the steps and sat down heavily, reaching into Ferius's pack that was still slung on my back and pulling out a small flask. I opened it and drank without checking the contents – possibly a mistake since it burned my tongue at first. A moment later the warmth snaked down my throat and into my belly. After that I started feeling a bit light-headed. I'd just had my first taste of liquor.

Maybe I should get drunk before I go see the council.

A few minutes of drinking brought me to a strange clarity. Why was I still sitting there, on the steps of the court? I should have been finding another horse and getting myself out of town as quickly as possible.

It wasn't that I was afraid of being taken captive by the council at this point. I knew too much, and though sometimes that can be a dangerous thing, there were many other people who also knew something had happened. They knew there had been a conspiracy to take over the clan. Powerful people would want answers, and if I was suddenly imprisoned, that would just raise more questions.

So it wasn't fear of retribution that kept me sitting on those steps; I was just afraid of leaving everything I'd ever known behind.

'Kellen?'

I looked up to see Nephenia standing barely two feet in front of me. Her long dark hair was draped over shoulders left uncovered by her long white celebration gown – a garment identical to those of several other students waiting their turn in front of the council in anticipation of completing their trials. Her arms were crossed in front of her, each hand clinging on to the opposite elbow for dear life. She looked beautiful and miserable in equal measure.

'What's wrong?' I asked.

She opened her mouth to speak, then took in a breath and sniffed. Her lips started to tremble. 'I . . . I'm sorry, it's stupid. It's nothing.' She reached up a shaking hand to wipe at a tear that hadn't yet formed. 'I'm going to be Sha'Tep.'

'What? Why? You've had your trial? But you passed the tests. How could—'

She looked up towards the entrance to the court. 'I'm due to go in next, but Master Osia'phest already came out and told me . . . I think he didn't want me to be surprised. I have no secret to bring to the council, none that matters to them anyway.'

I almost laughed out loud at the ridiculousness of the situation. Most of the initiates here, standing proud in their celebration garb, had no secret that mattered to anyone. It was, as much as anything, a formality. *So why did they go to the trouble of deciding in advance that Nephenia would fail?* The answer was simple of course. She had made enemies by not siding with Tennat and Panahsi and the others. Their parents must have slipped word to the council members that they wanted Nephenia shunned, and her own family had little influence or power.

We are such a small people, I thought. *For all our magic, we're scared, paranoid little children trying to protect ourselves from the bullies of the world by becoming bigger bullies ourselves.*

I found myself just staring at her. I don't think I'd ever seen a person that perfectly and utterly despondent in my entire life. You can't sit in the face of that kind of pain and do nothing, so I decided to try a spell.

I stood, very slowly, and carefully extended both my hands, palms up. I waited for a long time as she looked at me, nervousness gradually changing to curiosity as she became more confident this wasn't some kind of trick. Finally I felt the warmth of her palms on mine. 'I have a secret for you,' I said.

The surprise and hope on her face didn't last long before she shook her head. 'Don't. Don't tell me something they can use against you. I won't be –'

I smiled. 'The council is going to find out anyway. Tennat and the others will be back here soon, and they'll tell them. Nephenia, what I offer is a coin that will be worthless in a few hours. I want to spend it now, on you.' She hesitated, still not wanting to be part of all this ugliness. 'Please,' I said. 'If you don't tell them, I will.'

Finally she nodded. 'All right.'

There were too many people around so I had to whisper in her ear.

Imagine being told that someone you care about has the worst disease imaginable, something so foul that you're convinced just being close to them will infect you. Now add to that the deep conviction that this disease also means that person is twisted, vile on the inside. Imagine finding out that someone you know is no better than a demon waiting to attack. What do you do?

Nephenia reached out and hugged me again, holding me close to her for a long time. Even when I tried to push her away she held on to me, gripping me so tightly I could barely breathe. I could feel her cheek against mine. 'I'm not afraid of you, Kellen,' she said.

I hugged her back, as gently as I could, fighting the urge to take her face in my hands and kiss her. Just hours away from turning sixteen years old and I'd never kissed a girl. How long would it be before I ever had a chance like this again? But as much as I wanted to, as much as I think she wanted me to, my awareness grew to take in the hundreds of people around the court, no doubt staring at us. If we kissed, things would go poorly for Nephenia once people knew about my shadowblack. They would see her as tainted.

I felt her face tilting up towards mine and I knew she'd decided to stop waiting for me. Very carefully, I stepped back out of reach. 'No matter what anyone says, you're going to be a great mage one day,' I said.

She smiled. At first it was the same shy, demure smile I'd seen on her face hundreds of times before. Then something strange happened. One corner of her mouth turned up just a little more than the other, making her somehow appear bolder, more self-assured. There was something faintly mischievous in her voice when she said, 'What I plan to be is a woman who doesn't wait for permission from anyone.'

Suddenly she was pressed up against me, her lips on mine, hands reaching up to my face. I felt her fingers sliding through my hair and I wrapped my arms around her, both of us holding on to that moment, that kiss, for as long as we could.

My whole life I'd thought I'd wanted to kiss a girl. Turns out being kissed by one is infinitely better.

'Nephenia, daughter of Ena'eziat,' a clerk called out. 'The time of your mage's trial has come.'

I felt her reach around and gently remove my hands from her waist. She stepped back and smiled at me. 'We're going to see each other again, Kellen.'

'First you need to pass your trial and become a mage. Become the best mage our clan has ever seen.'

'And then?' she asked.

I reached up and tapped a finger on the paste Mer'esan had given me to cover the shadowblack marks around my eye. 'Then figure out a way to cure me.'

I didn't see Nephenia come out of the court. By tradition, initiates enter the building through the front and leave through the back, where they are greeted by their families, either in celebration or consolation.

So I sat there on the front steps, waiting. About two hours later, after all the rest of the council's business was done, a clerk was sent to lead me inside.

There were seven seats in the court chambers, each rising nearly ten feet above the floor and set on its own thick marble pillar surrounded by a spiral staircase to enable those who sat in judgment to rise to their lofty perch. Three men, one of them Master Osia'phest, and two women occupied five of the seats. Two were left empty: the one reserved for Ra'meth, and the one normally occupied by my father.

'Family members must be recused from judging their own children,' Te'oreth, deputy leader of the council, said. 'Ke'heops cannot protect you now, boy.'

When has he ever? I wondered. 'As summoned, so do I appear before you, Lords Magi,' I said, using the formal mode of address as Osia'phest had taught us when we'd begun preparing for our trial. The old man looked slightly relieved at my passable attempt at etiquette.

They're all old, I thought. Te'oreth, An'atria . . . all of them. If you'd asked me even a day before to describe the lords magi, I'd have told you of their specialities in magic, of their strength and power, of the stories of wondrous spells they'd cast. I would have described warriors, shining on the battlefields of this world, protecting our people from the military hordes of the Daroman and the religious zealots of the Berabesq along with all our other enemies. Now, in this stifling, ill-lit room, what I saw were old men and women hanging on to power through nothing more than ancient stories and dirty secrets.

'Kneel, boy,' Te'oreth said, motioning to the *supplicantia*, a set of heavy wooden stocks set into a flat, circular stone surface in the centre of the courtroom. The initiate, or prisoner, or whoever else had come to plead before the council, would place his or her wrists, palm up, in the semi-circular grooves. A guard would then slide the block in place. This had both a practical purpose – a supplicant who disputed the council's verdict would be unable to attempt any spells – and a symbolic one: it meant you spent the entire trial on your knees with your hands out like a beggar.

'I'm fine standing,' I said.

One of the council members started to object, but Osia'phest cut them off. 'Let us not waste time on ceremony. Greater matters attend us.'

'Perhaps,' An'atria said, her dark eyes peering out from a thick halo of grey hair as she stared at me, 'but do we still pretend this one comes to pass his mage's trial?'

'Why not?' I asked, folding my arms across my chest and doing my best impression of someone entirely disinterested in the outcome of these events. 'Today is the last day of the mage trials, I am an initiate and, as it turns out, it won't be my sixteenth birthday for several hours yet.'

'You truly believe we would give you a mage's name?' Te'oreth demanded. 'You have proven nothing during your tests other than that you are a liar, a cheat and a weakling.'

387

'He has proven himself worse than that,' added Ven'asp. 'He has been directly involved in a conspiracy to destroy this clan.'

Osia'phest rose in his seat. 'He is the one who stopped the conspiracy against the clan!' he insisted. 'At great cost to himself he put an end to Ra'meth's attempted takeover.'

Te'oreth gave an unconvincing laugh. 'You would paint this coward as a hero?' He shook his head. 'No, until Ra'meth recovers from his wounds sufficiently to answer for himself, this council will refrain from making any judgments in the matter. I for one find it hard to believe this boy did the things his mother would have us believe. I suspect there is much more at work here than we yet know.'

'An excellent assumption, Magus Te'oreth,' I said. 'I've recently discovered that people rarely tell the whole truth.'

'Is that what you're here to do then, Kellen?' Osia'phest asked hopefully. 'Tell the whole truth?'

I smiled. 'No, My Lords Magi, I'm not here for that.'

'Why do we waste our time then?' Ven'asp asked. 'Put him in copper bindings and lock him up until we're ready to deal with him. The boy hasn't passed a single test; he has no business being in this hallowed place.'

'That's not quite true, Magus Ven'asp,' I said. 'In fact, I do believe I've passed all four of your tests.'

Te'oreth spat. 'You make a mockery of these proceedings. I will not—'

'Let the boy present his evidence,' Osia'phest said. 'As my student, he has that right.'

I looked up at my old spellmaster, grateful for his intervention but also curious as to his motives. Had Osia'phest been part of the Sha'Tep conspiracy, tired of watching arrogant and cruel children rise to become initiates and then mages year after year? I decided it wasn't my problem any more and, besides, I wasn't sure I wanted to know the answer. Instead I turned my attention to the men and women staring down at me in preparation for judgment. 'Four tests, My Lords Magi. Four corners to the initiate's trial. I passed the first when I won a mage's duel with magic.'

'Liar!' Ven'asp said. 'Your own sister revealed your trick. You used Tennat's—'

'I never said it was *my* magic.'

There were more complaints after that, but again Osia'phest raised a hand. 'We will get through this faster if we simply let Kellen make his case.'

'Thank you, teacher,' I said. 'The second test was to find a source of power. I'm not sure if you all heard, but I secured a power animal that no other Jan'Tep mage has in all our history.'

'A nekhek,' Ven'asp said. He turned to the others. 'We should put the boy in the stocks for that reason if no other. He made a familiar of our most ancient enemy.'

'To be completely honest, Reichis is more of a business partner than a familiar. Either way, you have to admit, he brings power with him.'

I wiped my hands on my trousers to get rid of some of the sweat that came from both the heat of the room and the fact that I was still more than a little terrified of what might happen next. Mostly, though, I needed my hands to be dry. 'Now, as for the third test, I combined two very different disciplines to create a new spell.'

Te'oreth peered down from his perch at the bands on my forearms. 'You have sparked only the breath band. What is this "second" discipline you used?'

'Chemistry,' I replied, and slid my hands into the pouches

389

inside my pockets, letting a pinch of each of the powders combine in the air before I formed the somatic shapes and uttered the words. I ended up burning the tips of my fingers and had to suck in a breath to keep from letting out what would have been an embarrassing squeal of pain, but fortunately no one was paying attention to me. They were focused on the supplicantia that I had just blown up into a thousand pieces. 'Not bad, as initiates' spells go, don't you think?'

Te'oreth's eyes turned to me, his hands ready to cast something that I suspected would be particularly nasty if I moved again. Part of me – no doubt the part that was already taking on too many of Reichis's less polite qualities – wondered if I could outdraw the old mage. *Probably best not to find out.* I knew it had been stupid to show off, but it mattered to me that these people understand there might be a cost to messing with me in future.

'The fourth test then,' Osia'phest said. I think there might have been a hint of a smile on his face at everyone else's discomfort.

Ven'asp, however, seemed delighted. 'How about his own secret?' he asked, his smirk mean and triumphant as he looked down at me. 'The girl betrayed you, boy. She sold you out to pass her tests. To secure her mage's name of Neph'aria, she revealed to us that you have the shadowblack. Do you still feel prideful now?'

'Mostly I feel relieved,' I said, speaking honestly for a change. I'd been afraid that Nephenia . . . *no, Neph'aria* . . . I'd worried she might not go through with it. She was a good person who'd been trapped by the same rotten circumstances as I would have been if I hadn't met Ferius Parfax. She deserved a chance to make a life for herself.

'And you kept this vile illness a secret?' Ven'asp asked. 'Even from Ke'heops himself?'

Actually they kept it from me. I was about to say as much when I saw the way everyone was looking at me now. *This is how they do it. This is how they rewrite history.* They knew my parents had concealed my having the shadowblack, but with Ra'meth out of the running to become clan prince, they would need to stay on my father's good side. That meant overlooking his crime, which meant blaming it on me. 'I suppose it hardly matters now, does it?'

'Spoken like a true coward,' Te'oreth said. 'So then, what secret do you have for us? You can't truly believe that your fabrications about the House of Ra taking advantage of this Sha'Tep conspiracy will buy you a mage's name.'

And there was the second part of the story that had to be rewritten. Ra'meth couldn't be branded a murderer and conspirator. His family still had power and influence. Why should any of the lords magi make an enemy when they could instead be owed a favour?

I looked up at their faces, these great mage warriors of our people, these wizened old men and women. I saw the hint of optimism in Osia'phest's otherwise carefully neutral expression. Was there a chance that, with all that had happened, the council might actually grant me my name and give me a place among my people?

'No,' a voice said. It was my own, which surprised me. 'No, Lords Magi, the secret I've uncovered isn't that Ra'meth tried to use the Sha'Tep conspiracy in order to take control of the clan. It wasn't even that our own people massacred the Mahdek tribes to take their magic and this very city we now live in.' I walked over to the small table with the pen and ink next to finger-length rolls of parchment upon which the supplicant had to write the secret they would submit to the council. I wrote down a single sentence before rolling it up and handing it to one of the clerks, who ascended the steps of Te'oreth's pillar and handed it to him.

The old mage gave it only a moment's glance before he whispered a spell, setting the parchment alight and sending the ashes raining down at my feet.

'What did it say?' An'atria asked him.

He didn't answer, so I did. 'It said that there's no amount of magic in the world that's worth the price of a man's conscience.'

It's customary at the end of testimony for the supplicant, whether bound or not, to close their eyes as they await the court's verdict. Success results in a second slip of parchment placed in the supplicant's hands upon which is written his or her mage name. Failure is emptiness. I didn't close my eyes, nor did I hold out my hands. I was done hiding and I was done begging. I turned and started for the door.

'You abandon the trial?' An'atria asked. 'You would set aside your chance at passing your tests, at being granted a mage's name?'

I paused for a moment, my hand on the door between the halls of magic and the wide world outside. 'I already have a name.'

As I walked out through the front entrance of the court, I made sure they heard me when I said, 'My name is Kellen Argos.'

Epilogue

I tromped the quarter-mile back to where my horse waited for me and checked on his leg. It didn't seem to bother him any more, but since I didn't know much about horses I walked him to the edge of town just to be sure. Not long after, I woke to a mouthful of horsehair. At some point I must've dozed off and slumped face first against the animal's rump. After that the horse and I agreed it would be less embarrassing for both of us if I rode. So I mounted, awkwardly, and set out in the direction of the shack Ferius had spoken of.

I only got as far as the arch that led out of town before a figure stepped out onto the road in front of me.

'You're not leaving,' Shalla said. She had tears in her eyes and glimmers of blue and yellow magical force drifted up from the bands around her forearms to swirl around her hands.

A glance at the movements of her fingers told me she was preparing a lightning spell. Figuring the horse had suffered enough already on my account, I dismounted. 'I'm glad you're okay, Shalla.'

She gave a terse nod. I was pretty sure that was all the acknowledgement I was ever going to get from her for having nearly died trying to save her life. 'Mother and Father healed me. We're a family.' The last part sounded like an accusation.

'You are,' I said, trying to keep the bitterness out of my voice. 'You, Mother, Father – you're a family. A proper Jan'Tep family.' I was going to leave it there, but then I realised that what I'd said was true, but not complete. 'And you're my sister, Shalla. You'll always be my sister.'

'Then come back!' she pleaded, her voice cracking and the flickers of light disappearing from her hands.

'There's no place for me back there.' I reached up with the sleeve of my shirt and rubbed at my left eye. I was going to need to apply more of Mer'esan's paste soon. 'It's over for me, Shalla.'

She ran up to me and grabbed hold of my arm, an oddly childish gesture for her. 'But you *can* stay, don't you see? Father has the support of most of the council already, and once people hear what Ra'meth tried to do—'

'And what our uncle tried to do too.'

She shook her head, dismissing the notion. 'He was Sha'Tep. Everyone understands that. Besides, people think Father sent you to put a stop to it – that our family dealt with the problem. It's a sign of our house's dignity.'

Dignity seemed like the wrong choice of word to me. 'I can't help but notice that Ke'heops isn't here to thank me personally.'

She looked uncomfortable, and I realised she had begged him to come. 'It's all right,' I said. 'It's better this way.'

'It's complicated,' she said.

I couldn't help but smile at that. I reached out and took a piece of her hair in my hand. It was one of those stupid things we used to do as kids – a kind of taunt that masked affection. We never were a hugging family, but I decided I didn't care for once what kind of family we were and pulled her into an embrace. Surprisingly she didn't strike me down with lightning or fire or even a nasty look.

'Things don't have to change,' she insisted, hanging on to me as if the wind was about to send me drifting down the road. 'Father said you wouldn't even have to be Sha'Tep. You can stay with us while he and Mother find a way to keep your . . . condition from—'

'Our laws state that anyone with the shadowblack can be killed without consequence. Why would Father ever allow me to live under his roof?' I asked. The answer came to me almost immediately: the great and honourable Ke'heops had come to see that protecting a house like ours sometimes became an ugly business. I had shown that I could do those ugly things for him. I could be our family's enforcer, the one he sent to deal with our enemies. *After all, it's not like my soul can be saved anyway.*

As gently as I could, I pushed Shalla away. 'I love you, little sister. I reckon that's never going to change.'

Her eyes narrowed. 'You "reckon"? Don't you dare start talking like that Ferius woman, Kellen. You're not some Argosi wanderer. You're a Jan'Tep of the House of Ke.'

I thought about the card that was even now sitting in my pocket, the one painted to look like me. The 'Spellslinger'. A Discordance. A disturbance that could change the direction of the world. It sure didn't sound like me.

But it didn't sound too bad either.

I turned back to the horse, took a firm hold of the saddle and put my foot in the stirrup. 'What I am, Shalla, is a sixteen-year-old with one spell, a squirrel cat for a business partner and a death sentence written in black shadow around my left eye.' I took the horse's reins and nudged him into motion. 'I need to find out if I can be something more than that.'

Shalla cut me off, hands out in front of her, fingers already preparing a spell for which I had no counter. 'Stop! I'll strike you down, Kellen. I will.'

The glare of her magic was so bright I could see it reflecting off grains of sand on the road between us. 'Follow your conscience, Shalla. It's all any of us can do.'

I nudged the horse again. Reluctantly, the beast started moving. Even more reluctantly, Shalla let us pass. We had gone only a few yards when she called out after me. 'You'll be hunted, don't you understand? Without the protection of the clan, every Jan'Tep mage on the continent will be duty-bound to kill you. The Daromans won't take you in and neither will the Berabesq. You'll be alone, Kellen! You'll spend the entire rest of your life as an outcast.'

I pulled on the reins, just for a moment, and turned to give my sister my very best smile before continuing on my way out of town. 'Reckon I prefer the term "outlaw".'

Acknowledgements

It took seven perilous and peculiar spells to bring the world of *Spellslinger* to life. Thankfully, the master mages of my literary life were equal to the challenge.

A Conjuration of Inspiration
My friend and occasional writing partner Eric Torin, as he does with all of my books, posed the questions that most needed to be answered in order to bring *Spellslinger* to life.

An Incantation of Purpose
I never tried writing a novel until I met my wife Christina, who makes marriage the best and most alluring adventure an otherwise aimless rogue could ever hope for.

An Evocation of Exploration
Members past and present of my excellent (and exceedingly nasty) writing group saw many different versions of *Spellslinger*, always telling me with (again, exceedingly nasty) candour what worked and what needed rewriting. My ongoing thanks to Kim Tough, Wil Arndt, Brad Dehnert, Claire Ryan, Sarah Figueroa, and Jim Hull of Narrative First.

Some of my favourite people took the time to read earlier drafts of the novel and help me see both what was working and what was not. My thanks to Anna Webster, Mike Church, Sandra Glass, Sarah Bagshaw, Dougal Muir, Kat Zeller, and Sam Chandola.

A *Binding of Clarity*
My editor, the delightfully kind and utterly persistent Matilda Johnson, forced me to answer all the questions about Kellen and his world until I was almost convinced the magic would actually work.

A *Spell of Sparkling*
The eagle-eyed Talya Baker at Hot Key Books not only brought polish and crispness to the prose, she also found holes that I'd missed.

A *Prestidigitation of Publication*
This book would never have seen print without my incomparable agents, Heather Adams and Mike Bryan, who found the perfect home thanks to the indomitable Mark Smith who took a chance on me both with my first series and now with this one. Thanks also to Jane Harris, for helping me solve the esoteric dilemmas surrounding certain homicidal furry creatures.

A *Summoning of Kindred Spirits*
Thanks to all of you who take chances on new authors and books. One of the great pleasures of this business is meeting and hearing from readers who aren't simply fans but rather fellow travellers down the strange pathways of fantasy and adventure.

Turn the page for a preview
of Kellen's next adventure . . .

SHADOWBLACK

The way of the Argosi is the way of water.

Water never seeks to block another's path, nor does it permit impediments to its own. It moves freely, slipping past those who would capture it, taking nothing that belongs to others. To forget this is to stray from the path, for despite the rumours one sometimes hears, an Argosi never, ever steals.

1

The Charm

'This *isn't* stealing,' I insisted, a little loudly considering the only person who could hear me was a two-foot-tall squirrel cat who was, at that moment, busily picking the combination lock that stood between us and the contents of the pawnshop's glass display case.

Reichis, one furry ear up close to the lock as his dextrous paws worked the three small rotating brass discs, chittered angrily in reply. 'Would you mind? This isn't as easy as it looks.' His tubby little hindquarters shivered in annoyance.

If you've never seen a squirrel cat before, picture a mean-faced cat with a big bushy tail and thin furry flaps of skin between his front and back legs that let him glide through the air in a fashion that somehow looks both ridiculous and terrifying. Oh, and give him the personality of a thief, a blackmailer and, if you believe Reichis's stories, a murderer on more than one occasion.

'Almost done,' he insisted.

He'd been saying that for the past hour.

Thin lines of light were beginning to slip through the gaps between the wooden slats in the pawnshop's front window and beneath the bottom edge of the door. Soon people would be coming down the main street, opening their shops or standing outside the saloon for that all-important first drink of the morning. They do that sort of thing here in the borderlands: work themselves into a drunken stupor before they've even had breakfast. It's just one of the reasons why people here tend towards violence as the solution to any and all disputes. It's also why my nerves were fraying. 'We could have just broken the glass and left him some extra money to cover the damage,' I said.

'*Break* the glass?' Reichis growled to convey what he thought of that idea. 'Amateur.' He turned his attention back to the lock. 'Easy . . . easy . . .'

A click, and then a second later Reichis proudly held up the elaborate brass lock in his paws. 'See?' he demanded. '*That's* how you pull off a proper burglary!'

'It's *not* a burglary,' I said, for what must have been the twelfth time since we'd snuck into the pawnshop that night. 'We *paid* him for the charm, remember? He's the one who ripped *us* off.'

Reichis snorted dismissively. 'And what did you do about it, Kellen? Just stood there like a halfwit while he pocketed our hard-earned coin. That's what!'

To the best of my knowledge, Reichis had never actually *earned* a coin in his life. 'Shoulda ripped his throat out with your teeth like I told you,' he continued.

The solution to most thorny dilemmas – to squirrel cats anyway – is to walk up to the source of the problem and bite it very hard on the neck, preferably coming away with as much of its bleeding flesh as possible.

I let him have the last word and reached past him to pull open the glass doors and retrieve the small silver bell attached to a thin metal disc. Glyphs etched along its edge shimmered in the half-light: a quieting charm. An *actual* Jan'Tep quieting charm. With this I could cast spells without leaving the echo that allowed bounty hunters to track us. For the first time since we'd fled the Jan'Tep territories, I felt as if I could almost – *almost* – breathe easy again.

'Hey, Kellen?' Reichis asked, hopping up on the counter to peer at the silver disc I held in my hand. 'Those markings on the charm – those are magic, right?'

'Kind of. More like a way to bind a spell onto the charm.' I turned to look at him. 'Since when are you interested in magic?'

He held up the combination lock. 'Since this thing started glowing.'

A set of three elaborately drawn glyphs shimmered bright red along the cylindrical brass chamber. The next thing I knew, the door was bursting open and sunlight filling the pawnshop as a silhouetted figure charged inside and tackled me to the floor, putting an abrupt end to a heist that, in retrospect, could have done with more planning.

Four months in the borderlands had brought me to one irrefutable conclusion: I made a terrible outlaw. I couldn't hunt worth a damn, got lost just about everywhere I went, and it seemed like every person I met found some perfectly sensible reason to try to rob me or kill me.

Sometimes both.

For news and exclusive writing

from the author of *Spellslinger*, join the

Sebastien de Castell Readers' Club.

Sign up today at

www.bit.ly/SebastienClub

to download a **free short story**

set in the world of *Spellslinger*.

Thank you for choosing a Hot Key book.

If you want to know more about our authors and what we publish, you can find us online.

You can start at our website

www.hotkeybooks.com

And you can also find us on:

We hope to see you soon!